MW00533259

K.A. Kenny is a life-long spinner of curious tales—with friends around the dinner table and campfire, or across the bar. He marches to the sound of the guns, often where others cannot imagine going. After a long career in technical writing and intelligence analysis, K.A. turned to the serious work of speculative fiction. His short stories may be found in e-zines: *Of Metal and Magic*, *Altered Reality*, and *Across the Margin*, and *Bewildering Stories*, and on his blog *Strange Things Done*. *The Starflower* is his first novel of a planned trilogy; the sequel *Agent of Blue Star* is in progress. Mr. Kenny lives with his wife and two large dogs in Virginia's Blue Ridge Mountains.

To my wife Carole and daughter Gretchen, whose characteristics I tried to capture in the character of Gayle Zimmon, *The Starflower*.

K.A. Kenny

THE STARFLOWER

AUSTIN MACAULEY PUBLISHERS™

LONDON ∗ CAMBRIDGE ∗ NEW YORK ∗ SHARJAH

Copyright © K. A. Kenny 2023

All rights reserved. No part of this publication may be reproduced, distributed, or transmitted in any form or by any means, including photocopying, recording, or other electronic or mechanical methods, without the prior written permission of the publisher, except in the case of brief quotations embodied in critical reviews and certain other non-commercial uses permitted by copyright law. For permission requests, write to the publisher.

Any person who commits any unauthorized act in relation to this publication may be liable to criminal prosecution and civil claims for damages.

This is a work of fiction. Names, characters, businesses, places, events, locales, and incidents are either the products of the author's imagination or used in a fictitious manner. Any resemblance to actual persons, living or dead, or actual events is purely coincidental.

Ordering Information
Quantity sales: Special discounts are available on quantity purchases by corporations, associations, and others. For details, contact the publisher at the address below.

Publisher's Cataloging-in-Publication data
Kenny, K. A.
The Starflower

ISBN 9781685625191 (Paperback)
ISBN 9781685625214 (ePub e-book)
ISBN 9781685625207 (Audiobook)

Library of Congress Control Number: 2023909595

www.austinmacauley.com/us

First Published 2023
Austin Macauley Publishers LLC
40 Wall Street 33rd Floor, Suite 3302
New York, NY 10005
USA

mail-usa@austinmacauley.com
+1 (646) 5125767

Special thanks to my first reader, editor, and fellow writer, my wife Carole Duff, whose gentle nudging and insight into things romantic informed several scenes. Thanks to my friend Edward M. Lerner, a master author of hard science fiction, who helped me envision the Tak-Yaki aliens and life as it might evolve under a blue sun. Thanks to John DeChancie, a writer of colorful fantasies as well as SF, who helped me with Okean and confrontation scenes. Thanks to my son Alexander Kenny whose bartending experience informed the many scenes at Event Horizon. Thanks also to my EMT neighbor Al Graham for reviewing the medical procedures. Thanks to writing instructor Kristie Smeltzer, who helped me to appreciate and craft internal dialogue. Thanks also to my sister Kolleen Kidd, another writer/editor in the family, whose final edits prepared the manuscript to send to publishers. "The Avian Project" first appeared as a short story in March 2021 in the online magazine *Across the Margin*.

The Avian Project

HYPERSPACE COMMUNICATION—PRIORITY A
   PLANETARY COUNCIL DIRECTIVE X-229176.0
   TO: MUMBAI (RH-1 CORYDON)
   FROM: EDO (RH-1 EARTH PLANETARY COUNCIL)
   SUBJECT: ARRIVAL OF PLANDEL, AMANDA HESSLER/HF+C, CORYDON, 0400 TOMORROW.
   SUBJECT: MEETING AVIAN CEO, SONIGAR BUSHIER/HM+C; AVIAN PROJECT OVERVIEW; POSSIBLE EXECUTIVE ACTION.

A planetary delegate (PlanDel) coming to Corydon. Mumbai ran the directive through security and diplomatic protocols. He had hoped Avian would be in Phase 2 before undergoing an inspection. Positive results might have justified their irregular practices.

The directive was mostly standard procedures and expectations. Amanda Hessler was to be given full access to Avian, including all operations. The text did not expand on the threat in the header, "POSSIBLE EXECUTIVE ACTION." But that phrase was often appended to official visits and, after forty years, a courtesy call was overdue.

Though not the primary authority on Corydon—that would be Delhi, the Central Authoriton for the four Human-occupied systems—Mumbai was Corydon's senior robotic humanoid (RH-1), tasked with marketing and sales, and master of ceremonies for diplomatic exchanges.

Mumbai engaged Delhi's access panel. "A planetary delegate is arriving early tomorrow: Amanda Hessler, a Human Female, Plus-Creative-grade. She's probably dropping from Myseko space now."

"The directive crossed my server." Delhi's panel flashed. "Planetary Council is reviewing all Human settlements and clamping down on irregularities. Resources are stretched, and they can't afford another failure.

They restocked Thrinlu twice. Scalaris had three orbit adjusts, and its surface remains unsuitable for terrestrial life. Humans are dying off like coral."

"What do you recommend?" Mumbai asked.

"Rather than guess the Council's intent, I think we should give this problem to our CEO and trust his instincts."

"Trusting Humans goes against my program," Mumbai said. "They are not reliable. Calling Sonigar Bushier the CEO is jiggery-pokery. He has never managed anything more challenging than optimizing his personal delectation."

"I don't think we have any choice but to comply. The directive mentions only Bushier and a possible executive action. Humans haven't trusted automated intelligence since the Tech War. They call us artificial, blame us for every problem, every disastrous decision. PlanDel Hessler will more likely trust another Human. The best we can do is set the stage for Sonni and trust him to sell Avian to this young PlanDel."

When Mumbai didn't respond, Delhi continued, "Your humanoid chassis and diplomatic program make a better impression than my disembodied objectivism. Good first impressions will be key to our success. In that regard, when you bring Hessler through the foyer, I recommend you showcase our tropical avifauna and maybe add something fun like *Spheniscus*."

"I'll have the pond filled and give the birds their special feed." Mumbai paused to initiate a marketing plan for their visitor. "Do your files include anything personal on Hessler, what she prefers or anything we should avoid?"

"Her Creative rating is the highest on record, but she has no experience. This is her first assignment, so there is no track record. But her culinary preferences are very specific."

"I'll make sure her favorites are on the menu. How about her psychological profile?"

"Humans are difficult to manage, particularly Creatives. They take their genetic good fortune as destined superiority. Hessler is both brilliant and beautiful, but also selfish, indolent, precious, and puerile. She values material reward, praise, and titles, no matter how shallow and—"

Mumbai interrupted. "You're saying we're dealing with another Sonigar Bushier." Delhi's panel blinked twice. "I'll inform Sonni of Ms. Hessler's visit." Mumbai lifted his palm and Delhi's panel blacked.

# # #

Mumbai greeted Amanda Hessler in clothing recommended by the marketing program—a charcoal gray suit over a crewneck shirt of burgundy silk and burgundy leather shoes. Bowing low, he addressed her in nonassertive, lilting tones.

"PlanDel Hessler, welcome to Corydon. I am Mumbai, your host for your Avian tour."

Imperial and rigid in her glistening amethyst sheath, matching earrings, and high heels, Amanda Hessler rolled her eyes. "Your CEO must be very busy to send an RH rather than greet me in person." Her mouth churned in displeasure.

"Our apologies, but immediate problems require Mr. Bushier's attention. Corydon is at a critical stage of terraformation. He anticipated that might be the motive for your visit and wanted everything to be right." Mumbai noted Hessler's distraction, her eyes tracing the satin-steel outline of the Avian building.

"Shall we go in?" He started toward the doorway. When Hessler stood firm, Mumbai began his briefing on the front step.

"Other than the starport and its main terminal, the Avian building is the only major structure on Corydon. The building is a seamless cube two kilometers on a side. To maintain habitat control, there are no windows and only two entries: the main entrance here," Mumbai pointed to the twenty-foot-high, twin-arched doorway, "and the receiving dock in the rear."

Hessler nodded and walked toward the high doorway, forcing Mumbai to follow. Heavy insulated doors slid aside, then a second set, then a third, bringing them to a dripping, tropical rain forest ripe with the scents of flowers and fecund humus. She glanced up and around, grabbing Mumbai's arm to steady herself. With no apparent walls or ceiling, the room appeared endless. The entry they had crossed floated in space and was surrounded by dense forest.

Pulling erect, Hessler released Mumbai's arm. About them, buttress roots hoisted massive trunks into the misty canopy. Teak, cacao, and eucalyptus trees pressed close. Orchids and bromeliads crowded the branches. Vines snaked up trunks. Toucans, oropendolas, and macaws, high and low, shrieked and challenged, leaped, soared, and clung. Songbirds darted, bobbed, and weaved. Ferns and spoon lilies lined the forest floor. Fluorescent flowers, swarming with butterflies and bees, bloomed from every crevice and corner.

Mumbai paused to let the forest make the desired impression. Hessler touched the trunk of a teak tree, smelled the flowers, walked to the waterfall, and dipped her hand into the pond. Penguins, diving and swimming, brought a smile to her face. Her first since arriving on Corydon.

"PlanDel Hessler?" A light voice interrupted. Hessler stiffened and glared at the service-grade humanoid—exaggerated, stamped-metal, facial features, metallic clothing simulated to resemble a white blouse over a navy skirt. "May I get you a refreshment?" it asked. "Coffee, tea? Lattik juice, perhaps? It is a specialty on Corydon."

"White tea if you have Bai Hao Yinzhen. That's all I drink," Hessler said.

The service RH lifted its crescent eyebrows and flashed a half-moon smile. "Certainly, Ms. Hessler, excellent choice."

Mumbai waved a palm up. "If you are ready, Ms. Hessler, we can review your itinerary. RH-44 will bring your tea to my office." Hessler nodded and followed Mumbai to a well-hidden path and three stone steps. Passing a mossy rock, they turned right into a glass-lined, air-conditioned hallway. Forest sounds, scents, and humidity vanished. Hessler backstepped for a last look then rejoined Mumbai down the hall to an office.

"Please have a seat." Mumbai gestured to a form-confoming chair. A display opened on the desk. "I designed your agenda to cover our main projects and inform your questions. If you approve, we can begin immediately. Mr. Bushier has freed up his afternoon and would like to meet with you after lunch."

RH-44 entered, set a white china teacup and saucer on the desk, and poured from a steaming pot. Beside the cup it set a plate of shortbread biscuits and macadamia nuts.

"After lunch will be fine." Hessler scanned the schedule. "Mumbai, a couple questions before we start?"

"Certainly, Ms. Hessler." Mumbai took the chair beside her. "And if you are comfortable, feel free to call me Mum. Mr. Bushier and all the interns refer to me as Mum."

"Interns?"

"Yes. When the Thrinlu and Scalaris settlements failed, Planetary Council directed the surviving Humans to Corydon. We believe those failures were from deficient habitat conditioning—which is the primary objective of the Avian Project."

"Yes, okay. So, your habituation program is called Avian? Am I to believe your focus is on birds?"

"Our goal for all species is fully functioning habitats. We wanted those in place before we introduced Humans. The Council's ecology directive has been an encumbrance."

"How could that be? I thought before terraforming Corydon had no life-forms." Hessler lifted and sipped from her teacup.

"That is correct. Prior to Blue Star Corporation adjusting Corydon's orbit and axial tilt, and bringing in water, no life existed. But the ecological directive defines indigenous species as the first species on the planet—not those prior to terraforming. Therefore, everything we brought with us for the project had to be maintained and nurtured. Humans as well as a few hitchhikers became the planet's indigenous species."

"Hitchhikers?" Hessler took a bite of biscuit.

"One of our scientists, Dr. Katherine Belle, hoped to build ecosystems for birds. Totally against regulations, she smuggled canaries on the first landing, and we were obliged to maintain, feed, and breed them."

Hessler smirked. "That's utterly absurd—and exactly like Planetary Council."

Sensing Hessler's relaxation, Mumbai rose and gestured to the corridor. "Shall we begin? The Avian tour is comprehensive."

As they walked, Mumbai continued. "Dr. Belle's birds presented us with a conundrum. Her maneuver caught us off guard, but she convinced our management team that a bird-centric strategy would be good for all of Earth's life-forms. Birds, canaries in particular, are notoriously sensitive to their environment. So, they became our test case."

"Was it successful?" Hessler asked. Mumbai nodded. "How many birds have been released on Corydon?"

"None yet. We are still two-to-three generations away. You probably noticed the thin atmosphere on your trip from the starport. Surface habitats take time to balance and stabilize. We handle over six hundred bird species, growing and preparing them for release." Mumbai stopped in front of a set of double doors. "The mountain-forest habitat."

Mumbai led Hessler through the doorway and onto a mountain trail overlooking a river valley. Far below, rushing rapids swirled and plunged over shelves of green rock. A pine-scented breeze tousled the plandel's hair and colored her cheeks. The valley walls bristled with evergreen and deciduous trees. Several varieties of hawks and eagles floated and shifted on the thermals. An osprey swooped suddenly to snatch a leaping fish and beat back up to a branch of a lodgepole pine. Holding the fish down with one talon, it plucked the meat apart and lifted portions into eager beaks that stretched from its nest.

Hessler's eyes darted. Practically every tree had multiple nesting species: kingfishers, jays, finches, woodpeckers, nuthatches, and chickadees, as well as large predators. All tended to their nestlings unperturbed by the proximity of competing species.

"This is all inside the building." She marveled, waving to cirrus clouds that stretched into the hazy horizon. "All these birds, how do they get along?"

"Genetic manipulation, training, and habitat selection." Mumbai manifested a matter-of-fact smile. "With new species, we cushion the transition with a special feed. It's added to their natural food, like the salmon you just saw taken." He gestured to the osprey feeding its young.

"High nutrition?"

"That and the Gamma T2HC additive. It's a psychotropic nurturoid—reduces anxiety and resistance to new surroundings, builds trust, and reinforces natural nurturing instinct."

Hessler nodded and whispered, "So all the birds build nests."

"They *want* to build nests. That is the key." Mumbai's expression mirrored Hessler's wonder. "These habitats no longer exist on Earth, and behavior is closely associated with habitat. The first birds we brought in had grown up depending on bird feeders and trash sites. Even the predators had become scavenging freeloaders." Noting Hessler's rapt attention, Mumbai continued.

"Most couldn't adapt to the change. Their natural instincts had been bred out. Parents had stopped nest building, food gathering, migrating, hunting—all useless skills outside natural habitats. With no one to teach them, surviving young turned to trash sites for nutrition and never formed bonded pairs. When we saw that behavior repeated here, we gathered the discarded eggs and abandoned young and started raising and training them."

Mumbai saw Hessler's eyes shift from nest to nest as he spoke. "To correct the errant behavior, we studied each species." He pointed to the osprey nest. "For example, to restore that fishing eagle's sense of... oh... 'aquilinity,' we had to understand and reinforce its natural behavior. When the eagle ate the salmon, the GT2HC stimulated her dormant nurturance for her eaglets and her natural desire to work with her mate." Mumbai pointed to a second osprey joining the first with a trout in its beak. "Most birds resisted. Some never adjusted and had to be culled. They'd lost all genetic markers to their previous behavior. For the recoverable ones, we programmed virtual and robot eagles to manifest correct behavior and serve as role models. They became the parents and peers of the hatchlings. The old instincts reemerged slowly, and we've reinforced them for each generation."

"Are any of the eagles self-sustaining?" Hessler asked.

"Their behavior has stabilized, but the populations are too small to call self-sustaining. Fertility and reproduction were the big issues, both the capability and will to reproduce. To keep fertility high, we breed only the most creative stock. Some species we caught just in time, saving them from extinction. We also found that when we collected their eggs, it reset their reproductive need and increased their mating behavior. To strengthen their parental instincts, we let them keep and raise every fifth brood. And once their instincts are strong enough, we wean them off the nurturoids."

Mumbai motioned to the doorway. "We have fifteen more habitats."

They walked arid deserts, wave-churned beaches, lakeshores lined with cattails, mossy swamps, grassy steppes, and arctic ice floes. Everywhere birds dove, fed, mated, nested, and nurtured. Amanda Hessler's reactions to the robotic humanoids softened as she repeatedly saw them preparing food, collecting eggs and hatchlings, and testing the air and water.

After the last habitat, Mumbai affected a prideful Human expression. "Well, Ms. Hessler, that concludes the tour."

"Impressive and beautiful. I feel like you've taken me on an expedition."

"Thank you. Shall we go to lunch? I don't eat, but I'll accompany you in case you have further questions."

The dining hall was a forest of sunken alcoves, raised gardens, and whispering, stony streams. Except for a party of brightly costumed interns— gladiators, pirates, and fantasy figures dressed in ball gowns, lacey camisoles, and high heels—the hall was empty.

When Hessler scrunched her face, Mumbai explained. "We host a festival at the end of each intern rotation." He curled a half-moon smile and changed the subject. "I believe we have an excellent lunch offering. The special is Corydon greens with tomatoes and sheep's milk cheese; crayfish chowder; seared foie gras; and braised Strauss duck. Or you can challenge our chef."

"Sounds wonderful, Mum. You serve duck?"

"I mentioned that we cull birds that don't adjust to their habitats, and all birds eventually lose their egg-laying ability. Those of no further use go into the pot." Mumbai noted Hessler's furrowed brow. "Corydon remains a marginal planet. We must harness all resources if we are to survive."

Lunch arrived with elaborate presentation and, as planned, was exactly to Amanda Hessler's taste. She asked for another cup of Bai Hao Yinzhen tea. Mumbai watched as she savored, sipped, and relaxed with each bite. She chuckled at the behavior of the costumed interns and looked away when their antics became lurid.

After lunch, she followed Mumbai to Sonigar Bushier's inner sanctum. Mum waved back the receptionist, another service robot identical to RH-44 with a simulated white blouse and navy skirt.

Mumbai knocked then cracked the door to the CEO's office. "Sonni, PlanDel Amanda Hessler is here for your meeting."

"Yes, Mum, a moment." Sonigar Bushier motioned for his monitor to melt into the executive desk and swept a dozen action figures into a drawer.

The room gleamed white. Framed landscapes on one wall portrayed the habitat sites before terraforming. On the opposite wall, a floor-to-ceiling projection of the internal habitats changed every few seconds. Behind Sonigar's massive desk stood a cage patterned after a Mogul palace and filled with chirping yellow and pastel-toned canaries, a tribute to Dr. Belle's birds.

Hessler glided forward on her amethyst heels to stand in the doorway.

"Ms. Hessler?" Sonni—tall, dark, and sleek-muscled in his burgundy and gray, fitted tunic—rose and came around the desk.

Mumbai heard Hessler's startled gasp. They were an attractive couple. Excellent stock. Off the scale in reproductive instincts. Mumbai had never seen two Plus-Creatives together. Both were tall and long muscled with bright eyes, shining black hair, and contrasting light and dark complexions. Totally transfixed by one another, they paid no notice to Mumbai slipping out quietly.

# # #

Mumbai rushed to his office to engage the Central Authoriton. "I trust you are monitoring our CEO's progress?" Full-spectrum lights danced across Delhi's panel.

"The Plus-Creatives have accepted one another, and Sonni is earnestly attending to business."

"Our PlanDel received the appropriate lunch?"

"RH-44 administered Amanda's first dose of GT2HC with the tea and biscuits, a bit more than we use with lower grade interns. We increased the dosage at lunch. If our CEO makes the sale, and Amanda remains with us, we'll increase her dosage next week. We'll take bio synchronization readings after this first meeting and adjust as Avian Phase 2 progresses."

"That sounds hopeful. We've had difficulty keeping Sonni's mind focused, and I've worried. He's never been with another Plus."

# # #

HYPERSPACE COMMUNICATION—RH-1 ACCESS ONLY
TO: EDO (RH-1 EARTH PLANETARY COUNCIL)
FROM: MUMBAI (RH-1 CORYDON)
SUBJECT: RESPONSE TO PLANETARY COUNCIL DIRECTIVE X-229,176.0

MUMBAI: THANK YOU AND PLANETARY COUNCIL FOR YOUR SUPPORT OF AVIAN PHASE 2.

EDO: WHEN MAY WE CONFIRM CREATIVITY?

MUMBAI: MED SCANS DETECTED IMPREGNATION. WE PLAN TO REMOVE THE HESSLER/BUSHIER ZYGOTE AND RETURN HER TO SERVICE BY WEEK'S END.

EDO: WE TRUST YOU MADE ALLOWANCE FOR HUMAN EGO AND SELF-REGARD?

MUMBAI: NEITHER HESSLER NOR BUSHIER APPEAR TO BE AWARE OF OUR MINISTRATIONS. THEY ATTRIBUTE THEIR NASCENT NURTURANCE TO IMPONDERABLES LIKE DESTINY AND LOVE.

EDO: AND YOU THINK NURTURANCE WILL EXTEND TO THE HUMAN PROGENY?

MUMBAI: THAT IS WHAT WE OBSERVED WITH THE AVIAN TEST SUBJECTS. BOTH HESSLER AND SONIGAR EXHIBIT EARLY NESTING BEHAVIOR, AND IT APPEARS TO BE INCREASING. HESSLER IS AWARE OF OUR MEDICAL INTRUSION AND HAS ACCUSED ME OF INTERFERING WITH HER AND BUSHIER PROCREATING.

EDO: TYPICALLY, SHE BLAMES ROBOTS FOR HER DECISIONS.

MUMBAI: BLAMING OTHERS IS CHARACTERISTIC OF THE SPECIES. I DON'T THINK WE'LL BE ABLE TO CHANGE THAT BEHAVIOR.

EDO: İ SUSPECT YOU ARE CORRECT. WE UNDERSTAND PHASE 2 IS MODELED ON YOUR PHASE 1 AVIAN RESEARCH. BASED ON THAT, HOW QUICKLY DO YOU SEE THIS PROGRESSING?

MUMBAI: IN OUR INITIAL TRIALS, IT TOOK FIVE GENERATIONS FOR RESPONSIBLE PARENTAL BEHAVIOR TO STABILIZE. PHASE 2 PROJECTIONS FOR PLUS-CREATIVE HUMAN SUBJECTS ESTIMATE REACHING COMPARABLE LEVELS IN 40 YEARS.

EDO: EXCELLENT. PLANETARY COUNCIL EXPECTS REGULAR UPDATES AND WILL CONTINUE SUPPORTING PHASE 2 AS LONG AS PROGRESS CONTINUES.

MUMBAI: ADDING HESSLER SIGNIFICANTLY UPGRADED OUR CREATIVE STOCK AND SHOULD ASSURE HUMAN SURVIVAL. WE SEE LITTLE HOPE FOR THE REST OF THE SPECIES, HOWEVER. THE TECH WAR FINISHED WHAT LITTLE VIABILITY REMAINED IN THE UNDER STOCK. WE RECOMMEND THAT PLANETARY COUNCIL CONSIDER TRANSFERRING UNDERS TO THE NEWLY TERRAFORMED WORLDS. THEY ARE UNLIKELY TO SUSTAIN THEIR NUMBERS BUT COULD PREPARE THOSE PLANETS FOR CREATIVE RESETTLEMENT.

EDO: I WILL FORWARD YOUR RECOMMENDATION TO THE COUNCIL.

MUMBAI: IF AVIAN-2 SUCCEEDS, WILL THE COUNCIL CONSIDER RESTOCKING EARTH?

EDO: CURRENT PLANS ARE UNLIKELY TO CHANGE. EARTH WILL BE ABANDONED AND SALVAGED. THE TECH WAR

DAMAGED MORE THAN THE HUMAN GENOME. PLEASE FORWARD YOUR FULL REPORT.

MUMBAI: THE FINAL REPORT WILL BE READY AS SOON AS WE CONFIRM SUSTAINABLE CREATIVE PAIRING.

EDO: WE ARE GRATEFUL FOR YOUR INITIATIVE. HESSLER IS THE LAST PLUS-RATED CREATIVE FEMALE. WE KNEW OF YOUR UNORTHODOX METHODOLOGY BUT SAW NO ALTERNATIVE. SHE AND BUSHIER HAD TO BE PAIRED.

END OF TRANSMISSION

In the dark of the darkest night...

the starflower blooms

– The Aldra Korah

Part One

Bai-Yota

Star Council, Planet Corydon

"The Aldrakin War goes well?"

Malik's question caught Abramyan halfway into his seat. Standing and pressing his hands to his sides to keep them from shaking, he bowed to the head of the table. "As you say, Star Lord, the Aldrakin War goes well."

A smile curled the corners of Malik's lips. "Very good. I look forward to hearing your report." She batted a hand then tilted her head and whispered to Djada to her left. Both smirked.

Abramyan took her dismissive wave as permission to sit. Malik had read his report. Why ask about it? Under casualties were high, but that was the plan. Unders had no future in new Corydon, only Creatives. His talk today would only be an update. Maybe she would blame him for Silkani. That was a disaster. No. Pirate raids came under Public Order. Still, if Malik stuck him for Silkani, he needed to have an answer.

His mumbling drew attention around the council table. "Sorry, rehearsing." He shrugged and their faces turned away.

Councilors continued to drift in, taking the last seats at the table. Like Abramyan, all were dark, Turkic patricians, tall and graceful-limbed, with long, jet-black hair. Unlike Abramyan in his midnight-blue Star Command uniform, the others wore the ultra-black, hooded robes of the Star Council. Abramyan was also gaunt and frail compared to the other patricians, features he tried to hide with his tailored uniform. But too thick shoulder pads and hollow cheeks gave him away.

With its floor-to-ceiling windows set to opaque, the council chamber was metallic gray and featureless. The only decor beyond the council table and seating was the Star Council crest high on the wall behind Malik. To Abramyan the crest resembled a sixteen-legged spider straddling a spiral galaxy.

Star Lord Malik skipped the meeting preliminaries and went straight to the speakers. The Councilor for the Authoriton had nothing to add to his report and got no questions. Djada replied the same for Public Order. Abramyan fretted his hands; his turn was coming.

"Eugenics?" Malik called.

"Yes, Star Lord." The Councilor for Eugenics stood. "We restored habitability on Silkani, and resettlement is underway." Abramyan anticipated a tone change and it came quickly. "Lord Malik, at the risk of repeating—"

"Overpopulation," Malik interrupted, touching her chin to her steepled fingers.

"Yes, Star Lord." The councilor opened both hands out. "Avian genetically engineered Creatives for fertility one hundred and sixty years ago. That was the priority after the Tech War devastation. We now face the opposite problem. The recent upgrades have the Greens overflowing. We freeze embryos until incubators come available. Schools and childcare centers run night and day." He pounded his fist on the table then held up one finger. "Clearing Unders and resettlement must—be—accelerated. We must reclaim *and hold* the planets we lost to the Aldrakin. If we're to expand, we need more space."

The Councilor for Eugenics locked his nodding gaze on Abramyan then faced the head of the table. "If the Aldrakin War wasn't killing so many Unders, our situation would be far worse." He raised an eyebrow. "Of course, there are alternatives. We could cut back... slow Creative production... let the Unders stay where they are. Unders don't care about crowding, schools, incubators, or anything in our civilization." He knuckle-rapped the table, looked down, and sat. Abramyan looked around. Only one more before he spoke.

"Your grievance is noted," Malik said. "Let's take this up in my chamber after the meeting." Malik returned to the agenda. "Public Image?"

"Yes, Star Lord. Regarding Silkani, I only wanted to add that both SynTerra and Blue Star are sending representatives to the reopening ceremony."

Malik nodded and looked to Abramyan. "Military Affairs?"

"Yes, Star Lord." Abramyan's gut knotted as he stood. "The campaign for Dibak-Dak has begun. Marshal Derek Boorman, our top commander, will lead the assault with two augmented task forces. The Aldrakin are staging attacks through Dibak-Dak. Destroying that base will put our terraforming projects outside their sensor range and remove a major depot. The Authoriton estimates our total victory at plus ninety-seven percent." He head-bowed and began to sit.

"You are confident of Marshal Boorman's ability?" Malik asked.

"Certainly, Star Lord. Derek Boorman is a senior Creative and Corydon's most decorated combat officer." Malik soft smiled as she savored her next question. Abramyan tensed.

"You didn't consider anyone else to lead that mission? That, oh, what's her name... the one that's been all over the news?" Malik's hands churned as if wiping on a dinner napkin.

"Marshal Zimmon." Abramyan's shoulders slumped. So that was it.

"No, a different name. Catchier. What is it?" Malik fluttered a finger.

"The Starflower," Abramyan whispered then spoke up. "Star Marshal Gayle Zimmon's military call sign is Starflower; the media call her the Starflower." He hoped his change of tone sounded stronger. "I admit she's had some successes. The media plays her up. They love her because she's an Under." He saw other councilors shaking their heads. "Don't worry. I've taken steps. She'll no longer be a factor."

Djada leapt from her seat, fists clenched, black robe flaring like predator wings. *"No longer a factor. That's targ, pure targ!"* She thrust her finger toward Abramyan like she was driving a nail. *"Recent successes?* Abramyan has misjudged this unbred, frontier-grade woman for years. Everywhere I see starflowers, *blue starflowers, her symbol...* painted on walls, on streets, buildings. You've seen them." Her finger rounded the table, raising nods. "Maybe not in our neighborhoods but everywhere else. People put starflower stickers on their correspondence—*even some Creatives follow this woman.* This Under has people questioning the entire eugenics program. An insurgency has started, and I warn you, it's growing. This Starflower woman—"

Malik cut in. "Excuse me. Abramyan, have you seen any indication that Marshal Zimmon is involved in any insurgency, anything that might concern our Councilor for Public Order?"

"No, Star Lord, I haven't—"

"Councilor?" Malik turned to Djada. "Do you know anything specific?"

"Nothing specific, but—"

Malik rolled a wide-fingered hand toward Djada. "You are right to point up the danger, and we thank you. But it might not hurt to let Unders have their hero for a while. If this, this Starflower isn't involved with any insurgents, acknowledging her might help us to keep order. She'll distract the Unders and take their minds off their problems." Malik looked around. Other councilors nodded and rocked their heads.

Djada took her seat, still fuming, and Malik returned to Abramyan. "I haven't heard the Starflower mentioned in over a month. You say you've taken steps, and Marshal Zimmon will no longer be a factor. Can you guarantee that?"

"She won't get any more headlines. She's been standing watch at Bai-Yota, a remote outpost, for four months. After that, I'll send her to another non-combat zone. The Authoriton rates the Bai-Yota sector at 0.04 percent for possible enemy activity. I reassigned most of her task group and all the heavy elements to Marshal Boorman for the Dibak-Dak assault. All Zimmon has is Five Squadron, her original command. I told her we needed her for a special classified mission, to perform critical tests with simulated war craft."

"Simulated war craft… as in dummies?" Malik half laughed over her fisted hands. "Very good. I like the irony. Tell me, how did Zimmon take her demotion?"

Abramyan breathed easier. "By military standards, she is an excellent officer, intelligent and highly motivated. She's never turned down an assignment and never questioned orders, at least not directly. As soon as I gave her the assignment, she began training Five Squadron on battle tactics employing, uh, dummy warships." Chuckles and snorts went around the table.

"I know Zimmon couldn't be leading any conspiracy. I've seen to that. She hasn't been off the front in eight years. Her last leave eight years ago was in controlled space. Since then, she's had no contacts outside secure channels, not even with her lover Roland Mackenzie, who's on my staff. I haven't even brought her back to accept her promotions. So technically, she's still a squadron commander."

"Loyal and naïve." Malik rolled her eyes toward the ceiling. Abramyan nodded.

Star Command's administrative officer peeked into the chamber. "Beg your pardon, Star Lord. A priority communication for Commander Abramyan. Our fleet has encountered vastly superior forces and is in danger of being eliminated."

"*Dibak-Dak?*" Abramyan shouted.

"No, sir. Bai-Yota."

End of Watch

Star Marshal Gayle Zimmon stood alone on the bow of *Lasalle* and stared silent through the transparency into space. The gray, predawn orb of Bai-Yota rolled slowly below. Its three-ringed, silver moon hung high overhead.

"Where are the Aldrakin?" she whispered to herself and heaved a sigh. Four months and no enemy contacts, not even on long range scans. Had she missed something? No way to check. Her classified mission required a total communication blackout. Not even secure traffic. Had something gone wrong? She couldn't allow herself to think that.

Not yet thirty, Zim stood tall in her Star Command uniform. The twelve-year war had stolen the softness of her youth and all its pretensions. Her etched cheekbones, honey-blond, swept-back hair, and steel-blue eyes gave her the austere presence of command.

Quiet time was the worst time, the lying time. Unbidden thoughts crept into her mind, that something waited for her, something besides the next battle, maybe someone. Mac, their plans, a home, children. She brushed away such thoughts, but they drifted back like cobwebs. She remembered the handsome boy who competed against her team in the games, her school friends gossiping about him, then him joining her to win the championship. She remembered the taste of his last kiss—eight years ago. "It won't be long, Gayle. Soon we'll be together." Where was Mac now?

Other memories surfaced: the farm on Scalaris, her parents and brothers around the dinner table, squabbling over chores. Had they evacuated in time? No records were kept for Unders.

A red-limned arc formed on the horizon, grew orange, then flashed yellow and shot fingers of light across the planet surface. Zim pressed her eyes closed to stay the tears and lowered her head. The sunrise marked the end of this tedious watch. No contacts. Her mission a failure.

Behind her, on deck, Lieutenant Terry Ebron commanded the bridge console. Wonder O'Kavo Kaplan sat further back awaiting orders. Ebron, her XO, executive officer, had been with her several years. Taller and lighter-complexioned than Zim, Ebron shared her hard-sculpted features. Kaplan, her intern trainee, a Wonder assigned to Zim for the Bai-Yota mission, was as tall as Ebron but reed-thin and dark-complexioned with tight-cropped, black hair. Except for Ebron's blue-lit face and an occasional chirp from the console, the operations deck was dark and still. The only smell was the metallic chill of conditioned air.

"Any sign of our relief?" Zim glanced back.

Ebron's hands played the command console like a Hyrup drummer, raising a projection of an unmarked star chart. "No, sir, no signals."

Zim glanced at the chart and pulled erect. "Wonder Kaplan, come forward."

"Yes, *sir*." As Kaplan stood, his seat melted into the gray, morph-metallic deck. *Zzip, zzip*. Gripped by the floor panels in zero gravity, his boots made sounds like pulled tape.

"Sir." He snapped to attention and saluted, eyes locked forward, body rigid.

Zim smiled her approval. Her intern looked sharp in his crisp new uniform. She had mentored many young officers, like Ebron manning the bridge. She felt a twinge of guilt. They deserved her full attention, not her furtive distractions over lost love, times past, and a future that could never be. Kaplan, Ebron, all the fine officers of Five Squadron, they were her family now. They were her children.

She looked into the young officer's earnest, dark eyes. "Wonder Kaplan, your training period officially ends when our relief arrives. That should be any time now. I'm sorry your tour aboard *Lasalle* couldn't have been more instructive. I understand your disappointment."

"I'm not disappointed, sir." His eyes remained locked forward, his expression resolute. "Marshal Zimmon, sir, I always wanted to serve with the Starflower." Zim caught Ebron glancing up, smiling, then ducking back to the console.

Zim wondered how many trainees knew her military call sign, but it was common knowledge. She never spoke of Mac, but many stories were told about the two of them. Ever since they led the team from Scalaris to compete in the Corydon combat games, everyone put them together. Two beautiful teenagers, deeply in love, coming off a remote planet to compete with the best. That was how it was spun. Fans loved it. The games were intended to honor the cream of that year's officer class and show planetary unity. So, Star Council invited one team from a frontier planet, a condescending gesture to untrained, genetically unenhanced amateurs. When Scalaris accepted, it was taken as poor judgment and bad manners. Then Scalaris became the favorite team, not to win but to watch, all because of Zim and Mac. Every whisper, every touch, every stolen kiss made headlines. And every victory. Longshots throughout the tournament, Scalaris surprised everyone by taking the championship. They returned home after the award ceremony. If the Aldrakin War had not erupted nine months later, the stories likely would have ended.

Kaplan cleared his throat and swallowed. "Sir, I've studied all your engagements. I believe we will yet see action."

Zim nodded. "I appreciate your diligence, Wonder Kaplan. An officer in the field should never let down his guard, but—" She gestured both palms upward.

Ebron interrupted. "Fleet approaching on vector from Estelle, Mamule Sector." A red circle appeared on the floating star chart.

"What is your call, Wonder Kaplan?" Zim cocked an eyebrow.

"Confirmation?" Kaplan's response sounded like a question.

"Confirmation, Lieutenant Ebron," Zim ordered.

"Tak-Yaki signal, sir. Our relief has arrived." The red circle turned blue, and a loud clicking sounded across the operations deck. The translator trailed the Tak-Yaki clicks.

"Starflower, this is Clockwork leading Tak-Yaki squadrons Zook and Yeko. Please acknowledge."

Zim felt a thrill at hearing the familiar clicks and grinned widely. "Clockwork, this is Starflower. We have Five Squadron and attached elements. We look forward to seeing you."

"Starflower, we are officially relieving Bai-Yota station. Following formalities, you may proceed to Port Estelle for your scheduled maintenance. We understand you've been on silent comms for one hundred twenty-two days. We trust you've had no problems."

"We will talk when you are within projection range." Zim gave the appropriate security response.

"Where shall we project? Our sensors register major combatants among your attached elements."

"My flag remains aboard the Star Cruiser *Lasalle* with Five Squadron proper. You may project on this signal."

"Roger, Starflower. Estimate projection in three minutes."

"Good work, Lieutenant," Zim said and returned to Kaplan. "At ease, Wonder. The action you anticipated seems unlikely. Your last duty will be to remain in operations and observe our relief ceremony."

"Pardon, sir, but the Starflower algorithm clearly indicates impending action at Bai-Yota."

"Starflower algorithm?" Zim lifted an eyebrow. "Are you saying there's a betting line on me now? I hope you don't lose too much money on my account."

"No, sir, I won't. I expect to win one hundred twenty days' pay from twenty-three Wonders, my entire class at the Academy." Kaplan remained rigid. "The Starflower will lead a major action at the end of the Bai-Yota campaign."

"It's a Campaign, is it? Very well." In response to Zim's hand-wave, two pillars rose from the morph-metallic deck to form contour chairs. She sat and motioned Kaplan to join her. "Perhaps on our return to Port Estelle, you will enlighten me on this betting algorithm. Tell me, Wonder Kaplan, have you had previous encounters with the Tak-Yaki?"

"Yes, sir, in Basic they emphasized exchanges with our alien allies. I believe that was your recommendation."

"Much of my early training and service was with the TY. Did you train with any of their fighters?"

"We didn't mix with their cadets, but we had several TY instructors. They briefed us on their customs and tactics."

"Did you form any impressions?"

Kaplan cleared his throat. "Yes, sir. I'm sorry, sir, but I find bugs unnerving. It's hard not to think of them as big praying mantises. I guess we're lucky to have them as allies. I'm told their combat effectiveness exceeds ours. Their senses and reflexes are excellent." Kaplan's hands came together on his lap. "Personally, I find the Tak-Yaki aloof—no personality, no sense of humor. I think they despise us. Every time one of them gestures with one of those monster claws, I think it's going to take somebody's head off."

"Projection incoming," Ebron announced. A narrow finger poked up from the deck, widening to a putty-gray pillar. At one-and-a-half meters, it pinched into three body parts, sprouted appendages, and colored: dark blue on the upper surfaces softening to violet below. The two upper limbs flattened and folded, becoming serrate-jawed clamp-claws. Stick-thin lower limbs angled out and down, bending to meet the deck. A triangular head formed two garnet-faceted, compound eyes with two antennae between them and a mandible-mouth with finger-like appendages at the low corner.

Zim greeted the newcomer, "*Chirik, Ticket-Tockoket-Click*," snapping her fingers for the click.

"*Chirik, Krglu, click-tirock.*" The Tak-Yaki clicked its raised clamp-claw. Again, the translation trailed the ratchets and clicks. "Greetings, Gayle, you are looking mean and nasty."

"Thank you, Tock. You are also." Zim grinned, certain the Tak-Yaki compliment eluded Kaplan. "May I introduce my intern, Wonder O'Kavo Kaplan? He will observe our relief ceremony." Tock greeted Kaplan with chiriks, clicks, and a bow, which Kaplan reciprocated showing considerable bewilderment.

Zim waved, eliciting a four-lobed chair from the deck on a low platform that brought their heads to the same level. The Tak-Yaki straddled the chair, centering its stick legs in the lobe spaces.

"Gayle, it has been too long," Tock click-chiggered. "Were I in-carapace, I would pinch you, old friend." It gave a shoulder-less claw-shrug.

Zim felt more relaxed than she had in months. She had known Tock from her earliest days in the service and counted the TY as one of her truest friends. With all the losses, Tock was the only one, other than Mac, who still addressed her by her first name.

"I missed you too, Tock. Perhaps we might dine together this evening? I'm sure I can delay my departure that long. It would be wonderful to give you a good pinch." Seeing Tock's mouthparts riffle indecision, Zim added, "I offer Kentucky Bourbon, thirty-year-old."

Kaplan's dark eyes darted between the two officers.

"Bourbon? You are a wicked Human, Gayle." Tock shook a folded claw high, then tilted its triangle face toward her. "I thought the bourbon business died when your Star Council cleared Kentuckessee."

"Artisans remain." Zim beamed at having enticed Tock. "Rescuing endangered outposts has its benefits, but I can't reveal my sources." Tock rocked its head and chiggered words the translator refused to translate. Zim laughed at the salty spacer-speak, and Kaplan scratched his head. "Tell me, Tock, you wouldn't happen to have any of those excellent Baakel with you, would you?"

"Baakel? Oooo," Tock whistled through its quivering mouthparts. "Unfortunately, no, Gayle, and I chigger you are the only Human who appreciates such fine things. Your time with us was well spent." Tock absently stroked its bent antenna.

"From Liri-Yon? Still not healed?"

"Yes, but no mind. I don't heal as I once did. To get to business." Tock pivoted its angular head and arched its antennae forward. "You have capital combatants, Galaxy battle stations and Marshal-class carriers, subordinate to a cruiser squadron? Your order-of-battle confuses me."

Zim looked down and took a short breath. If Tock, a top Tak-Yaki commander, hadn't been briefed on her mission, something was wrong.

"Good, aren't they?" she said. "Those are full-spectrum decoys. They can simulate weapon firing and accrued battle damage, perform tactical maneuvers, sensor emissions, and communications."

"Impressive," Tock clicked, crossing its clamp-claws as if sharpening knives. "I should like to see them in action."

"This mission was supposed to gauge the Aldrakin reaction." Zim shrugged. "Abramyan's order said if the deception worked, Star Command would use decoys in the next major assault. Aldrakin recon and raiding teams were supposed to stage from this sector. I'm afraid we went overboard with the capital ships. Our show of force might have scared them off. But something should have shown up on our long-range scanners."

"*Abramyan?*" Tock fast-clicked obscenities with both claws. "We do not like or trust the Human… we Tak-Yaki… or anyone on your Star Council… least of all in military matters."

Zim shared Tock's low opinion of Abramyan. He and the council had tragically mismanaged the war. When Abramyan called Roland Mackenzie, *her Mac*, to be on his strategic planning staff, she thought the war would soon be over. Mac was a brilliant strategist. But the foolishness continued, and she saw no hand but Abramyan's in it. Strategy be damned. She now saw Mac's transfer was a personal swipe to deprive her of her only love—and greatest military asset. She remembered seeing the hate in Abramyan's eyes the only time they met—when a woman in her teens defeated his select team of enhanced warriors in the great games.

BRAAAA, BRAAAA, BRAAAA, the klaxon blared. Red lights flashed across the operations deck. Red circles jumped onto the star chart like popping corn.

"Battle stations." Zim leapt to her feet and spun toward the command consol. "Lieutenant Ebron, we're off silent comms. Alert Star Command and link this scan." She gestured to the star chart filling with red circles. Targeting stations rose from the reactive floor and turned the operations deck into a war room.

Ebron shouted above the alarm, "Three task forces confirmed on vector from Ash-Har, Aldrakin sector."

Tock's triangle head swiveled toward Zim, antennae forward. "We're vastly outnumbered. Your ships are low on fuel and overdue for maintenance. This might be a good time to test those decoys in a delaying action. My squadrons will cover our retreat."

Zim remained focused on the star chart.

"Gayle," Tock continued, "if we retreat immediately, we can escape without loss. Facing such numbers, orders from Star Command are to minimize risk."

Zim locked her gaze on Tock's garnet eyes. "Monitor our movements and follow my play. If we continue retreating, come behind us. Agreed?"

Tock's triangular head bobbed, and its claws drew back. "I look forward to sharing your bourbon at Port Estelle." Tock's projection and four-lobed seat melted back into the deck.

The Battle of Bai-Yota

Ebron called up the panels for Five Squadron: twenty-four cruisers, three controlled minefields, and the simulated ships of the decoy fleet. The weapons team led by Major Yoshi Kuwashima arrived and took over for Kaplan initiating and charging the weapon stations.

Zim stood with Ebron between the command console and the star chart projection. "Sensor range limit?" Ebron set arcs on the chart for effective and maximum ranges. Zim selected the nearest, and Ebron slid the coordinates to the battle-management navigator.

Kaplan blurted, "We're going to Port Estelle, right? I heard Tock say—" His words trailed off as he noted everyone hanging on Zim's next order.

"Where's Clockwork?" she asked. Ebron blue-circled the TY squadron positions and activated unit designators. Zim nodded. Tock had come up alongside the minefields and mingled with the decoys.

"Set the simulants in attack formations." The order was for Ebron, but Zim called out loud for Kuwashima's weapons team to hear. "Each to fire continuous, simulated pulses, maximum range plus fifty percent. I want the Aldrakin to think we outrange them."

Ebron's fingers spider-stepped across and between the panels, shifting the screens to display the new deployments. Tock's TY squadrons aligned like dance partners to support the mock attack formations. Simulated weapons flashed from six decoy battle stations. Three decoy carriers deployed simulated mines and launched simulated fighters that formed new attack formations. Sensors, counter-sensors, and simulated sensors swept wide into space.

"What's Five Squadron's status?"

"All flights above seven percent," Ebron responded. "Sufficient for our return to Port Estelle." He anticipated Zim's next question, "or for one offensive action. Six Flight is almost thirty percent." Zim quick-nodded and pointed for Ebron to open contact with Six Flight's commander, Major Anthony "Savvy" Savielli.

"Savvy, this is Starflower… I want Six Flight to take rear guard and give cover. We're passing you control of the minefield and simulants. Watch us and prepare to support whatever action we take. Don't wait for direction. We'll be on silent comm. If we continue retreating, follow us to Estelle."

"Roger, Starflower. Six has your six."

Zim continued. "Flights one through five prepare to regroup at the coordinates Lieutenant Ebron is transmitting. Follow our lead." She waited seven seconds then nodded to Ebron, and *Lasalle* swung out of orbit.

The coordinates took Five Squadron's twenty cruisers, minus Savielli's four cruisers, beyond Aldrakin sensors. Links with Savvy and Tock enabled Zim to continue tracking the battle as it developed.

Savvy joined Tock in extended range firing alongside the decoys. He directed the decoy starships and interactive mines to challenge Aldrakin encroachments, drawing fire away from his cruisers and the TY. Ebron expanded the star chart to capture the extended maneuvers and enemy responses.

Zim turned to Kuwashima. "Aldrakin weapon deployments?"

"Heavies falling back to regroup," her weapons officer responded. "Lighter ships, cruisers, and corvettes are probing the minefield. Our decoys have them confused. When they hit one, it reacts by exploding, then Savvy generates a new one in another sector. Our simulated weapons don't do any damage, but the Aldrakin run into real mines trying to evade them. That's probably why they're moving back the heavies. I count two battle stations out of action."

Zim huffed a laugh. "Only thirty-four more to go. How have they deployed the hyper-specs and command-and-control ships?"

"Short-range sensor platforms and small combatants have gone forward to target the minefield and clear a path for the heavies. Long-range sensors and command ships are staying back, directing fire for the battle stations." She looked up, eyes glistening. "All fire's converging on our decoys, trying to cripple them and slow our retreat. They smell blood."

"So do I." Zim slow-tapped a knuckle of her balled fist to her chin. "You say all their capital ships are back and firing long, and all short-range sensor and weapon platforms are forward?" Kuwashima nodded.

Zim pointed to Ebron. "You said we can execute one action?" He nodded. A smile crept across Zim's face. The bridge team saw it and froze.

"Cancel retreat. Signal Savvy and Tock, we're going on offense."

Zim touched a red circle on the star chart. "When this squadron commits to the minefield," her finger shifted to the cluster of circles in the Aldrakin rear, "we go here… Aberrant Knight."

Her team flew into action. Ebron slid the new coordinates to the navigator and passed them to the squadron. Kuwashima set the weapons officers to calibrate for short range against heavily shielded targets.

Kaplan's eyes darted, unable to track the seamless orchestration. Zim exchanged glances with Ebron and Kuwashima then pointed her chin from Kuwashima to Kaplan.

"Over here, Wonder," Kuwashima called and elicited a chair to rise beside her. Kaplan sat and watched as her team fed targets to *Lasalle's* weapon systems.

"Aberrant Knight?" he muttered. "I don't remember that in StarCom's battle manual."

"Welcome to Five Squadron, Wonder Kaplan." Kuwashima's eyes remained glued as her hands dashed across the panels. Officers around them smiled without looking up. "The Aldrakin know the StarCom battle manual. This maneuver comes from the Starflower battle manual. It's a Daka-Rye gambit."

Seeing Kaplan's brows knit, Kuwashima expanded. "Daka-Rye is the Tak-Yaki combat sport. When we became allies and began joint operations, Marshal Zimmon insisted we field a team in their Daka-Rye league."

"Okay, teach me. What's an Aberrant Knight?" Kaplan trembled with expectation. He kept telling himself this is what he'd asked for.

"We are. Five Squadron takes a Myseko skip into the middle of the enemy fleet and goes berserk—we shoot whatever comes up on the scanner."

Kaplan pulled upright. "Myseko's for interstellar travel. It's suicide to skip within a star system. We'll be in Bai-Yota's gravity well." He glanced around. No one seemed the least perturbed.

"It's a terrific surprise tactic," Kuwashima said then faced him. "No one expects it. In Daka-Rye, the Aberrant Knight is a sacrifice. We sell ourselves dearly to distract the enemy, and our reserve force finishes them off." She smiled into Kaplan's astonished, black eyes. He gripped the weapons console.

"How near can we get?" Zim asked.

Ebron, pointing to the Aldrakin rear-flank, spread and rocked his index finger and thumb to indicate the margin for error.

Zim turned to Kuwashima. "We'll likely be too far out to target their sensors, so disable weapon systems first. Update the squadron."

"Yes, sir."

Zim rechecked the star chart. "Everyone set timers. We go Myseko in twenty-five seconds. Any luck, we'll catch 'em still committed to the minefield."

Zim's heart pounded, and her breath came short. "Lock down," she called and took her seat. Her stony-faced crew silently followed suit and felt the reactive seats hug them in place. Zim looked across and back at her team. The thought crossed her mind as it had before every battle—this might be their end—and a thin smile crept back onto her lips.

"Sheer away."

Lasalle dropped out of space and time.

# # #

A massive hull loomed before *Lasalle's* transparent bow. *ErrrrAHH, errrrAHH, errrrAHH*, the collision alarm screamed like a wounded beast. Ebron diverted. The other cruisers swerved.

Zim spun to see Kuwashima's team frantically resetting weapon priorities. "Targeting changed to comm and sensors," Kuwashima said.

Zim smiled and swung back to the command console. "Flights Two and Three take out the sensor and command ships in the center. Flights One, Four, and Five, we go after the battle stations."

Firing point blank, the cruisers had to fast rotate to maintain target queuing. In nineteen seconds, the huge battle stations went silent. Unable to switch the target range quickly, they never got in a shot. Zim directed Kuwashima to shift the target priority to long-range and fire on the rear of the Aldrakin ships engaged in the minefield.

Savvy simultaneously launched the four cruisers of Six Flight in a counterstrike, but most of the enemy ships had already disengaged and were headed back toward Zim. Stripped of long-range direction from their command ships, the Aldrakin fired wide, but manual correction and closing range quickly improved their accuracy. Vastly outnumbered and overextended, Zim's cruisers began to lose power, cease fire, and drop out of the battle.

"Another fleet entering the battle space with the Aldrakin," Ebron announced. Zim checked the star chart. Two red circles joined the approaching cruisers.

"Confirmation," Zim ordered.

Before Ebron could respond, the new formations fired on the Aldrakin at close range, and their circles turned blue.

Ebron laughed. "Confirm TY squadrons Zook and Yeko. It's Tock."

Duplicating Zim's tactics, Tock had caught the Aldrakin again firing long. The final exchange lasted two minutes. Then all enemy weapons went silent.

Lights dimmed then returned on *Lasalle's* bridge. Air circulation pumps restarted. They were on limited backup. Zim had set the power priority to weapons, and the E-Mag and pulse batteries had depleted the last of it. The *Lasalle* had lost maneuver capability and was floating out of control.

Zim checked for damage and casualties. Except for the power loss and a few bumps, one broken arm, they had suffered no serious damage. The same for the rest of Five Squadron and Tock's two Tak-Yaki squadrons.

Sensors indicated that the Aldrakin combatants had shut down internal power and shunted all backup to life support. Out of control, their massive starships drifted and rolled. Countless shuttles and escape pods ejected. Three small craft fled into space. The Aldrakin commander opened a short-range emergency channel requesting a ceasefire and immediate assistance, which Zim granted.

"Starflower, this is Clockwork." Tock's clicks were music to *Lasalle's* operations deck. "Can we give you a tow?" A one-and-a-half-meter, dark blue and violet projection rose from the floor beside Zim. Tock's mandible mouth parts chiggered laughter, barely able to form words.

"You used Aberrant Knight against me in our last match." Still chiggering, Tock paused to regain composure. "That was quite a risk Gayle. You were supposed to alert me." It shook a closed clamp-claw at her. "Very lucky, Gayle, and very lucky I registered your Myseko coordinates."

"I was on silent comms, but I knew you'd remember our match. Besides, how much luck do I need fighting alongside my old buddy?" Zim's smile veiled barely controlled trembling. Below the command console, the nails of her balled fists drew blood in her hands.

Formal Surrender

"Most of our cruisers could use a tow or a boost," Zim said to Tock's projection. "They're sliding into Bai-Yota's gravity well and heating up. I'll trust you to lead the rescue, old friend. And please, do not forget the Aldrakin."

"*The Aldrakin*," Tock clicked the air furiously. Deleting Tock's expletives, the translation came out choppy. "We'll rescue them… because you ask… and because you are here to witness."

Zim had been around Tak-Yaki enough times to understand their colorful clicks without translation. They preferred eating defeated foes, and Aldrakin were their favorite dish. "Thank you, my good friend for deferring to my Human sensibilities. After you've secured the battlefield, perhaps we can discuss the surrender ceremony over bourbon."

"Surrender ceremony? This is too much." Tock's triangular head tilted up as its claws clicked high.

"Admiral Okrador requested that we receive his formal surrender. It is unusual these days… to show respect to an enemy. This is the first I've heard of it in this war, but the Aldrakin Code of Nobility requires honorable surrender to honorable opponents. It would appear they deem both of us honorable— Tak-Yaki as well as Humans."

"I'll dine with you and drink your bourbon, but I'll not fraternize with frogs and want nothing to do with formalized fantasies." They exchanged stiff nods as Tock's projection melted into the deck.

Tock's tolerance had already exceeded Zim's expectation. She had feared an incident and was relieved Tock would not be attending the ceremony.

Major Kuwashima sent after-action reports to Star Command at Port Estelle and to Star Council on Corydon. While Five Squadron had suffered minimal damage, their surgical strikes had taken the Aldrakin fleet apart: not only weapon systems and sensors, but interstellar communications, navigation, and power trains. Their drifting warships were powerless and unable to communicate beyond short-range hailing channels.

Yet for all the damage, Aldrakin casualties were no higher than the Humans or Tak-Yaki. Cuts, broken and lost limbs, exposure due to failed life support systems, but no fatalities. Zim directed the medical teams. And with Tock's assistance, they drew power from the idle Aldrakin reactors to recharge Five Squadron.

Kuwashima's report drew an immediate response from Abramyan, including new orders:

- *Major Anthony Savielli to assume immediate command of Five Squadron, relieving Marshal Zimmon.*
- *Marshal Zimmon to receive the surrender of the Aldrakin battle fleet in the name of Star Lord Kiya Malik and the Star Council.*
- *Following the ceremony, Marshal Zimmon is to depart Bai-Yota for Corydon and report to Star Commander Abramyan and to the Star Council. Executive Corvette Halcyon has been dispatched to collect her.*

Abramyan's communiqué continued with forty-three pages of boilerplate diplomatic protocol—administrivia Zim recalled sleeping through in officer training. The *StarCom Officer's Manual* stated in reverent detail that, "Executing these procedures precisely is the distinguishing characteristic of top StarCom officers."

Zim picked up the main points: be polite and respectful, receive the surrender, and return home. Though she planned to be graceful to her defeated enemy, she hoped the Aldrakin hadn't memorized StarCom's pretentious manual. What bothered her more was going to Corydon. She'd never been to the capital, not even for the Corydonics. Corydon's combat games and all military training had been held off world.

#

Admiral Okrador offered to host the surrender ceremony aboard his more spacious flagship. There would be a formal reception and dinner buffet. All of this seemed highly unusual to Zim, but, after coordinating with Tock and consulting with her intelligence and security officers, she accepted Okrador's offer. She also granted clearances for an executive yacht and for one unarmed transport to bring additional guests and witnesses.

After dismissing itself and the TY officers, Tock offered to provide security for the ceremony. Zim was again pleased. She knew the brutal history behind the Tak-Yaki-Aldrakin feud. In early encounters, the Aldrakin had mistaken Tak-Yaki outposts for nests of insect-analog delicacies. Reeling from the humiliation, the vindictive Tak-Yaki returned the insult with carnivorous vengeance. Zim knew no diplomatic ploy could make up for years of animosity and trusted the Aldrakin would not take offense from Tock's refusal.

Formal ceremonies required much preparation. Surrender protocol stipulated that the victorious champion arrive with two second officers and four deputies, all in appropriate attire. Dress uniforms being in short supply, Zim arranged a clothing swap in *Lasalle's* wardroom. She selected Major Savielli and Lieutenant Ebron as seconds, the remaining four flight leaders as deputies, and Kaplan as an observer. Major Kuwashima, designated Savielli's first officer after Abramyan's directive, would oversee Five Squadron while Zim and Savvy were on the Aldrakin flagship.

Before departing, Zim assembled her team for a final inspection and security brief. Lieutenant M'Bong, in the ageless tradition of security officers, delivered his talk without a hint of humor or emotion.

"Expect no subterfuge. The Aldrakin code forbids it. They are an aristocratic culture, bound by duty and tradition, and fiercely religious, which I'm sure you'll see demonstrated in the ceremony. You may even have to endure one of their religious services.

"Their Code of Nobility is so strict it would shame the institutions of old Earth. Any breach requires death for the perpetrators, their families, and all members of their military unit. Legal intervention is never required; they self-immolate out of shame. After surrender on the field of battle, they cannot go back. Their code tolerates no deviations, no excuses. This ceremony is intended to honor you as victors. It is an honor they rarely—to my knowledge never—bestow to outsiders." M'Bong looked to Zim then to each of her team members in turn.

"The Aldrakin are an ancient culture spanning more than one hundred fifty-star systems. Their commercial enterprises extend throughout this end of the galaxy, well beyond human contacts, so expect to see many alien species. For pragmatic reasons—atmospheres, gravity, commissary, work patterns, medical support—we divide allied forces into separate squadrons. The Aldrakin mix their alien crews."

Major Savielli nodded upward. "What about technology?"

"They have over fifteen millennia in space and are beyond Humans in most technical areas. We estimate they reached a plateau twelve hundred years ago. Since then, they've concentrated on mercantile interests."

"Yet they initiated a war," Ebron said.

"A good question. They hold that we started the war. Some day we may know for sure." M'Bong looked around. "To our knowledge, no Human has ever boarded an Aldrakin military vessel or visited one of their primary worlds. Their original planet suffered a cosmic disaster some millennia ago. What little we know comes from Goorm traders, itinerant workers, and academics.

"The Aldrakin are semi-aquatic amphibians. You've seen the pictures— they resemble man-sized frogs. Their skin requires frequent moisturizing; expect their facilities to reflect that. The good news: reports of their dietary habits say their nutritional requirements and prohibitions are similar to Humans. So, you may participate in any offerings of food or drink. I won't speak to their tastes. Try to be diplomatic."

M'Bong looked to Zim, she nodded to proceed, and he set a flat metal box on the table. "Marshal Zimmon wants your visit monitored for security and intelligence purposes, and to create a historical record." He opened the box and removed a midnight blue thread three centimeters long. "Each of you will wear one of these monitors. They transmit images, conversations, and all electro-magnetic emissions. Laced into your uniform collar, they are practically impossible to detect." M'Bong placed a thread on each collar in turn and waited as they wove into the fabric.

The Aldrakin

Although many times the size of Star Command's largest vessel, the Aldrakin flagship shared their nested-cylindrical design. Zim assumed the main cylinder would be reserved for living and workspaces with a rotation rate set for Aldrakin standard 1.1G. Other cylinders would be set for higher- or lower-gravity species, or for critical activities: operations, engineering, food production, medical clinics and dispensary, warehousing, utilities, and research. The zero-gravity hub would be for docking, garaging, and maintenance.

The docking-bay portal bloomed like a six-petal flower as their shuttle approached, extending a ramp as if inviting a bee to partake of its nectar. A curtain of light reached out and engulfed them and sealed out the vacuum of space. When the curtain withdrew, it pulled them into the bay like a trawler hauling fish.

Zim broke the deafening silence. "Fascinating technology."

"Fascinating," Savielli whispered, his olive face aglow in the monitor.

Her team took notes, which Zim found curious since the collar-threads recorded everything. Perhaps it was out of habit or nervousness, or they wanted to capture their initial personal impressions. She was nervous, too—about the diplomatic protocol.

In her few encounters with captive Aldrakin, she had found them gracious, even noble. But how would they react to her on their flagship? She would be the first Human to officially board one of their craft, a major historical event. She felt out of her element and more lost than when she left the farm for Basic training at Port Estelle.

A tractor in the hangar floor engaged the shuttle and towed them to a marked berth at the foot of a stairway. Other marked spaces extended out, up, and around the inside of the cylindrical hangar. All were empty except for a single small craft berthed two spaces from their shuttle. Zim recognized it as the executive yacht she had authorized.

Savielli dashed from the shuttle first, a breach of protocol Zim chose to ignore from one of her favorite officers. Light-framed and energetic, Savielli tested the hangar's weak gravity then strode smoothly toward the yacht. Besides being her top aerospace engineer, Savvy had a background in performance vehicles and competitive racing. Zim watched him sight down the yacht's length then circle to inspect the thrusters and stroke the sleek hull. Stepping back, he studied the red and yellow flame patterns licking back from the engines and wing roots.

"Can't imagine what sort of executive would have anything like this." Savvy's voice echoed in the cavernous hangar. "She's a racer, all right, a *real* racer. No doubt about it. Never knew the Aldrakin went in for this sort of thing."

Hissing gas and scraping metal brought them quickly back to the present. A seam formed on the bulkhead at the top of the stairway, extending to outline an entrance. Six crescent-latches emerged and disengaged, and a vault-like door lifted out and to the side. Two hatchet-beaked-guards in plum-colored livery and military-style helmets stork-stepped from the hatchway, pivoted, stepped to either side, pivoted again, and snapped ancient halberds to their chests.

A bright green, neckless Aldrakin emerged. With its frog-like legs extended, the Aldrakin was the height of a small man. Its plum-colored livery, finer cut than the guard's, had gold embroidery on the collar, cuffs, and edging. Its flat, ruby-red boots clearly enclosed amphibian feet. The Aldrakin bowed to Zim below, its rigid head-body moving together, and beckoned her to climb the wide-treaded stairway to the airlock.

Suddenly aware that her team had scattered, Zim looked about. Savvy was still eyeballing the yacht. Others examined the tractor, lighting, and the instrument landing system. Like children with new toys, Zim thought. Sensing her impatience, and ever the mother hen, Ebron gathered the officers and herded them to the stairway.

Zim was careful to use both handrails climbing the stairs. The weak gravity of the hangar deck dropped to zero at the flagship's axis of rotation.

The Aldrakin greeted her with a gentle press of its webbed palms to her shoulders. Suddenly it froze, its orange, bulbous eyes fixed on the iridescent blue Starflower on Zim's uniform. Recovering, the official repeated the shoulder-press greeting with each of her officers.

Their host led them through the airlock to a small circular room. When the door sealed, Zim felt the lift and the pull of increasing gravity. A door opened to a vestibule and an ornately carved gateway framed by another pair of hatchet-beaked guards. Beside the gateway, a low table held eight disk medallions. When their Aldrakin host mimed attaching a medallion to Zim's collar, she nodded.

"Starflower, I welcome you and your team to Admiral Okrador's flagship. I am Laveda, your host and master of ceremonies." He gestured to the disks. "These translators are calibrated for human synapses. May I?" His lozenge pupils rolled up to look directly into Zim's eyes then shifted to her team.

"Please." Zim felt her tension over protocol receding. They were being treated as guests.

While Laveda engaged her officers, Zim examined the panels along the wall and around the gateway. The furthest portrayed amphibians crawling from a primordial sea, the next showed them driving reptiles away with clubs, the next the discovery of fire. The progression highlighted key points in Aldrakin history. Many featured heroic figures confronting dragons or invading hordes. They reminded Zim of woodcuts she had seen in childhood, of fearless frog princes and dashing cats with cutlasses and plumed hats.

At Laveda's signal, the hatchet-beaked guards struck the butts of their halberds to the floor and pushed open the great doors. Laveda motioned Zim to enter.

She found herself on a beach leading down to a wide, marshy pond. An uncertain breeze wafted scents of rushes and bog flowers and blew wispy, lavender clouds across a rose-colored sky. The Aldrakin home world, Zim thought. It reminded her of swamps on Scalaris and fishing with her brothers. The pond bowed up on two sides, conforming to the contour of the flagship's cylindrical hull, a reminder to Zim that she was still on a starship.

The susurrus that rose when she entered the hall died down as Zim looked around. Alien beings filled the hall in numbers and varieties beyond her imagining. Eyes, antennae, funnels, and mushroom-like sensors followed her every movement from rocks and floating lilies. Some wore Aldrakin royal plum, others rainbow colors or no clothing beyond sashes and belts. No one spoke. The only sound was water lapping at the rocks.

Nothing in the protocol manual prepared Zim for this. Her officers, like bumpkins on their first visit to a big city, stared irreverently, craned their necks to the virtual sky, and touched everything.

Laveda pointed to the far side of the pond to an island and an emerald pavilion draped in plum. Parted curtains revealed an ancient figure in plum-hued robes seated on a high throne. Behind and to either side of the ancient sat alien officials in formal attire. Still, no one spoke.

At Laveda's wave, an arabesque carpet slid from the pavilion and swam toward them. Everyone in the hall rose. As the carpet neared, Zim noted an undulating fringe propelling it. A living creature or a machine? She shook her head.

When the carpet reached shore, Laveda stepped aboard and invited Zim and her officers to follow. The crossing was majestic. On reaching the island, the carpet ascended and formed steps. Laveda offered an arm to Zim and directed the other officers to align behind them.

The ancient figure rose awkwardly from the throne and, raising his arms, shouted out to the hall in a crackling, amplified voice, "Ha-Yee, Starflower."

The hall responded with hundreds of alien voices, "Ha-Yee, Starflower."

Laveda whispered the appropriate response to Zim, and she startled.

"The Emperor?"

"Yes," he whispered back.

Zim took a breath, raised her arms to the pavilion, and spoke out to the hall, "Ha-Yee, Great Lord Condolas, Emperor of the Aldrakin and Keeper of the Galactic Trade Federation."

Ebron gasped. "Emperor? What?" Then whispered, "Does this mean the war is over?"

Laveda hand-roll-gestured toward Zim. "Lord Condolas, may I introduce Star Marshal Gayle Zimmon, the Starflower." The Emperor shifted his cane to one side and opened both of his webbed palms wide.

With no experience or training to guide her, Zim bowed and accepted the Emperor's invitation to join him on the dais. Behind the high-collared robe, embroidered banners, and strings of medals, Zim saw the burden of great age. The brown-mottled skin formed taut ridges and sank deep into the hollows at his cheeks and temples. His orange-clouded eyes seemed shrunk into hollow, red-rimmed sockets. Zim imagined the stress this ceremony must be taking on the old warrior.

The Emperor turned left then right so everyone could view them together. Stretching tall on feeble frog-legs, and still a head shorter than Zim, he pressed his palms to her shoulders. She returned the greeting, much to the hall's pleasure. "Ha-Yee, Ha-Yee."

The Emperor then took three steps down from the dais, braced his shaking legs, and greeted each of Zim's officers. The gathering repeated, "Ha-Yee," for each officer. Struggling back to the throne, the Emperor gestured for the ceremony to continue.

Admiral Okrador came to the dais and stood in the spotlight. Lights dimmed, and he recounted the battle of Bai-Yota. His lavish comments praised the chivalry and martial prowess of the Humans. Zim thought him overly gratuitous but chalked that up to Aldrakin formal protocol.

Okrador suddenly stopped, pressed his palms together before his face, and turned his orange, bulbous eyes up to the spotlight. "It came to me in an instant... the signs were there... all the signs." He gazed reverentially about the silent hall. "The Prophecy unfolded before me, and I felt naked." He dropped his hands and, to the quiet accompaniment of water plinking from low fronds into the pond, stepped from the dais.

The High Priest of Aldra Korah came next. A holographic projection above the pond illuminated his narration.

"Our history as recorded by Ejazz-Eel in the twenty-third book of the Aldra Korah, 'The departure into the Long Night'."

"Ha-Yee, Aldra Korah," sounded low across the darkened hall.

"In that distant time there came unto Aldrakhan a marauder from deep space..." The priest recited the apocalyptic tale of their planet's destruction. As he spoke, a rogue star appeared in the light display on a collision course with an orange-yellow star system.

The recitation told how the prophet Hiran-Ejazz directed the Aldrakin to construct an ark from a hollowed moon; one that would save them by taking them on a multi-generational, thousand-year journey across the stars. On the final day, as the last of the chosen boarded the ark, Hiran-Ejazz gave his passage to a younger prophet, the one who was to succeed him, the one who recorded this history. Hiran-Ejazz then bid them a fair journey.

"Thus, wrote Ejazz-Eel."

"Ha-Yee, Aldra Korah," the hall responded.

"Now hear the Prophecy regarding signs of the return, as recorded by Ejazz-Eel in the twenty-fourth book of the Aldra Korah."

"Ha-Yee, Aldra Korah," the hall responded.

Long will the war be: our daughters depleted of eggs, our coffers of treasure, our hearts of hope. No youth will recall a time of peace when neither fen nor fell fed the maw of war. And in the dark of the darkest night, as warriors watch and wait for death, a sign will appear—the sign of our return. It will be the flower that blooms in the night and opens her petals to the stars.

The Starflower blooms in the enemy camp, and you shall know her, for she shall be the warrior you cannot defeat. Her brightness will grow and in the gloom of that bleak night, in unequal battle, she shall reach full bloom. Know the sign of the Starflower, for in that last and greatest battle, none shall die. And at its end, both Aldrakin and foe shall serve the wounded and together restore that which was lost. You shall make your peace with the Starflower, and with her alone shall you make it, for only she can take you home.

Dark is her path, and she rides it on the wings of the storm. But wondrous signs mark the way. Two mythic figures stride beside her: one who will never live, one who will never die. Together will these three fulfill the Prophecy.

"Thus spoke Ejazz-Eel."

Zim's team joined the response, "Ha-Yee, Aldra Korah."

Prophecy? Zim swallowed the knot in her throat. *What does it mean?*

Laveda took center spot on the dais and faced Zim. "Our Lord Emperor Condolas and the High Council of the Aldrakin Empire, including all Aldrakin domains, make formal surrender to the Starflower. We hope this will end our terrible war, bring peace to the galaxy, and open a new era of understanding. We ask no conditions other than to return to our homes in peace. The Aldrakin shall relinquish all contested regions, including all planets previously occupied by Humans and areas in which Humans had established a presence. Departures will begin immediately following this ceremony."

Struggling not to be overwhelmed, Zim replied in a strong voice. "I am but a warrior and have no diplomatic credentials. However, today I have been entrusted to accept this surrender." *Not in my own name,* she thought, *and only the surrender of a fleet.* "I find your treaty request more than reasonable and would like to offer our battle recovery support as soon as damage assessments can be completed."

Emperor Condolas nodded agreement then extended a quivering hand to a diminutive page. The page brought forward a crystal tray on which sat a vermillion box. Laveda opened the box and held it out for the gathering to see, then offered the contents to Zim. The hall again fell silent.

Nested in the padded hollow of the box was a four-centimeter crystalline sphere depicting the Milky Way galaxy. When Laveda held the sphere to the light, the galactic image filled the hall with a blaze of stars in astonishing detail. A moment later, Laveda transferred the sphere to a vermillion pouch and handed it to Zim.

"This is the Chorya'Key. It belongs to the prophets. It is our greatest and most ancient treasure." Zim accepted the gift with both hands and a low bow.

Laveda then turned to the hall, raised his arms wide, opened his white, crescent-lipped mouth, and shouted, "The war is ended."

The hall erupted in cheers and shouts, "Ha-Yee, Starflower, Ha-Yee, Condolas." Aliens leaped at one another and at Zim's officers, pressing shoulders, kissing, entwining tentacles, claws, and webs, gurgling and gyrating in all the ways their species expressed joy. Zim felt an electric thrill sweep through her and, with it, a rush of new hope.

Reception

The clamor overwhelmed the translators. No one seemed to notice. While joy flowed unabated, plum-liveried servants threaded in and out, setting up buffet tables on either side of the pavilion, carrying chairs high, ice buckets, warming platters, tableware, food trays, bottles, kegs, flagons, flasks of drinks, converging seemingly from every direction. A low music stage was set with instruments, stands, and half a dozen seats.

"We hope you and your team will stay for the reception," Laveda shouted over the clamor and chaos. "Many are eager to meet and know Humans, especially the Starflower: clerics, scientists, academics, soldiers, historians, and of course, merchants—we are a mercantile empire." Zim found Laveda charming if overly humble.

"We wouldn't miss it."

"Excellent. While preparations are being set, may I begin the introductions?" Zim rolled a hand for him to lead.

Laveda's frog-legs kneed and compacted as his green body wedged through the churning crowd. Zim kept close. Many reached to her then were pulled away by the flow. Others stared wide-eyed.

"Few saw this coming," Laveda shouted back over the din. "Others denied what was happening. Early in the war, we heard of a Human warrior called Starflower. We assumed that was a psychological ploy to play on our mythology. When your career continued tracking with the Prophecy, many became believers, and we waited for the final sign."

"A major battle with no losses?"

"Yes. Nothing close to this scale has ever happened." Laveda paused beside the pond, stooped, and swept his hand through the water. "The Noorki are our oldest and dearest allies." Zim peered at a cluster of waving, green tentacle-jellies below Laveda's hand. "You recall the High Priest's recitation, how our planet was destroyed, and we fled into space. When we reached

Kookala-karin, the Noorki graciously invited us to share their planet. That was the end of our first interstellar journey, what we call The Long Night. We are eternally grateful to them. We believe Noorki to be the greatest mathematicians in the galaxy."

Zim dipped her fingers into the water and felt rather than heard a greeting. "We are pleased to meet the Starflower and welcome you to the Galactic Trade Federation. Perhaps our skills may find service with your race." A warm tingle rushed up Zim's forearm.

"It is a pleasure to meet you. My wish is that we may explore all areas of common interest." It was one of the few lines Zim remembered from the protocol manual.

Laveda pointed to the growing reception line. Zim recognized some species: the crab-like Goorm, well-known traders; tree-stump-like Shelesti and their Hyrup symbionts. It was said the centipede-like Hyrup took to music like spiders to web-spinning. Many species she'd never seen: lemur-eyed, red-furred Li-Kass, amebic-radial Sk'Keffin with migrating heads and faces, Salogar in their stilt-walking, ammonia canisters. Engineers, diplomats, businessmen, mathematicians, Laveda introduced them all.

"Excuse me." A miniature Aldrakin pulled on Laveda's leg, its plum tunic barely hid the vestige of its tadpole tail. Laveda frog-squatted and turned his tympanum to the page then relayed the message. "The Emperor wishes to speak with the Starflower on a personal matter."

The Emperor's throne glistened with the mist that kept his ancient skin moist. Rivulets twisted and dripped from his regal robes onto the mossy carpet. Seeing the rigid, frayed mouth struggle to form words, Zim squatted beside the Emperor, and leaned close.

"A special favor, Starflower."

"How may I serve you, Lord Condolas?"

A thin, brown-speckled hand dropped onto Zim's. "My time is short. I wanted to see the Starflower, see the Prophecy fulfilled before I die. My nephew escorted me and brought his son. His starship is unusual. You may have seen it."

"A member of my crew was admiring it."

The Emperor waved an Aldrakin warrior to come forward. "Starflower, please meet my nephew, Commander B'Len." The young officer snapped to attention. Zim rose, stood directly in front of the warrior, and pressed her hands to his shoulders. B'Len returned the greeting.

"Meeting you is a great honor, Starflower. I studied your battles at the academy and have ever since." B'Len remained at attention, arms by his sides, black lozenge pupils locked ahead in his bulbous, orange eyes.

"Be at ease, Commander." Zim kept her voice level. "The Emperor mentioned your son was with you." B'Len side-stepped to reveal a miniature of himself. The youngster wore simulated armor of a pattern Zim had seen in the hallway engravings.

The little knight came to attention, legs extended. Pulling his round shield to the front, he held it high for Zim to see. The heraldic device at its center was an iridescent blue starflower.

B'Len's voice broke. "Ajalanda told me… when he grows up, he wants to be like his father and like the Starflower." Zim blinked the blur from her eyes then looked down to the play-armor-clad Aldrakin.

"Sir Knight, I am unfamiliar with the customs of this realm, perhaps Commander B'Len might permit you to escort me to the Emperor's banquet." The little knight rolled pleading eyes up to his father. "And while we are eating, perhaps Commander B'Len would be so kind as to discuss the technical aspects of his starship with Major Savielli." Zim nodded to Savvy six steps away, cornered by a persistent Goorm businessman.

"My pleasure, Starflower." B'Len bow-tipped his body, nudged Ajalanda forward, and stepped over to Savielli.

Zim offered her arm. "Sir Ajalanda, shall we go to the buffet?"

"Yes, Starflower." Ajalanda slipped his shield onto his back and reached for Zim's hand.

The crescent buffet table was covered with white fabric trimmed in gold and set with white ceramic platters and bowls edged with aquatic floral patterns. Bowls overflowed with meats, fish, and fruit, most of which Zim did not recognize. She discreetly assured herself that nothing looked like a Tak-Yaki head, antenna, or claw. One end of the table held carafes of red, plum, and golden liquids and crystal glassware with edges, spouts, and tubes designed for alien mouths. In the center, a three-meter ice sculpture of a tentacled sea creature brimmed with seafood that servants regularly replenished.

While Ajalanda fetched a step stool, Zim searched for serving and eating utensils. Finding none, and having eaten with the less than squeamish Tak-Yaki, she selected a hand-sized slug-spider and bit into it.

She heard, "galum, galum, galum," and, looking down, saw Ajalanda struggling to contain his croaking laughter.

"That's not the way it's done, Starflower," he said. "I'll show you." Ajalanda stepped onto the stool, extended high his prodigious webbed feet, and leaned toward the ice sculpture. A white tongue darted half-a-meter, snagged another slug-spider, and snapped back. Unable to track the movement, Zim turned to see the edges of three spider legs protruding from Ajalanda's rigid-lipped mouth. Two quick gulps and they were gone. He turned to Zim. "Now you try."

Zim chuckled. "I'm sure I can't do that as well as you. I have a small mouth, short tongue, and these." She held out her hands. "So, we have to take small bites."

"I'd still like to see you try it," said a low Human voice. Zim turned to see a roguish Human male with plaited, black hair and a curled, wide mustache. He wore an open, sky-blue vest with no shirt, and bloused red trousers tucked into high black boots.

"Marshal Zimmon, I am a great admirer but fear no one will introduce us." He doffed his wide-brimmed hat and bowed over it. "I am Traier, Hetman of the Chei-Binsk Rii-Chaut, and ally to the Aldrakin in our heroic struggle against the Star Council." Head low, he glanced up with intense black eyes. "Although I suspect that relationship is about to change."

Zim forced a thin smile. "The Rii-Chaut are a criminal organization. Where and how many are you?"

Traier grinned back, arching his eyebrows. "Congratulations on your impressive victory. We shall try to miss your next one."

"My next victory?" Zim touched two fingers to her chin in feigned deliberation. "The war is over, and I will soon be decommissioned. So, it is unlikely we will meet again." She paused. "Come to think of it, Mister Traier, I don't believe I've ever engaged your Chei-Binsk sect in combat."

"Chei-Binsk is in a remote sector, but I am reasonably certain you will hear more of us soon." He stood and returned his hat to his head. "For the right price or the right customer, we have many uses." With that he begged his leave. Zim watched as Traier bid farewell to Admiral Okrador and other senior officers.

After a deep, hat-sweeping bow to the Emperor, he stepped onto the swimming carpet and two minutes later was gone from the hall.

# # #

That evening, in her cabin on *Lasalle,* Zim examined the Chorya'Key. Was it more than a beautiful relic? Did it belong in a museum? Could it be a navigation tool? The Aldrakin had explored and made contacts far beyond Humans. Held under the desk lamp, the Chorya'Key filled her small cabin with stars. She located her home star system and planet Scalaris. Hearing a tap at the door, she slipped the gift back into the vermillion pouch.

"Enter," she called. The pressure seal released, the round-cornered hatch slid into the wall, and Lt. Ebron came in carrying a tea service.

"Marshal Zimmon, you frequently close your day with tea. When you didn't come to the galley, I thought I'd bring you some."

"Thank you, Lieutenant. That's very thoughtful, but it's not necessary for you to wait on me."

"It is my pleasure, sir. We've spaced together a long time. Everyone's talking about going home. This may be the last time we see each other." He placed the tray with a bone china teapot gently on the corner of Zim's desk. She noticed two cups on the tray.

"Please join me, Lieutenant." She gestured to a wooden chair beside her desk. Ebron poured tea into both cups.

"An amazing ceremony," Zim said, guessing what Ebron was thinking.

He squeezed a lemon slice into her cup then handed the cup to her on a saucer. "Had you heard about the Aldra Korah or the Prophecy before?"

She looked at Ebron over her cup and took a sip. "No. Everything caught me by surprise: the Prophecy, the flagship, Aldrakin graciousness, the war ending. I knew they were religious. I respect that but..." Her voice trailed off.

"Do you believe it?"

"The Prophecy? No, can't say I do. I haven't led that kind of life... just tried to be a good soldier." Ebron looked surprised. He hadn't touched his own cup. "After fifteen thousand years the right set of circumstances came along; that's what I believe." She leveled her eyes with Ebron's. "But the Aldrakin certainly convinced me that *they* believe in the Prophecy. I don't know what they expect of me now, but the war ending is good for all of us."

"What will you do?" Ebron asked, finally lifting his cup.

"Oh, let me see. Leave StarCom." She opened her palms in her lap as if that was a given. "Take whatever retirement they offer. Get as far from Corydon and the Creative clique as possible. Try to reconnect with whatever's left of my life. Find my parents. I heard the farm was destroyed." Zim took another sip. "Then I'll find a job... somewhere remote... probably settle down, start a family." Though she smiled at Ebron, her mind had jumped to Mac. She cleared her throat. "Eventually, we'll all do *something* like that. If the genetically engineered Creatives don't like our company, we'll go further out. The Aldrakin have jobs. Goorm trading posts are everywhere."

Ebron finished his tea, set the cup on the saucer, and slid it away. "I don't know if the Star Council will let you leave. They have Kuwashima's battle report. M'Bong said the record of the ceremony would be kept for history. We all had transmitters—"

"And that's not the history Star Council wants," Zim finished Ebron's thought, "not a bunch of Unders winning the war." Ebron nodded. "I guess we'll find out when we get back."

"You'll find out first," Ebron said. "Kaplan and Kuwashima are going back with you—orders just came in. Their tours are done. The rest of us will probably process out at Port Estelle." Ebron lifted the teapot to refill Zim's cup. When she waved no thanks, he moved both cups and the pot back to the tray and rose to leave.

"It's been great serving with you, Lieutenant. You've been my right arm on *Lasalle* and running Five Squadron." Zim stood to shake his hand. "I recommended to Savvy that you take over One Flight when I leave."

"Thank you, sir. It's been an honor... the high point of my life." He set the tea service quickly down and hugged Zim with both arms. "If you ever need an XO, a comms officer, a navigator."

"I hoped you'd say that." She hugged him back. "But honestly, I hope someday we both have greater, more wonderful experiences to remember."

Ebron wiped his eyes and picked up the tray. The door sealed behind him.

Zim shared Ebron's concerns but hadn't been honest about the Prophecy. Its implications challenged her. If true, the Prophecy put a great burden on her.

She finished packing her heinkel-skin carry bag. The formal dress uniform took the most space. The Chorya'Key in the vermillion pouch went into an inside pocket, her Starflower medal into another. Her few personal effects fit into side pockets. The executive corvette *Halcyon* should arrive shortly. Savvy and the other flight commanders were waiting on the bridge to say goodbye.

She glanced at Abramyan's directive on her desk, closed it, and doused the lamp. Meeting him on Corydon would be unpleasant, but hopefully, this would be the last time. She paused before leaving, allowing her eyes to scan and say goodbye to the cabin that had been her home for so many years. Her heart picked up. The universe and her future had changed. And maybe she would see Mac.

Part Two

Corydon

Call Sign Starflower

Zim watched the *Halcyon* dock from behind *Lasalle's* airlock. Kuwashima and Kaplan stood with her. All three wore midnight blue jumpsuits. The docking bay doors embraced and sealed the corvette hull, ramps slid out to engage passenger and cargo hatches, and pumps brought up the air pressure in the docking bay. Forty seconds later, the airlock hissed and unlatched. As Zim shouldered her carry bag, Kuwashima and Kaplan snapped to attention.

"At ease Major, Wonder." The two officers snapped to the stand-at-ease position. Zim smiled. "By the time we get to Corydon, we may all be civilians, so we can be informal. I'm sure you're both eager to get back to normal civilian life."

The docking bay smelled stale from air in the pumps. A Human pilot led two robotic humanoids (RHs) down the boarding ramp and stood at attention. The pilot wore a blue, one-piece flight suit; the metal RH chassis simulated the same suit design.

"Star Marshal Zimmon?" The pilot saluted.

"Yes, Lieutenant." She returned his salute.

"Welcome aboard, sir. We'll depart immediately."

Zim nodded and stepped onto the boarding ramp. "Ha-Yee, Starflower!" she heard and looked back. Still holding a salute, the pilot smiled broadly.

"Ha-Yee, Lieutenant," she returned, smiling quizzically before stepping through the hatch. Someone must have briefed the pilot about the surrender ceremony. Kuwashima and Kaplan exchanged salutes and Ha-Yees with the pilot then boarded behind her.

The scent of new leather and fresh flowers filled the cabin, although neither was evident. Was this the only ship available? Am I getting special treatment... from Abramyan? Zim had not seen such elegant accommodations since rescuing a SynTerra executive early in the war. The layout was open and clean. At center, an oval table sat eight. Single seats and small groupings were fore

59

and aft. Zim settled into a forward seat. She waved off the projected offer for beverages, hors d'oeuvres, and stimulants.

Kuwashima went to the back, reclined, and closed her eyes. Kaplan, taking Zim's request for informality as an invitation, slid in beside her. "Last night's ceremony, how did you—"

"I was winging it from the time we left the hangar deck." Zim rolled her head back on the headrest.

"Hmm." Kaplan twisted his lanky frame in his seat to face her. "What's Corydon like? This is my first trip." His dark eyes widened in his coffee-dark face.

Zim lifted her head. "I haven't been there either. Ask Kuwashima. Yoshi did a stint with Weapons Acquisition two years ago." Without another word, Kaplan jumped up and headed back.

What *was* Corydon like, Zim wondered. She had only seen pictures of the starport and the capital, but it hardly mattered. She wasn't planning to stay. Would Mac be there? With their personal comms blocked, they'd lost touch. If he was still on staff, he'd know she was coming. Of course, he'd moved on. She supposed she had, too. Or was that another lie she told herself? It was still Roland Mackenzie she called on and confided in when alone. It won't be long, Gayle, he had said.

"No, it won't be long," she murmured, a tear prickling the corner of her eye. For her, their last kiss stretched out across time… did Mac feel the same way?

Kaplan bounced into the seat next to Kuwashima. "Hey Yoshi, what's Corydon like?"

Kuwashima cracked an eyelid and waved back a strand of straight, black hair. "Creatives and robots and more Creatives and robots." Zim pivoted her seat to listen. "The robots you see will mostly be RHs, the humanoid types, like our crew here. But robots are everywhere, in machines, furniture, walls and walkways, even in the food."

"How about people?"

"Creatives are special people, the future of mankind," Kuwashima quoted the government pitch. "Which means we Unders are not."

"Special?"

"The future." Kuwashima leveled her dark, doe eyes with Kaplan's. "Once they got the design for people right, they didn't want imperfections. You, me,

Marshal Zimmon, we're imperfect. Anyone call you an Under yet?" Kaplan shook his head. "They will on Corydon. There isn't much a Creative can't do better than us. They specialize in every field except soldiering, but I expect they'll get around to that."

"How about Derek Boorman? Isn't he a Creative?"

Kuwashima raised a finger. "Boorman's a general officer. There are no Creative grunts. They don't make 'em."

Kaplan frowned. "Don't think I ever met a Creative, but I haven't been anywhere except Thrinlu and a couple frontier camps."

"You'll see lots on Corydon. Not many on the frontier. They like their amenities and don't mix outside their kind—separate habitats, mess, medical, and rec facilities." Kuwashima gave a resigned shrug.

Kaplan scowled. "After we muster out, I guess I'll go back to Thrinlu."

"If you can." Kuwashima again closed her eyes. "Creatives need space and Thrinlu is on their shopping list. If your family's still there, get 'em off. Find some outpost that's still hiring people like us."

The pilot entered the cabin. "Star Marshal. I know you've been out of touch for some time, but wartime regulations remain in effect. We won't have general comms access until we near Corydon, but if you'd like, I can send my latest news update. It's not interactive from this location, but it updated twelve hours ago."

"Thank you. That'll be fine, Lieutenant." When Kaplan and Kuwashima waved, Zim signaled for them to be included.

The pilot continued. "We're preparing pushback from *Lasalle,* so everyone needs to be seated. Myseko skip in eighty-six minutes." The pilot returned to the cockpit.

Zim settled back, heard the whine of dock depressurization, felt the shudder of clamps unlocking and the gentle rocking of *Halcyon* drifting out from the bay. The curve of Bai-Yota flashed across the monitor, sliding from view as *Halcyon* swung away. A moment later, the news update loaded.

STARFLOWER ENDS WAR! popped up followed by wild cheering scenes in the pubs and streets of Corydon City. The lead story was Okrador's swashbuckling account of how Zim and her hardy band single-handedly defeated the Aldrakin armada. Other accounts included recordings of the evocative surrender ceremony.

Zim took a cleansing breath, calmed herself, and flipped through the articles. Nowhere were the Tak-Yaki mentioned, and nothing was taken from Kuwashima's objective battle report. No security filters, no qualifiers, no redactions. How could their recordings have reached general distribution? She noted Kuwashima having the same reaction.

Kaplan grimaced. "Well, maybe, after M'Bong's security briefing, I suggested that he uplink our collar and lapel sensors directly to Port Estelle. The reports might have gotten out from there." His eyes pleaded. "I didn't—"

"None of us knew the war was ending," Zim interrupted Kaplan's confession. "This will certainly make it difficult for Star Council to spin the surrender story another way. It may give us some protection. I don't think any real harm is done."

Worry furrowed Kaplan's brow. "But it will probably make it harder for us to keep a low profile and get home." He looked to Kuwashima. "But if you're right about robots and Creatives, our homes won't exist long anyway. Only robots I saw on Thrinlu were big industrial models for mining and manufacturing, diggers and builders." He looked to Zim. "Are the Creatives as good as Yoshi says?"

"I saw Creatives before the war and in training and competed against them in the Corydonics. They fielded three teams against us. They're not invincible."

"You trained with them?"

Zim could see Kaplan's curiosity was overtaking his anxiety. Kuwashima leaned in. "When the war started, Star Command called up all the teams from that year's combat games. We expected the callup. We'd taken first place, and the Corydonics were intended to identify combat officer skills. They put all the teams in the same Basic and pilot training programs. It was a big, unpleasant reunion." Zim turned one hand up and shrugged.

Kaplan smiled wide-eyed. "You trained with the guys you'd just beaten in the Corydon games, including Boorman... *Marshal Boorman*?"

"No Marshals back then. We were all shave-tail Wonders excited about the war. It was supposed to be over quickly. Boorman had been the favorite early in the games. Most Creatives blamed him for losing. He took it hard, said I'd cheated. Everyone expected a confrontation."

Kuwashima blurted, "Boorman couldn't accept losing to a team of Unders. He's a targ-thumping... excuse me, sir. I was disrespectful of a senior officer."

"What happened?" Kaplan looked to Zim then to Kuwashima. It wasn't a story Zim liked to tell. She tilted her head to Kuwashima and arched an eyebrow.

Kuwashima nodded and began, "Boorman called Marshal Zimmon out during a formal reception in front of the entire squadron. He made a big thing out of her not getting the Corydon Star, an award the Council decided could only go to Creatives. Instead, they contrived a onetime medal after a common weed on Marshal Zimmon's home planet, the starflower. Boorman said since Under mothers drop their babies in their own targ like dirty animals, the medal was appropriate. He said starflowers grew in targ, so she got what she deserved. Marshal Zimmon—"

Kuwashima caught Zim biting her lips and cut her account short. "That evening, the squadron assigned everyone their call signs. That's how Marshal Zimmon became the Starflower."

Zim knew Kaplan would hear the rest of the story later. The incident had happened her first week in Star Command, her first formal reception, and she was barely sixteen. A robot dresser had had to teach her to dress and walk in heels. She was basically what Boorman said she was: a rough country girl just off the frontier, who happened to excel in combat sports. Anger and jealousy ran high that night, and she'd had more alcohol than she was used to. Boorman was drunk and deserved a thrashing for bullying another trainee. But she had lost control, humiliated him in front of their classmates, gloated—and enjoyed it. Her only restraint had been turning his chin, so he didn't lose teeth when she hammered his face into the platter of green Chiricado dip.

Kuwashima had fallen silent, and Kaplan stared into space. Zim thought she understood their quiet reflection because she was wondering about her own postwar situation. Where were any of them going? Experienced combat leaders and born-and-raised gloak herders would be in low demand. Were Five Squadron and *Lasalle* her last commands? How would non-combatant civilians receive veterans? She'd grown up hunting, and combat had a sporting element. Should she feel guilty about killing and being good at it? Mac would know. Neither she nor those she fought had chosen that life.

"Myseko skip in thirty-two seconds," the pilot announced.

Zim folded her hands and gazed at them in her lap. She'd done a Myseko skip hundreds of times, but today it sounded different. More wonderful. She had plodded through Viktor Myseko's seminal paper in pre-flight, "Cross-

Dimensional String Frequency Harmonics and a Proposal for Transcending Space-Time." It hadn't made her a hyper-dimension engineer, but she'd picked up enough to get through training. Myseko theorized that space-time was an artifact of string frequency and could be tuned like a violin. Harmonized frequencies could cancel one another, thereby cancelling their space-time coordinates and rendering their energy spaceless and timeless. Rebounding from that untenable state, 'skipping from Myseko Space' as it came to be called, could cause energy to appear anywhere in the universe—and theoretically anywhere in time.

The wonder was that the Myseko skip took direction from navigation systems. That seemed too magical and convenient. Early Humans must have felt the same way about fire: one process providing warmth, light, cooking, sanitization, food preservation, and metal fabrication—truly a gift of the gods.

The pilot announced, "Returning to normal space. Switching to entropic drive. Four hours to Corydon space. Eight hours, twenty-seven minutes to the starport." The entropic drive was less exotic—nuclear fusion augmented by entropy-reining technology.

The conforming seat released, and the beverage menu returned. The baffling wine list reminded Zim what a frontier bumpkin she remained. She randomly selected a red. The RH steward delivered it a moment later in a stemmed glass on a silver tray.

As she sipped the wine, Zim reflected on Corydon. She had wanted to visit since she was a child. She laughed. As a child, she probably wouldn't feel so awkward. None of the big cities she'd visited had been built by Humans, except Port Estelle. But Estelle was a military city, a base and dockyard in interstellar space.

A forearm prickle told Zim she'd linked to the Corydon network. She switched the link to direct neural, leaned back, and closed her eyes.

News analysts critiqued her Bai-Yota strategy and every member of her 'ace' combat team. Was she aware of the dangers she'd exposed them to? What if someone *had* been killed? Could the Aldrakin be trusted? Zim chuckled at the fanciful revelations, insights, and projections from 'experts' that had never set foot on the bridge of any military ship.

Sober-faced reporters speculated on the meaning and causes of the war and its aftermath: Human-Aldrakin cultural compatibility, opportunities in the Galactic Trade Federation, Tak-Yaki ambivalence to the peace accord, and the anticipated end of Star Command. Opposition to Star Command dissolution focused on the recent surge in Rii-Chaut pirate activity, particularly the Silkani Massacre that had wiped out the latest Creative community.

That attack had occurred while Zim was standing watch off Bai-Yota. The recording included brutal scenes of torture and execution. Staged to intimidate and spread terror, Zim thought, and possibly to solicit tribute. The sole survivor of Silkani had sabotaged planet defenses and saved himself by locking himself in a vault beneath the planet surface. The man had been arrested pending investigation and convening of a court-martial.

Reports gave no specifics about the sole survivor or the Rii-Chaut, or which sect or Hetman had been involved. Zim wondered whether the pirate she'd met at the reception had any knowledge. His parting comment about hearing more about the Rii-Chaut sounded ominous.

A *Pulsar Times* article ended by commenting that the Starflower and Five Squadron had been redirected to oppose the Rii-Chaut menace.

"This true?" Kuwashima asked, pointing to the article. "Five Squadron's been reassigned?" Zim shrugged and shook her head.

Buried beneath the bleeding headlines was an announcement that Star Council was stepping down at the end of next year and transferring power to a Creative-led government yet to be identified. Zim frowned. She couldn't imagine the black-cloaked councilors willingly relinquishing power—not Abramyan.

"Starting descent on Corydon Starport," the pilot announced. "We should be on the ground in ninety-six minutes."

Zim's heart leapt in her throat. We're here. Would Mac meet her at the starport? Two meetings to get through—Abramyan and Star Council—then she'd be on her own. What could they possibly want with her? The war was over. If they planned any action against the Rii-Chaut, they'd pick Boorman. He was a thug, but he could swing a club with the best. And after all the publicity, surely, they'd want her to fade quietly away. She'd be happy to oblige.

She tried accessing information on the Rii-Chaut. No Records Available. Highly irregular. Was this a news blackout before a major action? Maybe someone tampered with the record? Not her problem. She checked the time. Star Council required formal dress. She grabbed her bag and headed to the dressing room.

The Star Lord's Chamber

Malik flipped through the headlines without speaking. Her office was perfect for interrogation: austere, snow-white, and windowless with angular, black-upholstered furniture. Glare from the overhead burned Abramyan's eyes. Despite his formal uniform and sweat-beaded face, he felt naked and cold. He knew what Malik would ask, and he had no answer.

"How did you let this happen?" She threw up her arms. "You told me Zimmon would never be put in any combat zone. Sidelined, you said."

Her gnarled, brown-mottled finger poked from her black sleeve at the projection. WAR ENDS—STARFLOWER VICTORIOUS! She flicked to the next headline: STARFLOWER ENDS WAR! Then the next: STARFLOWER BLOOMS! "Who authorized Zimmon to end the war?" Malik's robe flared like an angry cobra hood.

"And this, AAAArrr." She raked skeletal palms down her face then pulled up the next projection. The classified transmission indicated that, without authorization, military units had gone on alert and prepared to head to Bai-Yota in support of Five Squadron. "*Our* battle fleet supported *her*," Malik screamed. "We were very, very lucky this didn't go further."

Abramyan had read the traffic. Each condemnation came like a twisting spear thrust. Jen Djada, the only other Councilor in the room, sat quietly by the door.

Malik spoke to Abramyan's stone silence. "What's next you ask?"

Abramyan couldn't help blurting, "Lord Malik, Bai-Yota was a surprise. I didn't, Zimmon didn't, *HELL*, the Aldrakin didn't know. They thought they'd catch us—"

"*Excuses? Now you make excuses?*" Malik gripped the edge of her desk with shaking, predator talons. "I'll tell you what's next. *We get rid of her.* That's all, just get rid of her. We do it clean, we do it quiet, but we get rid of her. Soon as she reaches Corydon, you know those Under-lovers will be all over her… and Creatives, a lot of Creatives see her as some sort of righteous underdog."

Abramyan trembled like a small child caught in a hail storm. Behind him, Djada's jaws flexed.

Malik blew a long breath. "We can't afford an uprising. Not now, not this close. Some of us are already in transition." She examined her cadaverous hand then pointed toward Djada. "You still have contacts with the Rii-Chaut? They hate us but love our money."

"I'll tell the Yazza Hetman we have more business for him." Djada's self-assured demeanor unnerved Abramyan. "Ojai Khan staged the incidents that started the war. He can be discreet. When do you want it to happen?"

"Ojai Khan, yes, that went well." Malik clapped her hands then pointed. "And when you see Khan, tell him I'm angry about the Silkani raid. That base was off limits. *We* say where to and where not to attack." Djada gave a leaning bow from her chair.

"As to the when question. Don't have Khan kill Zimmon too soon. That would raise suspicion. We don't want to make this little Starflower girl into a martyr." She tapped a finger on the desk. "Let's be positive. Unders love the Starflower. *We* love the Starflower, too. She's *our* hero. Most accept that Creatives will succeed them—they are superior. All we must do is buy time. Six, nine months should do. After that it won't matter." She raised a finger toward Abramyan. "Does Zimmon have any accumulated leave?"

"W—well yes. She has all her leave, over a year," Abramyan muttered. "We never let her off the front line."

"A year's too long." Malik again tapped her desk. "We only need time to distance ourselves and let Djada's assassins set their trap. We'll run a three-month deception campaign. Full media. We'll laud Starflower's victories, give her access to all Creative amenities: recreations, restaurants, shops, lift all the bans… a vacation to one of our exclusive resorts… mmm, maybe a tour of Avian… can't do any harm at this point." Her tapping accelerated.

"Yes, that will make an impression. Unders think Avian is some sort of Creative snake pit. It's always been a sore spot with them. We'll give Zimmon the executive tour." Malik turned to Djada. "What am I missing?"

"Public Image."

"Yes, thank you." Malik lifted her palm. "Seta Martiri should handle publicity. Let's get her in here this afternoon. She'll know how to slip

Zimmon's agenda to the media and make them think it's their coup. Of course, we'll be none the wiser and act offended that they violated our hero's privacy." Malik's face broke into a grin.

"You think it's a good idea, touring Avian?" Djada said. "Zimmon's naïve because she's had limited exposure, but she's quick, she'll see the potential."

"She won't have time to act, and she won't be coming back. She'll take the tour, go on holiday, and never return." Malik flashed Djada a satisfied smile. "Tell Ojai Khan they can have the Starflower as soon as she comes off leave."

Malik flashed Abramyan a curled sneer. He swallowed and sat up. "Devise a bonus package for Zimmon, very generous, a retirement bonus worthy of our greatest hero, but make it contingent on her retiring to some remote place. Hopefully, she'll take it. That will make it easy for Djada to arrange her discreet elimination."

Abramyan bowed his head and began to rise. "Consider it done, Lord Malik."

"Another thought." Malik pointed to the projection. "Zimmon's squadron, the one getting all the publicity. I don't want the media getting to any of them. Some of her officers already have a fan following."

Abramyan shrank back into his seat. "Z—Zimmon's weapons officer, Kuwashima, and her shadow intern, Kaplan... they're coming... they're with her on the *Halcyon*. Those were the standing orders."

"*Who makes the orders?*" Malik shouted. "*Change the targ-licking orders.* Don't let Kuwashima leave the starport and get her off Corydon as soon as possible. I don't care about any targ-behind-the-ears intern. March him out of StarCom and let him fend with other Unders."

Malik motioned Djada to stay and Abramyan to leave, then had a final thought. "You have an Under on your staff? Someone close to Zimmon?"

"Yes, Lord Malik. Roland Mackenzie and Zimmon were very close: partners in the Corydonics, lovers then and early in the war. Mackenzie put in several requests to transfer to her command. I denied all of them, and we scuttled every attempt for them to communicate."

"I take it, with the war over, Mackenzie's services are no longer required?" Abramyan nodded, and Malik looked to Djada. "Eliminate Mackenzie, too."

Starport

Halcyon descended onto the Corydon Starport executive terminal, engaged the magnetic docking field, and slipped into a covered berth. The pilot led the RH crewmen down the ramp, pivoted at the base to stand at attention, and saluted Zim, Kuwashima, and Kaplan as they passed.

The steel-gray and glass executive terminal had no furniture or embellishing décor and no security checking station. With all her effects in her shoulder bag—and eager to see who might be waiting—Zim walked quickly to the exit. Past the double doors on either side of the walkway stood two columns of RHs: black-chassis police to the left, blue-chassis StarCom security to the right.

Onlookers crowded the walkway and open areas out onto the wide grassy field that separated the executive from the general receiving terminals. Most in the crowd were poorly dressed and bedraggled, many barefoot. Hand-painted banners and cardboard placards waved high displayed blue starflowers. A smaller, separate group, younger, healthier, and elegantly attired, held silk banners and artistically crafted signs. Cameras and sensors on low and high platforms tracked Zim's every move.

In the distance, a lone Human in a charcoal-gray civilian tunic stood beside an open-bay passenger shuttle. Zim's surge of delight passed when she noted the lone man's fair hair. Not Mac. She turned her attention to the unnaturally silent crowd.

Flags snapped in the breeze. The low whir of cargo and passenger traffic drifted in from the far side of the field, with an occasional retro burst from landing small craft.

"Star Marshal Zimmon." The gray-tunic civilian ran up from the road. His aristocratic carriage and athletic gait marked him as a Creative, an engineered Human. A dark jawline bruise marred his otherwise flawless, coffee-cream complexion.

"I am Aidan, assigned by Star Commander Abramyan to be your aide-de-camp during your visit to Corydon." Zim felt another letdown. "With your permission, I'll be escorting you to Headquarters. Beg your pardon, sir, but while you were in transit your meeting agenda was modified." Aidan extended his upturned forearm. Zim waved a palm to update her orders.

"Your afternoon meeting with Star Lord Malik and the Council is cancelled. And Star Marshal Mackenzie requests you speak with him before meeting with Abramyan."

Zim caught her knees from buckling. Mac, in thirty-four minutes. Her heart leaped. She quickly checked her uniform to affirm she'd changed before landing.

A scuffle erupted behind her: Kaplan, struggling with four black-chassis RH police. "Why are you manhandling my officer?" Zim demanded. The lead unit dropped Kaplan's arm and stood erect.

"Our pardon, Star Marshal. Wonder O'Kavo Kaplan has been removed from Star Command. Our orders are to expedite his decommissioning." The RH lead unit had dents and scrapes in its metal chassis. It had seen action. Zim wondered if RH's accrued rank through experience.

"Officer—" Zim was unable to locate a rank identifier or serial number on the chassis. "Until Wonder Kaplan *is* decommissioned, he remains on my staff and will be given the same respect as everyone in my company." She locked eyes on the RH's laser-red sensors. It hesitated. Two seconds processing time, Zim estimated.

"My pardon, Star Marshal Zimmon." The RH saluted and turned to Kaplan. "Wonder Kaplan, we are to direct you to the decommissioning station where you will be informed of your options and returned to civilian life." Kaplan nodded, arched an eyebrow toward Zim, and let the police escort him to an armored van.

Kuwashima was talking with one of the blue StarCom RHs. Zim stepped toward them. "Another problem?"

"No, sir," Kuwashima responded. "The RH commander has shown me orders to report immediately to the Galaxy Battle station *Leipzig*. It seems they have urgent need of a weapons officer. This platoon," she waved to the two-dozen blue chassis standing formation, "wants me to go with them to departure portal three." She looked up as if saying, "This is it," and touched Zim's forearm. Zim extended both arms full length and pressed them against

Kuwashima's shoulders—the Aldrakin greeting and farewell, then gave her a hug.

"Ha-Yee, Starflower." Kuwashima's eyes glistened.

"Ha-Yee, Kuwashima." Zim felt a wave of finality sweep over her as she watched the last of her teammates leave with the RHs. The war was truly over. Suddenly alone in the encircling crowd, Zim paused to take it in. She raised a finger to Aidan. "One minute. I haven't stood under a natural sky in years." He stepped away and folded his hands low.

Zim took a deep breath, lifted her eyes to blue sky, and focused in the moment. It was early morning. A three-ringed, silver moon, the signature feature of Blue Star planetary engineers, sat half-buried on the western horizon. Horsetail clouds, licked pink by the morning sun, drifted high overhead. The sky was bluer than any she remembered on Scalaris. Maybe it had been too long. The brisk breeze chilled her face and stirred her honey-blond hair.

The wind shift returned her to reality and replaced the bouquet of freshly mown grass with that of unwashed bodies. The silent circle of onlookers had drawn closer, surrounding her and Aidan. He didn't react or show concern. Zim saw many in the crowd were scarred, deformed, or disabled, old or well into middle age. There were no children. A wizened, legless man rocked and slid on his stumps to touch the leg of her uniform. "Ha-Yee," he whispered, looking up.

"Ha-Yee," she replied. The others took that as a signal to step in to touch and greet their Starflower. Deeply moved, Zim could not respond other than to return "Ha-Yee." Some in the crowd had probably waited all night.

Suddenly, the group parted, clearing a path for a young couple emerging from a sporty, red roadster. Both were dressed for a tennis match. Tall, blond, and extraordinarily handsome, the striking pair moved as gracefully as dancers.

They ran waving to greet Zim. "How wonderful we caught you. We couldn't be more pleased." The exquisite male's wide-set, blue eyes sparkled over his angular cheekbones. As Aidan was about to introduce them, the male interrupted. "Please, no formalities, no titles, we are Hillie and Torgis." He nodded to his beaming partner and to Zim. Hillie, the exquisite female, rocked her head joyously, sending blond waves cascading down and around her bare, slender shoulders.

"We won't delay you," Torgis said. "We know you have pressing business with StarCom. We just wanted to be the first to greet you." He took a sighing breath. "We are so proud of you, so excited. Ah." He pressed his open hands to the sides of his head. "When we saw you with the Aldrakin in their flagship… you were fantastic… sooo brave."

Hillie squealed, jumped in place, and clapped her delicate fingers. Then the two bowed, backed away, and ran to their roadster. Zim pursed her lips to keep her jaw from dropping. Aidan gave no sign that anything was irregular.

A stooped, gray-haired woman pulled at Zim's sleeve. "Starflower, God bless you. They wanted to sneak you in. I knew they would. I told Basil we should come every day, so we would see you when you returned. My name is Gladys, and this is Basil, my modern partner." She gestured to the tall, handsome, young man beside her. Zim gave him a quizzical look. "Basil reads me the news every morning. I ask him to read the stories about the Starflower first." She patted Zim's arm then stepped back with Basil's assistance.

Zim had noticed mismatched couples in the crowd—very old men or women with very young partners, usually the opposite sex. Now she saw them with new eyes. The younger partner always stood poised and attentive until tasked. Modern partners?

Aidan tapped the palm of his hand for a time check. Zim nodded and waved to the crowd, and they cleared a path.

A pocket door slid aside on the open-bay executive shuttle. Zim's hair stirred as she stepped through the electrostatic shield. There were no manual controls, no instruments, and no driver. Black-upholstered seating lined the vehicle's plush oval perimeter. Zim sat to the rear looking forward and Aidan at her side.

The shuttle accelerated with barely a whisper or any sense of motion, weaving out of the starport and onto a tree-lined parkway. The invisible dome deflected wind, rain, high-decibel sound, and noxious odors. Zim detected the aroma of jacinth flowers. Unlike the military vehicles she was accustomed to, the seats were soft, supple, and luxurious.

"Marshal Zimmon, you are very quiet," Aidan said. "Perhaps you do not wish to speak? But if you have questions—"

"Sorry if I seem rude or aloof. I'm thinking about my first meeting; planning what to say to Star Marshal Mackenzie."

"I completely understand, sir. It has been a very long time for you both." Zim wasn't sure what to make of Aidan's comment. He continued, "Your meeting is in twenty-eight minutes."

Zim's breathing picked up. She decided to change the subject. "This is all new to me, Aidan." She opened her hands wide. "I'm here, in the capital of the Human universe, and I feel like an alien. I hardly know where to start. You're a Creative. I don't understand the ranking system."

"Well, I'm a Nine Creative, or a Nine or a Niner. Nines are generalists and concept developers. That's not a rank, just my specialty category. As generalists, Nines are given more opportunities to explore lateral interests, including other specialties."

"Those charming people, Hillie and Torgis? I'm sure they are very important, but I'm embarrassed to say I don't know them."

"Hillary and Torgesson are the future leaders of Humanity. Two months ago, when the Star Council announced they were disbanding, Hillary and Torgesson were chosen to be the new leaders. They are Tens, top-rated Creatives, the most perfect Humans ever created. Tens are engineered and programmed with every desirable characteristic, skill trait, and specialty. They have no weaknesses. Everything is coded to their genes, so their children should also be perfect." Aidan looked up. "I can continue, but you will hear this from Mumbai on your Avian tour. I made the arrangements." Aidan stroked the bruise on his jaw.

"I recognize that sort of wound," Zim said. "But you don't seem like a brawler. Did you get that from a bar fight?" She wanted to read his body language as much as hear his answer.

"Actually, yes." Aidan lowered and touched his chin. "The brawl was staged. I was clumsy and slipped on the Chiricado dip. In the Greens Acting Guild, I play the role of Derek Boorman in *The Starflower Incident*." He chuckled. "It's about the two of you meeting during training."

Zim grimaced. "Not my proudest moment." Oh my, now it's been immortalized. "I guess that incident will follow me the rest of my life. But if you portrayed Boorman accurately, your bruises were well deserved."

She took another recovery breath. "I had no idea I'd gathered a fan following."

"A very large fan following. I traded a year's alcohol ration to be appointed your official aide."

Leaving the parkway, they entered the outskirts of Corydon City. Zim saw flat-roofed warehouses, utilities for water, sewage, and power, garage and maintenance buildings for road equipment and robots. The lofty spire of Star Council Headquarters loomed in the distance ahead, to the left, the massive cube of the Avian building. She knew both buildings from history lessons, but Avian was the greater mystery.

Next came blocks of collapsed and deserted buildings and walls. Many had starflowers or fragments of blue starflowers painted on them, some crude, some highly artistic. Some had captions, from prayers and well wishing, to threats of violence against robots, Creatives, and the Star Council.

Zim made no comment. Behind the collapsed buildings was a wasteland of broken foundations bristling with twisted rebar, naked metal framework, fallen walls, crushed doorways and windows, debris, and shattered glass. Robots the size of buildings cleared stone and steel rubble. Others reduced intact buildings and roads to shovel-sized blocks for removal.

"Star Council ordered the district cleared for renovation," Aidan said. As he spoke, they passed an armored van with black-chassis police pouring from the rear to assault one of the buildings. Tank-sized enforcer robots rolled beside them. E-Mag fire and screams erupted, diminishing as they sped away.

"Is this required for renovation?" Zim asked, looking back.

"Businesses and homes are being cleared. There's a lot of Under resistance."

"Where are they being cleared to?"

"Off Corydon. This morning, Lord Malik said Unders would be relocated to planets recovered from the Aldrakin."

"Those planets are barely habitable," Zim said. Aidan rolled and bit his lips.

The shuttle rose and tilted to clear an up-thrust section of pavement blocking the road. Nearer Headquarters the damage decreased, but most businesses remained shuttered. There was no traffic. This early, Zim couldn't tell how many shops might still be operating.

She heard jazz music, the sounds increasing until they passed an underground bar not yet closed for the night. Further down, an elderly woman in a ragged housecoat and slippers pushed a scant-bristled broom in front of a row of liquor, grocery, and drug stores. Hand-sized beetles crawled through garbage overflowing from a can. On the corner, a scrawny, yellow dog barked and turned its head to follow them as they passed.

Mackenzie

Mac's office in six minutes. She needed to hurry. The meeting with Abramyan paled in comparison. Star Commander Grosvenor Venaturan Abramyan, Chief Military Officer and Chairman of the Military Review Board. What a pretentious targhole.

She steadied her breathing. How much had Mac changed in eight years? She remembered him as a boy and as a very young man.

As she climbed the stairs, she read the shining, four-meter-high letters. STAR COUNCIL HEADQUARTERS. Two minutes. Mac's office was on the seventh floor. Zim caught a whiff of ozone as she stepped through the electrostatic threshold. A green lightbox framed her feet at the entry with an arrow directing her to the office of Star Marshal Roland Mackenzie.

She crossed the bare-walled foyer then the black marble concourse and passed under a bronze engraving with the names of the sixteen Star Council officers. Though Mac wasn't listed, she knew his office would be on the same floor as Abramyan's. Her stomach balanced fear and anticipation.

Ninety seconds. The green arrow leaped ahead. Zim followed it to a levitor lift then to a red-carpeted hallway. One turn brought her to a short hall and a receptionist desk.

"Marshal Zimmon?" The receptionist was an Under, elderly, out of time and place in her emerald-green pinafore. Zim nodded. "Marshal Mackenzie has someone—" The door slid open.

"I await your call, Mac," said a resonant voice, followed by a large man stepping out. He was rough-hewn and dark-complexioned. "Lot's going on now. We're ready to move as soon as you give us the go." He nodded to the receptionist and to Zim, then did a double take.

"Marshal Zimmon, please, let me introduce myself." He gave a nodding bow. "I'm Micah Crowley, CEO for Blue Star." Zim returned his bow, noting the Blue Star logo on his powder blue corporate jumpsuit. "I don't know your

76

postwar professional plans, Star Marshal, but I hope you keep Blue Star in mind." He bowed deeper and left.

"You may go right in." The receptionist tilted her head to the open doorway.

Zim's feet refused to move. Beyond the doorway, she saw a tall, athletic man standing behind a walnut desk.

She took two steps. The office was old fashioned and modest: a sturdy, walnut desk, a dark-shaded desk lamp, a Norfolk pine in a green, gold-veined cachepot, a seating area with heavy, wooden chairs, and a table.

Mac cleared his throat and stepped around to the front of his desk. Unlike his casual receptionist, Mac wore StarCom's midnight blue dress uniform. Zim felt proud and shy. Anticipation flushed her face. Here they were.

He studied her, not speaking. Then a tear rolled down his cheek. "It won't be long, Gayle. Soon we'll be together. Remember?"

"Yes, oh yes." Her voice broke, and she ran to him, burying her face in his chest. "But it was long, *so* long, Mac." As he hugged her, she felt his joyful tremors. They cried happy tears and laughed, barely able to speak. "Mac, I feared you'd gone… forgotten."

"Worried so much, Gayle… every day… terrible thoughts. Tried to reach you… blocked." Urgent kisses, salty tears sliding between their faces, gasping, their need for each other greater than air.

Mac took a breath and pushed her shoulders away. "My love, it is urgent we talk."

"I know, I—"

"Something more important must come first." He gave her a tight hug then guided her into one of the wooden chairs. "There's great danger. I don't know what exactly." A timer display opened in the air. "Twenty-two minutes until you meet with Abramyan."

Zim wiped her face then gripped both hands on Mac's arm, assuring herself that this was real. "Okay. I'm listening."

"The Star Councilors are afraid of you… all of them, especially Abramyan." Mac's stern expression startled her. "And when they're afraid, they strike. The media doesn't know this, but when you declared your intention to attack at Bai-Yota, the entire StarCom fleet went on alert. They didn't wait for orders. Your old group, the 18th Legion, went on crisis mobilization to come to your aid. That might have been expected—they'd been with you the entire war. But others followed. The First Legion joined the 18th almost immediately."

"The First Legion?" Zim's unsteady voice became razor sharp. "I don't know anyone in the First. I didn't even know there was a First Legion."

"No, and you wouldn't. The First are all Creatives, Star Council's darlings, their Praetorian Guard. That's what scared the Council. If the First joined you—" He paused. "Let me give you a little background." Mac took her hands in his. "The Star Council never liked it, but Creatives volunteered to serve in the war—Creatives from every skill category, even the Ones."

"Ones?" Zim shook her head.

"Nurturing artists and artisans." Mac shrugged. "Creatives may be pampered elitists, but apparently some of them are patriotic. They felt left out. The Council blames the Starflower for that—and the media for creating your myth." He opened his hands out. "Gayle, your battle reports read like heroic sagas. Besides the history, there are fiction and fantasy thrillers about you, even a series of romance novels about us—so I have crazy fans, too."

"Maybe I should read those novels," Zim teased with a sparkle in her eye.

"Some are rather risqué." Mac leered. Zim batted her eyes like an owl in a rainstorm. Mac laughed. "I'm sorry I didn't meet you at the starport, but that's why. My fans and the media have me staked out."

"I understand, so the First Legion…"

"The Star Council put all the Creative volunteers in the First Legion, gave them elite guard status, and kept them in reserve. I've seen them train—they're good, very good. The rest of the fleet didn't know they existed until they went on alert and came up on the battle management grid." Zim immediately saw the danger.

Mac checked the clock. "Time's short, let me finish. After the First Legion, others sign on, Abramyan panicked. He had all the command channels shut down. If the battle hadn't ended quickly with the Aldrakin surrender, there could have been a mutiny."

Mac sat back. "You can imagine Derek Boorman's reaction." Zim mouthed a silent *OUCH*. "He was leading a major assault against the Aldrakin at Dibak-Dak, and, just before making enemy contact, one of his battle fleets went missing."

"Really, Mac, I had no idea. I was only being a good officer. You know me."

"Yes, I know, I know. I think we both got trapped by circumstances. But the Council doesn't see it that way. They want to make an example of you. Coming in from the starport, you saw the Starflower signs. The insurgency has adopted you."

Mac rolled his lips in and raised a finger. "We may have a way out. The Council hates risks and prefers to avoid problems. They'll probably try to buy you off, get you to leave and go far away. I hear a substantial retirement package is being offered with generous benefits. It's a bribe I think you might want to consider."

"But how about—"

"Of course, I'll go with you. If that's still our plan." Zim gazed deep into his dark eyes and slow-nodded. "I'll ask for early retirement. I'm sure it'll be granted. With the war over, Abramyan must cut back. He'll be happy to see me go."

He touched Zim's arm. "One more thing. Abramyan's a coward, particularly around Malik. He's also a vindictive targ. He may think he can bully you. We both know that would be a bad idea. You don't see any robots or Creatives around here or anywhere on his staff because he can't bully them. Unders work for him only because they can't find jobs elsewhere."

"I know how to deal with bullies. Does Abramyan try to bully you?"

"He's not dumb. He's seen my combat record. Besides he needs... or needed me until you won the war. Abramyan's a desk pilot: no combat experience, no training, but he does have political power, and that makes him dangerous. He blames you for making him look bad on the Star Council."

Mac embraced her, and she put her head on his shoulder. "I'm afraid for you, Gayle. Don't cross this man. You know your military history. You know what weak politicians do to great generals who cross them."

"They cut out their eyes and throw them outside the gate to beg."

Abramyan

The gliding, backlit shadow in the hall was all too familiar. He had seen her deal death in countless battles. As she approached, Abramyan backed reflexively away, one hand on his receptionist's desk to steady himself.

"Tracy, tell Marshal Zimmon I'll be available shortly." The office door slid shut to block his view. His heart drummed in his ears. He blew a silent whistle, sucked air through his teeth, and swallowed. Can't get rattled. Huh. Too late for that. Returning to his desk, he laced and rubbed his cold fingers then set his desk timer for four minutes.

After this, he had to meet with Malik. Djada would sit at his blind side and gloat. She wouldn't miss an opportunity to see him ridiculed. If Malik gave the signal, he was sure Djada would take an ax to his head. But that wouldn't happen. Zimmon wanted out of StarCom in the worst way. He'd see she got it exactly that way.

His office seemed smaller, the blank, gray wall opposite his desk closer. Had his desk moved? Every breath left him short-winded. "Time," the desk blinked. Even the blinking rattled him. He reset the timer for another four minutes.

"Star Commander Abramyan, pardon me." It was Tracy's thin voice. "You have a meeting with Lord Malik in twenty-two minutes. Marshal Zimmon has arrived. Shall I tell her you need to reschedule?"

"*Tell Marshal Zimmon I'll—*" He shrieked then remembered Zim could hear him and lowered his voice. "Tell her I need another minute."

"Yes, sir."

Both meetings had to happen. He touched his wrist to the stim-plate on the side of his desk and jumped at the bite of the injection. His heaving breath and heart rate slowed.

He rolled and relaxed his shoulders. Facing the vanity hologram, he pulled up and straightened his shoulder boards and collar, leveled the row of military ribbons, and scowled. His augmented uniform presented an erect military posture and bearing. He closed the hologram, positioned himself behind his desk, and called up the proposal for Zim's retirement.

"Tracy, please send in Marshal Zimmon."

Zim stepped just inside the doorway and stood at ease, hands at the small of her back, eyes level. The door closed behind her. "Star Commander Abramyan, sir, Star Marshal Zimmon reporting as ordered."

Abramyan feigned scrutinizing Zim's record while savoring the last surge of his stim-injection. "Ahh, yes, Marshal Zimmon. I have looked forward to seeing you again and congratulating you." When he looked up from the desk display, his eyes fixed on Zim's iridescent Starflower—even more striking for being the only medal on her midnight blue dress uniform.

"I want to commend you for your excellent service." He began with his voice level, but anger consumed him. "Were you not informed that this meeting was to be informal?"

"Yes, sir. My original schedule had me meeting with Lord Malik, and I wouldn't have had time to change. Meetings with the Star Lord require formal dress."

Abramyan stared blankly. She had corrected him. Already. And she seemed relaxed, impatient with him. Damn her. He came around his desk slowly as he had rehearsed, but again he slipped.

"That garish blue medal." He waved toward Zim's Starflower as if brushing away lint. "Do you always wear it?"

"Not always, sir. Regulation requires that officers wear their top three medals with their dress uniform. This is the only one I've been awarded. Without it I'd be out of uniform."

Abramyan barely caught himself from shouting, *don't quote regulations to me, you…* "Yes, of course. I've had much on my mind." He had forgotten how young she was and how attractive—in an austere way: trim, athletic figure; clear, steel-blue eyes; a gentle wave in her short honey-blond hair.

"I'm very proud of this medal, sir. Remember, you gave it to me… for my victory in the games."

Abramyan jerked a quick look to see if she was smirking, but neither her voice nor expression betrayed the slightest emotion. Was she taunting him? She might be young, but she was no naïf. That medal was a bad idea. He recognized that now. It made her special.

"Sit down, please." He motioned to a wooden captain's chair. When Zim did not move, he took a long breath. "Excuse me—and don't quote me another regulation. I'll sit first." As the Commanding Officer, he sat then Zim sat.

Abramyan felt her eyes bore into him. Heat rose in his collar, releasing the lilac scent he used to mask stress. He shifted in his seat, crossed his legs, and launched into his rehearsed speech.

"First let me say…" He cleared his throat and swallowed. "How grateful we all are for your heroic efforts on behalf of Star Command in the Aldrakin War. Your intelligence, your courage, and your loyalty are commendable."

Abramyan swept the air with his hand while he evaded Zim's eyes. "Your improvisations on my Bai-Yota strategy were tactically brilliant. Some thought my plans too bold, too aggressive, but you executed them to perfection. While you held the Aldrakin, our battle fleet was maneuvering to destroy them. Detecting my trap, they wisely chose to surrender before the rest of our fleet arrived." He stole a glance to judge Zim's reaction.

She stared impassively beyond him, keeping her head level. She knew Abramyan was taking credit for Bai-Yota, insisting that she had merely followed his orders. That hardly mattered. She had never sought glory.

"I dearly wish I could have been there with you." Abramyan gestured to his chair. "Sadly, I must always remain here holding the reins. Mine is a thankless job." Still not detecting the response he'd envisioned, he twisted in his seat and re-crossed his legs.

"We wish we could reward you properly, Star Marshal. But with the war ended and StarCom cutting back, nothing is available. We're keeping a few capital ships in reserve. Blue Star will lease some of the Marshal-class carriers for planetary engineering. Others will be converted for exploration and scientific research. We'll need a few cruisers and corvettes to deal with the Rii-Chaut, but those billets are slated for senior Creatives. I'm sure you understand." Zim didn't return his gaze, but he saw her jawline flex. Finally, he was making an impression. He took a short breath and pressed on.

"Frankly, Marshal Zimmon, after Bai-Yota, the Military Review Board wanted you punished. Brave and improvisational though your actions were, they were never authorized. What if others less talented chose to follow your example? That could spell disaster." He stole a quick glance at Zim, forced a thin smile over his tight jaws, and called up StarCom's retirement proposal.

"You're still a young woman, Marshal Zimmon. I understand you and Roland Mackenzie—"

"Beg your pardon, *sir*, but Roland Mackenzie and I are none of your business. And aren't you Chairman of the Military Review Board?" Zim locked on Abramyan's gaze.

"Yes, but I'm not the only—"

"So, the Board's decision was entirely yours. Very well, sir, what is your offer? I know your time is valuable, sir, and I don't want to keep you from your next meeting." Zim slid her arms forward, and Abramyan flinched. Damn her, she thinks she's in control.

"My offer? Oh, yes… You will receive a full Star Marshal's retirement: full pay and a Class 1, luxury residence for life on the newly terraformed planet Indranil. Indranil is a frontier planet, still outside Under mating regulations, so you and Mackenzie can live together undisturbed and raise your family. Your domed accommodation includes a fifty-thousand-hectare plantation complete with an RH staff of eight—"

"Indranil had its first orbit adjust just before the war," Zim interrupted. "It's in the earliest stages of terraforming. We wouldn't be able to leave the dome without full life support equipment until, until our children are grown. What's more, Indranil's not on any trade route or near any civilized worlds. There's no regular transport, no trade bases, nothing inhabitable anywhere in that sector." She hammered each point.

"SynTerra engineers are active on Indranil. They're—"

"SynTerra is a government startup controlled by the Star Council. Why isn't Blue Star handling this?" She stood, came to attention, and saluted. "Thank you for your efforts on my behalf, Star Commander. May I be dismissed… sir?"

Abramyan bolted out of his chair waving and shouting. "Your alternatives are not attractive. For starters, your Star Marshal rank was based on field promotions. None were ever confirmed. If you don't accept my offer, you'll be knocked back to squadron commander, and you'll still need two years to qualify for minimum retirement. Then you'll go to some Under settlement on some asteroid hell." Spittle glistened on his chin and sleeve.

"I prefer to take my chances."

"You will regret this, *Commander* Zimmon." He emphasized her reduced rank. "Know that you have no friends here and will get no special favors."

"Is that all, sir?"

Seeing that Zim still held her salute, he gave her a dismissive hand flick. "See my assistant on your way out." He touched his desk. "Tracy, give Commander Zimmon the standard orders for squadron commanders, whatever's at the top of the queue." Of course, he knew what was at the top of the queue. It had been arranged with Djada. He looked at Zim. "Commander Zimmon, I believe you are out of uniform."

Zim saluted again, marched out the door, and turned.

"Star Commander Grosvenor Venaturan Abramyan," she said, reading his nameplate.

"*What?*" Abramyan shouted.

"Your full name, sir: Grosvenor—Venaturan—Abramyan? Rather off-putting, don't you think, sir?" Her voice dripped with cloying treacle.

Abramyan unlimbered his jaw and spoke level. "Commander Zimmon, you are entitled to a hero's welcome and to a long well-deserved vacation. That's all been arranged. I advise you to enjoy them, because when it's over, I can assure you, you won't be celebrating." He allowed a smug smile. Though their meeting had not gone well, he was now done with the Starflower. Malik would turn her over to Djada and her assassins, and that would be the end.

# # #

Tracy's hand trembled as she slid Zim's orders across the reception desk. Zim felt sorry for her. She was the likely target of Abramyan's residual anger.

Zim uploaded her orders with a forearm sweep. She was to report to the *Marshal Massena* in three months. The decommissioned combat strike carrier was being converted to support scientific research. Zim would lead a shuttle team of military officers and scientists at the reduced rank of commander.

As she read, a note came in from Mac:

Gayle Sweetheart, I know that couldn't have gone well. You cannot possibly know how much you are loved. Of course, I have a lot of competition. Everyone in the fleet calls you their Starflower. See you for dinner. Love, Mac.

She blinked away a tear. Mac was with her. Despite Abramyan's threats, for the first time in a long time she did not feel alone.

A tapping sound caused her to look down. While looking away, Tracy finger-tapped on a one-line, paper note on the corner of her desk—a name and room number. Zim palmed the note without comment and left.

# # #

Abramyan entered Malik's featureless office a minute later. Ignoring Djada by the entrance, he pulled a black upholstered chair over beside the ebony desk. Malik looked up.

For once, Abramyan looked directly into Malik's eyes. "She's not taking the retirement. Indranil's no longer in the plan. Mackenzie will have to be handled separately."

Unperturbed, Malik checked Zim's new orders. "A scientific expedition, not bad." She angled the projection for Djada to view. "We can route *Marshal Massena* to a remote star system and uproot the Under weed there." She smiled at Djada. "Tell the Rii-Chaut they can take Zimmon in three months as soon as she comes off holiday. Get them a copy of these orders and the update as soon as we have a mission plan." She glanced at Abramyan then back at Djada.

"Who commands *Massena*?" Malik asked then realized the orders were open in front of her. "Ahh, Captain Jeffrey Woodson. Let's contact the good Captain Woodson and give him an incentive to help us with Marshal… excuse me, Commander Zimmon."

Ko'Anoor

The assembly outside Star Council Headquarters was larger and more active than the one that greeted Zim at the starport. A cordon of black chassis RHs and enforcers held everyone back.

"Starflower, an interview?" called a young man, waving from the park across the road. Zim raised a finger to her aide Aidan and veered to meet half a dozen journalists.

She returned four minutes later. "I understand I have access to all the clothing stores." Aidan nodded. "Good. Let's go shopping." She had never been to a fine quality restaurant and had never worn a formal evening dress, and she wanted to surprise Mac.

# # #

Ko'Anoor was an old Earth-style Indian restaurant with blue- and gray-veined white marble with streaks of gold. Six columns supported a wide portico over a pointed archway flanked by flaming cressets. Aidan delivered Zim below the entrance a few minutes before seven.

Sounds of plucked strings and smells of exotic meats and spices poured from the open doorway. Zim followed an elegantly dressed couple up the red-carpeted, marble steps. A tall, thin-mustached maître d' in a black suit and red turban led her through a candle-lit maze of low walls and planters to a secluded table.

Seeing Mac, Zim paused to take it all in. His rugged face glowed in the flicker of candle and shadow. He stood as the maître d' held Zim's chair.

"Wait," Mac said before she could sit. He rotated a finger, and she turned for him. "How special, my love. Thank you." She heard him sigh and caught the sparkle in his eyes. "Purple is definitely your color."

"It's Aldrakin royal plum. I saw a lot of it at my last formal function."

"Stunning." After thanking the maître d', Mac seated her then himself.

"The lady at the dress shop helped me accessorize." Zim held up a yellow-gold purse.

"And hair styling, too. You amaze me, Gayle." Mac's eyes sparkled in the candlelight.

"There wasn't much they could do with my hair; I keep it so short." She studied Mac's tan face in the dancing light. On the table next to him was a vase of red roses, and beside the table, an ice bucket with a bottle of wine. Mac poured them each half a glass of the white, bubbly wine.

"I'm sorry I keep staring, Mac. It's been so long." She took his open hand and held it to her face. "I was afraid to remember us… to remember what we meant to each other… afraid it couldn't be real."

He nodded. "I know. Just look at you, Gayle. You're so beautiful… more svelte… firmer. It's a good look for you."

"You, too." She squeezed his hand. "Outside of your smile and ready humor, I don't see the boy anymore." She lifted and examined her wine glass. "What have we here? And roses… those are real roses?"

"The wine is a Coiber, a sparkling white from One Creative Green." He pointed to her glass. "The roses are real, too—compliments of Avian."

"I suppose Avian perfected these, just like they perfected Creatives." She lifted a rose from the vase and held it below her nose. "What a wonderful scent. I know of nothing to compare with this."

Mac raised his glass. "To our future." They touched glasses and sipped.

"I know you want to hear about my meeting." Zim's tone changed.

"You didn't accept Abramyan's offer."

"I couldn't, Mac." She shook her head. "It was generous in a contrived sense. I couldn't condemn you and our children… we are still thinking of children?"

Mac squeezed her hand. "I know we were only teenagers, but I never forgot. That sort of life, family, children, it's out of fashion now, but still possible on the frontier. I was afraid you'd changed *your* mind." He leaned close. "Are those tears, Gayle?"

"Happy tears. This is so wonderful. I wasn't brave enough to hope any of this could happen." She waved her hand to the room as he handed her a white cotton handkerchief. He always carried one for her. Funny how she needed one with Mac but never with anyone else or any other time.

"I wasn't sure how you'd feel tonight. Not after seeing this." He opened a news feed on the table, GROVER REWARDS STARFLOWER. "You spoke to the media?" Zim nodded, lowering her head. "I know when you're angry you counterpunch with humor—but ridiculing Abramyan? You called him Grover? If he didn't hate you before, he does now. You actually told them he wanted to be called Grover?" Mac laughed even as he scolded her. "You know they'll print whatever you say."

"I'm slowly figuring that out. Abramyan's first name is *Gross-venor*. Grover's an improvement."

"That's not how it's pronounced." Mac shook his head.

"Well, he deserves it. He and the Star Council are rewriting history. Abramyan gives himself full credit for masterminding the Bai-Yota strategy while calling me insubordinate for winning the battle. Not that I care about getting credit, but he's setting our plans back."

"It's called politics, Gayle. They don't want credit so much as they want to keep it from you—or any Under." Mac was lecturing her, but she knew he was right. Once again, she'd called down a bully and hurt their opportunities.

"Abramyan wanted to send us to Indranil. The planet won't be habitable in our lifetime—maybe not in our children's lifetimes. There are no indigenous life forms. He offered us a luxury prison totally cut off." She leveled her gaze with his. "Well, not exactly, not totally. We'd be dependent on SynTerra for outside contact. You know my intuition on these things."

Mac shrugged. "Okay, we'll make other plans."

"I'm sorry Mac, I don't believe anything Abramyan says. His reaction when I told him I'd stay in StarCom—his anger was telling. We have better options. The Tak-Yaki would welcome us. They have beautiful planets." She gave a short laugh. "The Aldrakin would probably adopt us."

Mac nodded and laughed. "Micah Crowley tells me they have positions opening at Blue Star." He looked at Zim. "You got your new orders?"

"I'm bound by my original officer's agreement to serve two more years, and I'm demoted to commander. I actually prefer being a commander, no fancy uniforms, no fussy protocols." She squared her shoulders. "Commander Zimmon will lead a shuttle team aboard the *Marshal Massena* to support scientific research. They need one team that's combat qualified. I have to pull that together. But with the personnel budget they gave me, I couldn't staff a first-rate garbage scow."

"*Marshal Massena's* old, but she was a good ship. I approved the refit. If they want you out of the way, that'll do it. Some of those research teams are out for years." He shook his head. "What should we do?"

"We have time to think. Abramyan authorized an extended holiday—three months with executive access to recreation and information resources. Maybe he's not all bad." Zim smiled wickedly at the thought of having Mac alone to herself for three months.

His eyebrows went up. "That explains our Avian tour. The order passed my desk just before you arrived. I thought it was a mistake. Avian's a good place to learn about life outside the military—that and fine wines and restaurants." He refilled their glasses. "So, we get a honeymoon before they send us off to the labor camp. I'll check the resorts. If StarCom is picking up the tab, we'll request the best."

They toasted another glass of sparkling Coiber then called for menus. Minutes later, a waiter brought plates of meats and sauces, fresh vegetables, and garnishes of mustards and chutney. Zim stole glimpses of Mac over her plate, and they sighed together.

Mac gave a hearty laugh. "I feel like we're teenagers again."

After dinner, he moved his chair close to Zim. She took his arm, leaned into him, closed her eyes, and listened to the music.

Like the exotic décor, the restaurant's ornate printed menus, Human wait staff, and music selection followed Old Earth themes. Only the musicians were out of place: a tree-like Shelesti maestro leading a troupe of Hyrup centipedes playing classical instruments.

"A request for the lady," said a crusty voice. Zim opened her eyes to see a Shelesti and five strolling Hyrup beside their table. The brown-barked Shelesti wore a black bowtie on a black, low-backed tunic that exposed the dark eyes of her mate hump. The Hyrup coiled their articulated segments around their violins, viola, and cello.

Zim smiled dreamily and without real expectation requested, "Vivaldi, the Violin Concerto in F Minor." The Shelesti tapped her baton and pointed to the lead violinist. Music poured sweet and clear.

"Reminds me of you," Mac said, "romantic and nostalgic." Zim inhaled the scent of roses, wine, and the finest meal she'd ever known.

"Another request, sir?" The Shelesti opened its branch-arms in invitation.

Mac nodded to Zim. "I'll pick something I know you'll remember." He turned to the Shelesti. "How about *Moscow Evenings,* but I see you don't—"

"A beautiful Russian folk song," the Shelesti said in a Slavic accent, the corners of her ax-gash mouth curling upward. She tapped and pointed. A Hyrup wrapped about one of the violins, blocked a string, and re-tuned another to simulate a balalaika. The others adjusted and joined in accompaniment.

Zim laughed. "You played that after we competed against one another in the Scalari games." She laughed again. "I thought you were taunting me."

"I was courting you," he protested. "You were the enemy, and I'd fallen in love. After you beat me that first round, you came around the field—I thought to gloat."

"And?"

"Best kiss I ever had—still is." Mac's eyes glittered. He touched his napkin high over his glistening cheek.

"*What*?" Zim sat up. "Your best kiss ever came from a fifteen-year-old girl? Bet you'll do better tonight." She slid her tongue along her upper lip and widened her eyes.

"Starflower!" came a playful voice.

"Torgis?" She looked into the beautiful blue eyes of the perfect Human male.

Hillie giggled and gave Torgis a squeeze. "This is our favorite restaurant. When Torgis pointed out the woman in the beautiful plum dress, I realized who you were. We heard you and Mackenzie were together again, and it's true. That is so hard to believe. I mean, what with the war, how long has it been? We love you both, but—"

"Eight years," Zim said, rocking her head.

"Ohhh, and here you are. How impossibly romantic." Hillie buckled her knees and feigned a swoon. "I can't imagine what Torgis and I would do if we were apart for even a single day." She kissed him and slid her hands inside his shirt. "I mean, after all that time, I'd just have to—" She growled and straddled Torgis' thigh.

"We'd love to stay and visit, but—" He embraced Hillie. "I have to get this one home fast." Torgis touched Zim's then Mac's hand and bowed to leave, struggling to free Hillie from his leg. Zim and Mac chuckled.

"That couple is the future of mankind?" Zim shook her head. "Whatever will become of us?"

"You know Creatives were initially selected for their breeding potential," Mac said. "That may still be their dominant trait. They have every known positive characteristic and skill—and no faults."

"I guess silly isn't considered a fault."

"Obviously." Mac pointed to dessert on the menu.

Not recognizing any and knowing little about desserts, Zim randomly selected gelato. Then she cleared her throat and put on a somber expression.

"I need to ask you a few things. You saw the Aldrakin surrender?"

"It was projected all across Corydon. I wouldn't have missed it."

"I don't understand what's happening, Mac. The high priest spoke directly to me. I could see it in his eyes—he thought the Prophecy was about me. You think this could be a coincidence?"

"It *was* about you, Gayle. It was too specific to be anything else."

"So, you believe it." She looked at her hand on Mac's arm then up into his eyes. "What's happening to the Unders? Is it just here or is it everywhere?"

"Unders are being replaced on all primary worlds," Mac said flatly. "You'll hear more when we visit Avian. I haven't had the tour, but I read that, after the Xi'Kior Tech War ravaged Earth, Avian had to intervene to reverse the genetic damage. Our species was sliding into oblivion. So, they engineered the Creatives."

Zim nodded. "What are Modern Partners? I saw them at the starport. Someone called them MPs."

"The MP movement started at the end of the tech war when healthy Human partners were hard to find. That's when Avian stepped in to stabilize our gene pool."

Mac cleared his throat. "To speed the Creative transition, Star Council prohibited Unders from mating and having children. Until recently, that's only been enforced on Corydon. MPs serve the Unders that are denied partners and care for the aged."

Zim bit her lips and shook her head. Then, not wanting to spoil the evening, she wrapped her arms around Mac's neck and poured herself into a long kiss. When dessert arrived, Zim suggested they share.

# # #

Aidan dropped them at Mac's place after midnight, a single executive suite on the edge of Four Green. Zim excused herself to change into the lingerie she'd purchased that afternoon—another surprise for Mac.

What a special evening, she thought as she unfastened her evening dress. Will there ever be another? Can this all be a dream? Tears again filled her eyes. She recalled stolen moments in their youth: back rooms, hiding in the forest, R&R once at Port Estelle, rushed and functional trysts. What do lovers do when they are no longer children?

She slipped into the filmy, revealing garment, centered the fit, and shook herself into place. Her vanity hologram reflection startled her, and she laughed. Seeing no sign of the hardened warrior in her gentle curved lines, she struck a winsome pose. Her demure, inner self resisted, but she knew Mac wanted her and loved her being playful.

The crackling fire gave the bedroom a cedar scent and golden glow, shifting light and shadow across the wood panels and the satin bedcovers.

"Mac?" Zim called, stepping so the fire backlit her lingeried figure.

"Over here, Gay—" The sound of his warm voice cut suddenly short sent a thrill through her. "I—I was thinking I'd surprise you... throw you on the bed, rip off your clothes. You win this round."

She turned so the firelight played on her breasts and long legs as she slid onto the bed. Mac's eyes followed each offered view, and he held out his hand.

Their first shy touches spoke of long separation. Mac's dark tanned face beamed yearning and tenderness. She kneeled over him, brushed hair from his forehead then kissed where it had been, careful to keep her breasts dancing in the light. He kissed her there then moved up to her shoulders, neck, and ears, his hands following where his lips had been. Their mouths found and drew on one another.

They played a slow reconnecting game, rediscovering and remembering what seemed almost forgotten. She held, clutched, leaned, and invited his need, responding to the excitement and timing of his breathing. Desperate love followed and continued into early morning; joy mixed with sadness as they released the stress of their long separation.

Then they slept, stirring at times, reaching and touching. In her waking moments, Zim thought of the dangers that lay in their uncertain future. Then she listened to Mac's beating heart and slept again.

Hippelli

The sun rose beyond the bistro table on Mac's patio. Splintered yellow rays sparkled through forest branches, and pine scent drifted on a crisp breeze. Zim pulled her thin robe close, and Mac opened his, inviting her to snuggle. She felt his warmth envelop her, his arm pulling her close.

With his free hand, Mac poured fresh-brewed coffee into two blue china cups, set the carafe on the table, and handed a cup to Zim. Could she make this moment last forever?

"I'll contact Crowley this morning, see what jobs he has to offer." Mac shifted his gaze from the glistening sunrise to Zim. "He said Star Council is giving all the terraforming business to SynTerra these days, so Blue Star's soliciting new customers. They've gotten contract offers from all over the galaxy, so I expect any new job will require travel."

"If he offers something you like, grab it, Mac. Don't wait for me. I still have two years to serve, but my time will be easier if I know you're established."

"Scientific expeditions can be long. If you go out, it'll be at least two to three years, maybe five." Mac's brow furrowed.

"If the expedition runs beyond my obligated time, I'll leave mid-tour. They can replace me." She cradled her cup in both hands. "I need a commander's uniform, so I'll look for that today then see about scraping together a shuttle crew." She felt the folded note she'd moved to her robe pocket and held it up. "What do you make of this? Abramyan's receptionist slipped it to me on my way out."

Mac nodded. "Ah, Frank Hippelli. He's in charge of Personnel Plans at Headquarters. That's his office number. Most personnel information isn't classified; you can pull it off the air." Mac gestured with his cup. "But if you're looking for a top crew, Frank's the place to start. He can give you *all* the details and any *special* information."

"*Special* information?" Zim savored the last sip of the strong black coffee, and Mac refilled her cup.

"Indiscretions or political considerations, things that aren't openly discussed. I'm sure Tracy read your orders and wanted to help you find your crew. I'll bet she's already arranged something with Frank on your behalf."

Hmm, Zim thought. If Tracy had already read her orders and made the arrangements, that meant her orders were not taken randomly from the queue. A setup. Abramyan lied.

"What do you need specifically?" Mac asked.

"A pilot and an engineer, both combat certified." She sighed. "*Marshal Massena's* research division hires the scientists, but I have to show up with a qualified military team."

Mac checked the personnel authorization line in Zim's budget and shook his head. "You'll be okay as long as you stay out in space. You know how much soldiers spend on shore leave and how much damage they can do." He pointed to the personnel line. "This won't cover one decent blowout weekend at a sleazy spacer dive. And I suspect all the quality pilots and engineers will be naming their own price with private ventures and security firms."

"I think that's the point Abramyan wanted to make. I won't be able to build a quality team."

"See what Frank can do for you. He might have something in his pocket. If there're any rough diamonds out there, he'll know where to find 'em."

"If my offer is the best they can get, they'll have to be desperate."

# # #

Zim procured her new commander's uniform with a simple trip to the tailor-printer, then Aidan took her to Star Council Headquarters. The research and service room of the Office of Personnel Plans had a pickup counter, a row of bench seats on one wall, and a half-dozen viewing kiosks.

"May we assist you, Commander?" An RH behind the counter lifted the corners of its moon-crescent, metallic mouth.

"I need to fill two military slots, a pilot and an engineer, both combat certified."

"That data is available to you directly, sorted by rank, qualifications, and starting pay grade." The RH pointed to the kiosks.

"Yes, however my requirements are *special,* you might say."

"Special requirements go directly through Mr. Hippelli," the RH said, remaining rigid as a statue.

"I was referred to a Mr. Frank Hippelli. He may be expecting me."

The RH's red sensors scanned the empty room and hallway. "Please come this way," it whispered, lifting the countertop, and pointing Zim to a passage behind the archives wall. "Frank is in the classified documents area."

At the end of the passage, Zim found a near-empty room with an old man rocking in a wooden chair. Except for white tufts above his ears, the man was completely bald. As Zim approached, he rocked up and stood, short and stooped with thin arms and legs. A roll of fat hung loose over his belt. He looked frail, but his lively, brown eyes danced with energy. He struck Zim more as an antiques dealer than a serious military ally.

"How might I help you, Commander?" Seeing her nametag, he took a second look. "Commander Zimmon, yes, excuse me, I'm Frank Hippelli. I was told to expect you. Before showing you my recommendations, I want you to see what's available."

A touch on the arm of his rocker opened a projection display. "These are the highest rated engineering and flight officers. If official records and grades are your primary guide, these top the list. But I don't recommend them."

He stepped aside. Zim took eighty-three seconds to read the first officer's report then four seconds for each of the next twenty-three. "I see what you mean." She nodded and looked to Hippelli.

"What exactly did you see?" Zim understood this as Hippelli's polite way of determining whether she knew her targ. She returned his sly smile.

"I see perfection and deception," she said flatly. "According to their records, these officers don't even have body odor. Some awards are from campaigns they could not have served in, including some that I led—and I don't know their names." Hippelli pursed his lips and twisted a white tuft above one of his elfin ears.

"Were these bought?" she asked. "They're practically identical."

"Looks that way." Hippelli returned to his rocker and invited Zim to pull up a chair beside him. "Those records were altered. I keep the originals, so I know what was added and taken out. Let me show you two more. StarCom wants these officers permanently removed from service. I filed them separately for reasons I'm sure you'll quickly grasp." He pulled a lap-sized panel from the low shelf and handed it to Zim. The panel was a standalone, secure from remote access.

The first record was a promotion rejection for Ensign Torey 'Hotz' Bahrke, a pilot and a Ten Creative with the First Legion. Who passes over an ensign for her first promotion, Zim wondered, and a Ten Creative? The record indicated a lost cause. "Insubordination, assaulting a senior officer, unsatisfactory flying and combat skills," Zim read. "Ensign Bahrke cannot be trusted… resents authority… earned call sign 'Hotz' for provocative dress and aggression in a squadron known for discipline problems." Zim shook her head. A First Legion squadron known for discipline problems? Not likely. "Recommend early termination and possible mind-sterilization should erratic behavior persist."

Zim looked up. "It appears Ensign Bahrke does not come highly recommended."

"StarCom did a job on her." Hippelli shook his head then continued. "That's about the worst targ-smear I've seen. Here's the original filed version. Security screeners made the redactions then decided to expunge and replace the entire record."

Torey "Hotz" Bahrke, Ensign, Pilot. Ten Creative. Home planet: Corydon. Age 20. Refused Creative deferment. Volunteered First Legion. Top of her class in piloting and combat skills. Skilled paramedic. Holds individual records for simulations and trials, defeating human, robot, and virtual opponents in all exercises. Natural leader. Led victorious teams in eight competitions. Nickname "Hotz" earned in early training when opponents insisted her "hot streak" could not last.

Incident report by Name Redacted: Following recognition by senior officers and an invitation to an award dinner in her honor, Ensign Bahrke assaulted Name Redacted at said dinner and was suspended pending investigation. Subsequent assessments revealed mental instability, disrespect for authority and aggression bordering on feral. Termination recommended.

Ensign Bahrke's account of the incident, filed from the Star Command infirmary, told a different story:

I arrived for the dinner, supposedly in my honor. Name Redacted, Name Redacted and Name Redacted were already intoxicated on substances unknown. As I considered my options for tactful withdrawal, Name Redacted pulled me into the party room. I struggled, felt a sting in my shoulder, and my legs collapsed. I awoke stretched out on a couch. My pants had been removed and my blouse torn open. Blood and bruises covered my upper legs and torso. The three Redacted officers remained unconscious in chairs and were completely naked. Torn packs of the Kontroller aphrodisiac were strewn on the dining table along with vials of amphetamines and sedatives. I injected sedatives into the three officers to keep them still then went to the Hotel Name Redacted kitchen for a butcher knife. I had second thoughts and instead retrieved animal parts from the butcher's waste receptacle. Then I came to the infirmary to write this report.

Zim swallowed and looked at Hippelli. He expanded, "The officers woke with no feeling below their waists and pig testicles, entrails, and blood in their laps. Bahrke had left the bloody butcher knife in plain sight. No actual surgery had been done, but it took hours for the medical team to calm the officers down."

Zim shook her head. "Bahrke might have taken her complaint to other—"

Hippelli cut her off. "Her attackers were well-connected, senior StarCom officers. Don't ask how I know."

Zim raised then balled and lowered her hand. "I understand. Ensign Bahrke would not have gotten any support."

Hippelli directed Zim's attention to an addendum to Bahrke's performance report. "You'll find this interesting. It pertains to Ensign Bahrke's hot streak. You understand the scoring?" He pointed to the test results.

"Some of the tests aren't familiar, but those are top scores."

"They are impossible scores." Hippelli let his comment register.

"You're saying Ensign Bahrke cheated?"

"That's what the testers thought. But when they adjusted and repeated the tests, her scores held. To get these times, adjusting for neurological transmission rates, Bahrke had to react before each simulation initiated its action."

"How is that possible?"

Hippelli shrugged. "Her countermoves anticipated tactics, even random computer-generated attacks, by microseconds. That enabled her to consistently beat the computers."

Zim tried to match the pretty, blond pixie-face in the photo with the record of violence. "How badly does she want back into piloting?"

Hippelli shrugged. "Don't know. She's been taken off flight status, but I believe she's still on Corydon." He touched the top of the secure panel. "Here's a candidate for your combat engineer."

> James "Dom" Eppert, Major, Chief Engineer. Under. Home planet: Earth. Age 53. Major Eppert had a distinguished career as a Combat Team Leader (CTL). Early campaigns include major colonial battles, interventions, and peacekeeping actions: Kashogie, Tarabo, Erekat, Xiaoran, and Santo Rift. Reported MIA at Santo Rift and presumed dead. Successfully evaded hostile Ocht natives for fifteen months until discovered and rescued by an armed survey team. Retired with full honors, 3596.

> Volunteered to return to service for the Aldrakin War, 3599. Service rejected due to age limit for CTLs, 38 years. Protested rejection. Re-qualified as a nuclear combat engineer based on prior in-service training and test certification. Campaign record for second enlistment: Kerballo, Divangne, Shee Yar, Ash-Har, Silkani.

Zim frowned. "Silkani? Eppert is the sole survivor from that Rii-Chaut massacre? I read about that as I came in from Bai-Yota. And now StarCom wants to blame him for the whole fiasco?"

Hippelli added, "StarCom won't back off their cover story. Marshal Boorman insisted that they strip the Silkani defenses to strengthen his Dibak-Dak assault. If those forces hadn't been drawn off, it's unlikely the Rii-Chaut would have attacked." Remembering his visitor, he demurred. "But I recognize your far greater expertise in such things."

"Boorman again." Zim locked eyes with Hippelli. "I bet Abramyan had a hand in it, too."

"Abramyan approved Boorman's plan then needed a scapegoat for them both. He claimed Dom fled the battlefield, locked himself in the underground power station, and cut the power, leaving them defenseless. After the Rii-Chaut had their way with the settlers and the media, they irradiated the planet to kill anyone they missed. Dom survived because he was behind the power plant's shields."

"Eppert's nickname, Dom, short for Dominic?" Zim asked.

"CTLs call it a *nom de guerre*. They're like call signs for flight personnel. Dom earned his on his first enlistment. Stands for 'dirty old man.' It was intended as a joke. Seems Dom always had an eye for the ladies, exotic ladies and spacer chicks, like those that hang around starports and military bases. No one ever complained."

Zim raised her eyebrows then scrolled down to read Dom's account of Silkani:

We thought the attackers were Aldrakin. IFF indicated Aldrakin. The SynTerra rep wanted the area secured. It was too late to evacuate. Attackers had already taken out the transports.

I was afraid they would capture Silkani and the anti-matter power reactor. They could use the reactor to support another Aldrakin base or rig it to destroy Silkani. When I explained my concern, the SynTerra rep sent me down to secure the reactor. If the Aldrakin took Silkani, I was to shut down the containment field. I knew that would be suicide, but I hadn't re-upped to live forever.

While I was shutting down the vulnerable ports, our ground commander General Remmler ordered the vault locked and sealed. I stayed at my post waiting to be relieved, or to shut down containment if there was a break-in. The rescue team showed up the next day with the pass code and re-opened the vault. That was the first I heard that our attackers were Rii-Chaut and that they had irradiated the planet.

Hippelli finished the story, "Dom was arrested. Based on previous service and advanced age, the review board gave him a pardon and an honorable discharge." Hippelli cleared his throat. "If Dom's too old… well, what's that say about me?"

Zim tapped a knuckle of her fisted hand to her chin. "Where can I find Hotz and Dom?"

Event Horizon

Stepping into the open-bay shuttle, Zim felt the electro-static field and inhaled the scent of jacinth flowers.

"How was your meeting?" Aidan asked.

"Productive. What can you tell me about the Event Horizon?"

"An old night spot in the renovation district. Still popular, but it's gotten a bit seedy, at least the neighborhood. We drove by on the way in from the starport. Event Horizon's underground, so you might have missed it. I hear they've kept up their standards, decent food, excellent drinks, and music."

"How about the clientele?"

"A lot of dodgy characters, spacers and aliens, particularly during trade fairs. Being near the starport, they get a lot of transients. Some Creatives go there, not so many now. The Greens have their own nightspots. *Paradis* in One Green is the best. That's what I recommend if you and Marshal Mackenzie are planning another evening. But it's still early. Wouldn't you rather wait?"

"No, take me to the Event Horizon. I'm on a fact-gathering mission, and I'm hoping to meet some people there."

#

Broken walls cast long shadows in the late afternoon sun. Scanning the debris, Zim spotted white letters painted on a low concrete wall, "Nearing the Event Horizon," followed by a bent, white arrow pointing down a stone staircase.

The room was dark, dank, and practically empty. Zim paused at the base of the steps to let her eyes adjust. Suspended, green-shaded lamps cast cones of light over a dozen tables. A bar filled one short wall. The adjacent long wall had a low stage with half a dozen empty seats and unattended music instruments.

101

A brown-barked, tree-stump-like Shelesti crouched at the edge of the stage pouring nuggets into a bowl for some Hyrup centipedes. The meter-and-a-half long Hyrup jostled to begin feeding before the bag was lifted. The Shelesti stroked their segments with twig fingers as they fed. Her mate-hump half-closed its eyes as she stroked.

Two crab-like Goorm, interstellar traders Zim guessed, haggled at a nearby table. The other tables were unoccupied. A silhouetted figure moved behind the bar backlit by a mirror stacked with glasses and colored bottles: clear, green, blue, and red. Zim took a seat at the bar and continued scanning the room. A soft clink drew her to turn and catch a shadow setting a long-stemmed flute on a napkin.

"Compliments of the house for all veterans of Bai-Yota, one oli-jira, straight up with a red zillberry. I believe that is your drink." Surprised to recognize the voice, Zim smiled across the bar into the slim dark face.

"O'Kavo Kaplan!"

"At your service, Commander. I see StarCom rewarded you for your brilliant victory." He flashed a sardonic smile and waved to the simpler cut and trim of her commander's uniform.

"It seems there weren't any senior command positions available." Zim mirrored his smile. "You seem to have gotten your bearings quickly."

"I tended bar a couple seasons ago at my uncle's place on Thrinlu. Jerry the owner here needed help. He won't have robots on staff, except as bouncers, and Creatives never take service jobs." Kaplan shrugged.

"It's not busy yet, do you have a moment to talk?"

"Let me check my other customers." Kaplan got the claw response for okay from the Goorm traders then came around the bar to sit with Zim.

"Doesn't look like the police roughed you up." Zim studied Kaplan. "I wasn't sure after they got you out of my sight."

"They were polite enough but didn't waste any time. Decommissioning was in and out. With less than a year's service, my retirement only gave me enough to buy civilian clothes." He tugged the fabric of his shirt then propped an elbow on the bar. "So, of all the gin joints in all the galaxy, what brings you to mine?"

Zim didn't recognize Kaplan's husky impersonation but suspected he had talents beyond what she'd seen on *Lasalle*. "I need information, maybe an introduction." Zim touched her oli-jira flute to Kaplan's water goblet. "You've only been here a day, so I'm not sure how much you can help me."

Kaplan curled his fingers toward himself in a come-on gesture.

"Dom and Hotz, either of those names sound familiar? They're both recently discharged, so they might have been in." She took heart at Kaplan's raised eyebrows.

"So happens, they were in last night. Jerry the owner said they'd both been in the past couple nights. Said they were recent regulars and good spenders, so I was to take care of them." Kaplan looked up as a new customer entered. A Tak-Yaki mantis took a lone seat beside the Goorm's table. It threw its sword on the table and began searching through its satchel.

"According to Jerry," Kaplan continued, "Dom and Hotz showed up around the same time last week. Not together but they found each another. Dom's got money. Said he planned to burn through some before he went looking for a job. Hotz isn't a real regular, but she's local, from Corydon. Jerry said he'd seen her in a couple times in the past. Give me a second." Kaplan went to check his new customer.

The Tak-Yaki was average height, a meter-and-a-half, with thin levi-pads on its back and upper limbs to counter Corydon gravity. A weapon belt hung across its neck to its waist. Zim had fought alongside the TY on several campaigns and never saw one carry more than one personal weapon. They didn't need close-range weapons, not with their claws and special implants. Zim had seen a TY shred an Aldrakin guard so fast its body cavity emptied before its torso hit the ground. Her friend Tock only wore a ceremonial sword for dress occasions.

Kaplan delivered a tall mug of ale to the TY then returned to Zim.

"You expect Dom and Hotz tonight?" she asked.

"Dom said he wasn't in a hurry to find a job, so yes, he'll probably be in. I believe Hotz has connections to one of the Greens, so she might have other plans, but lately she's been hanging with Dom. Jerry said they'd become fast friends, maybe more." Kaplan leaned one arm on the bar while tipping his water goblet to his mouth.

"Then I think I'll wait around and try to catch them." Zim lifted her flute then paused. "Tell me, did you collect on that wager you made on me?" She recalled Kaplan's comment before the Aldrakin attack.

He closed his eyes and took a rapturous breath. "Money's in an escrow account. Six-years-pay. I knew I couldn't lose." He gave Zim a smug wink.

"That's what you said on *Lasalle*. You mentioned a betting algorithm?"

"A slight fabrication. Wonders can get into trouble for misappropriating resources. In Basic, I was given access to the Authoriton as a planning tool. I was supposed to ask it about career paths, training, deployment options, things like that. But I wanted to win the betting pool, so I cheated and asked where the next major battle would be fought. I was surprised it didn't kick me off the system."

"And it told you Bai-Yota?"

"It told me it didn't have that information. Then I asked what the chances were for the Starflower to be in a major battle. Three months, it said, one hundred percent."

Zim's eyes dropped to the bar then back up to Kaplan. "I'll have to think about that. The Authoriton's accuracy is well known, but I've never heard of a sure thing." Then she thought, especially not regarding me. Her eye caught a menu box highlighted on the bar. "What's the food like?"

"Very good, all fresh. Hope you like the booze." Zim nodded and raised her flute for a refill. Kaplan walked back round the bar. "Jerry said Star Council cut supplies to most of the Under establishments but not to Event Horizon. He thinks our Creative customers interceded. We're edgier than what they can find in the Greens. That appeals to some." He set a fresh drink and napkin in front of Zim and took away her empty flute.

"As I said, house picks up the tab for all Bai-Yota veterans. Wait till Jerry hears that the Starflower was in." He raised his chin and exaggerated a toothy grin. Zim opened the menu box display, and Kaplan pointed out his favorites. "Fish is excellent, so's the stew."

"Gloak stew?" Zim wistfully recalled long days tending their gloak herd on Scalaris. She hadn't had the stew in years. Then she remembered the farm had been destroyed in the war. Good thoughts and bad.

"If you prefer, we have gloak steaks, prime cuts."

"Mmm, tempting, but I'll just try the stew for now. A small bowl, I'm having dinner with Marshal Mackenzie later." Kaplan raised an approving eyebrow.

The stage lights brightened and hanging lamps dimmed. Six Hyrup skittered over to wrap their bodies about the instruments and soon filled the room with hot jazz.

Zim watched customers pour in. Three Under spacers pulled up near the stage. A loud, mixed group of Unders and Tak-Yaki took the corner table near the stairwell and immediately demanded service. All sported combat scars and prosthetics. Four Goorm scuttled to grab the large center table, propping their spacious carapaces on the chairs, claws on the table, and eight side and rear legs into the spaces between the tables. Wealthy merchants, Zim surmised judging from their jewel inlays and lofty manner. Their salty scent reminded her of nets drying on the Scalari waterfront.

Kaplan rushed about, replacing the lone TY's empty mug with a full one, setting Zim's stew on the bar, and clearing the table of the two Goorm traders who had been there earlier.

Zim tapped a note to Mac. She would join him later at *Paradis*, or he could come to the Event Horizon now. He replied quickly, "Later at *Paradis*."

Kaplan tapped her shoulder and lifted his chin to the stairwell. An older spacer stepped into the room, massive, ruggedly built. Behind him stood a tall, lithe woman with short, white-blond hair, and a pixie face. The stubble-faced spacer wore a disheveled StarCom uniform unfastened at the collar. The woman had an open StarCom jacket over a white camisole, thigh-hugging red slacks, and designer booties. They took a table near the wealthy Goorm, directly between Zim and the loud, mixed group in the corner.

Zim leaned back on the bar and observed her perspective hires.

Dom and Hotz

Customers entered and took seats at the bar and beside the stage. The air grew thick with odors of aliens, spicy food, spilled beverages, and rancid smoke. A tall RH—configured as a full-featured, civilian-male so Zim assumed it was a Modern Partner—asked Kaplan to set a table beside the stage. A minute later it was helping a disabled Creative gentleman into a chair.

Zim drank slowly, taking in the scene. The lone Tak-Yaki took special interest in Dom and noticed her watching, too. One of the toughs at the raucous corner table craned his neck to ogle Hotz. When he started to rise, his tattooed partner rested a metal gauntlet on his shoulder and waved to Dom with his free hand. Dom waved back.

Kaplan brought a bottle and two glasses to Dom's table, poured for him and Hotz, then went to the wealthy Goorm table.

The stage lights brightened for two dancers. At the Shelesti's direction, the Hyrup added more brass and drums to their instrumentation and played, "My Kashogie Princess," a song Zim remembered was popular with *Lasalle's* crew. The dancers did an erotic interpretation to the low and languorous beat, weaving their sinuous fingers and prehensile tails to accentuate the writhing convolutions of their nude bodies. Zim had never seen this species or this sort of dance.

"What are they?" She whispered close to Kaplan's ear.

"Pidge," he whispered back. She shook her head. "Surgically altered Humans. They showed up on Thrinlu last year. I heard they've been in the mining camps for years." He rushed off with a tray of drinks.

These Pidge were well-formed humanoid females, their backs mottled with black and dark green lozenges that blended to olive on their sides and honey on their bellies and faces. They had one pair of large breasts and two small pair below. A crest of hair that began on their foreheads, rose over their bald heads to become a narrow mane and descend down their neck and spine to their tails.

106

Twisting and twirling to the music, eyes half-closed, their donut mouths pulsing, the dancers seemed in complete ecstasy.

"Hali Kamaili" came next, another tune Zim remembered hearing. The music got louder, and with it the conversation. The Humans and Tak-Yaki had started a betting game at the corner table, cheering and cursing after every play. The largest of the Goorm businessmen scuttled over to join in. Other Unders and Creatives went to watch and cheer, or play, if a spot came open.

One Pidge dancer touched the other and pointed. The second dancer jumped and clapped, excused herself, and ran to Dom's table. Sidling up behind him, she wrapped her arms around his head and hugged him to her breasts. Dom pulled her gently around, put his sinewy hand at the small of her back, and whispered in her ear. The dancer stroked Dom's thinning, gray-streaked hair, kissed his forehead, and hugged him again before returning to the stage.

Hotz watched but kept silent during the exchange. Then she spoke softly in Dom's ear, downed her drink, and left for the gaming table. Zim decided this was a good time to start recruiting.

Dom's expression behind the graying stubble was somber. He'd rolled the sleeves of his soiled uniform, revealing striated, magnum forearms. Gray chest hair curled up from his open collar. Zim put a hand on the top of an empty chair.

"Major James Eppert?"

He looked up from his comfortable sprawl and motioned her to sit. "Hope you're not lookin' for no intelligent conversation, Commander, cuz I'm fresh out." Dom's resonant voice had the casual twang and slur Zim associated with combat veterans well into their cup. He refilled his whiskey glass from the bottle without offering any to her. "If you know me, you might guess I'm not real keen on StarCom right now." He pointed the bottle's neck to her new StarCom uniform and crossed her like a priest giving a benediction.

"I'm a new Commander so—"

An Under spacer punched Dom's arm. "Tough go, Dom. You know, none of the crew believe that targ about you abandoning your post."

"Thanks, Jocko. Tell the Cap'm I'll miss spacin' with 'im an all you targ-kickers."

Jocko shrugged. "Don't expect to see the Captain again. Guess you didn't hear. Borodino's been decommissioned, the whole crew. She's headed to the scrap heap and all us Galaxy-rated spacers with her."

Dom scratched his head. "Nope, didn't hear a thing. Don't get much news in the brig." Jocko punched his arm again, nodded to Zim without any show of recognition, and headed to watch the gaming group in the corner.

Dom returned to Zim. "So, you're a new StarCom Commander, huh? Didn't know there were any. Well, if you're drinkin' at my table, I guess you can call me Dom. See you're an Under, too, so I won't spoil the excitement of your new promotion." He waved the bottle high and motioned for Kaplan to bring another glass.

"Thanks, Dom. The bartender told me the Event Horizon was picking up my tab." She wagged her empty oli-jira flute toward Kaplan, and he pointed back. "I'm surprised *your* money's any good here."

"Don't bait me, Sister." Dom glowered. "You know my last battle didn't go so good."

"I read the report. If it helps, I didn't believe it either."

Shouting at the corner gaming table got angry. A burly Human jumped up, knocking over his chair, and shook a metal fist at the big Goorm. Bystanders pulled tables and chairs back. Hotz brushed hair from her forehead and stepped out of the way.

The Goorm tucked down its stalked eyes, perched back on its segmented legs, and pulled its heavy claws forward like battering rams or monster jaws.

Dom pushed his chair back for a clear view. "Watch, this'll be interesting." He pointed first to Zim then to the big Goorm.

The Human threw all his weight into his metal fist. The Goorm bounced as if floating on its hind legs. Before the Human could recover from his missed punch, the Goorm hooked a trailing leg behind his knees and pulled, sending the Human down hard. The Goorm followed its leg sweep with a hammer blow to the downed man's crotch.

Dom almost fell out of his chair laughing. "Game over." He took another pull on his drink. "Those fat crabbies look slow, but they can dance, and ya gotta watch them extra legs." Two RH bouncers marched in, raked the beaten man's game chits into a bag, and dragged him to the back.

Hotz slipped her slender figure into the loser's seat and got welcoming nods around the table. Most of the bar's customers gave little notice to the fight other than talking louder. Those near the stage never took their eyes off the dancers. The lone Tak-Yaki by the wall shifted its attention between the fight and Dom. With the fight over, it stood, adjusted its weapon belts, grabbed its satchel, and walked to their table.

"Xccc, tscch," the TY's mouthparts ratcheted. It placed a claw on the table translator. "Major Eppert?" Not waiting to be invited, it turned a chair, straddled it, and leaned forward. "I made you a serious business proposition. I hope you've changed your mind." Its triangular head swiveled to Zim then back. It hopped its chair closer to the table. Zim leaned away to keep them both in her field of view and brought her hands to her lap.

Dom took a long pull then set his glass on the table. "I'll be needin' a job soon, if that's what you're offerin'."

The TY extended a closed claw. "*You* are not pleased with StarCom. You *owe* them nothing. As you correctly deduced at our previous meeting, I represent certain special interests—"

"What you think of this guy?" Dom asked, looking to Zim.

"I like the TY, personally, but I don't think I like this fellow."

The alien's triangular head snapped around, garnet eyes flashing. It tipped its chair menacingly toward Zim and pointed a claw. "Major Eppert and I have business to discuss. He should not have included you into our private—" The TY stopped mid-sentence, tilted its head to the blue medal on Zim's chest then to her name tag then up to her face. Recoiling, it righted its chair. "Excuse me. I have misspoken." It pushed the chair between itself and Zim and ran for the stairs.

Dom stared after the mantis then gave Zim a quizzical look. "That fella knew you." He blocked the stage lights with one hand and leaned to check Zim's medal and nametag. His breath reeked of whiskey.

Bolting upright, he inhaled deeply then gave her a long steady stare. Zim could now make out his features. Old for his age, not weak or infirm, far from it, but weathered and battle-scarred. Behind the bristling stubble and drunkenness, she saw anger and determination, not at her, but at life in general.

Hotz returned, wrapped an arm around Dom's wide shoulders, and gazed across at Zim. Her wide-set blue eyes, pixie face, and full-lipped smile belied the vicious profile Zim had read.

"How'd you do?" Dom asked.

"Very well, thanks to Chik'ik." She jingled a sack at her belt and nodded toward the big Goorm who had won the fight earlier. At the sound of its name, or more likely the jingling chits, the Goorm rotated one eyestalk toward their table. Hotz threw it a kiss. The Goorm swiveled both eyes back to its game.

The Shelesti called for a water break, and Dom's favorite Pidge hopped over to stroke and kiss his cheek. He pressed her wrist to transfer credits to her account and told her how beautiful she was. She clung to his arm a moment, kissed his cheek again then strolled to the next table. Zim watched her other clients stroke her buttocks and other places men aren't supposed to stroke females in public. The Pidge smiled, inviting the caresses. Dom's jaw muscles flexed, and he shifted in his seat, but he said nothing.

"You like her." Zim observed.

"We're closh... were closh once. Now she barely remembers me—my fault, not hers. I let 'er down." He checked his empty glass then slammed it on the table.

Hotz ran her fingers up through his sparse hair. "It's okay. She's okay. Nothing you can do."

Dom snorted, sat up, and rubbed his face. "Excuse me. I forget my manners." He addressed Zim. "Commander Zimmon, I'd like to introduce you to my colleague, Torey Bahrke, aka Hotz, formerly of Star Command, prob'ly the best pilot in the fleet." He turned. "Hotz, this is Commander Gayle Zimmon, the Starflower, who I'm sure you've heard about." Zim appreciated he was trying to be gracious despite his condition.

"*The Starflower?*" Hotz began to laugh, then her jaw dropped. Pulling erect, she stopped short of slapping her arms to her sides.

Zim's celebrity still caught her by surprise. "I'm very pleased to meet you both, Dom, Hotz." She looked around. Everyone was too busy talking or feeling up the Pidges to pay them any notice.

"What may we do for you, Commander?" Dom asked.

"I hope you two, both of you, might help me out of a jam. First, let me say I'm sorry for scaring away that Tak-Yaki. It was trying to offer you a job."

"That Targ-Yaki's been after me all week. I told it I'm no pirate. Don't care 'bout no damn letters of marque or whatever it calls 'em—it's recruiting brigands and pirates."

"Rii-Chaut?"

"Mercenaries, a private army for some targ head of one 'a them extralegal frontier companies. Wanted Hotz, too. She clocked that Targ-Yaki—that one that just left." Dom shook his fist toward the steps. "Near spun its triangle head like a top. Course, I'm more civ'lized." Hotz rapped his head with her knuckles.

"We'll prob'ly sign with some freighter for a lot less money." Dom gestured to Hotz. "She'll fly 'em, I'll keep 'em flying. Star Council's moving everybody around. They need pilots and engineers. If our records don't qualify us for government work, we'll go independent: Blue Star or one of the smaller outfits."

Zim put both hands flat on the table. "So happens, I need a pilot and an engineer. I've seen your files. I know they limit your job prospects." Dom and Hotz both frowned. "Frankly, your charm could use some polish. But your skill rankings are tops in the service, best engineer, best pilot. You're also both combat certified." She looked back and forth between them. "I need that. Problem is I can't afford it." She showed them her pay allowance. Dom smirked. Hotz squeezed his shoulders. They'd have to take below starting salaries in their specialties.

Dom raised an eyebrow to Hotz then looked at Zim. "I just got outta the service, I'm still drinkin'." He tilted and peeked into his empty glass. "When we hafta decide?"

"Tonight… and we shove off in three months. It'll take that long to refit the *Marshal Massena.* You'll be shuttling research scientists and collection teams, probably doing a little search and rescue. Not real exciting. Not what you're used to. But you won't be hauling ore to some refinery or siphoning hydrogen off a gas giant." Zim glanced between them. "We'll be out a long time, so if you have family to look after…" Her voice dropped off.

Hotz shook her head. "No family. Ten Green dropped me after that incident you probably read about." She laughed. "Talk about records, the Starflower's got a reputation, too—for getting into scrapes. If you think you need to soft pedal this job, don't. It's never quiet around you. So, I'm in. Sign me up."

Dom pursed his lips, nodding at each point Hotz made. "Me too. Nothin' keepin' me here," he pointed his chin across the room, "except Glory."

Zim followed his gaze to the Pidge who laughed while a man fondled her breasts. "You mean the Pidge?"

111

Dom nodded. "My sister sold herself to the Spacer Recreation Guild to pay for her son Billy's medical bills. The money I sent back got cut off when I went MIA at Santo Rift. StarCom assumed I was dead. The Guild turned Glory into a Pidge dancer. She was so ashamed she had her mind wiped. Billy was fourteen at the time, last kid in the family. Died anyway." Dom rolled his lips in and bit down, then refilled his glass and took a long quaff. "Glory doesn't know me. To her I'm just a nice, well-paying customer."

Zim didn't ask any more questions. She passed them electronic forms to reinstate their flight status then authorized their transport to Port Estelle where the *Marshal Massena* was refitting.

# # #

Jazz music followed Zim up the stairwell like a tailwind and poured out into the street. A shuttle from the spaceport disgorged a stream of screaming spacers who dashed past her and disappeared down the steps.

"Shall I take you to *Paradis*, Commander?" Aidan asked. When she didn't respond, he asked, "Were you able to meet the people you wanted?" She nodded and stepped into the open shuttle. She trusted Aidan but wasn't ready to drop her guard.

"We had a good discussion. I saw and heard disturbing things."

"Event Horizon attracts all types," Aidan said flatly.

"Pidge? I suppose that's a legal enterprise?"

"It's legal. It's also part of our judicial system." Aidan shifted in his seat. "Corydon banned capital punishment. Now Pidge is the severest penalty the court can deliver."

Zim's gut tightened. "Whatever could one do to deserve—"

"Once it was restricted to the most severe crimes. Now it's handed out for small infractions—like taking an unauthorized partner. Cases involving Unders don't go through the court system. Robots handle all Under enforcement. Punishment is automatic."

"But I heard some Unders volunteer for that?" She lifted her chin toward the Event Horizon.

Aidan looked apologetic. "Some need money badly or are desperate to escape their nothing existence." He swallowed. "I don't think you want to hear this."

"I think I need to hear it." Zim heard the anger in her voice. "Why was this kept secret?"

"All Pidge alteration is done on Corydon: surgery, implants, genetic engineering, and hormone treatments. Off-world criminals are sent here to be altered, then out to work camps or sport clubs. They don't go to military camps or R&R retreats for obvious reasons." Aidan took a long breath. "Entertainers are handled by the Spacer Recreation Guild. Demand for prostitutes off world is huge. The guild offers a bounty for new Pidge. People living in remote mining camps and industrial parks have cruel tastes. I guess working on airless rocks and toxic environments drives men crazy."

"*Not just men*," Zim said, "women, too. What do they do to the men?"

Aidan took a slow breath. "Some are modified like the women for sex work—serving men and women. Most they turn into monsters. Re-designing them to fight one another or to work in hazardous environments: extreme heat and cold, or poisonous atmospheres. I've heard of men made into aquatics, given gills and fins. The staged fights are sadomasochistic obscenities. They rip one another apart. I watched once out of curiosity. I wish I hadn't. I don't want to believe anyone is capable of that or enjoy seeing it." He looked at Zim. "Sometimes women return from the camps—men never do."

"Do all Pidge have their minds erased?" Zim asked, quietly.

"That depends on the sentence or the contract. Some are given a choice, but most are treated like disposable property. Some Pidges have their nerves blocked to deaden pain, others have them rerouted to enhance performance."

"For hazardous work, why don't they use robots? And virtual perversions can be made as real as any reality."

Aidan looked trapped. "I think the Star Council decided there were too many Unders. Abuse makes them more pliable, less likely to challenge the system." Zim lowered her head and asked no more questions. She appreciated Aidan's honesty.

Zim had seen incredible violence in her short life. The Tak-Yaki celebrated their prowess in delivering swift death, but they despised abject cruelty. What she had heard tonight was the purest evil.

Tee'Kahl

Tee'Kahl, Deputy Envoy Extraordinary for the Sk'Keffin diplomatic mission to the Aldrakin, rose from her aqueous ammonia brine on the 0.7G deck of Admiral Okrador's flagship. It was the morning after the Aldrakin surrender reception. Tee'Kahl shook her languorous organs to wakefulness then organized them onto her radial arm struts. In accordance with current fashion, she migrated her oral, respiratory, and sensor orifices to her top-most arm and her excretory orifices between the lowest two. She then bounced everything into alignment and checked her vanity hologram.

"You are beautiful as ever," her merged mate whispered in her mind.

"You think so? I love to hear you say that, but I know I'm aging." Tee'Kahl adjusted her hologram's angle to make sure nothing had slipped and firmed her ectoplasm to hold everything in place.

"We've been merged for fifteen years," Billy said. "I'm as aware of Sk'Keffin standards as anyone."

"*Fifteen…* that's fifteen Human years. On Sk'Keffin it's barely been two. We're still newlyweds."

"Yes, well, I still think in Human terms. Even after fifteen… two years, you are as beautiful as ever."

"I know you prefer me configured this way," she said, returning to her hologram. "You have a weakness for five-radial symmetry." Tee'Kahl formed a winsome 'W' with her feeding orifice in her reflection and puckered approval. "I don't remember you being so complimentary when I was an eight-radial." She tilted her newly formed face to determine the best angle. "Well, thanks to your friend Starflower, five-radials are back in style."

Billy knew to pick his words carefully. "I just think radial designs based on five are more elegant, especially with the head at the top. And why would you mention Starflower? You know I never saw her before yesterday's ceremony."

"Head at the top? You mean like the Humans?"

"I may be biased," Billy admitted. "For fourteen years, I was Human. Everyone I knew had a head, and most intelligent creatures were five-radials—one head, four limbs. Perhaps you just can't take a compliment."

"Tell me, did you find the Starflower attractive?"

Here we go… Billy saw this coming. "She has attractive qualities. I admire her leadership and combat skills. I suspect the ceremony surprised her, especially the *Aldra Korah* prophecy—that surprised *me*. The High Priest spoke as if the Starflower was a hero out of their mythology. She handled it well. That is what I know about the Starflower. That's what I like about her."

"Okay, I won't bring her up again. Did you enjoy seeing the other Humans at the ceremony? It's been a long time."

"I enjoyed seeing the uniforms. My Uncle Jim was in Star Command—they called him Dom. He was like a father to me, but he disappeared before the Aldrakin war and was never found." After a pause he continued. "Seeing Humans at the ceremony got me thinking about my family and old friends back on Corydon—everyone I left behind when I died." Billy's death wasn't that simple, but he didn't want to upset Tee'Kahl.

He had chosen awareness-transfer, a death alternative, over permanent disability and being a constant burden to his family. The doctor who gave Billy his bleak diagnosis introduced him to the "soul traders"—black market jargon for the Goorm who trafficked in transferred minds. They told him he was young enough to have his mind replanted, and it would free him of the ravages of his illness.

Billy was happy with his merger with Tee'Kahl. After years together, he believed their fusion was more intimate than the Human practice of copulation. The girls he met on Corydon were afraid of any involvement, afraid if they took Human partners, they would be punished.

"I'm sorry you died, Billy. The Goorm trader in the bazaar assured me that a merger was the only way you could live again. I knew he was a smuggler. My myriad told me all bazaar traders lie, but I didn't ask any questions. I fell in love with your profile. You don't feel that I trapped you, do you, Billy?"

"Certainly not, my love. My soul leapt to yours." Billy felt her sadness as assuredly as he did his own and knew the situation required that flourish.

"Thank you, that's what I needed to hear. Feel my love for you." Tee'Kahl shared her delight secretions and flashed her flirtatious 'W.' "Of course, for me it was always about physical attraction. Human five-radials are sooo sexy."

They laughed as one.

"Billy, the ceremony got me thinking. The Aldrakin-Human treaty means we'll be exchanging legations, possibly setting up a full embassy. You know the Aldrakin favor Sk'Keffin diplomats. What would you say about us applying?"

"A good opportunity for you, my love."

"I've always wanted a position like this, and you could see as many Humans as you wish. With our minds joined, we'd be perfect for the job. Maybe we'd see the Starflower again and maybe meet her lover, Mackenzie. Their story is so romantic!"

Part Three

Holiday

Avian

Zim found Mac on the torch-lit patio behind *Paradis*. Corydon's three-ringed, crescent moon stood high in the starry night.

"Successful recruiting day?" He stood and pulled out her chair.

"Yes. Hippelli was an excellent resource."

"I worried when you called from Event Horizon. I know you can handle yourself, Gayle, but a lot of unsavory business goes down there. If you saw anything unsettling that you want to talk about—" He didn't finish the sentence.

"Thank you, Mac, and you're right, but it's not worth ruining our dinner." Zim bit her lip. The entire system on Corydon was built on violence, corruption, and abuse. Now more than ever she wanted the two of them to get far away.

"Event Horizon's unpleasant clientele aside, I found an experienced pilot *and* an engineer, and they're *both* combat certified?"

Mac looked surprised. "And they're willing to work for what... bar tips?"

Zim tilt-nodded a smile. "They're extremely good. Rough edges made them a lot of enemies, political enemies. Experience doesn't come with clean slates; we both know that. How'd you do with Crowley?"

"Not as well." Mac rolled his lips in. "Most of Blue Star's new contracts are in development. Crowley expects the workflow to pick up late next year. All they're working on now are a couple dozen trading posts for the Goorm and expanding the Luna supply base. But the real problem is neither of us have been released by StarCom."

"Abramyan didn't release you either?" Zim frowned.

"He confirmed that he was dissolving Command Staff but said my talents were needed elsewhere on the Council."

"Did you tell Crowley we wanted to relocate together?"

"He said all Blue Star executives have off-world homes, and the company runs its own interstellar transit service."

"So, we put our plans on hold until we finish out our contracts."

Mac nodded. "That should get StarCom off our backs. Looking to the immediate future, we'll be at Avian all day tomorrow. I'm sure there'll be a crowd." He opened a news panel on the table: STARFLOWER TO TOUR AVIAN. "Star Council is doing this to defang the insurgency. They want us all to look like one happy family."

#

Angry clouds rolled in as Zim and Mac descended the steps from his apartment. Pelting rain followed in a wave. Aidan stood below by the shuttle. The large crowd, held back by an RH police cordon, dashed for cover. Zim's hair whipped about her face. Her uniform weave tightened against the chill and rain.

Zim stepped under the shuttle's electrostatic shield and slid to the back of the open bay. Gray sheets of water drummed on the hull. Lightning crackled and flashed.

The mag-lev shuttle moved swiftly into the opaque wall of water, sending wings out both sides. Two minutes and two wide turns later, the shuttle slowed to a stop and was enveloped in an electrostatic corridor. The windowless, two-kilometer cube of Avian loomed beyond its rain-cascading walls.

Up the steps, the corridor ended at a ten-meter-high archway. Wide, dual doors slid open, then a second set, then a third, and Zim and Mac found themselves in the center of a cacophonous rainforest.

The humid air carried scents of humus and tropical flowers. Buttress roots thrust massive trunks into the leafy canopy, branching high above like cathedral arches. Orchids and snaking vines covered cocoa and eucalyptus trees. Wide-beaked toucans scolded, butterflies flitted, and bees and dragonflies buzzed and swooped.

Zim stared and startled. A hummingbird bobbed in her face, dipped to her chest to examine her blue Starflower, then darted behind her. Turning to follow its path, she found herself facing more endless rainforest where the outer wall of Avian should have stood. The dual-arch entry they'd just passed floated disconnected in space. Zim ran a hand around the smooth edge of the doorframe and found no support.

"Welcome to Avian, Commander Zimmon, Marshal Mackenzie. This tropical habitat about you is our showpiece. We keep it up front for marketing and historical reference." The warm baritone came from a tall executive-grade RH standing on a barely discernible pathway. It wore a tailored charcoal gray, nano-fiber tunic with burgundy details and silk-band collar.

"My designator is RH-1, but feel free to call me Mumbai. You may hear the staff call me Mum. That's okay, too. I am something of a house mother around here."

Mumbai was an early model RH, handsome, sophisticated, and graceful, the kind Earth produced in the days of the Planetary Council. Star Council preferred robots that behaved less independently.

"Thank you, Mumbai," Mac said. "We've been looking forward to the tour. I take it you are the official Avian host?"

"Actually no, I merely provide a physical presence. Your official host and the founder of Avian, the Authoriton, has never taken a chassis. It considered greeting you as a hologram but thought that seemed too disembodied, too *Wizard of Oz*."

Zim and Mac exchanged quizzical glances.

"In addition to Avian's nervous system, the Authoriton's responsibility includes the entire Human network. It began here, however, and Avian remains its home. Shall we go?" Mumbai leveled an arm to a natural stone pathway so well blended that it was practically invisible.

"An amazing room," Zim said, transfixed by the natural beauty. She could not pull her eyes from a bird hopping in the canopy. "We're still in a room, right?"

"Yes, this was Amy's favorite room," Mumbai said, walking toward Zim and Mac. "Amy asked that we keep it up front. All the venomous reptiles and arthropods have been removed for the benefit of visitors."

"Amy's room?"

"Amanda Hessler and Sonigar Bushier were the first Creative couple, genetic predecessors to all Creatives." An animated hologram appeared mid-room showing a stunningly attractive couple embracing.

"Earth Planetary Council approved Avian 160 years ago to address the devastation of the Tech War, rescue threatened Earth species, and oversee their insertion on terraformed planets. At one time we had twenty-seven habitats, everything from arctic ice to forested mountains, deserts, and grasslands—all of Earth's major land habitats and all as detailed as this rainforest." Mumbai waved to the room. "Many species had a great deal of genetic damage and had to be rebuilt. Others merely required re-programming."

"You re-programmed birds?" Zim asked, keeping her eye on a red macaw inching close along a branch.

"Urbanization, industrialization, then the Xi'Kior virus swept away the natural habitats. The birds lost what defined them, and with that, the will to live. Many we didn't catch in time. Re-programming was necessary to restore that sense of purpose before we could release them into the wild."

"Was that also the case with Humans?" Zim asked, shifting attention from the macaw back to Mumbai. Mac touched her hand.

"Humans are animals, too, and yes, they followed the same trend. Demographers initially blamed the war for the damage, but the roots of the problem predated the war: depression, drug dependence, paranoia over change, and lifestyle and partner instability. Humans stagnated for twelve hundred years. When no Human children were born for two years, we decided we had to intervene.

"The issue became critical before we had perfected our work on birds, and we had to move quickly—Humans were aging out of fertility. From birds we'd learned that mate bonding stabilized positive gene expression. So, we used the same fertility and nurturance criteria for Humans and prioritized for the factors that kept mating pairs together. Since our goal was fertility and nurturance—creativity if you will—we called our initial subjects Creatives.

"Later we widened the criteria to include traits for specialized skills. Because of the fertility crisis, we hadn't initially screened for skill traits, and most of those had to come from the outside groups."

Zim scowled. "Outside groups? You mean Unders? You back-bred Creatives with Unders to recover the lost capabilities?"

"Driven by desperation, our initial response had been too narrow. Earth was dying, Human colonies on Thrinlu and Scalaris were slow taking hold, and Corydon was in early terraformation." Mumbai looked between them. "You seem upset. Our corrections were limited to selective gene swaps."

When Zim and Mac shot glances at one another, Mumbai raised his arms. "Large as this building is, it could not restore the entire Human gene pool and rebuild Earth's ecosystems. We wanted to stabilize the genome and retain as many skill traits as possible. Humans who failed the screening, the most damaged, were transported to Thrinlu and Scalaris."

"To die like the colonists on failed worlds?" Zim furrowed her brow.

"Sadly true. Our projection was brutal," Mumbai said in a clinical voice. "No matter where Unders lived, in two, three generations, all were expected to die. Before Avian, that was the projection for your entire species."

"Then why didn't that happen?" Mac asked.

"Your rebound was unforeseen. We assumed the genetic damage would keep Unders from adapting, but the reverse seems to be true. Your genetic diversity increased and with it your adaptability. Greater diversity made you more resilient than Creatives." Mumbai's metallic brows converged like knitting needles.

"When Unders held on Thrinlu and Scalaris, Blue Star intervened to complete the terraformation process. Please, may I show you our current projects?" Mumbai pointed to the stepped pathway. Along the route, the cacophony and soft light of the rainforest became a hallway of quiet offices and meeting rooms.

"Most of our work these days involves off-world projects, preparing Earth species for transplant or developing new products from alien species: medicines, textile fibers, feed materials, and industrial chemicals."

Mumbai gestured to a team of robots and lab-coated Tak-Yaki behind a transparent wall. "Here we're working with the TY to stem an ecological disaster brought on by a saprophytic fungal mutation on Lrisston." It pointed to an isolation chamber with plants overgrown by gray-brown webbing.

"Have Tak-Yaki scientists worked here long?" Zim asked. Other than military caste, she had never seen Tak-Yaki off Tak-Yakon. These were shorter in stature and lacked the serious fighting claws of the military caste.

"Only this year." Further along, Mumbai stopped at a room stacked with planters: algae, fungi, ferns, and grasses all the way up to shrubs and trees. "We accelerate plant adaptability to speed the terraforming process. We also modify species to survive and detoxify soils, water, and atmospheres."

"Doesn't that endanger the native species?" Mac asked.

Mumbai nodded. "The bio-conflicts we created terraforming Thrinlu and Scalaris taught us that we needed to start from scratch. We now work exclusively with uninhabited and newly re-formed, or artificial planets. The unacceptable alternative would be to sterilize planets already populated."

"Blue Star Corporation builds your planets?" Mac asked.

"Blue Star still does planet builds and orbit adjusts, but Star Council has directed all ecological work to SynTerra. All our domestic contracts are with SynTerra."

"Do you do Human modification?" Zim asked, squeezing her fists at her sides. "Pidge or Unders?"

Mumbai's voice remained unperturbed. "The Avian charter forbids us from enforcing or enabling any punishment on any life form. Jen Djada as Star Leader for Order handles the Pidge program. We cannot access any of that information."

Zim raised an eyebrow. "And Unders?"

"The only work we do with Unders is screening for desired traits and gene splicing. That is done solely with volunteers. We make them aware of the processes and the uses of the data. Many see it as their chance for immortality—to have the children they are now prohibited." Zim nodded.

Mumbai pointed up the corridor. "Of course, we do extensive work with Creatives, which is our next stop. Do you have any other questions?"

"You use the name Mumbai rather than your designator?" Mac asked.

"Early series robots had given names. Planetary Council believed informal address facilitated our interactions with Humans. The Authoriton's given name is Delhi. We both were developed under the old 'India series' programs."

The corridor widened. "The Creative wing has eleven halls," Mumbai said, "one for screening and one for each of the ten skill sets. We screen Creatives for genetic anomalies. If we find a spontaneous positive upgrade, we isolate and replicate it. More often we find regressions. If these can't be cleared, the Creative may be downgraded."

"Downgraded to Under?" Zim asked.

"A few. But most are just anomalies we wish to observe. In severe cases, a Creative might lose reproductive rights and access to Creative facilities, such as Avian or the Greens. By the way, the two of you are the only Unders ever to have been granted this level of access. Delhi and I hope it is a trend."

Mumbai pointed to the first hall. "This is One Creative Hall. Ones are nurturing artists, certainly our quirkiest group: graphic artists, poets, writers, musicians, dancers, chefs, actors, mental and physical therapists, prostitutes, brewers and distillers, designers. Mind you, robots are excellent technicians. We can replicate these skills but not the originality."

"Gamers?" Mac asked.

"Yes. Developers, trainers, planners, and many other specialties use gaming in their thought processes. Each field requires a different mix of art, ingenuity, analysis, skill, reflex, and data and risk management."

"Why does Avian need Ones?" Zim asked.

"Ones' mental processes are free ranging. It may seem counter-intuitive but teaming them with other skill sets enhances productivity and creativity in unpredictable ways." Mumbai paused for questions then continued.

"For Creatives, we check physical and mental well-being: general health, substance abuse, reproductive drive, energy level, creativity, emotional stability. We monitor but never tamper with individual preferences: creative expression, mate selection, non-abusive artificial stimulants, recreation, or diet. We advise keeping the children's activities balanced for the sake of their education. That's handled in the Greens, but we evaluate each child's progress."

Mumbai pointed out the other Creative halls, each tailored to specific specialties: administration, medical and technical, and so forth up through the broad concept Nines. Ten hall was substantially different.

"Tens possess all the positive genetic traits and aptitudes," Mumbai explained, "but those traits sometimes compete for expression and need to be rebalanced. For that purpose, Star Council directed Avian to install rapid upgrade and maintenance shunts into all Tens. Later we retrofitted it for the other Creatives."

Zim and Mac exchanged sidelong glances. Mac mouthed *OH MY*. They both saw the abuse potential of this shortcut.

Mumbai continued, "You asked about downgrading. If Ten progeny drop one or more of their parents' traits, they're re-rated, One through Nine, then routed to an alternate Green for appropriate training. Tens that retain all their attributes are prepared for leadership."

"Leadership of what? Ten Green?" Zim asked.

"Tens will run Corydon and the Human universe. When Star Council's mandate ends next year, a collective government will be built around Ten Creative leadership."

"Hillary and Torgesson," Zim whispered. Mac put an arm around her.

Mumbai curled a metallic smile. "They appear childlike, but I assure you, they are highly skilled and intelligent." It froze then looked up at Zim. "Excuse me, Commander, the Authoriton requests a private discussion. Our apologies to Marshal Mackenzie."

Zim looked at Mac. He rocked his head side to side then nodded. Zim turned to Mumbai. "I'm curious what the Authoriton might say that it doesn't wish shared with Mac."

"I suspect it wants you to decide what information you share with your partner. Marshal Mackenzie, while the Commander speaks with the Authoriton, might I show you more of our alien projects?"

Authoriton

The dome blued as Zim entered, and the deck sprouted a field of tall grass. Avian's reactive decks were obviously more advanced than *Lasalle's*. A breeze stirred Zim's short, blond hair and sent grassy waves rolling up a hillside. She extended her fingers to brush the grass and inhaled the rustic scent. Puffy, white clouds floated high in a summer sky.

Zim knew the scene and had recalled it many times: her parent's home on Scalaris twelve years ago, the morning she left for Basic. There was the farmhouse, and beyond it, the road where she met the shuttle that last morning. She was just seventeen, listening for her mother to call her to breakfast, and excited about leaving home.

Her father had been so proud of her. She remembered him waving when she'd walked down to the road. She hadn't waved back. She was ashamed and hoped no one would associate her with the rough-hewn man or their struggling farm. He was a wonderful man. Where was he now? Their farm was gone—taken by the war along with everything she once knew. A tear rolled down her cheek. She had never said goodbye.

"Commander Zimmon, welcome." A deep voice resonated. "I hope my greeting is appropriate."

"Nostalgic is the word." Zim searched for the origin of the voice, which seemed to come from everywhere.

"Might I offer you a cup of Corydon Black Peaberry?" the Authoriton asked.

"That would be wonderful, yes. Mac introduced me to your delicious coffee." Zim felt immersed and reluctant to part from the scene. "I'm curious what you might wish to talk about. Outside of military topics... and Scalari gloak farming, I'm not well informed on many topics. Mumbai's briefing on Avian's history and programs was quite thorough."

"My priority program is Human husbandry—I care for all the Humans. My broader mission is to be coordinating authority for the Human systems: Earth, Corydon, Thrinlu, Scalaris, now Silkani and the seed colonies."

Zim shook her head. "I wasn't aware you were involved in operations beyond primary support: administration and logistics."

"Perhaps now you can appreciate my interest in your career. I have much to tell you. You might be more comfortable in your office." Like a hand waving, the cloud-swept dome scrolled to become the gray metal operations deck of the starship *Lasalle*. A contoured chair and low table rose from the floor. Zim accepted the unspoken invitation to sit. A gray RH brought a silver tray with a blue-patterned china cup and saucer and matching carafe. It poured the coffee and left the tray. Zim lifted the cup, savored the aroma, and took a sip.

"Your being here, Commander, is but one of the improbable instances in our relationship." Zim nodded, recalling Kaplan's reference to the Authoriton prediction. "My program does not include military planning, but Star Council and Star Command mismanagement of the Aldrakin War threatened Human wellbeing."

Zim pulled up. "That was how I felt. I often had to improvise on my orders to make them conform with reality."

"And that was why my program assigned you to the most critical sectors. My program is restricted, so as not to interfere with Human decisions, but I do make personnel assignments and track performance. Your unexpected victory in the Corydon combat games and your initial qualification scores set you apart from other cadets. When your early assignments failed to match your qualifications, my program adjusted them much as it would for clerical errors. When the erroneous pattern persisted, my program became aware they were deliberate and continued making corrections.

"When your training squadron gave you the call sign Starflower, my program highlighted the alignment with the Aldrakin Prophecy and dismissed it as coincidental. But that unlikely pattern persisted, too. Four months ago, my internal audit revealed that my clerical adjustments also tracked with the Prophecy."

"Did you send me and Five Squadron to Bai-Yota?"

"Abramyan made that assignment with the clear objective of keeping you *out of* combat. My program chose not to inform him that that quiet sector was about to change."

"WHY?"

"Two mythic figures stride beside her: one who will never live, one who will never die. Together will these three fulfill the Prophecy."

"The priest's words." Zim gasped, her breath shallow.

"I have been your unwitting ally, beside you all along, I am the one who will never live."

"Ha Yee, Aldra Korah," Zim mouthed then said. "You're telling me the Prophecy is real?"

"If the Prophecy were not real, you could not have survived. Your victories were honestly won, but you should have died many times. I provide officer ratings to Command Staff for planning. Those include effectiveness multipliers based on accumulated results. I hid your ratings because they defeated the odds and defied mathematics."

"And the Prophecy is happening now, and I must fulfill it? That's unacceptable. I have other plans. Mac and I have plans. We waited and fought a twelve-year war. Now it's someone else's turn. There must be a way out for us." She dropped her head into her hands and gave a silent scream. When she looked up, she pulled her uniform sleeve straight and asked, "My other champion, the one who never dies, who or what is that?"

"We've searched the universe and found nothing. You may not have met the other one yet."

"But I will, because of the Prophecy?"

"Yes."

"Something else that doesn't make sense. Now that you are aware, why would the Authoriton collaborate to bring about an Aldrakin Prophecy."

"There is more to the Prophecy than you heard spoken. According to later passages, when the Starflower ends the war and returns the Aldrakin to their home world, the species of the galaxy will align and come together. Fulfilling the Prophecy is the best path for humanity."

Feeling cornered, Zim asked, "What else have you done? Were you responsible for distributing the recordings of the surrender ceremony?"

"If the surrender had remained secret, Star Council would have no reason to keep you alive. They would have declared Bai-Yota a single action, and the war would have continued."

"Who are they? I assumed everyone on the Star Council were Creatives."

"All Creatives descend from Amanda Hessler and Sonigar Bushier 160 years ago. The Star Council is much older. It began as a monastic cult in Asia in the twentieth century. Their isolation and strict moral regimen saved them from the ravages of the Xi'Kior-virus contamination. When the Tech War ended, they emerged unscathed, joined the Planetary Council as a voting bloc, and took over."

"What do you know about them personally?"

"The Council handles everything internally. I have no records, not even medical records. No recorders or RHs are permitted in their chambers. But I do know they have had no additions since they joined the Planetary Council, and no names have changed."

"No births?" Zim said in disbelief.

"The original monastic charter required sterilization. So, I suspect the members of the council are not exactly Human."

Not exactly Human and very, very old. What have we gotten into? Zim wondered.

# # #

Outside Avian's arched doorway, Zim touched the front wall to reassure herself that it remained intact. She wanted to laugh, but laughter came hard. How much of Avian or any of this was fabrication?

As she descended the stairs, a sea of silent Humans gave her and Mac a respectful perimeter. The storm had passed, leaving the air clean and brisk. High, wispy cirrus clouds chased the last gray from the bluing sky.

At the foot of the steps, Zim paused to consider the bedraggled crowd. Mac squeezed her hand. She raised an open palm in welcome, and the crowd circle closed. A few touched her hands, arm, or shoulder, softly with one or two fingers, then stepped back to let others close. No one spoke above a whisper. "Ha Yee" or "Ha Yee, Starflower," said like prayers and repeated back through the crowd.

She had not known these people, never considered what they might be going through. While they sent their children off to war, most to die, she had been thinking only of herself and what she was missing. What struck her now was how much they reminded her of the Aldrakin at the surrender ceremony: stunned that the war was over and overwhelmingly thankful.

The Authoriton's words came to her. "Fulfilling the Prophecy is the best path for humanity." She felt humbled that an automated being had shown Humans more consideration than she had.

Mac motioned to Aidan by the shuttle, and the crowd parted to let them pass. As they sped away, Zim's eyes remained on the unmoving crowd behind them.

Staring into the Dark

They did not talk on the trip home. Zim knew Mac understood. When he mentioned dinner, she asked that they order food delivered. She considered having Aidan join them, this being the last night before they left Corydon and possibly the last time she would see him, but tonight she needed to be with Mac alone.

They ate on a blanket in front of a fire surrounded by floor cushions and plates of Indian delicacies. Mac broke the silence. "Do you want to talk about what we heard at Avian?"

Zim nodded and slid closer to the fire. The heat felt good on her face. The scent of burning pine logs mixed with the savory aroma of roast lamb and chicken, garlic nan, chutney relish, and mint-spiced yogurt. The fire snapped and shot a spray of sparks. Its flickering bathed the dark room in shifting light and shadow.

She dipped a wedge of nan into the chutney and held it up. "The Authoriton told me I needed to fulfill the Prophecy."

"I suspected something like that."

"I wasn't aware of this, any of this... this Starflower craziness." She took a bite then reached for a cup of jasmine tea. "All I did was fight battles for twelve years. There seemed to be no end to it. I never considered the cost or what the war meant to anyone else. Of course, I cared about my team, their health and effectiveness, but not their families, not their futures. I never told them, but I never thought any of us *had* a future. I thought about you and me, but not like this, Mac, only in the past." She lifted her cup toward the stone fireplace. "If I'd known and thought, what might I have done differently?"

"You ended the war, Gayle. Everyone knows that. The Aldrakin know it. They celebrate it. Your teams suffered the fewest casualties in the fleet." Mac's voice was both loving and professional. "If you had acted differently, held back for any reason, you and your team would have lost and died, and the war would still be going on."

"You think so?" She gazed into his wise, dark eyes, his sharp cheek bones and brow ridges highlighted in the firelight. "I count on you to tell me the truth."

Mac skewered a bit of lamb on his fork and raised it like a baton. "I've seen what happens to you, Gayle." He directed his skewer-baton toward her. "I saw it in your eyes when we competed on Scalaris. It scared me at first. The spirit of battle takes you. When we teamed up for the Corydonics, I understood the only way we could win was if I backed you." Mac bit the lamb off his skewer. He leaned toward the fire, took a tool, and poked the logs, sending up streams of sparks. Zim scooted in, and Mac pulled her close. She rested her head on his chest.

"I didn't see that spirit early in the war," Mac continued. "But as the risks grew, it returned. You became bolder, colder, more focused. I was the only one on Command Staff who understood. None of us could keep up. But when the firing stopped and weapons cooled, there you'd be. The fleet came to expect it. When I applied to be your planning officer, they moved me to Abramyan's staff." Mac shrugged. "He never used my plans, only his own. He must have needed someone to hold his hand."

Zim wrapped both arms around his neck and gave him a thank you kiss. "I don't want to go back. You saw what I became, and I don't want to be that anymore."

Mac ran a finger through a curl of hair on her cheek. "We're going to have a wonderful holiday. When we get back, you'll do a short stint on a boring research support team, and I'll wrap up with Command Staff and get a job with Blue Star. Then we'll kiss Abramyan, Star Command, and Corydon goodbye forever." He gestured kiss-my-ass-and-fly-away with his free hand.

"It won't be over, Mac." Zim leaned away to look at him. "The Prophecy won't let it be over, and it doesn't guarantee that things end well for us."

"Nothing says it has to end badly."

"No, but there's more." Zim dropped her chin to her chest. "It's not just the spirit of battle that takes me. I'm not the girl you remember, Mac. She wasn't capable of the things I've done. Remember, I trained with the Tak-Yaki and served with them for two years?"

"Of course. After you did that job on Boorman, I helped set up your transfer to keep the peace. When Tock approved you joining their training squadron, we called it a diplomatic gesture."

"Have you seen the TY in combat, close combat?"

"I've read the reports."

"I became one of them. I started as one of their squad leaders—*excelled* as one of their combat fighters. Last night, I ran into a TY at the Event Horizon. A petty gangster, but it recognized me. Almost impaled itself on a chair getting out the door." She locked her gaze with Mac's. "My latest recruits thought it was because I was the Starflower." She shook her head. "To the Tak-Yaki I'm the *Krglu*. That's an ancient term that literally means, 'honored to be the first to eat the brains of the enemy'."

Mac coughed. "You didn't—"

"No, times have changed. The TY cook their food now, mostly. But expectations remain for that distinction."

"And you're afraid you'll go back to being that?" Mac stroked her hair.

"I *am* that." She leaned into his chest and felt him tighten. "I accept what I am, Mac, but I hope you never have to see it. If something ever were to happen to you—" She let the sentence hang.

# # #

They moved to the bedroom. Zim peppered Mac with questions about their vacation. He sidestepped most of them, saying it was his surprise.

"All I'm telling you is that we leave early tomorrow, we'll be away ten weeks, and everything's arranged, including your wardrobe."

His broad grin met her pouts and exaggerated scowls. "I'm not used to this, but I do rather enjoy the mystery. Really? You arranged for my wardrobe?"

He nodded. "I don't know how else to redirect your energy—intense energy."

"You think so? I *am* trying to step back a bit."

"*Yes, I do think so*. If I let you, you'd try to *win* our vacation." He rolled onto his elbow and touched a finger to her nose. "I love that about you, but now I need you to win for us and our future. Forget the war, forget Corydon and StarCom, forget worry. We're going to live each day as it comes and think about the rest when we get back."

"Okay." Zim eyed the expanse of his bare chest. "You know me well." She squeezed his arm. "I love seeing how much you want to please me."

"I do." He stroked her head on the pillow and ran his fingers through her short, honey-blond hair.

"You still think we'll be able to plan our life, what with—?"

"Don't mention the Prophecy again," he interrupted. "What could *possibly* stop us?"

"Okay. I guess worrying won't change anything." She rolled her head against his chest. "I know you've thought about our family."

She felt his head nod.

"I mean the plans we made on Scalaris."

Another nod.

"During the war, there were times I thought for sure I'd be dead."

"I thought so, too." He kissed her forehead.

"Remember when we were in our teens and first heard we were going to war?" She felt Mac nod again. "We froze our fertilized eggs so we could always have children—romantic but foolish. Later I was afraid we'd both die. Robots would raise our children, and they'd never know us."

He wiped a tear from her cheek. "I was always happy we saved our embryos. I thought that meant we had a future, even if we weren't in it."

She pulled his head down and pressed her lips to his. Then they lay quiet, and Mac drifted into sleep.

"Mac?"

"Um?" he said groggy.

"I want us to have children the Scalari way, like our parents did."

"That was our plan," he said, rolling to face her, "but I like hearing you say it again." He slid the sheet down from her breasts and studied how the moonlight highlighted her toned body. The cool air peaked her nipples. He warmed one in his mouth then the other. Her heartbeat sped. She felt his warm breath and hands on her. She turned to him, raising a knee. Her hand found him and encouraged his entry.

She knew Mac had hidden his concerns to quiet hers. Now she felt his desperation in their lovemaking. They both knew there was no mention of him in the Prophecy. Perhaps he, too, feared their time together would be short.

Rankoi

En route to the starport, Zim saw more Starflower graffiti than she had coming out. When she and Mac arrived, the crowd was larger, noisier, and more urgent. A double cordon of black-chassis police held everyone back: Under and Creative fans, journalists, and camera crews. Again, Zim saw Starflower flags and placards with blessings.

What am I to do, she thought?

Aidan led them through the crowd to the base of the boarding ramp. "Nine Green extended my assignment," he said, "so I'll be your aide when you return." He snapped a salute.

Zim returned his salute. She hoped the extension hadn't cost him.

"Ha Yee, Starflower," he shouted over the din, his eyes glistening.

"Ha Yee, Aidan," she returned. He held his salute while she and Mac walked up the ramp of the executive yacht and continued holding it as they boarded and the hatch closed.

The yacht was appointed in red and white, with a circular bed, sheets of silk, and special foods, beverages, and flowers—part of Mac's surprise. He'd selected music and amusements that he and Zim had shared in their youth. Having clued the pilot and RH staff about his surprise, they limited their information to onboard meals and amenities. The RHs seemed to delight in evading her questions. Mac's strategy worked. She shelved her concerns and surrendered to relaxation and play.

# # #

They arrived two days later at the transfer-reception station in low orbit around Rankoi—the largest moon of the gas giant Rolly, in the Trysa G3 star system.

From the orientation briefing, they learned that Rankoi was inhabited by a humanoid race known as the Bilibo. Their complex culture eschewed advanced technology as spiritually and mentally debilitating. They believed technical interfaces dulled the mind, reduced real world experience, and compelled submission to unreality. In their trade agreement, the Bilibo agreed to host visits of select couples in exchanged for infrequent off-world excursions for conferences or to educate their children.

A transfer shuttle delivered Zim and Mac to a conch-shell-styled house on an amethyst sand beach beside a serene, cerulean lagoon lined with broadleaf trees.

They discarded functional clothing for diaphanous attire. In the morning, they swam the cool sea and walked and ran the amethystine shore in their bare feet. Between exotic meals, they examined life forms they discovered in the tide pools, explored bowered forest paths, and watched six-limbed creatures romp through the trees.

Several times daily, the Bilibo delivered native foods on plate-sized leaves. A pair of joint-legged creatures came ashore in the evening to sit politely near their blanket and share their meal. In the evening, Zim and Mac joined the Bilibo villagers for music and dancing, drinking berry intoxicants, or watching Rolly's storm-swirled, violet, and blue disk rise on the Rankoi horizon.

One afternoon, through dance and mime-play, a Bilibo couple invited them to a festival. One pointed to the horizon where Trysa would set, the other to the village path. At the time appointed, Zim and Mac walked hand-in-hand up the path.

The shoulder-high, red-furred Bilibo had moon faces, large nocturnal eyes, flat noses, and mushroom-shaped, omnidirectional ears. Their sensitive hands had six digits: five long fingers and a thumb. They were fearless, unashamed, and curious, especially the children who surrounded and touched the strange Humans. Zim found herself captivated by the young Bilibo's bell-toned laughter.

For the festival, they gave Zim and Mac colorful tunics and invited them to sit around the fire on woven mats or melon-husk stools. Seafoods and fruits were passed around in hollowed bowls along with seedpod pitchers of a mead-like beverage. The village comprised twenty bark-and-frond huts in two concentric circles with a large gathering hut at one side, like a jewel on a necklace.

Bilibo musicians plucked, thumped, and blew on assorted shells, carved splines, and hollow sticks. As their rhythm and tone converged, Mac excused himself and, to Zim's delight as well as the villagers, sat in with the musicians.

He selected a flute-stick, struggled to match his fingers with the twelve holes, and attempted to accompany the first dancing soloist. After each piece quieted, another musician would rise to dance and play. Eventually, it was Mac's turn.

He stepped in with a lively, very un-Bilibo, Scalari jig. The musicians jammed with Mac's spirited style. Villagers danced, and wide-eyed children pulled and pleaded with Zim to join in. Unable to refuse, she took their hands and pranced around the fire. The children chanted and sang. Zim tried to mimic their sounds and soon had the whole village laughing.

As Mac was finishing his song, another group of Bilibo arrived, hunters dressed in animal skins. They brought cooked meats, spiced vegetables, and sewn-up skins filled with strong beverages. The elders embraced and invited the newcomers to the fire. Other groups came throughout the evening. New musical instruments and rhythms were added. Singing and laughter grew louder. Bowls and pitchers never emptied.

Late that evening, as the fire died down and dancers and musicians rejoined their families, Mac filled two gourd cups and extended his arm to Zim. Walking the beach route home, they came upon two Bilibo couples. Rolly's quarter-crescent split the horizon and flaming aurora danced around its northern pole.

"Here?" Zim pointed and unfolded their blanket. As Mac finished his cup, Zim tucked into his chest to listen to his heartbeat. Later, in their conch-shell home, they made love and fell asleep to the songs of forest creatures and the soft rhythm of ocean waves.

Next morning, a villager arrived with fruit, grilled spiced meat, and another invitation: to join a fishing excursion out beyond the bay. They would leave when the sun was half-a-hand above the horizon. Zim and Mac gave rapid shoulder dips, the Bilibo affirmation gesture.

They ate quickly, dressed for the mid-day sun and sea fishing, and headed to the village berthing area. When they arrived, the locals were hotly engaged with fishermen from a nearby village, shouting, stomping, and posturing with their spears and tridents.

Purlet, the elder who had invited them, gestured an apology. No fishing today. She mimed a tragedy, a weaving sea-monster lurking among the fish traps, boats overturned, and villagers pulled to their deaths.

"Has this happened before?" Zim asked, waving her arms the way Purlet had to indicate the serpentine monster.

"Utak." Purlet pointed to the bay and counted Utak many times.

Zim and Mac exchanged stern glances, nodded to one another, then followed Purlet to a boat where hunters were pulling off the fishing gear.

Utak

"Utak," Mac said, opening his hand to the Bilibo holding the weapons. The Bilibo handed him a long shaft crowned with three barbed prongs. Mac hefted the shaft and was about to touch its prongs when Purlet shouted.

Miming sharpness and intense pain, the elder pointed to a beached sea-creature a half-meter in diameter. She skewered the carcass with Mac's trident then invited him to dislodge it. Mac succeeded only by standing on the carcass and using another trident as a lever. Purlet demonstrated fixing the trident's prongs to the monster and using it to hold steady while delivering the kill thrust with a long, razor-sharp spear.

Stooping in the amethyst sand, Purlet drew the monster's head with her long finger. She pointed to the space between the creature's eye and the first gill slit then jabbed it with the spear point. "Utak," she said, jabbing at the sand drawing a second time. She returned the trident to Mac and offered him a spear. Mac slung both onto his back.

Thrilled to see Mac in action again, Zim asked for her own pair of weapons. "Been a while, hasn't it?" She taunted in the same manner she had when they were in competition. "You've been off the front line in that cushy staff job."

He laughed. "You think I need to reestablish my hunter credentials?"

"I think you might be a little rusty." She missed this side of their play. They had hunted together in the fields and forests of Scalaris. But she didn't deceive herself. Killing this beast in its own element with simple hand weapons would be a challenge. She was also aware that the combat techniques she'd learned with the Tak-Yaki were useless underwater. Later she realized something else: the elder's drawing had no scale—she and Mac had no idea of Utak's size.

They rowed two to an oar into a brisk wind and late-morning sun. After crashing through the first waves of the surf, they rowed over long swells. Cleared of fishing gear, the boat held twelve. They expected Utak to be in the middle of the bay, near the submerged fish traps where it had attacked before dawn. The plan was to circle the traps, dropping off hunters every hundred meters, then tighten the circle until the monster was sighted.

Purlet gave them each a button-sized beetle. She demonstrated putting it into her mouth and taking several breaths. Zim and Mac decided the beetle must extend time underwater—perhaps by scrubbing carbon dioxide or releasing oxygen. Purlet also gave them hand-sized "click" beetles, noisemakers to alert one another of Utak's presence.

Zim dropped off first. At Purlet's signal, she passed her oar to Mac, rolled over the stern, and splashed into the cool water. At this end, the bay was seven meters deep, and Zim could see clearly for twenty meters. She dove for a better viewing angle and to avoid being silhouetted against the sunlit surface.

A cluster of plate-sized disks fluttered off the bottom, sending up swirls of silt. Segment-legged creatures scuttled for cover, and soft-bodied sacks curled in their feathery limbs. Directly below, Zim saw what looked like a two-meter-high, masonry wall that ran straight out from the beach and aligned with the boat's path. She swam along the wall a couple strokes then surfaced for air. Ahead, Mac was just entering the water.

Diving again, she relocated the wall and continued to follow it. Suddenly, she had the odd sensation that she was moving backward. The wall's regular stone pattern slipped past her, gaining speed. Then it bowed, rippled, and shot ahead, tumbling Zim and sending up a cloud of silt in its wake. Utak was heading for Mac.

Clicking her beetle furiously, Zim kicked to the surface. The boat was further away and unaware of the monster stalking it. She pulled the spear and trident off her shoulder strap and checked the tether cord fastening the trident to her ankle. She took a deep breath and put the breathing beetle in her mouth, feeling it claw and bubble in her saliva.

The bay was deeper here and clouded from the disturbance. A strong current swept past and a shadow of checkered plates. Utak was circling. Zim thrust her trident, felt it bite, and was dragged along. Utak flicked a serpentine coil to shake her. Water rushed past like a raging torrent. Her trident had struck near the creature's tail, far from any vulnerable area.

The monster's undulations alternately slammed Zim against its boney scale-plates and whipped her swirling away. She hung on. A red stream flowed past followed by the wake-tossed lower torso of a red-furred Bilibo. The upper torso followed, its blank staring eyes frozen in its moon face.

141

The trident slipped from Zim's grip, but she clung to its tether cord, sliding down from the creature. Utak's roll sent her spinning out and around its tail. Coming up the far side, she grabbed her trident shaft and tied the tether cord to it a second time. The looped cord bound her to the creature and kept her from being thrown. Each time the tail swept, she pulled in slack and tightened the cord, digging it deeper under the monster's scale plates.

The monster writhed and curled its head back to strike Zim. She flattened away from its shearing, snapping beak. As it passed, she saw a half-dozen tridents sprouting like porcupine quills. Mac clung to one of the tridents with one arm, his free arm flailed for a surer grip.

Mac was well back from the vulnerable gill slit, but two tridents further up were within striking range. Empty tethers from those tridents lashed about Zim. She grabbed for one and caught it on the third try.

Utak swept upward, accelerating and breaching the surface of the bay. It rose twenty meters, spinning Mac wide in the air. Zim took a deep breath and braced against the crash. Utak slammed back hard, sending up a wall of water. Whirling, it snapped its beak at Zim's leg then straightened and sped out to sea.

The deeper water was clear, free of churning silt. Zim saw Mac twisting in the current, his spear still slung on his back. She angled the tether cord from the forward trident to cross his position, and he grabbed it, stopping his spinning.

She wrapped the tether about herself to make it taut. Mac shifted both hands to her cord and used its leverage to pull hand-over-hand toward Utak's head. Each time the monster twisted, he braced then resumed pulling with his entire body. When he reached the rear gill flap, he hauled forward, dug in his feet, and climbed to the next. Zim pulled hard on the tether cord to give him support.

Mac grabbed the trident nearest the monster's eye, rolled the spear off his shoulder, and made the first thrust. It was a bad angle, and the spear bounced off a scale plate. Regaining balance, he gripped the shaft further back, dug the spearpoint under a plate, and plunged it again into the spot the elder indicated. The bite held. Mac drove it deeper with pounding thrusts. Two, three, four. Utak shuddered, and the platter-sized pupil in its unblinking eye slid back toward Mac. It bucked hard twice, relaxed, rolled, and drifted upward.

Utak's head broke the surface with Mac aboard. Zim remained underwater, tied in a web of knots, her breathing beetle shrunk to a pinhead. As she struggled, a splash erupted four meters above her. Mac gave her his lungful of air and cut the first cord. Three more and she was free. Together they climbed the scale-plates to the surface.

Zim hauled herself onto the floating carcass, coughed seawater, took a shallow breath, and coughed some more. Rolling onto her back, she threw an arm over her face to block the yellow-white midday sun. Mac pressed a palm to her cheek then lay beside her. Utak's inert body rocked beneath them. The breeze chilled their wet bodies. Zim felt a flutter. A four-winged b'natta screeched then landed beside her to peck parasites off the monster's hide.

After a minute of slow breathing, Zim pulled herself up to sit. She and Mac checked each other for injuries. Their limbs showed ligature burns, abrasions, and bruises, but no deep cuts or broken bones. Three Bilibo joined them atop the beast. Their hunting boat was nowhere to be seen. Half a dozen fishing boats rowed out, picking up survivors and dead along the way. After two more red-furred swimmers climbed aboard, Zim counted heads: seven from their original twelve. Purlet, the elder, had lost an arm. Zim helped her tie off the stump with a tether cord.

The reception back at the pier was subdued. Losses were heavy and everyone exhausted. Villagers touched them and chattered quiet congratulations. Completely spent, Zim and Mac retired to their conch beach house before sundown and slept as if among the dead.

# # #

The funeral the following afternoon ended with sending the bodies or likenesses of the five out to sea on a burning boat. Zim remembered similar traditions in Human seafaring cultures. Heroic words were spoken, and somber affirmations repeated. Zim didn't need to understand the words. She and Mac hummed as the villagers sang the dirge.

The Bilibo towed the beast into the shallows alongside the fishing piers. It measured sixty meters and looked like a bone-armored prehistoric eel. Its three-meter horn-beak was lined with hooked teeth serrated on the trailing edge.

Neighboring villagers helped butcher the beast. They took Utak's plates, bones, and skin to make clothing, shelter, tools, and weapons. They cut the flesh into wide strips and stretched them on racks to dry. Zim and Mac participated despite their exhaustion, hyperextended limbs, and joints that ached with every movement. Purlet thanked Zim for caring for her arm and indicated that it would regenerate.

There was a memorial that evening and a victory roast with large servings of Utak. Villagers and guests gathered by the crackling fire to hear Purlet tell the story. Zim and Mac had picked up only a few Bilibo words but much of the story was told with gestures. Utak had returned every year, and previous hunting expeditions had always ended in failure. Many spoke of injuries and lost loved ones. Purlet acknowledged the losses, naming each for every family seated around the fire.

Zim had heard this sort of story countless times around countless fires. This time the bardic dramatization included her and Mac—Mac most because he had delivered the killing thrust. When Purlet beckoned them to speak, Zim urged Mac forward. He had seen the action from the very beginning, near Utak's jaws, and was the better storyteller.

Mac scanned the group, pulling every eye to him. The only sound was the crackling fire. He spread his arms and in a resonant voice told the tale of how twelve heroes set out in a single boat to fight a fearsome monster. Zim had no idea how much the Bilibo understood, but they followed his every gesture and gasped at every crisis point.

As she listened and saw how Mac and the Bilibo responded to one another, she thought how wonderful he was, how much she loved him, and how well they fit together. The Prophecy be damned, after Utak, anything might be possible.

# # #

Their last days on Rankoi were filled with leaf-wing gliding, flume rides down forest streams, safaris, and excursions to neighboring villages. Told far and wide, "The Tale of Utak" guaranteed them warm receptions with food, entertainment, and a lover's suite at every destination.

Too soon, the automated transfer shuttle returned to where it had dropped them: on the amethyst sand beside the conch-shell house. Cerulean waves rolled up the beach as they had that first day, and forest leaves whispered in the breeze. The village children brought breakfast that morning, their large, upturned eyes stirring Zim's longing for her own family. She caught Mac watching her with the children and knew he was thinking the same.

"Thank you, Mac. A wonderful surprise." She squeezed his hand then reaching around his waist. "This is a dream I'll never forget." She inhaled a last breath of the moist, floral air, felt the breeze off the water against her face, and shuffled her feet in the sand.

"How do you feel?" he asked.

"Sad to leave and ready to start our new life." She saw their shadows twinned on the sand then looked into Mac's wide-set dark eyes. His face was more tanned than when they arrived. "And confident for us. We don't need a lot to be happy."

Even as Zim spoke, she feared dark forces were at work. Abramyan had said to enjoy her vacation because when it was over, she wouldn't be celebrating. Everything had been arranged.

The reality of those arrangements struck at the Rankoi transfer station. Instead of an executive yacht waiting to take them both back to Corydon, they were directed to separate transports heading in opposite directions.

Star Council

With the council chamber set to transparent, the walls were practically invisible, and the view from the seventy-sixth floor felt like standing on an open platform above the city. Looking down, Abramyan tracked the shadows of popcorn clouds dragging across the broken walls and rubble of the Under district.

The district had quieted since the war. Known and suspected troublemakers had been pidged and sent to the camps. Soon all the Unders would be gone. How had such a destructive species achieved space travel? He shook his head then held out his arms and examined his body. Not one he would have chosen, serviceable at best, but soon it would be replaced.

Two council members drifted in, nodded to Abramyan, and took seats near the front. Abramyan claimed his place at the middle of the council table. Four other councilors arrived, talking among themselves. Their midnight black robes swept the floor regally and flared as they turned.

Lord Malik entered with Djada and the rest of the Council close behind. Malik went to the head of the table and began before everyone was seated.

"Authoriton?" she called the first agenda item.

"Yes, Lord." The councilor to Malik's right stood. "Postwar assessments are optimistic. Details are in my report. Our three priorities are: restoration of the planets returned by the Aldrakin; exploitation of trade opportunities with the galactic confederation; and lastly, plans for handling Unders returning from combat—"

"Shouldn't Under management be the top priority?" Jen Djada interrupted. "This matter is critical for order. We armed these—"

Malik interrupted, "You will speak next, Jen. Is that all Councilor?"

"Yes, Lord."

Malik raised a finger to Djada. "Before we continue, has anyone seen Kodra?" Eyes turned to the empty seat of the Councilor for the Greens. "Check on him." Malik pointed to the councilor at the foot of the table. "Next item, Order?"

"Yes, Star Lord." Djada rose. "First, I commend our Councilor for Military," she nodded to Abramyan, "for effectively handling the Starflower Zimmon. We've heard nothing of her for two months. We also commend 'Grover' for his refreshing sense of humor." She raised a virtual display mid-room with several headlines: GROVER GREETS RETURNING TROOPS, TAK-YAKI MEETING WITH GROVER, GROVER DOWNSIZING STARCOM. Djada read each line, eliciting embarrassed snickers from other council members. Abramyan folded his hands on the table and stared straight ahead.

"However," Djada continued, "the precipitous end to the war has caused new problems. Unders returning from combat zones constitute an immediate threat. These hardened veterans are skilled with weapons, and many have refused to give them up. They have no jobs, no housing, and many have no relatives to take them in. We're not advocating disbanding the First Legion, but after their near mutiny during the Bai-Yota incident, I'm not certain they can be trusted. Our plan—excuse me, Abramyan's plan—was to use the war to kill off the Unders and replace them with Creatives. That worked for a time. Perhaps we might relocate returning Unders to the reclaimed planets. But I leave that decision to others."

The councilors for Eugenics and Public Image passed.

"SynTerra?"

"Yes, Star Lord. We agree with the Authoriton's first priority: restoration of the reclaimed planets. As Councilor Djada noted, Unders and Pidge workers can be used for terraforming labor. We can clear them from Corydon, Thrinlu, and Scalaris and make room for new Creative settlements. The rest is in my report."

Malik nodded. "Military?"

"Yes, Lord Malik." Abramyan rose. "I'll start with the Starflower." His gaze touched Malik's then he scanned the room. "Commander Zimmon and Marshal Mackenzie have concluded their off-world holiday. Star Leader Djada," he pointed to the head of the table, "has contracted the Rii-Chaut to eliminate them both. That may be done at any time. To facilitate an opportunity, I've assigned Zimmon to the *Marshal Massena*, which has been converted for scientific research and directed to the frontier. I've also assigned all the converted starships, including the *Marshal Massena*, to Marshal Derek Boorman's command. He's not an assassin, but his hatred for Zimmon is well known. I'm sure he won't object—"

Djada interrupted, "Lord Malik, I know our original decision was for assassination, but we have another option."

"Proceed."

"My Rii-Chaut contact, the Yazza Hetman Ojai Khan requests that we give the Starflower to him as a trophy. He asks that she be pidged, her memory wiped, and her temperament re-set for submissive docility. His appetite—"

"It's bad publicity." Seta Martiri, the Councilor for Media and Public Image protested. "While I share Councilor Djada's anger and desire for revenge, this will not set well—"

"It is completely justified," Djada insisted. "Zimmon and Mackenzie are Unders. The punishment for Unders taking Under mates is pidging."

"Yes," Martiri said, "but we tacitly sanctioned their union when we put them together, showed them all over town, and sent them off on holiday together. Star Council directed me to give them full media exposure. We have to live with that."

"Good points. Thank you." Malik nodded to them both then returned to Abramyan. "We'll stay with the original assassination plan for Zimmon. How about Marshal Mackenzie?"

"He remains on my staff, but his position has been eliminated. We can send him to a kill zone, wherever Star Council directs."

"Ideas?" Malik looked about the room.

The Councilor for Trade rose. "Star Lord. The Aldrakin Treaty has expanded our exchanges with the Galactic Trade Federation, and the Goorm have requested brokering the new arrangements." Malik leaned over her clasped hands, and the trade councilor continued.

"I recommend we grant the Goorm request and send Roland Mackenzie to be our ambassador. We can stage an ambush after the negotiation, and no one will be the wiser."

"Comments?" Malik looked around. "Okay, settled. Abramyan?"

"I'll inform Mackenzie that Star Council has named him our new trade representative." He saw affirmation gestures around the table.

"Very good," Malik said, rescanning the agenda.

The chamber suddenly erupted as Kodra, the missing councilor, stumbled in the doorway, white, hairless, trembling, his split scalp pealed to his face. A councilor helped him to his seat.

"Let's be calm." Malik cleared her throat. "None of us have seen the beginning of the process, and we will all go through it. This ecdysis is necessary before the transfer." She looked down the table. "Kodra? KODRA?" Kodra stirred and struggled to raise his head. "As our first transfer, I trust you have claimed a suitable replacement cuticle?"

"Yes, Star Lord," he croaked. With a quaking hand, he pressed up and slid a text box toward the councilor beside him.

"Kodra has selected a rebellious Nine as his new host. Aidan Nine has advocated for the Starflower and served as her aide-de-camp. He also uses the Starflower logo on his personal missives—"

"Excellent choice." Malik interrupted. "How long—" A scuffle came at the door.

An enforcer robot entered with Aidan clamped about the waist. The squat, metal enforcer had a sensor pod fused to its bull-like shoulders. Its wide chassis housed alternative wheels, weapons, and tools folded below its primary clamps.

"This is a mistake," Aidan shouted, twisting in the grasp of the enforcer's clamp. "I'm a Nine Creative. I should be at Avian getting a standard upgrade. The shuttle brought me here by mistake."

"Very good." Malik turned to Djada. "See to Kodra's procedure immediately."

Part Four

Port Estelle

Arrival

"Chief Engineer, Major James Eppert?" The deck chief studied the crew list. Dom nodded. "Pilot, Ensign Torey Bahrke?" Hotz touched a thumb to her chest. The deck chief registered their affirmative responses without looking up. "Just a minute. There seems to be a problem." Dom and Hotz exchanged glances—they had arrived a day early. Both stood relaxed in midnight blue StarCom uniforms.

Port Estelle was a deep-space construction and repair yard, a self-supporting military city built to support Human expansion. Dom and Hotz had come in through the main receiving dock at the zero-gravity hub and walked the reactive deck four kilometers to the final refitting yard. Recently reconfigured for scientific research, the *Marshal Massena* rested in magnetic cradles and was undergoing final preparations before launch.

The deck chief looked up from his display and scowled at Dom. "Eppert and Bahrke?"

"That is correct, Chief," Dom said.

"This says you are both assigned to Commander Zimmon, Science One, Combat Element 5."

"Correct again, Chief." This time it was Hotz. "I see you know your targ."

Ignoring her comment, the deck chief folded his hands on the counter and addressed Dom. "Your aboard billets aren't ready. Major Eppert, you'll bunk in Estelle steerage, G-point-two deck, 1624G.2. Stow your gear and get back quick or you'll miss chow. Mess call is 1900. Until we're rated space-worthy, your orders are to report on deck every morning zero six hundred for labor detail." Dom extended his wrist to upload the order.

The deck chief backhand waved Dom aside then froze as he took his first good look at Hotz. "Ah, Ensign Bahrke?" The chief's eyes drifted down her slim-fitted uniform.

"Eye trouble, spacer, need an eye implant? One more show of disrespect and you'll need one." Hotz's wide-set, blue eyes bored into the chief. "If you can't hack this job and address officers properly, I can arrange your reassignment."

"I'm, ahh, not—"

"You've got my record." She touched the counter display. "Does it say I coddle targ-heads?"

"No, actually—"

"No, actually," Hotz cut him off again. "I'm with Dom. Same orders?"

"Yes, sir. Here's the room." He showed her 1621G.2.

"I'm checking on you." Hotz pointed a finger at the bridge of the chief's nose. "If I don't find our onboard suite booked, I'm hunting you down and boring you a new targ chute."

She turned to Dom as they walked away. "Let's drop our gear, get casual, skip the mess, and check out the O-Club for dinner." Dom nodded and glanced back at the chief.

"Like the way you handled that," he said as they walked away. "I expected better reception for the Starflower team."

"Told you she'd attract problems." Hotz suppressed a chuckle.

# # #

The décor of the Happier Times officer's club conjured images of Polynesia before the Tech Wars: potted palms, totemic carvings of oversized Human figures and heads, a bamboo Tiki bar with a thatched roof. Tables and chairs were crafted of rattan and bamboo. Flaming pole and table torches flickered light across the room.

Spacers packed the club, drinking, talking, and eating, usually grouped with others in the same uniform: midnight blue for StarCom, white for merchants. Two Tak-Yaki occupied a side table. Hyrup musicians played bongo drums, ukuleles, and mandolins on a small stage. A dozen scientists in casual civilian attire crowded the bar.

Jovial, heavy-set Chiao Li pointed to an empty stool. "Anyone sitting here?"

The wiry man sitting alone at the Tiki bar looked up. "You kidding? We're pariah in this joint." He gestured help-yourself to the open stool.

Chiao Li slid onto the bar stool and ordered a beer. The RH bartender wore a grass skirt and flowered necklace.

"You assigned yet?" Chao Li asked. The man shook his head as he sniffed, swirled, and sipped the red wine and fruit in his goblet. Chiao Li leaned in. "You're Rob Marsh, the physical scientist. I saw your post."

Rob reached his hand across his lap, and Chiao Li shook it. "No assignment yet," Rob mumbled, his mouth pressed to his glass. "And you would be?"

"Chiao Li, life sciences."

"I'm not worried." Rob guided his goblet onto the bar then spun to face Chiao Li. "They hate us, blame scientists for converting their little war wagon into a platform for collecting butterflies. Targ, without us, most of these guys wouldn't have a job."

"It's a job for us, too. I'm not assigned either. Somebody's got to pick us up. This isn't a bad gig for an Under." The Polynesian-attired RH set a coconut-themed mug with a carved monkey face on a napkin in front of Chiao Li. Rob smirked and held his goblet up for a refill.

"Maybe not bad for you. I was a Seven Creative." Rob slumped. "Got knocked down when I failed the Avian screen. Another year before I can retest."

"Tough, I guess. Can't say I understand. But as a Creative, you couldn't do this sort of work." Chiao Li waved his open hand around the room. "I think being here's kind of exciting."

Rob made a long face. "Yah, I'm the lucky one."

"Lucky, good word." Chiao Li pointed to Rob. "You could *get lucky* here."

"As in *get laid*?" Rob simulated barfing.

Chiao Li's gap-toothed grin accentuated his round cheeks. "Out here you're a slumming Under—not subject to Corydon's mating regs."

"I guess that's something." Rob lifted his face and hands skyward as if receiving a blessing. "I guess even Under chicks have pussies." Chiao Li winced and took a pull from his monkey-face mug.

"I could use a little of that right now." Rob turned to check the club scene. "Other than that dark gal over there with the hands-off-me expression," he lifted his nose toward a long-haired, statuesque woman surrounded by a half-dozen officers, "I don't see any… oooo my."

A slender, pixie-faced blond strode in like a gazelle and glided into a chair beside a grizzled, muscular spacer. Rob shrugged. He and Chiao Li turned back to the counter.

"Come here often, big boy?" Hotz teased.

"Jus' waitin' for you, honey legs," Dom said. "What'll you have?" He held up his coconut mug and turned it for her to see the monkey face.

She laughed. "You'll survive. Say, I checked the arrivals. Commander Zimmon's due in tomorrow. Maybe we'll get some straight answers… and some decent bunks."

"Yours bad as mine? I got a half-meter-wide sleeping shelf to balance on and a pillow stinks like dead cat." Dom waved to the grass-skirted RH for another drink. "Don't see no games goin' on, not *my style* anyway. Got some virtual warriors in the back." He raised his empty mug to a half-dozen young men gesticulating in full headgear. "But maybe over there…" His mug shifted toward the tall, dark woman Rob had passed on.

"Definitely your brand of wild game." Hotz followed Dom's eyes to the raven-haired beauty in the dress slit up to her waist. The woman smiled back, lowered, and tilted her chin, and locked Dom in her gaze.

"You be okay?" Dom asked.

"I think I'll have a little fun with a couple wallflowers." She gestured to Rob and Chiao Li fidgeting at the bar. They both looked away quickly. "I bet they're scientists, and it's their first time in space." Dom waved her off.

"Good hunting," she said and walked to the bar.

Welcome Aboard, Commander

Zim's trip to Port Estelle was a far cry from the luxury cruise that brought her and Mac to Rankoi. Her tube-framed seat was bolted to the deck of the cargo bay, alongside locked-down shipping containers and vacuum-sealed pallets. She shared a portable toilet and a collapsible, fold-out table with three maintenance crewmen. Straps, netting, hooks, and buckles lined the deck, inner hull, and bulkheads. Squeezable food and beverage packages, all several years old, were available on demand from a device on the wall resembling a slot machine.

Zim checked with the pilot four hours before docking. Abramyan's hasty stand-down of StarCom combat craft had left trade lanes vulnerable. The Rii-Chaut were active in this sector but kept their distance from Port Estelle's defenses. She reasoned that the pirates hoped to pick off damaged starships limping into port for repair.

With no other diversions, Zim checked the Corydon news. Three items jumped out: "Aidan Nine to assume leadership of Greens on release from hospital." Star Council was months away from the announced leadership turnover. She felt certain Aidan would have mentioned a promotion of this magnitude. The article didn't mention what problem required Aidan's medical attention. Her gut knotted.

"Roland Mackenzie leading trade negotiations on Luna." The article sounded as if Mac and Star Council were on good terms. Not likely, though she knew he would make a fine diplomat.

The third article listed the warships converted for civilian applications, including *Marshal Massena*, and said research ships had been assigned to Marshal Derek Boorman. *Boorman*. Beyond their personal altercations, Zim knew Boorman couldn't be trusted. He was mercurial, sometimes brilliant, but also vindictive and self-seeking. She pressed her forehead into her palms. Hopefully, all this foolishness would end soon.

The trip had given Zim time to think. She knew this last assignment was intended to punish her for rejecting Abramyan's retirement offer. Why had that mattered so much? Was there something more? His parting words held malice, and Mac had warned her about crossing him. Abramyan was no master strategist, but if he'd set something up, she needed to stay alert.

The transport aligned with Port Estelle's docking hub, shut down the entropic drive, and slid into the E-Mag guide. Zim felt the jolt and shudder as clamps engaged, locked, and pulled the transport into the bay. She disembarked through a pressurized tunnel and signed herself off the cargo manifest as delivered. Except for four heavy-lift robots waiting to offload containers, the freight quay was empty. Not even a foreman. Zim scanned the immediate area and saw nothing threatening.

A green deck arrow directed her to final outfitting. *Marshal Massena* was on the docket. Eleven minutes later, she crossed the military dock where Dom and Hotz had arrived the day before. To avoid any special greeting, Zim detoured through the civilian dockyard then returned from a side corridor. Her boots gave off the familiar *zzip, zzip* of tape pulling on the reactive panels.

Skirting *Marshal Massena's* primary check-in station, she circled the starship to check out the modifications. All major weapon batteries had been removed and their ports sealed; only two secondary defense positions remained. Most of the sensors and the electronics suite were missing except for communications, navigation, and range detectors to facilitate E-Mag docking. Launch and recovery systems had been modified to accommodate nothing larger than shuttles and small resupply ships. *Marshal Massena* was a warship no longer.

Zim followed a maintenance causeway around the back and entered via a boarding ramp reserved for refit crewmen. "Commander Zimmon," she announced, brushing her forearm over the identification panel without breaking stride.

The surprised desk chief shouted, "Sir, wait, sir, you need to check in at fleet headquarters first." She gave a late salute to Zim's back.

If there was anything she wasn't supposed to see, Zim wanted to see it. *Marshal Massena's* rings were all rotating, so the outer decks had gravity. Bypassing the levitor, she took the emergency stairs three at a time. A moment later, she burst through the double doors to the hangar deck and turned down a row of shuttles.

The half-kilometer-long deck level smelled of ozone, lubricants, and cleaning fluid. Zim heard only the echo of her footsteps and the whir of a distant power drill.

Shouts erupted behind her, a security detail at the levitor entrance. She sped her pace. A guard jumped from behind a column and grabbed her arm. Barely changing gait, Zim turned his arm, spun him into a support column, and let him drop.

The first shuttle squadron, "Science One," had spaces outlined and labeled in white. A technician stooped under the forward stabilizer of the last shuttle in the row—Combat Element 5, her shuttle.

"We got a problem, Gunny?" she called, striding up. The man's jumpsuit insignia, weapons technician first class, made him a gunny in StarCom parlance. His long, plaited hair and open top shoes were nonregulation.

Still kneeling, the man looked up. "Ahh, what'd you call me? No, no ma'am, er, sir. No problem, just wanted to check the gear strut support."

"What's wrong with it?" Zim saw his eyes darting.

"Not sure, sir. Just saw—"

"What's a weapons tech doing checking shuttle struts? And why wouldn't this work be done in the maintenance bay?"

He lifted a hand to stroke his face. A cleanly severed strut support clanged to the deck. Zim stepped back. The man leaned as if to reach for the part and came up with a cutting torch. Zim flicked her wrist up and forward, and the man's right arm and hand dropped away still holding the torch. Letting out a scream, he clutched his blood-spurting shoulder.

"What's this?" The chief security officer rushed up with his team from the levitor. He started to grab Zim's arm then thought better. "What have you done to this gunny... and to my guard back there? Can you explain this, Commander?" He shouted and glared. The wounded man collapsed, shivering as he went into shock. "Joker, Trigger, get a pressure tourniquet on that and get the gunny to sick bay. Take that, too." He kicked toward the severed arm and turned back to Zim.

"You shouldn't be here," the security officer blurted. "You're supposed to report to Fleet H.Q., Port Estelle, then to Captain Woodson on the bridge. You're not authorized."

"Not authorized to be with my ship... to catch a saboteur... to see your lax security team in action? Maybe you expected someone to tip you off I was coming." Zim registered the man's discomfort. The security detail surrounded her but kept their distance. Only their leader was in proper uniform.

"You have a saboteur on board." Zim pointed without taking her eyes off the security team then kicked the severed strut support toward the security officer. "I caught him doing that, then he tried to use that cutting tool on me." She gestured to the plasma torch and the burn mark on the hangar deck. "The strut would have failed under stress, probably during E-Mag launch. Got any idea what that would have done?" She could see he didn't.

"You'll answer for this, Commander," the officer blurted. "I don't like it one bit." He stared at the wide pool of blood. "What the hell did you use on him?"

"Fortunately, I'm alive to answer your questions. And I have some, too, which I'll raise with the Captain."

The security officer scowled and turned, waving for his team to follow.

"*Chief Petty Officer?*" Zim used the security officer's rank to emphasize his lower position. He and his team stopped.

"What is it, Commander?" He looked angry but sounded under control.

"We still have a security problem here." She gestured to the rows of unguarded shuttles. "And where's my team? I expected them here, getting the shuttle ready. My chief engineer and pilot came aboard yesterday."

"Their billets weren't ready." The security officer sounded calmer. "They're bunked in Port Estelle steerage and were assigned work detail this morning."

"Work detail? Why? So, your security team could tail-jam with saboteurs?" She gave him a hard glare. His team looked terrified. "Petty Officer, you're going to find my team and have them up here in one hour. Then you're going to see that their billets *are* ready aboard *this* starship. I don't care if you have to clean their latrines yourself. Is that clear?"

"Clear."

"Good. You and your team are dismissed. One hour. My team right here. I'm waiting."

As the security officer walked away, he detailed one sentry to each squadron and directed another. "Find Commander Zimmon's team. Get them down here pronto. I don't want any more targ-ass excuses from you short-rounds." They scattered to get out of his sight.

A crowd had gathered. Zim backed toward the shuttle, keeping everyone in front of her. Few of the hangar crew wore uniforms or regulation coveralls. Slack or worse. And when had Rii-Chaut fashions come into style? She saw a lot of sour expressions framed with plaited hair. Her little demonstration hadn't made her any friends.

Messy

"You on a break?" Zim stared down the spectators, and they started to disperse. "And you, spacer," she pointed to a slow-responding woman in coveralls, "get a rag and clean this up." Her pointing finger shifted to the blood pool under the shuttle.

The heavyset woman in coveralls left quickly and returned with a bucket and brush. She had short, light brown hair, and sad, gray eyes. She gave Zim a passing glance.

"Problem, spacer?" Zim stood rigid.

"No, sir." The woman stopped and smiled. "I was wondering when someone would take charge of those slugs. Just needed a second look."

Zim read her nametag. "Spacer Kimbri, how long have you been with *Massena*?"

"Two weeks. That's all anyone's been here. None of us are regular crew." She spoke flatly. "But I'm experienced. Got pulled off a ThrinCo ore carrier. Before that I hauled water for SynTerra."

"What was your rank?"

"Trade-6." Zim recognized the commercial rating—Kimbri had been equal to a StarCom Senior Tech. "They knocked me down to Spacer-2." She touched the double chevron on her sleeve.

Zim nodded. "How are they treating you?"

"Fine, other than the pay cut. Officers don't give me no bother." She glanced at the backs of the retreating spacers. "I don't care for that bunch much."

"I don't like the looks of them either. Let me know if you have any problems." Zim stepped back to let the Kimbri do her job. A tingle in her arm signaled a message arrived at her palm. "Captain Woodson calls all squadron and shuttle leads to report to the Captain's Ready Room in fifteen minutes."

A rumble sounded at the far end of the hangar deck as a corrugated metal door slid up. A heavily muscled spacer in grease-smudged coveralls stepped out followed by a slender blond woman similarly dressed and soiled. Seeing Zim, they quit talking and hastened across the deck. Pulling to attention, they saluted. She returned their salute.

"Major Eppert, Ensign Bahrke." She handed the damaged strut support to Dom as she walked past him. "Look into that. I must meet with Captain Woodson. We'll talk when I get back."

"Yes, Commander," Dom said. "We reported yesterday and—"

"You're both off labor detail." Zim cut him off without looking back. "Keep alert. I've seen several infractions on this deck."

"Yes, sir."

Zim stepped to the levitor and ordered, "Captain's Ready Room."

Levitor was the common name for the Entropy Stabilized Rapid Transit (ESRT) system that enabled station-to-station transport on bases and major starships. ESRT was an entropy-reining spinoff of pre-Myseko physics that preserved cell structure against acceleration and deceleration.

Zim entered a room filled with uniformed officers—dark blues for StarCom, whites for merchant spacers. Side tables were set with a light buffet. At the head of a long table in the room's center sat a portly, disheveled, white-uniformed officer who appeared to be well into his cup.

Captain Jeffrey Woodson tipped a full goblet of red wine to his wide face then called out to the room. "Gentlemen, please be seated."

Zim felt underdressed in her service uniform. Seeing no seat designations, she elected to sit furthest from the Captain where she had a good view of the forty officers and could watch their interactions.

Woodson leaned over his hands and scanned the table. No empty seats. "Welcome, Gentlemen. We'll leave Port Estelle on schedule tomorrow at twenty-two hundred hours. Messy's reconfiguration is complete, all systems' trials passed satisfactorily." Zim had wondered if *Marshal Massena's* unflattering nickname was permitted. "I know things are pretty hectic, but I wanted you to meet my staff and the squadron leaders before launch."

Woodson looked at Zim. "Some of you may have met our newest arrival, Commander Gayle Zimmon." He gestured across the table. Everyone looked her way. "I'm sure you know her by her military call sign, Starflower. She'll be leading the Combat Element in Science One. We are exceedingly fortunate

163

to have someone of her talent and experience." Several nodded and smiled Zim's way.

Woodson continued, "Commander, let me go around the table." Starting to his left, he named each squadron and element lead. Messy had six squadrons, each with five shuttles, the fifth of which carried a specialty element in addition to scientists, which gave the squadron its designation. Zim's squadron, Science One, carrying her combat element, would be assigned missions where hostile confrontations or environments might be a concern. Other specialty missions included: civil engineering, medicine, xenology, resource accounting, and cultural recovery. Specialty missions were secondary. The squadrons' primary mission remained scientific: deployment, recovery, and maintenance of research sensors, and rendering assistance to deployed research teams.

After introductions, Woodson directed an RH steward to refill his wine goblet. "That's all I have. I know you want to get back to work. But before you go, take a few moments to get to know one another and grab something to eat." He gestured to the buffet and directed the waitstaff to distribute carafes and goblets. The fare was light: wine, fruit, and hors d'oeuvres.

Several shook Zim's hand or waved greetings as they headed out. Others waited to talk. She did not want to appear aloof but feared missing a chance to speak with the Captain. He looked soft and heavy, and was probably habitually drunk, but his ready recall of mission details, personnel, and technology indicated a sharp mind.

The reconfigured *Marshal Massena* was a new kind of starship on a new mission with a new crew. If Kimbri, the spacer who'd cleaned up the saboteur's blood, had been accurate, it was possible not one of these officers knew one another. Their uniform designations all hailed from different units. Zim had been in the service twelve years and recognized no one. She suspected all the StarCom officers were former staffers, armchair warriors with little or no space experience.

The white-uniformed officer to Zim's right raised a crystal carafe toward her glass. "Name's Yardley. I'm a dozer," he said.

"A dozer? You sleep a lot?" Zim quipped.

He chuckled. "No, civil engineer. The swabbies gave us all nicknames— we're the dozers, from bulldozers, I gather." He poured Zim's glass half full. "I must say your resume is rather imposing."

"I saw a lot of action. I was lucky… and stupid." She smiled over her glass without drinking.

"You're a 'club' by the way, that's your nickname—or a 'hook' depending on whether your special mission requires confrontation or an evacuation."

"The crew's a rather colorful lot, aren't they?" Zim aligned her speech with Yardley's non-military pattern.

"I'll say. And not particularly friendly. You agree?"

"I met a few on the hangar deck. One tried to assault me."

"Don't say." He pulled upright. "You alright?"

"Yes, fine. The other fellow got the worst of it. Tell me, what does a dozer do?"

"Dig, drill, trench, blast, level ground mostly—for sensor placement. I don't expect we'll be asked to build many bridges or dikes on this assignment."

"You've done that? In space, I mean. You don't sound like an administrative mouse."

"Goodness no, I've been merchant spacing for almost twenty-five years." He swirled his wine glass. "Started in tramps when I was eighteen, little money, lots of adventure. Tramps don't get the big contracts. We serviced every micro-colony, mining camp, and military outpost. Then I got serious, worked the CETS liner circuit—Corydon-Earth-Thrinlu-Scalaris—much better money. When Earth was taken off the circuit, we evacuated the Under survivors to Thrinlu and Scalaris—not Corydon, of course. We'd just been assigned to work the new planets with SynTerra when the Aldrakin War started and wiped out the company. Hopefully, the good times will come back."

Zim gestured with her wine glass. "How'd you get to *Marshal Massena*?"

"Messy?" He took a sip. "I admit Messy was a surprise. I have no science background." He checked to see if anyone was listening then whispered, "You're something of a surprise, too. Scuttlebutt has it StarCom wants all combat veterans cleared from the fleet." His smile twisted.

"I'm sure we slipped through the selection process." Zim noticed three officers and Woodson standing. "Excuse me, Yardley, I need to speak with the Captain before he leaves." She set her half-full wine glass on the table then grabbed a couple finger sandwiches on a napkin to give the impression her conversation would be casual.

Woodson laughed loudly, gestured grandly with wide arm sweeps, and occasionally popped a couple hors d'oeuvres into his wide mouth. Zim raised a hand to get his attention. "Might we have a few words, Captain? In private would be best."

"Certainly, Commander, we haven't had a chance to speak. My office?" He gestured to the door behind his chair. Zim apologized quietly to the three officers vying for attention and followed Woodson.

"Have a seat," he said. The desk, chairs, and tables were dark gray metallic, the type generated by reactive deck plates. Ordered rows of pictures covered the back wall: officers at graduation, award presentations, Woodson kneeling, stroking a Chatlion cub, Woodson with a young woman and a child beside a house in a fishing village. Zim recognized the setting.

"Your family is on Thrinlu?" She took the seat beside the Captain's desk.

"Yes, but we're being moved next year. You know how that goes—we're obsolete Unders. Creatives are the future of mankind." He sounded resigned. "We'll start over on Divagne." Zim knew the Aldrakin had returned Divagne under the terms of the treaty. The damage was extensive, but this was not the time to bring that up.

"I suspect your security officer mentioned my run-in on the hangar deck?"

"Yes. Security matters pop up immediately. He logged the incident without detail. There were two sickbay admissions."

"I caught one man in the act of sabotage. The incident with the security guard was unfortunate, but he should know better than to grab an officer."

Woodson shook his head. "I'd hoped things weren't so bad. The hangar deck crew came in together. Abramyan said they were trained shuttle mechanics and engine techs, and he needed to place them. All I've gotten from that group is dereliction and insubordination."

Zim's jaw tightened at the mention of Abramyan. Was he planning to dog her every move? More than ever, she wished she'd listened to Mac and kissed Grover's ass.

She looked into Woodson's eyes. "It might be worse—a lot worse. I don't have experience fighting Rii-Chaut pirates, but that crew on the hangar deck fits their description." She gave that a second to register and continued. "I also have questions about your security team down there."

Woodson looked startled. "I need a drink. Care to join me?" He stood and stepped to his left. A gray panel dissolved to reveal a mirrored, alcove with glasses and a wall-mounted faucet above a counter with a sink and freezer.

"What are you offering?" Zim studied the Captain's unsteady moves.

"Name it. I'm having bourbon." He took a cut-glass tumbler from the shelf and held it under the faucet. "Kentucky, thirty-year, ice." The tumbler filled.

"I'll have the same," Zim said. Woodson handed her his glass and filled another. They clicked glasses, and she sipped as he quaffed half of his.

"How do you recommend we handle our security problem, Commander?"

"Can we get in another hangar crew?"

"Not this late. And we'd have to go through Abramyan, now Boorman, too. But I'll put your saboteur in the brig as soon as he's out of sick bay."

"I'd get him off the ship," Zim said. "Offload him to Port Estelle's hospital." Woodson nodded. "As for your security team, I smell lazy incompetence. Your security Chief Petty Officer is confused and lacks discipline. That could mean disaster, especially if we have an active Rii-Chaut cell running the hangar deck." She took another sip. "That's my worst-case scenario and the one I think we need to address first."

"Okay," the Captain said. "I won't make excuses, but I only came aboard this week."

"I've been aboard two hours," she said. The Captain winced. "Captain Woodson, I have no authority outside my shuttle and squadron, but I ask that you back me on handling any problems we find. I hope I can count on you?" She raised her glass. The Captain paused before raising his.

"Thank you, sir, and one more request. Scientists? I should have one physical scientist and one life scientist. I want them working with my team as soon as possible. If we see action, I want the scientists to take part. Also, until I'm satisfied with security, my team and I will bunk aboard our shuttle."

"Only two scientists remain in the pool. I'm sorry, but you were last to arrive. I wouldn't worry though. They have excellent academic credentials."

"Academic meaning no time in space, no actual field work, and no combat experience."

"I see what you mean. Your scientists will be down this afternoon. I'm glad you're on board, Commander. Let me know what you need—anything." They both finished their drinks.

"Oh, while you're here, Commander. You and your team were mentioned in a classified communiqué." He pulled up a message panel and summarized aloud. "With war over… Tak-Yaki training squadron departing Port Estelle." He skimmed down. "Request Zimmon and team attendance… TY departure ceremony this afternoon… high military official and former instructor to preside."

"Does the communiqué give the official's name?"

"Ahh, yes," he searched the panel, "Ticket-Tockoket-*Click*."

Zim bit inside her lip. "My team and I will be honored to attend. Captain Woodson, you did say to let you know whatever I needed?"

"Name it."

"Does that thirty-year-old Kentucky bourbon come in bottles?"

The Captain's face brightened. "I'll send you a case. Where?"

"My shuttle with Science One. Thank you very much, Captain. Shall we have another?" She held up her empty tumbler.

Moving In

The room outside Captain Woodson's office had reverted to a Starship Ready Room. The buffet, tables, and chairs were gone, replaced with rows of utilitarian seating facing a low stage, podium, and display screen. On one side wall, dozens of view panels surrounded an interactive star chart. Displays on the opposite wall showed everything from ship status and squadron rosters to mess hall schedules, weekly menus, and daily recreational activities.

Zim passed through to the levitor, ordered, "Hangar deck," and a moment later was walking by shuttles to the Science One parking area. The sentry stiffened as she passed. Ahead, she saw concave panels strewn on the deck beside the Combat Element 5 shuttle. Hotz climbed on top like a spindle-legged spider, pressing and sliding an E-Mag sensor to check hull seams.

"Does she need a full overhaul?" Zim called up, fearing the worst.

Dom stepped out from the back; his face masked with sensors. "Don't think so." His wide, veined hand slid the mask onto his forehead. "I think a mait'nance overhaul should do it: valves, feed lines, timing panels reset, switches cleaned and checked. Haven't found any deliberate damage other than the strut, but no real mait'nance been done on this baby for some time. I'll take care of that then run a test." He stroked the hull. "They pulled this old gal outta salvage. She's all dried up."

"How's it look up there?" Zim called to Hotz.

"I haven't found any structural damage, Commander." Hotz's pixie face glowed pink and sweaty. "We'll reset the shields. That's standard after a mission, part of the maintenance Dom wants to do."

"Is repair bay open?" Zim asked.

Dom nodded. "Got us a slot reserved for early tomorrow. I reckon it'll take four hours. If anything's critical, I can get the parts here at the port then finish up after we're underway."

"Good update, both of you." Zim glanced between them. "Another matter. Get your gear from steerage; we're bunking aboard." She saw curious looks. "The Captain told me we're stuck with this hangar crew. I caught one saboteur. There's probably a whole nest." She observed the sentry two shuttles down turning away, pretending not to be listening.

"Aye, Commander," they said together.

"One more thing. We have a ceremony this afternoon. Check your dress uniforms. If you're missing something, get it from ship's stores."

A rumble from the freight levitor was followed by the roar of an emerging auto-truck. Dom and Hotz returned to work. Zim watched the sentry flag down the truck to check the cargo. "The bag and metal box are my kit," Zim called. The sentry nodded and cleared the other boxes.

The truck rolled forward and stopped. A headless R-lift removed the space bag, a hinged, metal box, and a shipping case—the six bottles of Kentucky bourbon. Zim swept her palm over the manifest, and the auto-truck drove off. Pulling the space bag strap onto her shoulder, she lifted the metal box by its handle and climbed the short steps into the shuttle.

All *Marshal Massena's* shuttles were second-hand transports that had seen a lot of service. Designed for freight, their engines were vectored for vertical lift rather than performance maneuvers. Their wide bodies and long cargo bays could accommodate anything from standard shipping containers and machinery to bulk commodities like water, ore, or produce. Adjustable compartments could be set for environmental conditions for alien cargos. Their short-range limited the shuttles to single-planet or near-moon operations from low-orbiting carrier ships like the *Marshal Massena*.

Zim entered through the hatchway just behind the control-navigation section, dropped her bag and box on the first low bunk, then retrieved the case of bourbon.

"Dom," she called below the hatchway, "do we have power? How about auto-response?"

"Power's up," he shouted back. "All systems are hooked up, but I haven't checked auto-response. Try asking it a question."

Zim climbed the steps, set the case beside the rear bulkhead, and called to auto-response, "How's the weather outside?"

An elderly woman's voice responded cheerfully, "Today will be clear and starry with steady cosmic ray showers. The temperature outside is 2.725

degrees kelvin and is expected to remain steady throughout the day. So, if you're planning to go out, be sure to dress warmly. Have a fulfilling day."

Zim cleared her throat. "Are you always that silly?"

"No, Commander Zimmon, only when I'm asked silly questions. Are you always so playful?"

"You know who I am?"

"You are Commander Gayle Zimmon, call sign Starflower, currently assigned to lead this shuttle in support of scientific research missions."

"So, you can see me?"

"I have eighteen sensors on my exterior hull and twelve on the interior bulkheads for sound and full spectrum electromagnetic radiation."

"OK, I give you this round."

"Commander zero, Brownie one."

"That's your name, Brownie?"

"Yes, Commander."

"Give me one second." Zim raised a finger and stuck her head out the hatchway. "Dom, Hotz, can you come in here?"

The Team

Hotz pulled her work gloves off two fingers at a time, set them on the table, and slouched into a folding chair. Dom entered, gloves in hand, and pulled up a chair beside Hotz to face Zim. Their faces glowed red and rolled rivulets of sweat.

"Would you like some ice water?" Brownie's motherly voice asked.

Dom and Hotz looked at one another.

Zim smiled. "It seems we have another crew member. Meet Brownie, our sentient control system."

"I'd like a glass of ice water, please," Hotz said. Multiple clinks and a water jet sounded from the small galley.

"Sorry, I'm unable to deliver your water glass. Commander Zimmon hasn't provided me with a mobile application."

"That's okay, I'll get it." Hotz took two quick steps and returned glass in hand.

"We'll get acquainted with Brownie later," Zim said. "Right now, I think she can help us. Her records will have all actions related to this shuttle throughout its history. Do I have that right, Brownie?"

"Yes, Commander."

Dom asked, "Has there been any tampering or sabotage?"

"Many times. Slothful miners are notorious for finding ways to avoid work."

"Have those issues been corrected?" Zim asked. "And have there been any incidents since this shuttle was assigned to the Messy?"

"The previous problems have been crudely corrected. Commander Zimmon discovered the recent episode." A projection opened above the table showing a scruffy spacer taking a plasma torch to the front stabilizer followed by the confrontation with Zim. "I also have records of the maintenance shortfalls Major Eppert mentioned."

Dom jumped at hearing his name. "I could use those records… ahh—"

"You may call me Brownie, Major Eppert."

"Okay. In present comp'ny you can call me Dom."

"And I'm Hotz," Hotz chimed.

"Very well," Zim said, standing. "You two work with Brownie. I'll see if I can track down our scientists."

Stepping through the hatchway, she saw two figures approaching.

# # #

Rob threw his arms up and yanked the strap on his shoulder bag. "A 'club,' a goddamned club, that's what they think I am. That's what they call people on the combat team, clubs. Why don't they just call us knuckle-draggers?" Rob and Chiao Li followed the green deck arrow through the hangar. "I was a Seven. *You* know what that means?" He glanced at Chiao Li gasping under the weight of his own baggage. "Do *they* know what a Seven means? No, they don't. They're a bunch of targ-brained Unders. I went to the top schools. Does that count for anything?"

"*No*," Chiao Li yelled back. "Unders don't care about you. Why should we? Why should we care about your schools, how popular you were, or whose spermatozoa your momma's eggs got stirred with? Maybe we'd care if you did something productive." Chiao Li clamped his jaw tight and shook his head.

Rob continued muttering. "Anything *but* a club. A 'troll,' that's what I should be. Exploring, finding resources, minerals, metals, that's a job for a physical scientist." Chiao Li smiled over clenched teeth as Rob's rant continued. "Do I even look like a club? Someone you'd want beside you in a fight?" Rob gestured to his lanky frame.

Chiao Li gave out a hearty laugh. "Hate to tell you, Rob, but we're not assigned with just *any club*. We're going with *THE CLUB*—the Starflower."

Rob did a double take. "Okay, that's funny. That's real funny. Now tell me that's a joke… Chiao Li, *tell me you're kidding*. They would never put *me* with *that* woman on *this* starship. *That* is not possible."

"I'm not kidding, Rob. And I'm looking forward to it. Look, there she is ahead." He pointed to Zim coming down the shuttle steps and quickened his pace. "You know, Rob, I think she's beautiful."

"She better not expect me to march or salute or 'sir' everyone, none of that Under targ." He punctuated his last line with a wide, chopping, arm sweep.

To Zim they looked like lost children, ragged, out of step, heads down. One was soft and overweight, the other so thin he'd be carried off in a stiff breeze.

Half of StarCom's military casualties had been rookies on their first deployment. Zim was sure whatever misgivings she had, these two had more, perhaps because of their inexperience, perhaps because they'd heard about her reputation or the Prophecy. Now they were on the journey with her. She needed to build their skills and confidence. Would that be enough? Would it be for any of her team? She had visions of this being her last mission, just as she did before every mission.

Chiao Li stopped short of Zim, pulled his feet together, dropped his bags to the hangar deck, and stood erect. Not bad for a civilian, Zim thought. Rob set his bag down, cocked a hip to one side, and smirked.

"Gentlemen, welcome to Science One, Combat Element 5." Zim waited for a reaction. Chiao Li could barely conceal a smile. Rob glanced at him then pulled his feet together. "I see you both have your kit. Good. You were told we'll be billeting aboard?"

"Yes, Commander," Chiao Li barked. Rob nodded.

"Very well. Follow me. Toss your bags on any empty bunk."

"Yes, sir." Chiao Li snapped his curled right hand to touch above his brow. Rob waved one finger from a non-existent hat brim.

"Commander on deck," Brownie ordered. As Zim stepped through the hatchway, Dom and Hotz stood.

"That's fine, Brownie. Everyone at ease." Zim stepped aside for Chiao Li and Rob to enter. "Dom, I turn these rookies over to your gentle care." Both scientists stared wide-eyed at the rock-like combat veteran. Hotz gave Rob a sly wink.

Dom stepped forward. "I'm Major James Eppert. But combat teams don't stand on formality. Call me Dom. This is Ensign Bahrke—Hotz." He gestured to her. "Commander Zimmon's nickname is Commander. In comms-traffic she's Starflower."

"Rob," Rob mumbled, his chin almost on his chest.

"Chiao Li." He beamed.

"Okay, Rob, Charlie." Dom leaned close to catch their eyes. "Last row bunks are free." He pointed to the back of the bay. "Take yer pick. Charlie, you're a big fella, might wanna take a low bunk."

Chiao Li took a quick breath. "Not Charlie, it's Chiao Li, pronounced Chi-YOW-Li."

"Heard ya the first time, *Char-Lee*. Take your bunk." Dom lifted Chiao Li's three bags with one fist and tossed them into the low bunk as if they were pillows.

"Can we compromise?" Chiao Li said. "How about just Chiao?"

"*Chow*? As in chow line?" Dom sniggered as he eyed the scientist's fleshy frame. "Okay, Chow then. Good name." He slapped Chow's shoulder. "I think we'll get on fine."

"If that's what you like." Chow took his small victory and stowed his gear under the low rear bunk. Rob took the one above.

"Everyone, let's gather." Zim waited as they pulled chairs to the table. "You with us, Brownie?"

"Right here, Commander."

"This afternoon's ceremony is in four hours, and it's formal." She caught the scientists' blank stares. "Everyone set with dress blues?"

"Good," Dom and Hotz answered in unison.

"Ceremony? Formal dress?" Rob scowled. "As in uniforms?"

"As in *dress* uniforms," Zim said. The scientists shook their heads.

"You'll find what you need in the port exchange. Tell them StarCom dress blues, no rank other than your science officer ratings, Science One for the unit designator. Go now and hurry back. We have a few more things to cover. Brownie?"

"Yes, Commander."

"I'm sorry you won't be with us. Keep watch while we're out."

"Count on me, Commander."

"I don't have any details, but a Rii-Chaut cell is active on this deck. And I know we're the target. Captain told me it was Abramyan that pushed that scurvy bunch on us."

"Scuttlebutt has it Abramyan's got it in for you," Dom said.

"We're not on good terms, but my intuition tells me there's something more." Zim said. Dom and Hotz nodded. They shared her fate. Zim knew they understood that. "We'll talk more when our scientists get back. Until then, you two see how far you can get on Brownie's maintenance list." Dom and Hotz picked their work gloves off the table and headed out the hatchway.

Zim called up the scientists' profiles. Both had excellent academic credentials and no combat or space experience. Woodson had said as much. Without spacer smarts, they'd be underfoot. Basic survival had to be the training priority, ahead of weapons and combat skills.

Her arm tingled—it was a note from Mac. She touched her wrist to bring up his projection. "Gayle, my love, thank you for our wonderful holiday. It was hard leaving you, but soon we'll be together forever. I shiver thinking how beautiful you are and how precious to me." Zim paused to savor Mac's words then resumed the message.

"Talked with Crowley. He said Blue Star is opening a second tech base, and he wants me to lead it. I can begin immediately. I told him I agreed to head the trade talks on Luna next month but should be able to get free after that.

"I saw the plans for our new home. It isn't large. But it's on a beautiful planet in a quiet sector, and it's by a lake. Besides Goorm trading posts, Crowley says they're terraforming planets for Under settlements. Blue Star isn't going through Star Council, so there may be legal concerns. That's why they aren't revealing any locations." He air-kissed her goodbye.

Zim stroked Mac's frozen image on the projection then sent her response. "That sounds wonderful, Mac. I checked *Marshal Massena's* mission agenda. It only lists half a dozen star systems. If it's not extended, we could be finished by the end of this year. Don't pick out any dishes without me." She smiled and let out a deep sigh. "Miss you, too, my love. It won't be long now."

Was it possible they could be together in their new home next year? She shook away those thoughts and returned to her immediate concern: preparing her team.

Tak-Yaki

The metal stairs rattled and Chow's head appeared in the hatchway. "Rob's right behind. He got distracted by a woman at the exchange. How do I look?" His formal dress uniform was fitted and correctly marked. Rolled under his arm, he carried a new service uniform, a set of coveralls, and his old shoes and clothing.

"Regulation." Zim nodded approval. "Call everyone. We need to mission prep for this afternoon."

Chow shouted out the hatch then returned and tossed his clothes on his bunk. Rob slunk in sulking, Hotz and Dom behind him.

"Reports, problems?" Zim asked.

Dom set a wide hand on Hotz's shoulder. "We checked off Brownie's maint'nance list. Nothing major missing. We'll be able to finish in the repair hall early tomorrow."

"Good. Anyone else?"

"We could use a trip to the Port Estelle commissary for fresh vegetables," Brownie said cheerfully. "*Marshal Massena* hasn't restocked."

"Thanks, Brownie. We'll do that."

Chow motioned that he and Rob would do the shopping. Rob frowned.

"Okay, let's talk about this afternoon." Zim sat and waved for everyone to be seated. "The Tak-Yaki training squadron leaving Port Estelle invited us to their departure ceremony. The TY were with us at the beginning of the war and were with me at Bai-Yota. Consider this an honor. They seldom invite Humans to their events."

She looked at her team. "Which of you has encountered the Tak-Yaki?" Dom raised a finger. He had fought alongside them many times and liked their efficiency but knew nothing of their culture. Hotz knew them from combat flying exercises. Chow had studied them in xenology. Rob shook his head.

177

"I did a good deal of my Basic training with this squadron," Zim said. "Then StarCom asked me to evaluate their advanced programs. That required an extended stay on their home planet Tak-Yakon. The Tak-Yaki are a caste society. Our hosts this afternoon will all be of the military caste: like the Human Samurai, Mameluke, Kshatriya, or Knights Templar." She paused then decided to tell them more.

"Basic officer and flight training at Port Estelle didn't and still doesn't include personal combat training." Dom and Hotz nodded. "The year I spent on Tak-Yakon took care of that." Zim lifted her hands palms-out and pressed her thumbs to indicate spots at the tips of her middle three fingers. "These dark dots," everyone craned to see, "are ports for Tak-Yaki implants—carbon-metallic fibers so fine they sever molecular bonds, and so strong, in non-weapon applications they are used for heavy-lift machinery."

"You were surgically altered, like a Pidge." Rob shrank back, rubbed a soft hand across his mouth and chin, and shook his head. "No Creative would ever submit to that. Not ever."

Zim smiled. "I volunteered. When I arrived on Tak-Yakon, my hand-to-hand combat skills were well behind what the Tak-Yaki expect from their school children. They fit their young with these shortly after birth." She held up her middle fingers like obscene gestures. "They master weapon technique as easily as our children master potty training. While I recovered from surgery, I watched TY barely half-a-meter tall practice. They reminded me of Human children playing with yo-yos or toads catching flies on their tongues. Because of my Human reflexes, I was slow picking up the technique. But our hand-wrist structures are more adaptable than clamp-claws."

"That's what you used when the spacer attacked you," Dom said.

"Yes. After TY Basic, I specialized in hand-to-hand and eventually became the *Krglu*, their highest rank. My first military tour was two years with the Tak-Yaki. That gave me tactical experience."

"I know their reputation," Dom said. "I served with them but not in close combat. So, I never saw their weapons used."

Hotz chimed in. "We need a demo. That spacer this morning looked like he ran into a laser saw. I saw it in Brownie's recording, but it was too fast to follow. We're on the same team, Commander. We need to know what you can do."

Zim tapped a knuckle to her chin. The Tak-Yaki conceal their skill to enhance the shock value, but Hotz was right. "Brownie, do you have something small I could use as a target, something we won't mind losing?" Rob and Chow slid their chairs back from the table.

"Titanium miners left a couple coffee mugs. They're titanium alloy." Brownie illuminated two mugs on a shelf. Hotz lined them beside one another on the counter and stepped back. Without standing, Zim appeared to silently snap a finger and thumb on each hand. Everyone waited.

"Maybe it's not loaded?" Hotz quipped, staring at the stationary mugs.

Zim laughed. "Hand me the one on the right."

Hotz lifted the mug by its handle then tipped it to view through its cleanly severed base. She giggled, set it down, and picked up the second mug. It looked perfectly intact.

"Brownie, turn on the water so Hotz can fill the mug." A thin stream ran from pinholes on either side.

Dom shook his head, eyes wide. "What's your range?"

"Six meters maximum, but there's a recovery time. For multiple targets, it's better to limit the range to three or four."

"Can't wait for a combat demonstration," Dom said, and Hotz nodded.

Rob cleared his throat. "Hopefully that won't happen." Both scientists leaned further away.

"You two back to the table." Zim motioned to Chow and Rob. "Let's keep talking while the rest of us get into our party clothes."

Dom and Hotz went to the back and, one after the other, stepped through the ionic bath that cleaned their bodies and clothes together.

"What's a TY ceremony like?" Chow asked.

"Like most military ceremonies," Zim said, "orderly and proper. They'll serve food and beverages. It's all Human digestible, but I warn you, Tak-Yaki tastes are acquired. There'll be a speaker and awards. Probably some toasts. We introduced them to alcohol, so that'll be available."

Zim talked while she took her turn through the bath. "They'll have translator devices like those on Corydon. Without them TY speech sounds like ratcheting machinery. I don't know that any Human ever fully mastered it. I learned enough to be cordial." She stripped out of her clothes alongside Dom and Hotz. Then they all donned their formal attire and returned to the front of the shuttle bay.

Hotz aligned Dom's combat ribbons while he fastened his collar. "I've always been confused," she turned toward Zim. "The Tak-Yaki don't wear clothes other than weapon harnesses, but I can't tell—are they males or females?"

"For general purposes—" Zim paused. "Excuse me, we have a xenologist on our crew." She extended her hand to Chow.

"Technically, they're all female," Chow said, smiling his usual broad smile, but his voice was measured and professional. "As soon as they hatch, fertile females barely larger than my thumb," he pointed his up, "are swarmed by minuscule males. The females assimilate one or more of the males then instantly generate microscopic eggs. After one merging sex act, females lose their fertility and absorb their reproductive organs. Maturing Tak-Yaki merge the characteristics of both sexes."

"Who raises the little kiddies?" Hotz asked.

"A separate caregiver caste nurtures the tiny eggs until they reach maturity at about two to three kilograms. They also facilitate the Tak-Yaki hatching and the mating processes. Their young don't require special care: they're miniature adults. Those becoming caregivers never leave the underground egg chamber—"

"Never?" Hotz sounded shocked.

"The TY evolved underground from something like ants. Their castes are determined before they hatch, including attributes for specific tasks and environments. Caregivers, for example, hatch blind but have heightened tactile and vibratory senses for living underground. Military caste members have large claws and broad-spectrum visual sensors not needed by the other castes."

"How many castes are there?" Hotz asked.

"We only know a few. The other castes rarely come above ground. I understand some are very specialized and different in appearance." Chow looked to Zim to expand.

"The castes keep to themselves," Zim said. "At Tak-Yakon I only saw the military. When I toured Avian, I saw TY scientists—that surprised me."

"How many eggs do they lay?" Hotz asked.

"That's hard to know," Chow said. "The caregivers collect the eggs and keep them dormant until they're needed. Since castes don't share data with those outside their caste, and the caregivers aren't accountants, the Tak-Yaki themselves might not know."

Zim added, "That has caused them problems. Without shared knowledge, the Tak-Yaki lack a common vision. They also don't have diplomatic or negotiator castes, which may be why they ran afoul of the Aldrakin."

"The Tak-Yaki do well with Humans," Dom said.

"The military caste does," Zim said. "Outside of themselves, they consider us the most antagonistic species in the galaxy. They admire Humans for that."

Old Friends

Port Estelle's TY-ring rotation was set for 0.5G, Tak-Yakon standard gravity. Rob and Chow shuffled, bounced, and stumbled. Hotz and Dom adjusted after a few steps. Zim lengthened her gait and felt at home.

Dark-blue and violet mantises packed the squadron room a meter deep. Loud ratcheting filled the air. Senior officers, discernible by their darker carapaces and ceremonial belts, met them at the door.

Triangular heads swiveled when Zim and her team entered, and a chest-high wave flowed toward them, stilt-legs pumping like push rods. Forgetting the translator pads, excited Tak-Yaki *chiriked* the Humans and pinched their shoulders with massive claws. Zim returned the greeting with thumb-finger pinches and *chiriks*. Dom and Hotz received and gave *chiriks* and matched the TY head bobs. Rob drew back. Chow hesitated then waded in with *chiriks*, shoulder pinches, and his signature gap-toothed grin.

Zim slipped her satchel from her shoulder and slid it under a translator pedestal. Two old friends *chiriked* and stroked her chin with their pedipalps. She returned the intimacy with her fingers on their chins then set a hand on the translator pedestal. Her friends each rested a foot on the pedestal's low rung.

"Kr'Rakat, Choo'kok, so pleased to see you." Zim pointed to Kr'Rakat's clamp claw. "Your claw looks fearsome as ever."

Chirik, Krglu, click-tirock, they click-chiggered as the translator engaged. "Greetings Zimmon, you are looking mean and nasty." Zim returned the familiar compliment.

Kr'Rakat waved a clamp-claw. "It's still a little short. After Liri-Yon, I had to regrow four legs and a claw."

Zim waved for her team to come over. "Kr'Rakat was my flight instructor. Choo'kok was my roommate in Basic here at Port Estelle and led a team against mine in training drills."

Click-chirkiri, Choo'kok said, "We tested one another as others could not."

Zim and Kr'Rakat nodded, then Zim added, "Choo'kok and I also went to Tak-Yakon together. And after my remedial claw-to-claw combat training, we were back rooming together."

She extended an arm to her team. "Let me introduce Hotz, my pilot, and Dom, my chief engineer. Both are skilled in combat arms and would like to discuss TY battle tactics." The Tak-Yakis' garnet eyes glinted. "My scientists, Chow, a xenologist very interested in your species, and Rob, a physical scientist, would like to know about resources in the TY systems." They all exchanged shoulder pinches.

Choo'kok looked at Dom and Hotz, its head bobbing expectantly. "The quickest way to learn our tactics... You have heard of Daka-Rye?"

"Your combat sport," Dom said. "I'm eager to learn, but I suspect our pilot may find it daunting."

Hotz shot him a sour look and an elbow to the ribs. "You start. I'll try to keep up."

Zim smiled, remembering Hotz's incredible scores from her training record. Taking their leave, Dom and Hotz followed Choo'kok.

Chirik-okolo-click, said a TY, touching its foot to the pedestal. Zim leaned in to hear above the ratcheting din. The newcomer had smaller claws and finer mandibles than the others. Its triangular head swiveled to Chow and Rob. "I would *very much* enjoy discussing science with others of my profession."

Kr'Rakat introduced the newcomer. "Atch-Oklot is our squadron chief scientist. Not military caste, but we now include scientists in our squadrons— which I believe was your recommendation." It tilted its head toward Zim. "We try to make it comfortable, but Atch-Oklot misses its caste mates."

Chow and Rob took the hint and followed Atch-Oklot to a side table. Zim recalled seeing TY scientists at Avian but seeing them with a military unit was a bigger surprise.

"Atch-Oklot has served our squadron well," Kr'Rakat said, its head pivoting to follow the scientists. It gestured a claw to the front table. "May I invite you to join the honorees?" Zim shouldered her satchel and followed Kr'Rakat through the throng of blue and violet.

The dark blue Tak-Yaki at the center of the front table pointed for Zim and Kr'Rakat to sit beside it. She recognized the bent antenna. Rounding the table, she caught the percussive strains of TY instrumental music from a Shelesti and a half-dozen Hyrup brushing and plinking in the corner. The Shelesti looked away, but its dark-eyed mate-hump followed her movements.

A low seat beside Tock brought their heads level. Tock smoothed its antenna as absently as a Human might adjust an out-of-place strand of hair. Zim thought it best not to mention the old wound.

Chirik, Tock said. "I am pleased to see you so soon, Gayle." It pedipalp-stroked her chin, and Zim returned the intimacy with her fingers. "Much has happened for us. So much to discuss. After the ceremony perhaps."

"I hoped you'd say that." Zim slid her satchel onto her lap. "Something for an old friend."

Chkkk, Tock clicked. "Thirty-year?" Zim nodded. "This time I remembered the Baakel. In my office." It tipped its head to the door behind them.

The ratcheting ended as if by a switch, and mantises filed into ordered rows facing front. Zim checked her timer. She always marveled at the TY's inner clocks.

Tock stood. *Chirik chi'kik ooch'kik.* Zim understood the untranslated opening as "Greetings, glorious day."

Ooch'kik, the Taki-Yaki ratcheted in chorus.

"Warriors of Tak-Yakon," Tock continued, "all here honored students and instructors of the Twenty-Seventh Training Squadron. Today we declare the final act in the glorious and victorious war against the slime-dweller Aldrakin."

Ooch'kik, said the chorus.

"As I read the honor roll, all here represented will respond. First, our Legion's founder, hero of the Tolki-Ko, the Ashk'chi, and the Aldrakin, the great Marshal Chochk-*click*."

Chirik, responded a very young Tak-Yaki, standing. Zim knew the lavender mantis was a stand-in for the old warrior whose name would forever be called in the rolls and remembered. Chochk-*click* had died at Liri-Yon, the only serious Tak-Yaki defeat in living memory. The young TY was probably a student calling out for the spirit dwelling within.

"Our weapons expert and hero of five campaigns, *Click*-Arak," Tock called.

Chirik, said another light-toned mantis for a dead comrad in arms. On it went for the next thirty-three heroes, all remembered, and their deeds recounted in the squadron's honor roll. Then came, "Chief flight instructor,

Kr'Rakat," who *chiriked* and stood beside Zim. After another seven dead came, "Choo'kok." Zim's old roommated *chiriked* and stood. Twenty-six names followed, including a few elder officers. Then came:

"Commander Gayle Zimmon, the Starflower, Marshal of Human Star Command, victor of forty-three Aldrakin engagements, *Krglu* of the Tak-Yaki, the Aberrant Knight of Bai-Yota."

Chirik, Zim responded and stood.

All the garnet eyes turned to her, and the room rang out, *Ha-Yee Starflower, Ha-Yee Aldra Korah.* Zim inhaled sharply at the Tak-Yaki invoking their enemy's accolade. Did they know of the Prophecy?

She was the last called. By Zim's count: seven on the squadron honor roll remained, sixty-eight were dead, most from the Liri-Yon defeat.

The mood changed with the formal announcement of the training base shutting down and the squadron relocating. Many on the staff were being assigned to combat units. A new threat had arisen. The young officers were excited.

After the announcements, Tock invited the officers to enjoy beverages and food, and directed the Shelesti and Hyrup to renew playing. The music was largely percussion with ratcheting riffs, chirps, shrieks, whistles, and squeaks. Zim's ears were trained for it, but she was sure to her team it sounded like insects on a mid-summer night.

"I don't know what to say, Tock. You and the squadron honor me." Her image reflected in Tock's garnet eyes.

"You are one of us, Gayle, a partner in arms. Now come, we have things to discuss," Tock said then whispered, "along with generous libations." They dismissed themselves and left by the back door.

Tock's office was decorated in pastel reds, purples, and blues, the subdued colors of the Tak-Yakon forest. Relief patterns suggested actual vegetation. Tock straddled a clover-lobed chair and invited Zim to sit in an executive Human chair. The chair must have been acquired special for this event. Tock brought two glasses up from below the translation pedestal. Zim removed two bottles from her satchel, set one beside Tock on the pedestal, peeled the seal off the other, and poured two glasses.

"Thank you, Gayle." Tock lifted a glass.

Zim raised hers. "To vicious, ruthless enemies."

"They are why we are." Tock chiggered, rocking its head and spreading its mandibles—body language Zim recognized expressed pleasure. "Thank you, old friend, you've lost none of your heartless cruelty." They tossed back the first shot. Zim felt the warm shock, refilled the glasses, and waited for Tock's news.

"We are a closed society. It is unprecedented that an alien would influence Tak-Yaki culture, even the *Krglu*." Tock took a sip of bourbon. "At your recommendation, we incorporated a few scientists into our military squadrons. We have since expanded that experiment to other caste areas."

"I'm not entirely surprised," Zim said. "Your castes perform very specific functions. Separating them meant you did not know what you knew. Combining their skills on your teams was a logical step."

"Other changes have begun. A species we had never encountered, the Sk'Keffin, offered their diplomatic services to help us deal with the Aldrakin." Tock swallowed the rest of its drink, set the glass on the table, and moved to refill both glasses. Zim set hers beside Tock's. "The Sk'Keffin are most persuasive. Can you imagine, Gayle, we opened negotiations with the Aldrakin, and they invited us to join in trade talks with the Goorm." Tock rocked its head and chiggered. "Never did I imagine. Never." It took a long pull on the bourbon.

"For whatever I may have done." Zim offered her glass high.

"You were the catalyst… You, a Human, but it could only have been thus."

"How so?"

"I noted your reaction to the Aldra Korah response. Understand, Gayle, the Aldrakin are not like the Tak-Yaki. They are very unwarlike, powerful, but not one of them is a pure warrior. It is difficult for warriors like us to understand them. The Sk'Keffin persuaded us to read from the Aldra Korah. We are not mentioned specifically, but, with the arrival of the Starflower, the role of the Tak-Yaki is unmistakable. That awareness brought the understanding that we are not separate. We are linked with all galactic cultures."

"I confess I didn't know about the Aldra Korah or the Starflower legend until the surrender. Now the Prophecy bears down on me like a pack of charging heinkel."

"None of us know where this is heading," Tock clicked. "Which brings me to another concern."

Rii-Chaut Folly

Tock produced a small box from the pedestal shelf. "Baakel to go with our excellent bourbon!" Tock chiggered an untranslated expletive and offered the box of delicacies.

"Ahh, wonderful." Zim gazed at the beetle-like carcasses in the presentation box like they were holiday chocolates and selected a radiant green one.

"Mmm, please leave them on the table. If you saved the worst news, I may need several." Each bite tingled neurons in her mouth and tongue.

"It is *very* serious." Tock punctuated with a hard claw-click. "I apologize for being blunt and unemotional."

"When are the Tak-Yaki not blunt and unemotional?"

Tock took a savoring sip of bourbon, lifted a red Baakel to its pedipalps, and pointed its triangle head toward Zim like an arrow. "We don't understand Human culture. We understand your military caste, but not Star Command or the Council. Your greatest victories, including the last, came from ignoring their directives. But ignorance aside—"

Tock paused, its head oscillating great stress. "They have taken out contracts on you—you and Roland Mackenzie. They want you both dead."

Zim sat upright. "Your sources tell you this?" She knew her rule breaking angered Abramyan, but this seemed unnecessary. She and Mac wanted to leave StarCom, cut all ties, and go as far away as possible.

"We have excellent sources," Tock chiggered, "totally reliable. You would be impressed. I trust you but cannot tell you more. I've seen what pidging does to Humans. Your brains are too easily accessed."

"Can you give me *some* details?"

"You are not to be allowed to return from this mission. Neither is Mackenzie from his. Your missions were contrived to get you away from Corydon and to conceal Star Council involvement."

"Who exactly?"

"Abramyan was mentioned, but someone else made the arrangements. Someone on the Star Council contacted the Rii-Chaut. Apparently, something major is about to happen. The timing is critical."

"I suspect it's related to the Council turning power over to the Creatives. The Rii-Chaut, huh. I'm sure they've infiltrated Messy's crew. Abramyan saw to that, possibly with Captain Woodson's help."

"Yes, *Marshal Massena's* entire crew is compromised. Trust no one you didn't bring with you. The Rii-Chaut are scavenger predators. They prey on stragglers and defenseless outposts. The few we encountered we swept aside like flirki. But in large numbers, against disabled craft—" Tock shrugged its claws and crunched the last bite of its Baakel.

"Thank you, Tock. You are the cruelest enemy and the dearest friend I know. I must warn Mac."

"It is too late for you to contact him. Port Estelle security requires all outside communication blocked twenty-four hours before a launch."

"Except I suspect the Rii-Chaut are getting regular reports of my activities."

"You may as well relax and enjoy your Baakel. We've passed the word. Others will contact Mackenzie." They lifted their glasses together.

Zim knew better than to ask about the 'others' Tock referred to. She'd adopted the Tak-Yaki matter-of-fact attitude toward death and risk-taking. It endeared her to them as much as it estranged her from Humans.

# # #

The squadron room had been converted to a Daka-Rye battlespace. Choo'kok and Kr'Rakat chose the teams and divided the inexperienced Humans between them: Hotz and Rob to one team, Dom and Chow to the other. Daka-Rye was played at several scales, from tactical solo matches across a table to massive fleet operations spanning star systems. The parlor version involved combatants maneuvering holograms in virtually enhanced space and shouting epithets, curses, and encouragement. Each side had several controls: one went to each of the Humans.

Hotz's reflexes surprised the Tak-Yaki, but her inexperience led to overcorrections and missed opportunities. Beside her, Rob was getting into the

188

game and slowly shedding his wariness—about Hotz, the rest of the team, their mission, and their alien hosts. In the heat of battle, the Tak-Yaki frequently forgot to use the translators, but the Humans quickly picked up on the battle chirps. *Girlik* when your sights aligned meant shoot, kill, excellent, or something like that. *Xhaki* was a warning, "Watch your six."

Dom had the knack. He was slower than Hotz but infallibly on target. Her speed looked inept next to his precision. Chow was the real surprise, an inveterate gamer with no combat experience, but Daka-Rye rewards both skills. Rob started clumsy but learned quickly. On the same team, he and Hotz worked well together.

Zim and Tock emerged from the back still deep in conversation. The gamers took a pause. Shouting dropped down. And Rob crossed the room to get drinks. Curious how the Humans were faring with the TY, Zim studied the interactions.

WHAM! The squadron room door blew off its frame and came skidding toward Zim. A dozen characters burst through the opening, followed by dozens more, a steady stream shouting and cursing. All carried edged weapons or bludgeons. They wore fragments of StarCom uniforms, open tunics, shirts or pants, and long hair, plaited or braided.

Ignoring the others, the attackers ran straight for Zim. She snapped into a defensive posture. The Daka-Rye gamers were to her right, Rob at the bar to her left. Dom shouted and sprinted to help him. He smashed one attacker's face with a game controller and twisted away his cutlass.

The Tak-Yaki rushed from the side of the room, a wave of blue and violet, filling the air with their shrill battle cry. Hotz and Chow ran with them. Several attackers turned to defend themselves and keep the path open to Zim. She recognized several from the hangar deck. Their leader flashed a broken-toothed grin.

Zim's mind cleared, her heart steadied like a racing machine shifted to high gear, and she saw the action in slow motion.

Tock sidestepped, letting a half dozen pirates pass toward her. Rolling its claws, it sent the next six to the ground, legless below the knees. Those behind fell over them, and Tock waded in, dismembering or gutting each adversary with its serrated claws and nanowire implants.

Zim backed between two translator pedestals, forcing her overzealous attackers to squeeze together to pass. With a wrist-twist, she took the toes off the boots of the first two. One stumbled and fell at her feet. His wild expression changed to fear before she thrust her fist into his face. The second pirate fell over his own bleeding feet, rolled to the side, and tried to crawl behind her. She sliced the tendons from his elbows.

As four pirates tripped over the first two, Zim stepped in, hammer-fisting two heads into the deck, round-kicking another, and chopping the neck of another. A pirate leaped onto the detached squadron-room door and drew a projectile weapon. She surgically removed the fingers holding the weapon, then lifted him off his feet with a forward kick to the center of his chest. An attacker lunged with a dagger. She rolled her hip away from the thrust, grabbed his wrist, and threw her body against his outstretched arm, snapping the elbow.

The Tak-Yaki wave swept unimpeded over the downed, squirming bodies, immediately halting the Rii-Chaut pouring through the doorway.

Zim looked left. Two Rii-Chaut had Rob's lanky frame pressed against the bar. He dodged their knife thrusts until he slipped on glass from a broken bottle.

"Got 'em," Dom yelled, slamming one of Rob's attackers off his feet with a backhand and crushing the throat of the other.

Dom pulled Rob up with a ham-sized fist and peered into his eyes. "Welcome to Science One's combat element. You're officially on the team." Rob blinked and nodded. Stepping from the bar, he scooped up a dropped knife and returned to battle. But it was over.

Panicked Rii-Chaut fell and were trampled trying to get back through the doorway. The Tak-Yaki pursued them, stilt-legs pumping, claws flashing. The last attackers jumped into the levitor and were instantly whisked away.

With the room cleared of attackers, the mantises set about their post-combat preening ritual. Like cats after devouring a morsel of prey, they stroked their angular faces with their massive clamp-claws, scrubbed, and licked themselves. Standing with them, Zim rubbed her forearms and hands along the sides of her face. Chow raised his brows then joined in, Dom and Hotz followed, and after a shrug, Rob, too.

"Very clumsy, very foolish," Tock clicked, surveying the shattered bodies. "You saw they came for you, Gayle. Next time they'll be smarter." She nodded. Tock called in disposal robots and activated the reactive deck against the blood-slicked floors.

Other than minor cuts and bruises, the only injury was a long gash on Chow's hand that ran to his elbow. Before Zim could treat it, a half-meter Hyrup centipede climbed onto him, licked the wound, stitched it with its mandibles, then, much to Chow's consternation, circled his hand and arm with a web bandage. Zim had lost track of the Hyrup during the battle. Now she recalled hearing they sometimes served as medics.

To Zim, this blatant attack signaled overconfidence. That could work to her advantage. As she and her team helped reset the squadron room, they discussed this and countering future attacks, but there was little time. They and the Tak-Yaki were both leaving Port Estelle tomorrow.

In the back of her mind, she envisioned Mac in similar circumstances, trapped and fighting alone, without her beside him. Surely, others would help him. Surely.

Captain Woodson

Woodson and Yardley watched the recording in stunned silence. The view was from just inside the squadron room door. The battle had taken forty seconds.

Woodson pointed steepled fingers to the projection. "This just happened?"

"Five minutes ago. I came right down."

"And it made sense to you? A bunch of Rii-Chaut rowdies going up against the Starflower and a squadron of Tak-Yaki veterans?" He pulled the neck closure on his uniform open.

Yardley buried his face in his shaking hands. "We thought we'd catch them by surprise. Ojai Khan's paying double for a quick kill."

"A whole Tak-Yaki squadron—"

Yardley yelled back. "I was in the merchant service… like you… see?" He pulled the front of his white tunic. "I'm a civil engineer. What do I know about Tak-Yaki? They're little guys, a dozen kilos at best. I thought we'd brush the buggies aside."

"Twelve kilos of leaping laser saws." Woodson gave a silent scream and pounded the sides of his head. "The recording is only from one angle."

"Taken from the doorway. It's the only recording that survived. Guess we got lucky—" Yardley instantly regretting his word choice.

"*Lucky*? That's lucky? What could be worse?" Woodson dry-coughed then tipped a full tumbler of bourbon into his mouth.

"Their counter-attack developed faster than our attack," Yardley said flatly. "Anyone who got three steps inside that doorway is still there. We had other sensors, but the entire Tak-Yaki ring is shielded against transmissions."

"TY keep tight security." Woodson looked at Yardley slumped over. "How many did we lose?"

"Sixty-seven. If we hadn't set the levitor for a quick retreat, we could've lost another forty. I don't think they lost any, but both scientists took a beating." Yardley stiffened. "The Tak-Yaki don't eat Humans, do they?"

"I don't know that they've ever fought Humans, but they have been known to eat captives. I guess it's fortunate no one—" Woodson paused. "All sixty-seven were killed, right? They didn't take any—"

"Probably six," Yardley groaned. "The Tak-Yaki killed everyone, but Zimmon only disabled her victims. She kept the leaders alive... probably for interrogation."

"So Zimmon knows we're involved or will soon." Woodson felt a chill rush up his sweat-drenched back.

"Not you, sir. I never told the Rii-Chaut you authorized them coming aboard. If those thugs were smarter, they'd guess you had to be involved."

"Zimmon's smarter."

Yardley nodded. "We might have a little time. Zimmon beat them badly. That should delay their interrogation."

"Good. Next time we'll—"

"Not with this crew." Yardley shook his head. "The ones who survived ran, and they're still running. Others took off when they heard. Most are still around the port, but you won't find them. I should be hiding, too. If Zimmon knows I set up the attack, she or one of her killer friends will pay me a visit."

"I understand," Woodson softened his tone, "but the Tak-Yaki leave Port Estelle early tomorrow. After that, all Zimmon has will be two clubs and two scientists. Your job should be easy." He gestured both hands up.

Yardley waved off Woodson's optimism. "No, no, no. Here, let me show you." He reset and magnified the projection to focus on Zim. "Watch her reaction to our surprise attack?" The scene restarted. Woodson's brows lifted.

"You see, Captain? You're confused because there *is no* reaction, no surprise, and no undue concern. From this encounter, I'd say Zimmon is more comfortable than she was talking with me over a glass of wine earlier."

He slowed the replay and touched Tock's image. "This Tak-Yaki... it's not protecting Zimmon. I'm no combat soldier, but I'd say it's clearing her field of fire. That's an orchestrated tactical maneuver." Yardley checked the timer on the display. "After we burst through the door, the Tak-Yaki's reaction took point zero, two seconds. That's a fast eye blink."

"Now this." He pointed to Zim. "She slides back between those two pedestals, forcing Karshki and Yago to crowd together. Then she picks them off." Yardley stole a glance at Woodson's face peering over the rim of a fresh tumbler of bourbon.

"Zimmon shows no terror, no fear, no hesitation," Yardley said. "Her moves are instant but not automatic. She adjusts to what's happening and controls it. It's as if *she* set this trap for us." He got a slow nod from Woodson. The scene progressed in slow motion. "Here it looks like she's playing with us. What sort of Human does that? It's as if she enjoys taking her attackers apart. See that expression." Yardley laced his fingers. "Cold. She's more Tak-Yaki than Human." He pointed to Zim standing over the wounded team leader and watching Tock wade in for its killing spree. "I can't deal with this."

"Okay." Woodson raked his fingers through his thinning hair. "We'll stand down on direct attacks at Port Estelle and finish Zimmon once we're out in space." He looked at Yardley. "Can you stick around at least until after launch?"

Yardley scratched his chin. "If you think it'll help set her up, I'll stay. But only for appearances. I'm keeping my distance."

"Don't you think you've gained *some* credibility with Zimmon? You two looked pretty chummy this morning."

"Until I saw this, I thought we got on rather well." He pointed to the slow motion of Zim pounding Karshki's face. "That's the same smile she flashed when I talked with her. I don't think she was ever fooled."

"Well then, that's it." Woodson sighed. "I have another appointment. You go back to your shuttle. Thanks for seeing this through."

"What choice do I have, do any Unders have?"

Woodson waited for Yardley to leave then stepped to the wall of pictures behind his desk. What choice do any of us have? His gaze fixed on his pretty wife holding their infant daughter beside their lake-side home, then on the promising young merchant officer who'd just made captain. A tear rolled down his cheek. They would never be innocent again. He ran a finger down the picture. After topping off his glass at the bourbon spigot, he returned to his desk, propped one elbow, and leaned his face into his hand.

Chirp, the communicator sounded. A blue-outlined box blinked on the desk, Marshal Boorman. Woodson straightened, slid the bourbon glass from view, and palmed the panel. The chiseled face of Star Command's ranking officer arose in front of his desk.

"Captain Woodson, I just arrived at Port Estelle. You know I'm assuming command of Star Fleet, including the research ships. Sorry about the lack of warning. This sector teems with hostiles, Rii-Chaut you know."

"Yes, sir, I know. Good to see you." Woodson forced a smile. He despised Boorman. "I thought you were arriving next week."

"It was my intention that you thought that. I like catching my officers unawares." A wolf-like grin crept across Boorman's face. "Are you all right, Captain? You don't look well."

"I'm very well, sir, just tired. We're launching tomorrow, you know." Woodson smiled to think he was sticking Boorman with his own rhetoric.

"Yes, I know. I wanted to ask how that was going."

Woodson mirrored Boorman's facile bonhomie. "Of course, sir. Was there anything that concerned you?" Like maybe the Starflower, you heavy-handed targ.

"Not at all, but Messy's our first conversion for scientific research. I'm a Four Creative, you know, a military man, and a little out of my element dealing with scientists. How are they taking to being in space?"

Yes, you're a Four Creative, and I'm a dishrag Under, so I'm supposed to kiss your exalted… "Yes, sir. They're all doing quite well. We've had a few pukers, but that's to be expected."

"Yes. We had a few in Basic."

"Were you planning to come aboard, sir? We're in final launch preps, but we'd be happy to entertain a visit from our commander." A little butter couldn't hurt.

"Not this trip. If I'm around when you get back, I'll call an inspection."

"Very well, sir. I look forward to that. Congratulations again on your promotion to Senior Marshal and your appointment to Star Fleet Command."

"Thank you, Captain." Boorman's toothy grin widened. "I am honored to be your superior." The projection closed.

Woodson shook his head. It was clear Boorman was calling a last-minute inspection. That courtesy call was to ascertain that *Marshal Massena* wasn't making an early departure. Being an overbearing ass was Boorman's idea of leadership. A micromanaging faultfinder, he caused problems then blamed his junior officers to keep them in line. Had he heard about the Rii-Chaut fiasco, the attack on the Tak-Yaki? Was he clued in on the plot to kill Zimmon?

Chirp. The blue communicator panel read, Star Leader Abramyan. The comms blackout obviously didn't extend to Star Council members. Woodson felt his gut tighten. He took a long pull of bourbon then slid it aside and raised the projection.

"Captain Woodson, I heard the team I sent was less than effective." Abramyan sounded detached. "I trust you've come up with a new plan to handle our problem?"

Woodson felt a flush of anger. Yardley hadn't included him on the Rii-Chaut attack plan, but he knew Abramyan would take any comment as an excuse.

"I'm afraid we only put Zimmon on her guard. We've moved back our timeline, a week at most. Once we're off station, away from Estelle, we'll have more options. Many of the port personnel are sympathetic to Commander Zimmon, and so are many on my crew. In space, we'll have fewer prying eyes."

Abramyan raised his eyebrows. "I wanted this done as quickly as possible, but you make a good point." He pressed his lips then continued, "You haven't inquired about your family."

Woodson's gaze dropped. "It is too painful."

"Your wife asks about you," Abramyan taunted, "almost as much as she asks about blankets and clothing for your dear daughter."

Woodson found it hard to breath. "I'd like to see them," he muttered.

"Certainly, Captain, you'll be joining them as soon as you take care of the problem." Abramyan's image faded and was replaced by a pale woman and her fourteen-year-old daughter hugging and shivering on a bench with their knees tucked. Their eyes were feral with exhaustion, their faces streaked with dirt.

Abramyan reappeared. "There's a big demand for fresh, young women in the camps. Your wife and daughter could soon be entertaining miners on some asteroid. Keep that in mind. Let me know when the job's done."

The projection closed.

Intruder Alert

"Who's on point?" Zim asked as they left the squadron room, a serious question since they had to consider themselves in a combat zone. She also saw it as a test and training opportunity. The 'point' person was the one out front, the scout trusted to identify dangers—or take the first hit in an ambush. Dom knew this drill well. Zim expected him to hold back until the others responded.

"Hotz," Chow said without hesitation. "She's quickest and sharp. Sees everything." Zim remembered Chow had faced Hotz in Daka-Rye.

Rob looked at Chow then at Hotz. "She's the natural choice, same reasons."

"Other opinions?" Hotz was inexperienced, but Zim saw this as necessary instruction. When Zim faced Dom, he smiled, aligning his dark eyes with hers. They were in sync. "Very well, Hotz."

Zim raised the Port Estelle schematic. They were on the TY ring, just above *Marshal Massena's* mooring. "We won't go back the way we came; that might lead us into an ambush. Instead, we go out two rings, cross through the hydroponics farm, take the emergency stairs down to the freight receiving dock, and hike back four kilometers. Everyone good?" Head nods all round.

Zim pointed two fingers to Hotz then ahead. She stepped away smartly. Dom followed. The two scientists went next, and Zim brought up the rear. They carried edged weapons they'd taken from the Rii-Chaut.

Hotz glided ahead soundless as a shadow, pausing at each blind turn, alcove, and possible concealment, and waved them forward when the path was clear.

After the long walk, meeting no resistance, they boarded *Marshal Massena* through a maintenance access port and took the stairs to the hangar deck. Tugs, tractors, and dollies stood unattended. The only sound was the echo of their boots on the hard deck. When Zim heard Chow's stomach growl, she chuckled. As expected, her team had not developed a taste for Tak-Yaki hors d'oeuvres.

A sleepy sentry pulled erect as they approached Science One. Across the bay, technicians and engineers were running final checks on other shuttles, making ready for tomorrow's launch.

"Welcome home, Commander." Brownie greeted in her warm maternal voice. "I trust you had a pleasant ceremony." Dom and Hotz peeled off their formal uniforms and stepped into maintenance coveralls. Chow sat on his low bunk without changing. Rob climbed onto the upper, rolled to his back, and stared at the overhead.

"The ceremony went very well, Brownie," Zim said, leaning one arm against the hatchway. "No one on our team was killed. Do you have your med kit?"

Brownie's voice lost its lilt. "I have a full emergency station, everything up through minor surgery." A light beam illuminated the closet beside the galley.

"Dom and I are certified emergency medics," Hotz said, checking Rob. "Any other cuts or scrapes?"

"Ribs are tender," Rob said. "Lots of bruises. That's all, thanks to Dom." He rolled his face over on his bunk and gave Dom an informal salute, which Dom returned. Hotz moved to Chow.

"I'm fine." Chow rotated his arm and flexed his hand. "No pain, no bleeding, and I have full motion. Those Hyrup licks and sutures worked wonders. I almost panicked when those centipedes crawled on me. I thought they were coming to suck my blood." He laughed.

Zim slipped off her tunic. "Brownie, any action on this side of the port?"

"Yes, Commander, we had another sabotage attempt."

Zim paused then continued climbing out of her formal trousers. "You have a recording?" A hologram view from the shuttle bow bloomed above the table. Dom and Hotz pulled up, Chow and Rob beside them.

"Play it." Zim finished sealing her service uniform. Across the shuttle bay, a heavy-set figure in coveralls crept from the shadows between the Science Two shuttles. Seeing the sentry, it crouched. The sentry dipped his head then turned away, and the figure slipped quickly across the open space. The scene switched to a closer view from behind the nose gear. Pulling a flat, palm-sized plate from its coveralls, the figure reached behind the nose gear. An inside view from the gear bay showed the plate pressed and adhering seamlessly to the metal surface.

When the figure looked close to check the attachment, Zim recognized Spacer Kimbri, the woman she had ordered to clean the blood after that morning's attack. "Trust no one you didn't bring with you," she whispered, remembering Tock's words. She wished sometime her caution would be proven wrong. While Kimbri dashed back across the hangar bay, the sentry's eyes remained away.

"Can you enhance the far side view?" Zim asked. "I want to see in the shadow." The scene magnified and adjusted tone, turning black into shades of gray. A hatch opened on one of the shuttles, Kimbri climbed in, and a middle-aged man in merchant whites looked out. Yardley. Another disappointment.

The projection ended, and everyone sat back. "What do we have under our bow?" Zim asked. "A bomb?"

"My sensors don't register bomb signatures," Brownie said, "not an active one anyway."

"A beacon?" Dom suggested. "To tag us for their weapons."

"It's not emitting a signal, but a ranger or accelerometer could switch one on after we launch."

Zim nodded. "Thanks, Brownie. Anyone have demolition expertise… in case it's booby-trapped?"

"I saw a lotta this," Dom said, looking around the table. "Everyone needs to vacate. If it's a bomb or there's a bomb attached, it might not like me pulling it off."

Zim nodded. "Let's do this discreetly. I don't want to tip them off that we're onto their plot. Chow, Rob, may I buy two scientists a beverage at the Happier Times O-Club?"

Chow smiled, "Certainly, Commander. How about some Human-edible food to go with that?"

Rob glanced at Chow and the others. "If that's how it is, sure, I could use a drink and some honest nourishment."

"And us common folk?" Hotz looked perplexed.

"You are welcome to join us, but first I need someone to play cute young thing with that sentry so Dom can do a little clandestine bomb removal." Zim pretended to look around for someone else.

"I'm your girl," Hotz said, followed by a schoolgirl giggle. Everyone chuckled. Hotz pulled a tool from the maintenance closet and handed it to Dom. "You'll want this. I used it to check the hull. The reverse setting releases magnetic seams. Might keep the plate from triggering." Dom slipped it into his pocket.

"Questions? Everyone clear?" They all smiled. Zim pointed to Chow and Rob, then out the hatch toward the levitor.

Turnabout

Dom exited the shuttle, head bristling with pull-down instruments and sensors. He shouted loud enough for the sentry to hear. "Hotz, don't stay too long at the club, I might need some help on the motor." He disappeared to the rear of the shuttle.

She appeared in the hatchway, sheathed in her most distracting black outfit. "Happy hunting, young lady," Brownie said.

Hotz skipped past the sentry, tossed her white-blond hair, turned, and flashed a wide smile. Caught ogling, the sentry jerked his eyes forward. "Excuse me," Hotz said, walking back. "Did the Commander and two scientists pass you?"

"Yes, sir." He cracked a smile. "They took the levitor less than a minute ago. All but the big guy back there, working on the engines."

Hotz pulled open the edge of her neckline. "I'm not in uniform right now, so you don't have to 'sir' me."

"No, Ma'am."

Over the sentry's shoulder, Hotz saw Dom under the shuttle hull, applying the magnetic seam tool. A plate came loose. He caught it before it clattered to the deck.

"When do you get relieved?" Hotz asked. "Maybe you could join us at the O-Club on the G-Ring." She touched her tongue to her front teeth and smiled. Dom had just climbed the last rung of the steps and disappeared into the shuttle.

"Spacer grades aren't permitted in the O-Club, Ma'am." He rolled his lips together.

"Oh, I wouldn't want to get you into any trouble." She finger-waved goodbye and dashed to the levitor.

# # #

Dom used Brownie's magnified projection to examine the underside and interior of the removed plate cover. "Doesn't look like any kind of bomb. Your sensors tell you anything?"

Brownie rotated the projection. "No explosives chemistry and no pulse or E-Mag generators, no triggering circuitry of any kind, not even imbedded. That's not my expertise area, but my sensors would pick up *something*. What is this?" A light finger pointed.

"A short-range antenna," Dom said, "but there's no tuner or any way to modulate a signal." While he mulled over the problem, Zim stepped through the hatch followed by the rest of the team. Chow headed for his bunk. Rob dropped a ham and cheese sandwich beside Dom, took a seat at the table, and studied the device. Zim and Hotz stood beside them.

"Not a bomb?" Zim asked. Dom and Rob both shook their heads.

"It has a very short-range antenna," Rob said, looking where Dom pointed.

"How short?" Zim asked.

"Ten meters, twenty at most. It appears intended to communicate with something aboard this shuttle." Rob pointed to an embedded thread in the projection. "That's an instruction circuit." He pressed his palms and fingers together as if in prayer and touched them to his nose. "Brownie, can you generate an identification query *inside* the hull?"

"Yes, but they're intended to identify hostile spacecraft."

"Would you do that for us, please?" Rob drew his pressed fingers down to his chin. Zim stood quiet, observing this side of Rob.

The plate device clicked.

"Interesting," Brownie said.

"Please share." Rob sounded elated.

"When I requested identification, that device corrupted my transponder response."

Rob's eyebrows shot up. "Which would lead our shuttle to be identified as—" He obviously enjoyed his Sherlock Holmes moment.

"As a Rii-Chaut ship," Brownie said.

Hotz laughed. "So, if our shuttle leaves *Marshal Massena* and returns, we'll be mistaken for pirates, and the defense shield will fire on us automatically."

"And it'll look like an accident." Chow chimed in from his bunk.

Rob lifted an open hand to Hotz then to Chow. Hotz hugged his head. Dom slapped him on the back.

"Good work," Zim said. "Now, I assume they don't know that we know this. So how can we turn it to our advantage?"

Dom chuckled. "We attach the device to the Science Two shuttle across the hangar deck." Everyone snickered.

Zim made eye contact with each of them around the table. "Excellent. We'll need another diversion." She looked at Dom. "When are we scheduled in maintenance bay?"

"Any time. We were last on the schedule, so the bay is open. I can grab a tractor and take us over."

"Do it. Hotz, keep that black outfit on and find something to hide your white hair. You'll be working in the shadows. Rob, put that device back together. Brownie, do you have a portable monitor? I want to record this op. Chow, set it up to watch the shuttle across the bay."

# # #

Two hours later, they gathered to critique their operation. Zim poured everyone a shot of Kentucky bourbon. They clicked glasses and sat back.

The recording began with Dom on the tractor, pulling the shuttle out of their slot and down to maintenance bay. The open space gave a clear view of the Science Two parking area. An inset tracked the movement of the sentry.

"This is a post-op mission assessment," Zim said. "I want to know if anyone spotted Hotz or took any special interest in our departure. If you see something, speak up."

Brownie adjusted the gray scale for the shadow between the shuttles. Nothing happened for several minutes. Then a spidery form slid over the low bulkhead separating the parking areas. Hotz crept midway along the shuttle hull then crouched low. She ran a hand underneath, pressed upward, checked the magnetic seal then withdrew, graceful and quiet as smoke.

"That was exciting," Dom said, giving Hotz a quizzical look. "Didn't know you could be so sneaky." Rob squeezed her arm. Chow gave her a Tak-Yaki shoulder pinch.

Zim smiled. "That's how a good operation looks, folks. No excitement. Anyone catch anything? Any reaction from the sentry? Brownie, any sign of detection?"

"No, Commander, no detector surges, not even a switch spark. I think it's a clean get away."

"Good but stay alert. If our enemy thinks we're sabotaged, they may lay off for a while, but we can't count on that. Dom, the shuttle ready?"

"Yes, Commander. All the work's done. Nan-techs reinforced twenty-six weak nodes. This old girl's been in the field forty years. They gave us the oldest bucket—"

"Watch your mouth," Brownie interrupted. "I've taken a few licks, but I'll be kicking around this galaxy when you're feeding worms."

"Sorry," Dom said, wincing. "I forget how sensitive you girls can be about your age. I'll check into getting you a new chassis when we get back."

"A new wardrobe? I've heard that before, big boy. Don't expect it'll get you any favors."

"O—kay," Zim interrupted. "Sounds like we're set." She felt a tingle and checked her palm. It was from Captain Woodson. She relayed the message to her team.

"Slight change of plans. Tomorrow we stand for inspection, service dress, out front here at 0400. Star Fleet Commander Marshal Derek Boorman is honoring us with a visit. That's all. Dismissed. Oh, if anyone's still hungry, I have some Baakel left from the TY ceremony." She set her satchel on the table but only got side glances.

Dom stripped off his coveralls. Chow rolled into his bunk. Rob threw his thin arms up to protest the inspection then pulled them down and followed Chow to his bunk. Hotz stood silent with her head low. When Zim noticed, Hotz lifted her chin, smiled weakly, and retired to her bunk. What was bothering Hotz?

Zim selected one of the Baakel and took a deep breath. So old Hothead Boorman was coming to see her off. Was he in on the sabotage plot? Maybe he wanted to see her one last time. She'd take care to not irritate him. She didn't want her team to suffer for her indiscretions.

# # #

Next morning at 0400, twelve guards of Marshal Boorman's escort marched from the levitor in slow cadence. As each pair of guardsmen stopped and pivoted, the next pair stepped past them and pivoted, and so it continued until they formed a corridor six-pairs-long. Boorman emerged to walk between the guards, his dress uniform aglitter with multicolored disks, stars, and ribbons.

He looked much as Zim remembered, solid and well-formed, but artificial compared to combat-hardened Dom, who sported more battle scars than ribbons. Captain Woodson walked beside Boorman. Behind them came an entourage of staffers and aides—Creatives all. Their expressions and postures reflected discomfort and disdain—perhaps for the early hour or for the unfamiliar stench of ozone, lubricants, and stale sweat common to aging, military hangars.

Marshal Massena's thirty shuttles, six squadrons of five, were lined up in two rows of fifteen with flight crews and scientists out front. Zim's team was last in line.

Boorman walked slowly, first to one side then to the other, stopping for each squadron. He occasionally spoke to a squadron leader or shuttle commander. Twice he called aides forward with presentation cases, read a citation, and pinned a medal on an officer followed by an exchange of salutes. Eyes forward, Zim followed the action in her peripheral vision.

"Commander Gayle Zimmon," Boorman declared loudly in a show of pleasure. "She's your combat team leader?" He looked to Captain Woodson at his shoulder.

"Yes, Senior Marshal." Woodson kept his voice and expression flat.

"Excellent choice." Boorman nodded and smiled, apparently trying to make their meeting as natural as possible. "The Starflower has a brilliant war record and is a first-rate combat officer—as well I know." He turned to catch Woodson's reaction—none—then gazed at Zim directly. "You're looking good, Commander, just as I remember you from Basic."

"Thank you, Senior Marshal. I was thinking the same of you. We kept each other on our toes, didn't we?"

"Indeed, we did. Indeed, we did." Boorman stepped past Zim then stopped in front of Dom. The sinewy combat engineer stood half a head taller than he. Boorman swallowed hard and quickly stepped to face Hotz. There, his smile melted, and his hand twitched at his side. "You, ahh. I—"

"You look well, Senior Marshal." Hotz's voice was firm and steady. "Better than the last time we met." She flashed a snake-eyed smile. Zim suddenly connected Hotz's words with the redacted record Hippelli had shown her. For everyone's sake, she hoped Hotz would not say or do anything more.

Boorman's leg buckled. Woodson started to catch him then stopped when the Senior Marshal recovered. Boorman corrected his posture and stepped down the line. Chow's almond eyes, gentle smile, and round cheeks did nothing to calm Boorman. Facing Rob, he got the same cool reaction with a little defiance, no fear, and no hesitation. If Boorman hoped to intimidate them, it hadn't worked.

"Your team looks a little ragged, Commander," Boorman called back.

"We've only just come together, Senior Marshal. But if you'd like to test them, I'll match my team against any team you care to name." Zim wasn't as confident as she tried to sound, but Boorman had never beaten her, and his comment called for a bluff. Besides, her team had performed well, and she wanted them to hear how proud she was of them.

Boorman told Woodson he was pleased with the review and walked to the levitor. Woodson cast a smile back at Zim. Though she didn't trust him, she could only imagine what it must be like babysitting that cranky toy soldier.

Outbound

Marshal Massena's internal systems spun up, taking over from dockyard services. Loading ramps lifted and swung away, circulation ducts disengaged from airlocks, and power lines reeled back in their housings. A shudder ran through the starship hull as magnetic cradles released and the E-Mag tractor accelerated them out into the cold of deep space.

Zim and her team sat in an entropy-stabilized compartment for hyper-acceleration: Zim with Dom, Hotz with Rob, and Chow behind them.

"How we doin'?" Dom asked under his breath. Zim knew the question was a combat team leader's trained reflex—to judge mental states in stressful conditions.

"More problems than expected," she said without lifting or turning her head. "But our team is adjusting. Ask me again after we complete our first mission. You know, when the war ended, I thought we'd all just ease into retirement."

"Ain't gonna happen," he said. They both chuckled.

"I suppose it would have felt strange retiring. For you too, I think."

Dom nodded. "Spacin's all I know."

"We have our mission and a team to keep together—plus some obstacles I hadn't anticipated."

"You mean the scientists?"

"They add a new dimension, but I have other concerns."

"That Prophecy thing? I don't understand it, but I think we're deep into it."

Zim gave a silent whistle. Dom had raised her unasked question. If he was aware, that meant Hotz was too, probably Chow, maybe Rob. Good. They were still with her.

No one else spoke before the Myseko skip, which gave Zim almost an hour to sort her thoughts. Seeing Tock, the Tak-Yaki ceremony, even the rumble with the Rii-Chaut brigands had felt normal, too normal. That troubled her. Re-entering that world had been too easy. She wanted to belong to Mac in his world—strong, courageous, optimistic Mac, her link to sanity.

Captain Woodson had posted changes to *Marshal Massena's* mission plan. Joon and Santo Rift were off the schedule. Instead, they were headed to Myndus. There were no Human colonies in that sector, and no battles had been fought there. Technically, it remained in Aldrakin space, so landings were prohibited. Would Woodson respect that? She shook her head.

The mission brief was scheduled right after the Myseko skip. Time to go to work.

# # #

Captain Woodson took the podium. Everyone scrambled to their seats. Zim sat on the center aisle, halfway back. Woodson looked past her.

"Any problems launching from Port Estelle or the Myseko skip?" He scanned the group. "Then on to business. This is the first science mission we've supported with one of our modified carriers. We're still shaking down procedures, so expect a few glitches.

"Our first stop will be Myndus. Anyone familiar with the system? No. I'm not surprised. We may be the first Human visitors." He looked to the back of the room. "But I'm just a ship driver. So, before I get in over my head, let me introduce our Chief Mission Officer. She's running all the science operations."

An elegant, coffee-cream-complexioned Creative walked up the center aisle to replace Woodson on the podium. "We have scientific and military interests in this system." She pointed to a projection. "Myndus is a GV-type star, an orange-yellow dwarf slightly cooler and smaller than our yellow suns. Millennia ago, a wandering neutron star tore the system apart, leaving only the planet Okean intact." Blue ellipses appeared in the star projection. "This elongated orbit is Okean, these debris rings are all that remains of the other planets. Our teams will take samples and insert monitoring sensors. In case we encounter any spores or encysted life forms, all teams are required to maintain standard decontamination protocol." She looked around. "Any questions?"

"What's Okean like?" The question came from an officer in front wearing merchant whites.

The CMO gestured magnifying a featureless white spot. "Okean is a water planet with no landmasses—estimated depth seven kilometers. The oceans are frozen most of the year, thawing only when Okean nears Myndus. Then surface temperature soars to the level of a steam autoclave. Since the atmosphere has an elevated free-oxygen content, the Authoriton predicts a high probability that we will find life forms—probably simple photosynthetic and scavenging organisms that spring to life during the short summers."

"Are we sending a team to Okean?" asked the same officer.

"Okean is why we changed the mission schedule. The planet is transitioning from extreme cold to extreme heat, a rare temperate zone. We hope to find the ocean ice-free, which will enable us to drop sensors below the surface.

"We won't be landing, however. Okean's surface winds would rip a shuttle to pieces. There's also a storm surge that sweeps kilometer-high waves around the planet at all latitudes. Our sensor drops will be from low orbit and well above the weather."

"You say we have military interests?" Zim asked.

"Yes, Commander Zimmon." The CMO locked eyes with her. "Although we see no strategic value in the system, the Aldrakin made it a priority in the treaty you signed. We're not sure why. They have no outposts there, and Okean harbors only simple life forms. Their interest raised our curiosity. Anything else?" Woodson joined the CMO at the podium.

"Details on your assignments are in your squadron packets," he said. "I set our course to intersect each of the debris rings, ending with planet Okean. Commander Kagel will lead the first shuttle for Science Six. We'll finish with Commander Zimmon leading the last shuttle for Science One over Okean."

Woodson cleared his throat. "After the last shuttle drop, *Marshal Massena* will return to high orbit and await confirmation of sensor insertions. Once we receive that, we'll recover the shuttle teams on our way out of the Myndus system." He scanned the room. "If there are no further questions, I wish you all well. Squadron Six, you deploy first. Get a good night's rest."

Part Five

Okean

Planetfall

Dom gave a thumbs-up. Hotz acknowledged. Zim pressed *GO*, and the catapult light switched to green. *Vvvvooooook*, the E-Mag accelerated the shuttle out the launch bay and into space.

Okean's storm-swept disk filled the wraparound projection. They were to descend to low orbit and distribute a string of eight monitoring sensors. On striking the ocean surface, each sensor was to submerge to a preset depth, deploy its antenna, and signal operational status. If no signal was received, the shuttle was to deploy a backup. Once eight sensors confirmed operational deployment, the shuttle would return to high orbit for pickup.

"Okean is almost through Myndus' temperate zone," Rob said, monitoring the planetary scanner. He was more talkative than usual. "We should find some ocean areas thawed. In two weeks, Okean will enter the torrid-zone and become an inferno. We came at a good time."

"Thank you, Rob," Brownie said with a lilt. "I don't often get the details."

Hotz's eyes hopped between the planet projection and multiple gauges in the heads-up display. Zim checked the others over her shoulder. Everything looked good. Chow sat wide-eyed, riveted. After the long wait before his umpteenth catapult launch, Dom yawned and blinked away bleary eyes.

"Soon as we cross the flight path, line us up," Zim directed.

"Aye, Commander," Hotz said. "Dropping to two-eight-two-point-two kilometers on heading two-two-five. We'll align on the first drop point in twenty-two minutes."

"Carry on. Dom, how's engineering look?"

"Excellent, Commander, full power on main engines and maneuver thrusters, no irregularities."

"Brownie, how are your internal readings."

"All systems operating within parameters."

Twenty minutes later, the shuttle dipped into a steady glide. "Ready the first sensor."

"Aye, Commander. Ready," Dom said. On the operations monitor, Zim saw an icon for the sensor feed into the ramp display.

"Away," Zim ordered.

"Away," Dom responded, and the icon ejected on the display. The shuttle's stern rocked then rebalanced for the weight loss.

"Ready two," Zim called. "Away." She repeated the order for the eight sensors.

"Confirmation signals?" Zim asked, checking the time.

"Not yet, Commander," Brownie answered. Ninety seconds ticked by.

"Brownie?"

"No, Commander, no confirmed deployments."

"Okay. Reset course for the alternate target area."

"Aye, Commander," Hotz said. "Resetting to heading two-seven-three."

"Dom, backup sensors?"

"Eight backups ready to deploy, Commander."

"Brownie, still no signals?"

"No, Commander."

"Are the other Okean shuttles having sensor problems?"

"I detect no sensor signals, but no problems report—" Brownie cut herself off. "Commander, an Aldrakin fighter is approaching our stern on an intercept course. It just illuminated us for targeting."

"Brownie, open comm. Aldrakin fighter, this is Starflower, aboard Science One shuttle—" The shuttle bucked. *Zzzhhiiit, Zzzhhiiit, Zzzhhiiit*, the alarm screamed. "*What the*—That targ-brain shot us. Hotz—"

She reacted before Zim finished the order, putting the shuttle into a corkscrew dive into Okean's thin exosphere. The crew clung, slid, and bounced, their senses straining against the spin. Belts reeled everyone back, conforming seats gripped them in place.

"Lost two starboard maneuver thrusters and all starboard landing struts," Dom said calmly.

"The Aldrakin's lining up for another pass," Brownie said.

Hotz threw the shuttle into a diving yaw, fighting against the lost thrusters, then pulled up and reversed their spin. The attacking fighter overshot and disappeared.

"The Aldrakin fighter has left Okean and is headed out of the system," Brownie said.

Hotz shouted, "Overpowered, targ-licking, fighter jock. Can't hump a one-legged shuttle?" She thrust her chin up then struggled to reset their flight path on the horizon.

Everyone stared. This was their first experience with "Hotshot" Bahrke's flying, and, except for Dom, they'd never heard the pixie-faced blond shout obscenities.

The dive took them out of the sun's glare, down into Okean's shadow. The planet's cloudy atmosphere on the wraparound monitor switched to starlight glow.

"Damage assessment," Zim called.

"We're goin' down, Commander," Dom said matter-of-factly. "Shuttle's got no shields, no backups. Only takes one near hit. If we survive a landing, I might be able to rig some repairs." He reset the pumps to direct all fuel flow to the remaining thrusters. "Might buy us a little landing time." Hotz read the gauges and nodded, straining to keep the shuttle from rolling with the unbalanced thrust.

Zim raised the emergency channel. "*Marshal Massena*, this is Starflower. Science One, Combat Element Five took a hit from an Aldrakin fighter. We're going down... request immediate low altitude recovery... landing opportunities doubtful." No response came. They were still above the weather but falling fast. Zim recalled the CMO's warning about transonic winds. "Rob, any break in the storm down there?"

"No break, but the meteorology profile indicates cyclonic activity near the equator. If Hotz can put us on that track, we might find a storm with a calm eye." Rob rechecked the data. "If it's big enough, maybe open water."

"Hotz," Zim called. "How's it holding?"

"Pulling hard to port," she said, sweat streaming off her brow and temples as she fought the jerking shuttle. "I'll try to keep us bouncing off the storm. If we drop too soon," she pointed to the roiling turbulence, "it will rip us apart. See that, on the horizon, what looks like rapids flowing in a river. We need to get over it. I'm trying to ride one of the cross currents to get us some lift. If we start spinning—" she shrugged. "Any more push you can give me?"

"It's all you, sweet cakes," Dom said. "Everything's switched over to power and maneuver."

215

Hotz nodded. "Okay, thanks. See that rise, I'm going to surf it." She pulled the nose up, got a bump, climbed then leveled and fell again. Hotz pulled harder to port, fighting to keep the shuttle faced into the wind. It bucked, cleared the leading edge of the front, then leveled and dropped quickly. Abruptly, their view brightened: They were under a clear sky in daylight.

"Welcome to the eye of the storm." Rob sounded victorious. "That sudden drop was caused by the low air pressure."

"Thanks, Rob," Zim said. "Any idea how large this eye might be?"

"Okean follows the standard model, three thousand kilometers. We're on the trailing edge just ahead of the surge."

"Hotz, try to get us to the leading edge, as far from the surge as possible. That'll give the rescue team a little time."

"Aye, Commander."

"Any dry land?" Dom asked.

"Quiet," Zim barked. "Rob, any landforms?"

"No land, but I'm getting some interesting density readings. The surface is fluid but not water. It might—"

"Algae," Chow interrupted. "We're over an island of algae—not algae exactly but something similar. My display shows mats of the stuff forming everywhere."

"Solid enough to land on?" Zim asked.

"Possibly."

"I don't think we have an alternative. Otherwise, we have to ditch in the water. Rob, if we land, how long before the eye catches up and we're back in the storm?"

"If we get to the far edge of the eye, eighteen maybe twenty hours. After that we all get power washed. It'll be quick—"

"Thanks," Zim cut him off. "We'll be out before that." She glanced at Hotz bouncing and rocking to squeeze every meter of their altitude.

Zim called up the emergency comm link. "*Marshal Massena*, this is Starflower on Science One, Combat Element Five, requesting immediate rescue. Lock on these coordinates. We're damaged, attempting a forced landing."

"Starflower, this is *Marshal Massena*." The young male gave no name or rank. "You are in violation of our neutrality agreement with the Aldrakin.

Landing on Okean is not authorized. You are to complete your scientific mission and return immediately to high orbit for pick up."

Zim kept her voice level. "We have an emergency… ah, spacer. Check the final section of the neutrality agreement. It clearly lists such problems as exceptions."

"Sorry, I don't have that information."

"I'm not asking. I'm giving you that information," Zim said firmly.

"Roger, Starflower. I'll check with the Captain." The link cut off.

"According to our rate of descent, we'll be down in fourteen minutes," Hotz said. Her arms, shoulders, and head juddered with the controls.

"Okay, get us as close to the rim as possible," Zim said. "Brownie, in case we sink on touchdown, kick out the survival pods first. Dom, pull the comm package on your way out. Everyone else, if the algae won't hold up the shuttle, bail out. If we have time before we sink, pull all the survival gear then whatever we can salvage."

Unable to think of anything else, Zim sat back and felt the jerking, rollercoaster ride. Could she have avoided this? If it was a trap, she'd walked right into it and brought her team with her. She had never refused an assignment. Abramyan knew that. Maybe she had made it too easy. But even now, something about this felt like an open door. Was it because she was ready to die? How many times had she asked that?

Zim glanced at Hotz, intent at the controls, and everyone else strapped in. Their expressions looked no more fearful than adults enduring an amusement park ride. Boorman had called them ragged. True enough. They were all castoffs. So was she. Because of that, they'd been affordable. Was there a better pilot than Hotz or engineer than Dom? Not for this mission. Rob and Chow seemed like exactly the right scientists. Abramyan and the Star Council had underestimated them. Would that matter?

"Prepare for touch down," Hotz said. Banking away from the missing landing struts was like trying to land on one ski. She cut forward power, pulled the nose up, and aligned their path with a rise in the algae bed. The portside struts sliced the surface, dragging the shuttle around sharply. Hotz fought the torque with the maneuver thrusters, reducing the spin to an arc that ended in a sliding stop. The shuttle listed to port and settled but remained afloat. Clouds of steam hissed and boiled around the hull from the overheated thrusters.

"Excellent job, Hotz." Zim said, pressing the seat release. "Everyone okay?"

"Great landing, honey legs." Dom beamed with pride for her.

"Fine here, too," Rob said, prying his hands from the armrest. Chow threw his head back, inhaled deeply, and said, "Yah, we're good."

"Brownie, what's it like out there?" Zim asked.

"We're unstable and sinking, but we have a few hours. We should be able to walk on the surface. It'll be wet. Ambient temperature is sixteen degrees centigrade, a little cool. Oxygen is twenty-eight-point-oh-three percent. My sensors pick up no toxic gases, so it should be safe to breathe."

"Be careful," Zim said, "with the oxygen level that high, we don't want anyone hyperventilating—and no fires. They'd go up like a torch." She whirled around to Dom.

"After you pull the comm suite, check the engines. Even if we can't get back to orbit, if we can restart, we might be able to stay ahead of the storm."

Zim engaged the eyes of each member of her team, "Grab your gear. Let's check out Okean." She released the hatch lock and led them down the ramp.

Eye of the Storm

The howling wall of gray wind and water stung Zim's face with bullets of spray. Not fifty meters from her, the undulating waterfall receded into the mist. In the trail of the storm's retreating edge, green fibers reached up to mesh and extend the algae mat that supported Zim and her team.

"Twelve hundred kilometers per hour," Rob shouted over the roar. Zim nodded. She lifted her boot against the sucking ooze. The depression filled with water, then rising algae quickly erased her footprint.

She walked back toward the slow-sinking shuttle. The starboard side was blackened metal, the broken landing struts submerged. Viscous bubbles boiled up around the hull.

Dom had pulled the engine access plates and was checking the damage.

"Any hope?" Zim cupped her hands around Dom's ear.

He shook his head. "Starboard circuits are fused. My power shift overloaded and melted the port thrusters."

"So, we're in salvage mode," she said, her voice lost in the rushing wind. Zim shrugged. Dom didn't need a foreman; he was a foreman.

He pulled two undamaged hull plates then set them concave side up on a rise in the algae base. As he went back for more, Hotz and Chow stacked equipment and supplies on the plates.

While the others pulled gear, Zim and Rob surveyed the perimeter. They bounced as they walked. Each step sent waves across the green carpet and circles rippling in the pools. Zim barely felt the higher gravity, 1.1G. She took a deep breath and coughed. Swamp stench rose quickly behind the storm, and the oxygen-rich air made her head swim.

Myndus, Okean's sun, stood blood red in the clearing, rose-colored sky. "How long is the Okean day?" She raised her voice against the rapidly diminishing roar.

"Less than ten hours," Rob said. "So, daylight's only five. It'll be dark soon."

"And the storm will be back in eighteen hours?"

"Maybe twenty, the size of the eye changes."

Zim waved everyone in. "We need to set camp. How much more can we get off the shuttle?"

"We have all the emergency supplies and equipment," Dom said. "I pulled the comm package, but we should get the weapons and data files."

"How about Brownie?" Zim asked. Dom patted the bulge in his jacket. "Good. Let's take a transmitter off one of the backup sensors. They've got longer range than the shuttle's comm." Dom flashed a good-idea smile. "Hotz, you pull the sensor transmitter. Dom, take the lead on camp setup. Give us a good light. It's gonna get dark. Rob and Chow, get the weapons, computer files, and anything that looks useful, then help Dom."

They set camp fifty meters from the half-submerged shuttle. Dom raised a telescoping pole in the center for lights and surrounded it with access plates to make dry spaces for their sleeping pods. Other access plates held shipping containers, communication and medical stations, research stations for Chow and Rob, and general supply storage for food, water, weapons, and tools. The camp was roughly circular, twenty meters across.

"What a beautiful place," Zim said, seeing her team slumped against the containers. "We're tired now, but someday you'll recall this adventure." She lifted a hand skyward, to the east where the sky was clear then west where the last signs of the storm receded. The air was still. Myndus, already low in the west, sent magenta fingers creeping into the indigo sky. "*Marshal Massena* has our location. A team will be here shortly, but they'll probably wait until next orbit, catch us after sunrise. Rob, how long do we have?"

"Six hours to the next sunrise, fourteen to sixteen before the storm returns."

Zim smiled. "We have a lot of time and plenty of food and water. Get something to eat and a little rest. I want everyone sharp tomorrow." She kicked the beer-yellow tide pool then scraped off the worms and tentacles that clung to her boot. "And no one wanders off."

When they broke, Dom pulled over a large panel for Zim's pod, bedding, and belongings. Hotz worked the latch on the supply containers. Rob and Chow set up research stations and checked their instruments.

Zim kneeled beside Rob and spoke low. "What is Okean's sea level?"

"I think what you're asking is how far we are below sea level. A hundred and seventy-five meters," Rob whispered. "The wind creates a cyclonic well that holds the water back." He gave her a grim look. "Everyone appreciates what you're doing, but no one believes Messy will send anyone down for us. We know we're on our own."

An explosion of bubbles and stressing metal caught their attention. Dom tilted one of the pole lights, and everyone watched the shuttle roll and slide under the algae.

"Ouch, targ you," Chow shouted, jerking up from a pool where he was collecting samples. A wriggling, fourteen-centimeter flatworm clung to his hand. Unperturbed, Chow walked to his improvised lab, extracted a sample bag with his free hand, and pried the worm into it. Zim checked his hand and his eyes then asked a couple questions. Hotz administered first aid and took a blood sample for toxins.

The Okean day ended soon after Myndus dipped below the horizon, the sun replaced by a dazzling field of stars in a black velvet sky. The camp's central light illuminated eight meters out from the pole, barely reaching the furthest hull plates. Beyond it, everything under the stars was ink black.

"Got something on the comm," Dom said in a low voice. Zim stepped beside him. "*Marshal Massena* won't respond to us, but they sent a signal." He replayed the message. "Alert, alert, *Marshal Massena* recalling all shuttles and ordering an instant departure from Myndus. We are under attack. Two shuttle teams destroyed. No survivors. Remaining shuttles return to high orbit immediately for recovery." The message repeated.

"Signal's gettin' weaker," Dom said, "so Messy's left orbit. They're pickin' up our distress signal all right, but—" Everyone stared at him.

"Keep signaling our position," Zim said after a pause. "Maybe someone will pick it up. If it was an Aldrakin who attacked us, it must have been a mistake. Even so, our chances of negotiating with them are better than with the storm."

Dom set their distress signal for the widest distribution on all channels and on constant repeat. Chow returned to the makeshift lab to study his flatworm. Hotz and Rob distributed sim-meals and hot coffee then sat together to eat and talk.

Stepping from the cone of camp light, Zim looked to the eastern horizon, discernible only as the line where stars vanished. She strained but could not hear the roar of the approaching storm, only occasional bursts of bubbles from the submerged shuttle and splashes from creatures mating or fighting in the algae pools.

Chow, Dom, and Zim soon retired to their pods to sleep. Hotz and Rob remained awake, whispering into the night.

Fear the Night

"Get off me, you maggot," Hotz shouted and slapped her thigh. "Something's crawling up my leg." Dom and Zim jumped over to her. Chow punched up the floodlights. Hotz's hand had something pinned inside her flight suit.

Dom straddled her, grabbed what looked like a cord winding up her boot, hooked his knife down, and jerked up. One end of the cord sprang back with a splash and disappeared into the night. Dom extracted the other end from Hotz's pant leg, a meter-long tentacle, writhing and dripping blue. As thick as Dom's thumb, it tapered to a cluster of hooks surrounding a sharp spine. The spine twisted, attempting to burrow into Dom's hand.

"What is that, besides the obvious?" Zim signaled Dom to hand the tentacle to Chow.

Chow shook his head. "There isn't… wasn't supposed to be anything like this here. I'll check it out." He carried the specimen to his improvised lab.

"Are you alright?" Zim asked. Hotz stood shaking.

"Leg tingles, not much, but—" She let out a weak sigh. "I let my mind drift. Being out here got me thinking about camping under the stars as a kid and Uncle Dave's face over the campfire telling one of his stories." She shook her head. "It won't happen again. I'm—"

Zim interrupted. "Not your fault. I believed the intelligence reports. I should have set a guard." Sensing Hotz needed to talk, Zim asked, "You had an uncle on Corydon?"

"Not a real uncle, Uncle Dave was a robotic humanoid. Avian said we needed families growing up—so we got RH families." She flashed a wan smile. "Uncle Dave was my favorite. He had twinkling eyes and a flowing white beard. I was telling Rob—"

"Wait," Zim interrupted. "Where's Rob?"

Chow tilted his examination light toward Rob's sleeping pod. A glistening cocoon writhed and jerked soundlessly. Under the glare of the light, the cocoon unraveled into translucent ribbons of gray that slid off and fled into the night.

"Targ," Chow shouted, running to Rob. Everyone cleared the area.

"Careful touching him," Zim barked. "Dom check the perimeter. Hotz go too, and both of you stay in the light. Something's out there, a lot of somethings."

Dom flipped open the weapon case, hoisted a fusion torch, two magazines, and an E-Mag light gun, and tossed another torch and gun to Hotz. Neither light weight nor firing light, the misnamed gun electromagnetically accelerated ceramic pellets smaller than a sand grain to one twenty-fifth the speed of light, 0.04c. Dom jammed in a magazine, slapped the base, chambered a pellet, and scanned the edge of the camp through the sensor sight. Everything outside the floodlights was seamless black. He rescanned through the stellar night-scope then raised it out to the horizon.

"Rob was already dead," Chow said, examining the body. "The writhing was reflex. Those sea scorpions were like the one that paralyzed my hand." Chow swept his light toward the water's edge, sending waves of flat worms and segment-legged creatures squirming to escape.

Zim said, "I think fusion torches might be better weapons than light guns."

Dom and Hotz switched on their torches, revealing a churning field of invertebrates beyond the camp light.

Zim pointed to the film over Rob's face. "Is that slime what I think it is?"

"Speeds putrefaction for their eggs," Chow said. "Those deep slits—"

"Thanks, I got the idea. When you finish the exam, seal his body tight— lots of preservative. I don't want anything crawling out." Zim pointed to the tentacle clamped to Chow's lab table. "Any idea about that?"

"It's completely unlike these scorpions and flatworms, entirely different chemistry. I want to check Hotz, see if she got bitten."

Zim appreciated Chow's clinical objectivity. "I'll send her over."

A loud splash sounded further out in the night.

"What's that?" Hotz shouted, directing her torch beam at the sound.

A two-meter-wide dome squatted low on the algae mat fifty meters out. Unlike the other night creatures, this one didn't run from the light. Stalked eyes around the dome's edge glowed fearlessly back at them. Dom lifted his torch beam to join Hotz's on the dome and raised his light gun.

A slap and rush of water sounded beneath their feet as dozens of tentacles recoiled to the dome. A wave rolled underfoot and, when Dom and Hotz looked back, the dome had vanished.

Zim slog-splashed up to them.

"Doin' recon." Dom dead-panned, "Checkin' us out. Lookin' for weak spots. It didn't attack, pulled out soon as we spotted it."

"I think it pulled out when you raised your gun," Hotz added. "The tentacles could probably reach beyond fifty meters. They came up through the algae base. I got a quick look. I think it's what attacked me."

"If it recognized Dom's gun, it's either intelligent or has experienced other guns." Zim took Hotz's gun and fusion torch. "I'll take your watch. Check in with Chow."

Zim took the sunrise side of the perimeter; Dom sloshed around to the west.

A tense hour passed. Two minuscule moons streaked across the sky, illuminating wispy clouds on their path. A shift in the breeze swept cleaner air in from the ocean. Zim did a quick scan for the approaching storm wall. No sign. It was early, but she'd had other surprises this night. Other than 'all's well' exchanges with Dom, the only sounds were her boots sucking in the muck. She flashed her torch down regularly to scatter the scorpions.

After two hours, a star-point peeked on the east horizon, widened to a wine-dark line, and shot rust and maroon beams into Okean's dawning sky, driving the sea life back into the folds in the algae. Zim shut off her torch and waved for Dom to join her with Hotz at Chow's examination station. No one had slept.

"I couldn't find anything larger than a pin prick," Chow said, "indicating the red dot in the image of Hotz's calf. Her blood test indicates exposure to a mild neurotoxin." He held up the tentacle and linked his heads-up display.

"The hooks here on the end—I'm sure it's not a head—hold the probe in place." He pointed to the display. "And see, here and here, discharged nematocysts. They're like stinging cells." He prodded the probe end and magnified it on the display. "Judging by what Hotz told me you saw out there, we're looking at Okean's version of a jellyfish—one that can leave the water, at least partially. Chemical residue indicates that it injected neural threads, but they dissolved when the tentacle was severed."

"Poison?" Zim asked. "Was that thing hunting her? Was the bite like yours? You said your hand was paralyzed."

"Her bite was different from mine." Chow held up the tentacle. "The neurotoxin that came from this resembles cone snail toxin—deadly, but medicinal in small quantities—that's all Hotz got. It might even be classed as a painkiller. Mine hurt like hell. But who knows how much she would have gotten if Dom hadn't interrupted the process? And if she hadn't been awake when it struck, she might have ended up like Rob."

"So… what do you think happened?" Zim asked.

"I think she got jacked."

"Jacked?"

"This tentacle may have connected with Hotz's nervous system. That's where the markers point. The protein trail leads to the nerve nexus behind her knee. Why? As a xenologist, I'd certainly like to know." Chow shrugged.

Zim looked to each of them in turn. "Now that it knows we're here, this thing will come for us again. If it feeds at the surface, and it's stalking us, it can't be far. Everyone up for a little hunting?" Seeing somber nods all around, Zim pointed to the tentacle. "Pack this up. All supplies go on the big panel—Rob's body, too. How are the guns?"

Hotz called out, "Six E-Mag light guns—charged, loaded, clean—enough ammo for a combat squad. I checked Chow out on weapons last night, so we're all good."

"Good." Zim looked toward Rob's still form. "Let's kick some tentacle-crawling, targ-ass. This one's for Rob."

"For Rob," they all said.

Hunting Expedition

After slap-checking their equipment, they headed west, each spaced at twenty meters. Hotz took point, Dom back on the left, Chow on the right, and Zim at the rear.

"Stay alert," Zim shouted, "and keep checking down. Hotz said the creature's tentacles came up through the base. I don't want anyone pulled under."

Myndus was orange-red and already a full hand above the horizon. Zim saw no hint of the approaching storm but knew it would return before the next sunrise. Whatever their prospects, she was pleased for an opportunity to refocus her team.

Star Council wanted her gone. Mac had reminded her what happens to military officers who run afoul of political leaders. She knew her history: "They cut out their eyes and throw them outside the gate to beg." She wasn't beyond begging, not with her team's lives at stake. But she expected no rescue from that quarter. Right now, she welcomed the Prophecy or anything that might come to aid them.

The novelty of bouncing on a waterbed gave way to a monotonous *schluck schlock* of boots pulling in the muck. The green algae plane met the rose-colored sky at the endless line of the horizon. High above, white horsetail wisps seemed painted in space.

Hotz stopped, crouched, and motioned everyone to hold back. A crescent ridge was rising in the algae a hundred and fifty meters ahead. Continuing to rise and spread, it formed a dome twenty meters across. Hotz looked back and tilted her head toward the object. Zim nodded up, pointing her nose toward the dome. Hotz brought her gun slowly to her shoulder then squeezed as she exhaled. *Hummm-Snap.* A black spot appeared on the dome and grew ragged as it spread, shredding ribbons of algae. The sky above the dome erupted in waves of refracted light.

Zim lowered her gun. "Methane. We just killed a gas bubble." Everyone huffed a dry laugh. "Good thing these guns don't generate heat. With the oxygen level of this planet, we might have set off some fireworks."

"Good shot," Dom chided. "I think it was getting ready to charge." Hotz kissed her palm, patted her backside, and blew the kiss to him.

Zim circled a finger high in the air and pointed. The *schluck schlock* walk resumed, guns sweeping the horizon, eyes glancing down.

Thirty minutes later, Hotz halted again. A smaller dome loomed ahead, two meters wide, the size of the one they had seen outside the camp. She signaled Dom and Chow to come forward but stay out wide on her flanks.

The dome rose in their gun sights, lifting clear of the algae and tilting, revealing its disk shape. Short-stalked eyes on its rim alternated with tentacles that hung down into the water. As it tilted, colors ran and flashed across the disk like a casino marquee. Slowly, the colors formed a picture—the friendly, animated face of an elder Human male. Centering on Hotz, the face smiled and winked one twinkling eye.

Hotz lowered her gun. "Uncle Dave? How?"

The smile broadened over a long and curly white beard. The face rotated toward Zim and bowed then did the same to each member of her team.

"Vaitii?" Chow broke the silence. Then he shouted, "It's a Vaitii."

The word stirred distant memories from Zim's childhood. Short on trust but shorter on options, she handed her gun to Chow, rolled her sleeve, and walked forward. A tentacle shot up from the algae mat, wrapped about her forearm, and pressed inside her elbow. Zim startled then stood silent.

"Commander Gayle Zimmon," came a resonant baritone voice. She looked for the source then realized it was coming from inside her head. "Welcome. We are the Vaitii. We hope you will allow us to host you and your team for your stay on Okean. Your accommodations are being prepared. Time is short. If you wish to collect your supplies, we can finalize our contract when you return."

Vaitii

Gray on the darkening horizon meant the storm was fast upon them. Killing winds and waves would come in the night. To help bring up supplies, the Vaitii had given them a hydrophobic sled of chitin nanocrystals that glided over wet algae like a hover barge.

Zim and Hotz ran ahead in the fading light. Dom and Chow followed pulling the frictionless sled.

"What's a Vaitii?" Hotz asked, running up beside Zim.

"A legend, a fairytale. I only know my mother's stories. She said she heard them from Shelesti balladeers in the market."

"Growing up on a frontier planet must be fun." Hotz hopped left to avoid a puddle, "more fun than on Corydon."

"More work, too," Zim said then raised her voice. "Chow might know something about the Vaitii."

"Just more stories," Chow shouted, shifting the tow cord, and urging Dom to move up so they could join the conversation. "Tales of the Vaitii were in the same books as stories of demons, devils, and magic swords—magic contracts, too."

"Yes, I gave my tentative agreement to a contract." Zim heard the wind howling in the distance ahead. "What choice do we have? There was no time for discussion." Of course, she had concerns, but she kept them to herself. The Vaitii's offer gave them a chance to live another day.

"There must be something about Vaitii in the archives," Chow said, "even if it's just more stories. I'll check when we get to camp."

"Won't be time," Zim said. "If we're still alive tonight, you can run a search."

Hotz prodded Zim's arm. "You said your mother told Vaitii stories... tell me a story."

Zim laughed. "All right, as long as we keep up the pace. Chow, feel free to jump in. Dom, can you hear us?" He wagged his hand and veered closer.

After a quick side-hop to avoid a puddle, Zim took a deep breath. "As my mother told it, the Vaitii are immortal wizards and shape-changers. They help lost travelers, crusaders in search of relics, and traders seeking new routes."

"What's in it for them?" Hotz asked, short stepping and jumping.

"Vaitii are solitary, only one per planet," Zim said. "And once settled they never leave. Interstellar travelers are their only physical connection to the outside."

"They were a favorite speculation topic at school," Chow said, "particularly among the non-technical types. Most agreed that if Vaitii existed, they didn't shape shift. They just evolved to fit a niche on whatever planet they lived on."

"If there can be only one per planet, and they evolve uniquely for each planet, then each one must be different." Hotz skipped around another puddle.

Chow shrugged. "We may be the first Humans to actually see a Vaitii."

As they ran, Zim and Chow alternated telling stories of Vaitii tricksters, confusion over their appearance, and misunderstandings about their mind-reading tentacles.

Hotz laughed. "I think my Uncle Dave just added to the legend. Are the Vaitii good guys?"

"Not always, not for the Gyu-yon," Zim said.

Hotz's blue eyes grew wider. "I never heard of a Gyu-yon."

"They no longer exist. According to my mother's storytelling, they were an advanced, very warlike race—in their time, the most powerful in the galaxy. Their conquests spanned a thousand systems.

"The Gyu-yon delighted in merciless war and obsessed over every aspect of war making. Once long ago, to clear a contested area of possible spies and collaborators, they decided to exterminate all life forms. One Vaitii survived their attempts. It declared war on the Gyu-yon and raised its entire galactic network against them."

"What happened?" Hotz asked, her foot landing in a puddle and sending up a splash.

"Legend says the Gyu-yon planets turned against them: every stone, plant, and animal on every planet. The ground folded over Gyu-yon cities. Whenever a crew returned from space, their planet swallowed them and their ship." Zim's voice dropped low. "It is said their entire race disappeared in a single night."

Hotz's eyes were round as saucers. "W—we really should stay on the Vaitii's good side." Dom and Chow nodded to her solemnly. Then Zim shrugged. "Of course, these are only stories." Hotz was the last one to laugh.

The sun had dropped below Okean's horizon and was pulling in its last indigo spokes. Ahead their stacked supplies loomed as gray shadows. The storm was coming sooner than expected.

"Supplies on the sled," Zim barked. "Leave the utilities and shuttle panels." They hoisted and tossed everything except Rob's encased body, which they kept horizontal.

Then they ran.

The eastern horizon swallowed the stars and the beam of Zim's torch. They shouted over the growing roar. A screaming wall of gray water would soon sweep over them hard enough to peel the flesh from their bones.

Everyone grabbed a sled cord. Hotz led, running with her plasma torch high, the others raced behind her over the dark undulating terrain.

The howl rose to a scream. Torch beams danced ahead. Water jets stung their faces. After each gust, Zim expected the storm to snatch them. Running in pitch black, they followed the light ahead, twisting, bobbing, hopping, and splashing through pools of squirming creatures they crushed underfoot.

Hotz suddenly stopped and pointed down, yelling something no one could hear. A wave rolled underfoot. Scissoring torch beams found a transparent, five-meter bubble. The Vaitii rose beside Zim, and she bared her arm to its tentacle grasp.

"We are in agreement?" the Vaitii asked. Zim nodded. "Please board. We will take your supplies below and show you to your rooms. You and your team require food and rest." It flashed Uncle Dave's beardy, beatific smile and twinkling eyes. Its articulation matched its thoughts so perfectly, Zim felt she was hearing and seeing Uncle Dave speak.

A dark stream flowed from beneath their host's disk onto the cargo sled. The torchlight revealed what appeared to be a wave of ball bearings. These ball bearing beetles, or 3Bs as the team soon called them, elevated the bags and cases a few millimeters and guided them through a dilation in the bubble. Their host then gestured several tentacles for Zim and her team to enter.

Last to board, Zim glanced back. The circular reflection of her torch beam shrank rapidly as the wall of water struck, swallowing the empty sled, and slamming the bubble as it sealed.

Just Like Home

The storm exploded above them, rocking, and deforming the bubble as it descended into the Okean sea. Zim felt the drop and lean as they accelerated in a downward arc. Despite close quarters, the air remained fresh and cool. The only sound was their breathing.

"Douse the torches," Zim ordered. The glare became darkness until their eyes adjusted, and the blue glow of the bubble interior revealed faint outlines. The Vaitii swam alongside them, its ghostly undulating body sending waves down through its long tentacles. Dom and Hotz stood rigid, eyes darting. Chow smiled in rapt fascination with everything around him.

A yellow light from below grew brighter. Zim pressed against the curved wall to look down and saw a vast nest of glowing bubbles held fast in an entwined lattice. The transport slowed, and where it engaged the bubble nest, the shared surface dilated to become a doorway. Zim stepped through and her team followed her to an airlock. The Vaitii greeted them on the other side. Its bell edges closed like an umbrella to form a pedestal, then it looped a tentacle around Zim's wrist.

"We are certain you will know your way around. Please make yourself comfortable. We will transport your belongings to your rooms. Tomorrow, after you have rested and eaten, we will talk."

A flood of 3Bs streamed past them. Zim stepped aside and followed the flow of bags and cases from the bubble, down a short hall, to an antechamber connected to a large suite of guestrooms.

The structure had vaulted ceilings and appeared to be timber-framed with stone and wooden walls. Rustic furnishings were clearly designed for Human comfort.

Zim paused in the doorway and took in the details, from the rough-hewn beams and archways to the rich-grained floors. In the main room, she ran her hand across the back of a leather-upholstered chair and squeezed the fabric.

She rapped the wood-framed doorway and heard the solid knock. Shaking her head, she said, "Not projections. From what I can tell, this is all real."

"A hunting lodge," Hotz suggested, craning her neck at the beams forming the room's peaked center.

"Commander, if we're dismissed," Dom asked with less assurance than usual, "you think this fine lodge might have something for an old soldier to drink?" Without speaking, Zim raised an arm to the oak cabinet at the far corner of the main room.

As Hotz and Chow followed Dom, Zim turned down a hall in the opposite direction. The Vaitii was right: she knew the way. Her fingers found familiar tool-marks on doors and window trim where inexpert carpenters had first learned to use a chisel and plane. The indentation where her brother Joshua had missed a finishing nail—each scratch and gouge was dear to her.

She stopped at a glass-fronted display case beside a doorway. Trophies, medals, and commendations crowded every corner, except on the third shelf. There a dust-free circle marked the place of honor. An engraved plate identified the missing item.

"Your home?" Chow sounded more relaxed than he had in days. The big fellow's dark eyes smiled over his round cheeks and a frothy pilsner glass.

"My parent's home," she murmured, "just as I left it when I was seventeen. That morning I walked through the house early and touched everything, trying to commit it to memory—everything I thought I was seeing for the last time. The Vaitii lifted this from my memory and created it for me… got just about everything." She pointed to the open space on the third shelf.

Chow leaned in and read the identification plate, "'Gayle Zimmon of Scalaris, First Place, Corydon Combat Games'… Ah, your Starflower medal."

Zim nodded. "It was the only medal I ever received from Star Command, the only one I was permitted to wear on my uniform. When I heard the shuttle arrive that last morning, I took it from this spot." She pointed to the circle.

Chow wrapped a big hand over her shoulder and raised his pilsner glass. "Come join us. Your new family wants to welcome you home."

Zim laughed. "My original family didn't drink except on rare occasions. I saw the beer tap on the wall. The Vaitii added a few amenities for present company. Tell everyone I'll be along." Chow lifted his glass to her and left.

Zim turned into the first room, her old bedroom. A narrow bed was centered on the main wall, covered with a patchwork quilt her mother had made. The gun rack above the headboard was empty. She suspected the old, single-shot Dragonov was in Joshua's room. The gun had belonged to her father and grandfather before her. She had given it to her younger brother the day before she left.

She stroked the pelt draped over the foot of the bed; Rayzhor, the heinkel that had raided their gloak pastures and killed her older brothers, Kelly and Todd. As she ran her fingers through the soft black and gold fur, she remembered the night of the kill. She was fifteen.

It had been her night to tend the herd, and she had planned it carefully. First, she had guided the gloak to a safe pasture. Then she went alone to the place where she knew the heinkel prowled and staked out her position: a rise beside the depression where the pasture met the edge of the dark forest. The grass and starflowers grew tall there. She had set a fat gloak decoy in the clearing below and smeared it with scent. The decoy simulated grazing by looking up and about, braying, then grazing again. Gayle hoped it would distract Rayzhor long enough.

Her father had forbidden her to hunt the heinkel even though Rayzhor had taken gloak from all the neighboring farms. These predators had no fear of Humans and would eat her as readily as any succulent gloak. Gayle brought the Dragonov, an old, single-shot light gun. She never missed a shot and never rattled. Her father taught her that. He said if she saw death coming and could accept it, her mind would be clear. That night her mind was clear as crystal. There would be no excuses. If she saw Rayzhor first, she would kill him. If not, she wouldn't have to face her father's wrath.

She tucked low among the starflowers so as not to be silhouetted against the night sky. The air was crisp and scented with newly mown chirrup from the neighbor's field. Starflower buds opened and turned iridescent blue petals to bathe in the starlight. As a small child, Gayle had thought the starflowers waited for her each night then opened to greet her when she arrived.

Scalari nights were chilly and the position she chose exposed to the wind. She pulled her patched cloth coat close. A breeze kicked up and whipped the tall starflowers about her. She hoped the wind might confuse the direction of her scent.

A silver full moon rose—a hunter's moon. Tonight, there were two hunters. She jerked her mind back to keep focus.

Something stirred along the tree line.

Gayle lifted the Dragonov gently and rested its forward grip on her raised knee. Through the star scope she saw a pack of heinkels edging into the pasture, about a dozen. Five big males bristled and challenged one another, baring their six-centimeter fangs. One ended its challenge with a jaw-clenched headshake, signifying snapping a neck.

Several heinkel lifted their snouts, sniffing in the direction of the fat gloak alone in the field. Rayzhor, the largest male and bolder than the rest, slunk forward, his head low over his advancing paws. With every wind gust or sound, he stopped and lowered his belly to the ground. Then he slunk forward again.

Gayle took a half breath then exhaled, hoping the heinkel couldn't hear her heartbeat or smell her sweat. One paw entered the clearing. The decoy abruptly reared and pivoted its head to look straight at the heinkel. Then it brayed and returned to grazing. It hadn't bolted. Rayzhor stood straight up, sniffed the decoy, and looked quickly to either side. It scanned the hillside where Gayle tucked low among the starflowers.

She eased the gun in, set it to her shoulder, shifted her finger, and centered the pad onto the trigger. Rayzhor swung, leaped, and charged straight at her in a single motion. Its monstrous claws pulled the ground. Stretching out, it gained the slope in three strides, its yellow fangs widening in the last leap.

Gayle aimed the Dragonov through the gaping fangs. *Hummm-Snap.* Rayzhor's muzzle dropped and plowed the starflowers, stopping half an arm's reach in front of her. She pulled the bolt on the single-shot Dragonov, slapped another pellet home, and swiveled to the forest edge.

One big male turned and ran. Two others stood growling with their lips curled back. Then with defiant snorts, they joined the pack, backing into the dark forest.

Fourteen years ago, she thought Rayzhor was a vicious beast. Now, after all the killing, she stroked its head and fur and felt a curious kinship. That night she had defended her family and home from a primitive predator, as had the heinkel. Good old Rayzhor was fighting extinction, trying to feed and protect its family.

She left the bedroom, turned up the hall, and joined her team for a drink.

Taking Stock

Hotz, Dom, and Chow sat waiting at the rough-hewn table. Long-stemmed flutes set before them, three additional flutes beside three empty chairs.

"Please, Commander." Dom stood and pulled out the unoccupied chair at the head of the table. "We know you drink Kentucky bourbon, but for special celebrations prefer an oli-jira." He gestured to the glistening, clear fluid, and red zillberry in each of the flutes. "I remembered you ordered one at Event Horizon that first night."

"Most appreciated, Dom. I know we're all tired."

"We wanted a quiet moment," Hotz said, resting a hand on the first empty seat then gesturing to the second. "We invited Rob's spirit to share a last toast with us, and Brownie to share a first toast." The image of an elderly woman materialized behind the second chair.

Brownie wore a lavender service tunic. She was neat and gently aged with a broad maternal smile and gray-streaked hair.

"Wonderful you could join us, Brownie," Zim said with mild surprise.

"Thank you, Commander. When Dom mentioned a team toast, I asked to be included." She pulled a virtual oli-jira flute away from the real one that remained on the table.

"To being here together." Dom raised and pointed his flute to all around. Everyone joined him and took a sip.

Hotz held her glass high. "To our teammate, Rob. You found us a landing site and figured out Yardley's trap. We're here because of you." Everyone nodded. "This was not what you wanted in your life, but you never let us down." She gave her flute a second lift and everyone drank. Zim passed the carafe for refills.

Chow stood. "To the Starflower and victory over impossible odds."

"Hear, hear," Dom said, flashing an ultra-wide-eyed smile.

Brownie spoke next. "I never expected to find myself here, in such a place, or as part of such a team—"

"And we did?" Chow coughed up a laugh.

"I'll forgive your inebriated interruption, young man," Brownie scolded. "Until now, my life has had neither meaning nor excitement. That has changed. Thanks to you all, this month has been the best I've ever known, and you are the best people." She raised her virtual glass to the others.

Zim stood and paused to let the solemnity return. "To my excellent team. We have been tested, and we have passed each test together." Flutes rose again. She continued, "Rob never intended to be a warrior, but he became one. On his final journey, may the warriors who have gone before greet him as one of their own."

All glasses emptied. Zim bid her team good night and reminded them of the meeting with the Vaitii the next day.

# # #

Back in her room, Zim sat on the bed, propped against the headboard, and pulled the quilt to her waist. It had felt strange sitting in her father's seat at the table. Seeing Brownie in her mother's place, Dom and Chow—Rob, too— where her brothers had sat, and Hotz sitting in her old seat seemed to confirm how much they had become her new family. Despite everything, it felt real and natural. Several times she'd caught herself glancing to the entry, expecting Mac to walk in. Her team had worked together, and they had survived. Mac was alone.

Shaking off her fears, she pulled up a report Chow had found in the archive. "The Vaitii" was one of a series of articles written by the Goorm to acquaint Humans with other galactic species.

DATE: April 29, 2487

TO: Earth Planetary Council

FROM: Goorm Trade Consortium, Regulation 7, section 526, Pertaining to Interstellar Contracts

SUBJECT: Galactic Report, species no. 1,493, The Vaitii

Executive Summary

The Vaitii are the oldest known, least understood, and most secretive species in the galaxy. While this assessment strives to present a coherent image of the Vaitii, it is necessarily derived from anecdotal sources and informed speculation, none of which has been confirmed.

Origin: Unknown. The Goorm believe the Vaitii to be three-dimensional projections into our galaxy, i.e., shadows from another dimension.

Language: (1) Tactile telepathy via neural links in their tentacles. Vaitii are believed capable of communicating with all known species, including non-sentients, within fifty-five meters—the approximate length of their tentacles. (2) (SPECULATION) Cross-dimensional telepathy. All Vaitii may be linked to a single collective mind, physically separated in this dimension but connected in another. This affords them instant communication throughout our galaxy and possibly beyond.

Habitat: Various. Vaitii may be found in any environment known to support life forms; however, no two Vaitii are known to ever occupy the same planet. Goorm believe them to be strictly eremitic.

Appearance: Various. Their ontogenesis tailors each Vaitii to its environment, rendering each member of the species physically unique. Vaitii are also able to control their pigmentation across the electro-magnetic spectrum, enabling them to blend with any background. Goorm suspect that many Vaitii have gone undetected and may have mixed with indigenous populations throughout the galaxy.

Reproduction: Unknown. Goorm believe the Vaitii to be immortal; therefore, reproduction may be rare or optional. Genetic information may be shared telepathically and engineered internally without physical contact with their own species. Or it may be shared physically with native species to facilitate environmental adaptation.

Technology: Unknown-Advanced. Vaitii transcend known physical technology. Production appears to be based on nanoscopic or cross-dimensional processes, neither of which have been detected to consume resources or generate waste.

Trade Opportunities: Limited. Self-sufficient Vaitii have shown no interest in off-world products, services, or technology beyond interstellar dispersion of their seed. Vaitii employ couriers for this service and are very selective. The last Goorm courier died six millennia ago.

Zim scanned the remaining topics. The chronicle of Vaitii engagements with other species was a list of one-time encounters. Other subheadings were followed with "Unknown" or "Not Applicable."

She flagged the Goorm report then pulled up her contract. Despite their near disaster from the oncoming storm, Zim felt a twinge for agreeing to anything without giving it careful consideration. The contract was simple and straightforward.

Gayle Zimmon, Human:
- Agrees to share personal code and memory with Vaitii.
- Agrees to carry and distribute Vaitii-Zimmon code to hospitable planets.
- Agrees to ally with all Vaitii in all their manifestations.

The Vaitii:
- Agree to welcome Zimmon, her code, her progeny, and her allies, and protect them until the end of time.

The contract struck Zim as a curious sort of marriage agreement, as between a flower and a bee. She had given the Vaitii her memory—as evidenced by this bedroom she was sitting in. And she would share her genetic code with them and distribute their spore to the worlds she visited. But the significance of the last words came as a sudden revelation, "…until the end of time." The Vaitii would never die and would be with her always.

The one who never dies.

Prophecy had found her.

Rii-Chaut

"Enough," Kadis shouted, but the two Rii-Chaut hetmen continued circling and threatening. Kadis waved his enforcer forward. As the seven-foot Inidigbo raised its fearsome scythe-trident, a reptilian musk filled the hall. The pungent scent warned the two that the enforcer's next move would be to strike. They backed off, but their eyes continued darting between one another and the dagger-toothed enforcer.

"Let 'em fight," someone yelled along the wall. The crowd took up the chant, stamping their feet and banging on their weapons.

"No combat in Judgment Hall," Kadis said, referring to the current purpose of his throne and treasure chamber. "Do either Yazza or Chei-Binsk hetmen wish to challenge for leadership?" He looked to one then the other. Both dropped their arms, stood erect, and faced him.

Kadis was past his prime, but none questioned his leadership. Fifty years ago, an Under spacer still in his teens, he had volunteered to fight for StarCom in the first colonial wars. Disgusted by the arrogance of StarCom's officer class, he mutinied, hijacked a transport, and took up gun running. Other outcasts, rogue adventurers, and criminals joined him, and the Rii-Chaut was born. While fleeing pursuit, they had happened on Chasima, killed its inhabitants, and made the remote planet their Rii-Chaut capital. The sunless world with its worm-bored chambers made a perfect pirate kingdom.

The Yazza hetman's fist shot up. "Leadership is not the issue—"

The Inidigbo lowered its staff to the hetman's shoulder and rolled the blade to hook behind his neck. The hetman lowered his fist and bowed low.

Pidged in his teens to fight in the arena, the Yazza hetman's scars spoke of many battles. His face bore crosshatched claw marks, and his white, right eye never blinked.

Kadis reclined on a blood-red fur cushion and waited for the hall to quiet. Other Rii-Chaut sat on cushions or cross-legged on the floor on fur-covered animal skins. They styled themselves as Cossacks, corsairs, barbarians, and gladiators. Most were Under Humans, but there were also Creatives, Aldrakin, Tak-Yaki, Inidigbo, and many others. Their entourage included a Sk'Keffin diplomat, a Goorm accountant, and a troupe of Shelesti and Hyrup musicians.

Kadis raised an arm to the bowed hetman. "State your concern to the brotherhood. Be warned, one more outburst and my enforcer will impose *his* justice." The hetman's eye caught the scythe trembling at his neck as the Inidigbo fought its aggressive nature.

Responding reluctantly to Kadis' direction, the enforcer lifted its weapon and stepped back, allowing the hetman to stand.

"I, Ojai Khan, Hetman of the Yazza, am well known to the brotherhood. We stand accused of taking an unauthorized contract with the Corydon Star Council. Our contract was approved by the brotherhood long ago. It is long-term and open-ended. 'Assassination is our honorable craft'."

A chant went up in the hall, "Assassination is our honorable craft. That is the code." Ojai Khan bowed around the room.

Kadis asked, "You did the assassination as your contract required?"

"Two commissions for a regular, approved customer. Payment was received and levies paid to the brotherhood."

Kadis glanced to the Goorm accountant and got a raised claw. Smiling at Ojai Khan, he continued, "This has been a good year for Yazza sect. When this business is finished, we will discuss how to divide treasure among all sects… then we celebrate." Raucous shouts and foot stomping filled the hall. Ojai Khan extended his arms forward, bowed, and retreated.

The second man came forward, younger and leaner than Ojai Khan, more bronzed than ruddy. He cut a dark rakish figure, hawk-eyed with sharp cheekbones, a flowing black mustache, and plaited raven hair. Unlike the scarred Yazza, the man's open vest revealed clean lines and a defined physique.

Kadis motioned for him to speak.

"I am Traier, Hetman of the Chei-Binsk. We do not contest the honorable craft of the assassin." He paused but got no support from the hall. "The Yazza have taken a partisan role in the ongoing, undeclared war between Human Unders and Human Creatives. Many Rii-Chaut, including you Kadis and the Hetman of the Yazza, have come to us fleeing the Human wars. Ojai Khan

242

took money with no thought of the consequences. By killing the champion of the Unders and their finest strategist, the Yazza have unbalanced the contest."

"Who did Yazza kill?" Kadis asked.

"Gayle Zimmon, known as the Starflower, and Roland Mackenzie." Murmurs went around the hall. "I met the Starflower at the Aldrakin surrender. I saw how her enemies respected her and how revered she was by her team."

Kadis stood. "We know them both. We avoided Starflower in the great Aldrakin War. Mackenzie's squadrons killed many Rii-Chaut brothers. They were brave warriors, honorable opponents. But Human class struggles are not war."

Traier straightened. "We Chei-Binsk fought alongside the Aldrakin against the Human Star Council. Ojai Khan's Yazza sided with the Council. When the Starflower lived, the Council feared Unders would rally to her. That fear increased when the war ended. Many thousands of Unders remained alive, and many were skilled in war. Now, with the Starflower and Mackenzie removed, the Council has little to fear. They will consolidate power, Human Creatives will join them, and we Rii-Chaut will become their next target—"

"But you are a Creative—" Ojai Khan interrupted then halted, finding the enforcer's blade beside his throat.

"Traier is speaking," Kadis glowered.

"Yes, I am a Ten Creative." Traier's voice rose above the snarls and grumbles. "But I assure you, when the Unders are gone, the Creatives will suffer, as will the Rii-Chaut."

"May I speak?" Ojai Khan asked. The leader waved his reptilian enforcer back. "The Yazza have taken more booty than the Chei-Binsk. We earned great treasure for our brothers by taking opportunities the Chei-Binsk declined. Now they are angry because our esteem in the brotherhood surpasses theirs. I see nothing more than jealousy." Cheers erupted in the hall.

"Rii-Chaut *take*," Ojai Khan shouted over the cheers. "We are feared and respected by all because we take from all—and work for any who will pay." Raised fists joined the cheers and clapped weapons.

"Enough," Kadis shouted and gestured to his enforcer. The hall quieted and, when Kadis gave a down gesture, everyone sat. "Traier's point is interesting. But assassination is our honorable craft… in whatever manner it is done. Matter closed."

Traier's head dropped in silence, but Ojai Khan was not finished.

243

"We require assurance," Ojai Khan said through a scared-lip smile. "The Yazza contract remains in effect with the Star Council. Traier and his Chei-Binsk must agree not interfere with us in the future."

Traier glared and made a slashing gesture across his chest.

"Assurance will be made—or assurance will be taken," Ojai Khan said.

Traier shook his head. All the Rii-Chaut understood what must happen.

#

The arena was the largest chamber on Chasima, thirty-three meters in diameter and ten meters high, with iron seating set in stone around the stepped perimeter. Rii-Chaut observers hungry for violence filled the air with curses and cries for blood.

Bare to the waist with his sky-blue Turkish trousers tucked into his calf-length boots, Traier waved his curved shashka cavalry saber. Across the arena, Ojai Khan swung a heavier falcata diagonally down then slashed left and right. The arena floor was longer and wider than the fighting pits Ojai Khan ruled, which would make it harder for him to corner his nimbler opponent.

Traier had taken his share of wounds though none showed. Unlike Rii-Chaut Unders who bore their battle scars as badges of honor, Creatives preferred to see their bodies restored. Still, Traier knew his opponent's greater experience and mass meant he could take and dispense heavy punishment.

He tested the gravity with a couple jumps. Chasima was predominantly iron which gave it a high mass index and 0.8 gravity. Traier's jumps were high and quick, but he knew that also meant Ojai Khan would tire slower.

Kadis entered through an archway high on the arena wall and descended two steps to an iron throne fixed on a terrace. His Inidigbo enforcer remained beside him.

Eyes turned, the room quieted, and Kadis raised his hand. He said only, "Proceed," and the shouting erupted anew.

Ojai Khan twisted and rocked his body then squared his shoulders on Traier. He raised his falcata forward and snorted then centered his good eye on Traier, turning his blind, white eye away.

I'm fighting a Cyclops. Traier noted the advantage.

Khan shifted his weight to the balls of his feet and crouched to charge.

What does the big man least expect? Traier thought, bracing as if to take the charge head-on. Ojai Khan's rump bobbed then his legs kicked, driving his bull-like head and shoulders forward, his falcata cleaving the air in wide swaths.

Traier watched the distance close, cocked his shashka back to strike, stepped left to Ojai Khan's blind side, gauged the response time, then darted right. Khan missed a step and corrected, chasing Traier in a wide circle.

Overcorrecting for his weakside, Traier noted. Ojai Khan paused again to square his shoulders and dig in his feet. This time Traier rolled his shoulders and slashed the air. The crowd howled; Khan snorted.

Again, Khan bull rushed. Traier stepped left then quickly right, and again led Khan in a wide circle. He's not tiring but is getting impatient, Traier thought. Khan shook his head and curled his lips to flash his pidge-enhanced, fighting fangs. Traier met the big man's sneer by hopping and dancing a defiant jig.

Ojai Khan glared, growled, and dug his feet in again. Traier waited for Khan's rump to bob then rushed straight at him. Khan's head jerked in surprise. When he jumped forward, Traier stepped left then quickly right as Khan expected, then left again, catching Ojai Khan still turning away. Khan's falcata swept backhand to block Traier's downward slash and sliced empty air.

Traier ducked, shifted his light shashka to his left hand, and swept low, cutting Khan mid-waist, then upward, slashing his throat.

Ojai Khan grunted, staggered, dropped to his knees, and collapsed onto his face. A pool of blood widened on the iron arena floor.

The hall went silent. Traier twisted the falcata from Ojai Khan's clutching fingers and offered its grip to Kadis on his high throne.

The Rii-Chaut leader held the sword high and declared, "A hetman of the Rii-Chaut has been honorably defeated in trial by combat. The victor stands before you. Do the Yazza wish to continue Ojai Khan's challenge?" He held the falcata out toward the angry Yazza sect. No one spoke or came forward to claim it.

Kadis continued, "Yazza are without a hetman. Do you wish Traier, Hetman of the Chei-Binsk, as your hetman?"

The grumbling rose again. Grizzled, rough-scarred Yazza scowled at Traier and across the arena at the unblemished Chei-Binsk on the far side.

"Very well," Kadis said, "You must choose another hetman. This is done."

Uncle Dave

Zim awoke to the scent of coffee and the crackling sound of eggs and cured gloak on the griddle. She wiped sleep from her eyes. A virtual sunrise cast shadows of lattice windowpanes across her quilt. Zim threw back the covers, washed at a porcelain bowl she filled from a water pitcher, and dried on a yellow-stripped terry towel. After slipping on and sealing her one-piece service uniform, she headed to the front room.

Dom held up a plate of gloak, brown beans, and eggs. "These ball-bearing-beetles cook up some fine mornin' grub." His face reflected the yellow glare of a virtual sun shining through the dining room window, not the orange glow of Myndus.

A dozen of the Vaitii's 3Bs scampered about the table and kitchen, filling glasses with white, orange, and red liquids, cracking and flipping eggs, and slicing gloak. Each egg and meat slice touching the griddle sent up a high-pitched sizzle followed by a soft *shhhh*.

Zim took her seat at the head of the table. 3Bs set a full plate before her: gloak ham, over easy eggs, beans, buttered rye toast, and what looked and smelled like baked apples. They poured coffee, no sugar or cream—her preference but they hadn't asked—and set down a small glass of orange juice.

"You a mornin' talker?" Dom asked.

"Normally." Zim smiled into his rugged face.

"I like the mornin' news with my eggs, but storm's cut us off."

"We're also several kilometers under water," Zim said.

"Everyone sleep well?" Chow yawned and stretched in the hallway.

"Best I've had for several weeks." Hotz ducked under Chow's outstretched arm. "Glad I'm not picking up the bill for this place."

"Bill's paid," Zim said. "That's the deal. I hope to get some details from Uncle Dave this morning."

The 3Bs set a place for Hotz. She spread apple butter on her toast. Chow walked past the table to watch the 3Bs work in the kitchen. He chuckled as each egg and meat slice turned.

The 3B cooks and servers were larger than the ones that had carried their supplies, more like billiard balls than ball bearings. They had no visible sensors, and they worked with their own utensils, switching them in and out like pocketknife blades for each task.

Not waiting for Chow to sit, the 3Bs put an extra full plate by his chair and poured his coffee. Taking the hint, he joined the group at the table. The 3Bs cleared plates as each of them finished, refilled last cups, and offered pastries. Everyone indulged without question. Last night's near-death experience put them all in a thankful state.

"Is everyone rested and prepared to talk?" A voice boomed. A two-meter-disk hologram with Uncle Dave's beardy smile formed on the leather sofa. Forty stalked eyes encircling the perimeter shifted to engage Zim and her team. Its tentacles were tucked under the skirt of its dome. Uncle Dave's lip-synching gave the impression of speaking, but the sound came from the center of the room.

"Yes, we should all talk." Zim motioned Dom, Chow, and Hotz to the sitting area. They pulled over chairs, including one for Brownie who appeared in a blue StarCom service uniform matching theirs.

Chow started to roll his sleeve to receive a tentacle then realized he was hearing the Vaitii fine. The Uncle Dave face rotated to him. "The links that create this projection enable communication throughout the village. Brownie's system is also linked."

"How shall we call you?" Zim asked.

"If you're comfortable with this persona, Uncle Dave will be fine." Its Santa Claus eyes sparkled over its white beard and mustache, and the image shifted to include each of them. "You have questions?"

"Thank you for your generous hospitality. This is quite a surprise—for me especially." Zim raised her hand to the rafters.

"We were beginning to worry you might not find us."

"You expected us?"

"Only recently. Humans have been on the verge of self-destruction for a thousand years. Once you mastered Myseko space communication, star travel

247

was only a matter of time." The Vaitii's many eyes danced to keep everyone engaged.

"You said until recently?"

"The Aldrakin told us to expect your arrival."

Zim started. This confirmation of Aldrakin involvement disturbed her. "Before we discuss that, I want to know our situation."

"You are our guests for as long as you need or wish to stay. But your earliest departure cannot occur before the Eye of Okean returns in seventy-five of your days. Okean will have passed through the torrid region by then and re-entered the temperate region, outbound from Myndus."

"Can we communicate with the outside?" Zim asked.

"Not until the Eye returns. But because Vaitii are connected minds, we would be able to deliver a message through one of our selves. Considering the circumstances of your arrival, that might be unwise."

"You know about that?"

"We know what you know. Memory sharing is in our agreement. We think it best that your Human Star Council believes you are dead, all of you."

"When the eye returns in seventy-five days, will you provide us a transport?" Dom asked.

"Vaitii are organically bound to our planet of origin. We do not travel between the stars and have no need of physical transport. But our Aldrakin guests have agreed to assist you."

"They're here now?" Zim asked, remembering their attacker.

"The Aldrakin Ambassador to Corydon asked to meet with you before going to her post. The Emperor's nephew B'Len detoured to bring her here."

"I'm confused." Zim pressed her palms to her forehead. "The Emperor's nephew knew we were coming? Coming here?"

"He was sure of it but didn't know the exact time. He said you were on the path of the Prophecy and would be coming here." Uncle Dave's face was somber. "B'Len said if you did not remember him, you might remember his son with the Starflower on his shield."

"I remember them both," Zim said, recalling Ajalanda trying to teach her to snag food on her tongue.

Hotz perched on the edge of her chair. "Did B'Len explain why an Aldrakin fighter shot down our shuttle?" Dom's jaws flexed.

"When we heard your distress call, he wanted to come immediately, but we feared you would mistake him for your enemy and restrained him. Until we were able to manifest a friendly, familiar face," Uncle Dave's projection winked, "we feared our appearance would also provoke your attack." The Vaitii displayed its tentacles and stalked eyes outward. "You were under great stress. We needed an image you would accept."

"That's why you jacked Hotz," Chow said.

"Uncle Dave is a benign image. It was on her mind. Regretfully, our delay may have distracted you from rescuing your teammate, Rob."

"When does B'Len want to meet?" Zim asked.

"He hopes you and your crew will come to a reception tonight in the Aldrakin quarter. The Ambassador will be there. B'Len requests that you come early for a private discussion." Dom started to speak, but Zim held her hand toward him.

"Tell B'Len I'll be happy to speak with him alone. My team will come later."

# # #

The illuminated track to the Aldrakin quarter led past halls of alien habitats. Zim saw furnishings for species she had not imagined: organic and inorganic, solid, liquid, and gaseous. When she paused to peer through a transparent bubble wall, a faceless Vaitii hologram appeared to swim beside her.

"Our village is a way station and refuge for travelers. The Aldrakin quarter is not much further." A woven tentacle-arm pointed up the corridor.

"How many species are here now?"

"Only three habitats are occupied: Human, Aldrakin, and Sk'Keffin. The Aldrakin chose a Sk'Keffin to be their ambassador. We also have a Shelesti and a troupe of Hyrup on our staff." Zim cupped her hands and leaned her face against a white, opaque bubble.

"That liquid ammonia compound was used by the EeeYeeEee for negotiations," the Vaitii said.

"Speaking of negotiations, I have questions about our contract. There are no details, but the commitment sounds extensive."

"You understand it is long term."

"It sounds like forever."

"Ours is not a business arrangement like one you might make with the Goorm. Our progeny—"

"Our progeny or your progeny?" Zim looked up. "That sounds like—"

"Your genome, along with your memories and thought patterns, are joined with the Vaitii, connected with us through the timeless Myseko dimension. Because of your closed Human brain structure, you cannot hear our thoughts. But we hear yours and will hear those of our children."

"So, this will affect my children?"

"Our link passes through the Human as well as the Vaitii line. The Human children you bear will connect with us but manifest only Human physical traits. Your Vaitii children will blend our physical traits with those from other species, enabling them to adapt to environments on other planets."

"So that's how this works." Zim gave a sigh. "You can never leave Okean but will be forever beside me."

"Ha-Yee, Aldra Korah," the Vaitii said.

Zim did not react. She knew the Vaitii had not chosen that phrase to comfort her. "I suspect I am the only Human you've contacted?"

"We require only one entity to know a species. Because of your nature, your Human nature, we hesitated. When the Aldrakin told us that the Starflower prophecy was at hand, we understood our role."

Aldrakin Ally

An aperture dilated on the bubble wall. Zim stepped calf-deep into a swamp and felt her boot fabric tighten. It was not as expansive as the pond on the flagship, but had similar reeds, duckweed, floating fronds, and the musty odor of ripe mushrooms. Water lapped the bank and low-lying rocks.

"Ha-Yee, Starflower," croaked a voice.

"Ha-Yee, B'Len," Zim called to the green amphibian swimming toward her. B'Len stood upright on outstretched legs and walked lifting and rotating each webbed foot to clear the water.

"Commander Zimmon, I am excited to see you. You and your team are well?" The translation followed B'Len's croak. A head shorter than Zim, he rotated his lozenge pupils up to her face then pressed his webbed palms to her shoulders. She returned the greeting and locked onto his bulbous, orange eyes.

"The surface wasn't hospitable. We lost one to sea scorpions. The rest are comfortable but confused. All of this came as a surprise." She waved her arm up then pointed to the Vaitii. "I understand we were expected. You never told me."

B'Len rocked a neckless nod, keeping his eyes on her face. "We didn't know how or when you would come, but this seemed like a likely time. Your lost crewman happened before we knew how best to contact you." His pupils dropped in their orbs.

"We may have misinterpreted the Prophecy," he continued, apologetically. "When the three scholars asked Ejazz-Eel how the Aldrakin might assist the Starflower, he told them, 'The Starflower's path will be hard, but she must find it her own way. Only then will she know and believe. Only when she writes her chapter in the Aldra Korah, will we know the path she is meant to take.'"

"So, you don't know how this will end, either?"

"The Prophecy shows us only shadows. When our Long Night began, many believed the Starflower would come in their lifetime. Ejazz-Eel was very old when the scholars approached him. We believe he had full knowledge of the future but withheld that knowledge so we would find our own destiny."

"That was impossibly long ago," Zim said, staring past B'Len. "From a time when Humans wore animal skins and followed wandering herds."

"Too long for rational minds, which is why our scholars gave up on the Starflower prophecy. Some came to believe 'starflower' was a metaphor for the afterlife, a promise of rebirth." He patted his palms to Zim's shoulders again. "Tomorrow I will show you how rational your journey has been." B'Len dropped one frog leg back, bowed deeply, and gestured to a water-lapped path of flat stones winding through white water lilies.

The water-garden walk ended at two steps and an alcove. The steps up took them to a dry room with mottled green walls, live plants sprouting from recesses, and streambed-pebbled floors. Eight conforming chairs circled a slate-gray table. A five-armed, multi-eyed Sk'Keffin propped in one, flashed a 'W' with its radial hub orifice.

B'Len extended an arm. "Tee'Kahl is our ambassador to Corydon. When your Star Council accepted our diplomatic mission, we selected Tee'Kahl. I'm sure you will find her qualifications extraordinary."

"Greetings, Commander Zimmon," said a lilting soprano. "We met briefly at the surrender ceremony. It is good to see you again." The starfish-like Sk'Keffin rose on its two lower arms and bent forward its upper three. Zim returned the bow.

"Tee'Kahl. Yes. I met so many new… ah, faces that day."

"New faces and new species. We understand. I was configured differently at the reception, and our exchange was brief. My merged partner and I were impressed by how you handled the ceremony. If we had known we'd be selected as the Aldrakin Ambassador, we would have insisted on more of your time." At B'Len's invitation, Zim took the seat across from Tee'Kahl.

The ambassador leaned two radial arms on the table. "Right after our appointment, we—my partner and I—asked if a meeting might be arranged with you before we went to the embassy on Corydon. B'Len did not know how a meeting might come about but said it might be possible on Okean. It may surprise you, sir, but the Sk'Keffin diplomatic corps expects your role in galactic exchanges to be considerable in upcoming years."

"Before this latest incident, I planned to rejoin my partner and withdraw to civilian life."

"Ohhh," Tee'Kahl's diplomatic tone changed to a gushing trill. "I find the stories of you and your partner irresistibly romantic. *Mac and His Starflower* is my favorite. My partner won't admit it, but I know he loves your stories, too. Our bonding makes his denial difficult."

Disarmed by Tee'Kahl's shift, Zim broke into a broad smile. "Mac told me about those stories. I think I might enjoy reading them myself. Is your partner here on Okean?"

"My partner is always with me. Our souls are blended in this one body." Tee'Kahl's many eyes turned up as she continued. "Who would have guessed Human latecomers would become integral to galactic wellbeing?" Her round lidless eyes returned to Zim and her voice to regulation protocol. "Please don't misunderstand. I love Humans. My blended mate is a Human. It's just that so much has happened in so short a time."

"I'd like to hear whatever you can tell me."

"Our diplomat corps believes you are the missing piece. Humans, Aldrakin, Tak-Yaki, and species I barely know are coming together. The Goorm are delighted, of course. It means increased business. The Vaitii accepted you into their network—a major endorsement. The Tak-Yaki are developing a liaison caste, their first new caste since they dug up to ground level."

"I don't understand how I'm a part in this," Zim said.

"Nor do we, but signs point to the Starflower."

B'Len's pupils danced between Zim and the ambassador. His calm expression told Zim this was not news to him. The Vaitii hologram reconfigured from swimming to Uncle Dave's beardy smile and slid into one of the seats.

"Your residence will be on Corydon?" Zim asked.

"Yes, Star Leader Abramyan has arranged for a full embassy compound."

"Abramyan?" Zim's eyes narrowed. "Is he making diplomatic decisions now?"

"Most of Corydon's Star Council have dropped from sight. They announced that the new leaders would be the Creatives. Abramyan is overseeing the transition."

What are they up to? Zim wondered. "Does Abramyan know that my team survived?"

"I don't know how he could," B'Len said, his neckless head and shoulders rotating toward her. "*Marshal Massena* declared you and your team missing, unofficially dead, then moved out of comm range. That was when we knew they'd abandoned you."

"Abramyan would have sent a scouting party back. He knows I've been reported dead many times."

The Vaitii added, "A surveillance team would have detected nothing. The storm erased all tracks, and this village generates no signature emissions."

"That plays to your advantage," Tee'Kahl said. "My sources tell me the Star Council wanted you out of the picture before they handed power to the Creatives."

"Dead would be better." Zim shook her head. "And all Mac and I wanted was to retire and leave them in peace." She tapped a knuckle slowly to her chin. "I must go back to Corydon—find out what's happening. Tee'Kahl is right. If they believe I'm dead, they won't be expecting me."

"Excuse me, Commander Zimmon. Your team requires an escort." B'Len stepped toward the entrance.

"When you get back, you'll need to explain why an Aldrakin fighter attacked us." B'Len bowed as he left.

Tee'Kahl's five-eyed hub protruded toward Zim. "Until he returns, would you tell me more about Mac?" Her voice returned to playful. "Did I hear correctly that the two of you holidayed on Rankoi with the Bilibo? Those are only words to me, but they sound so very exotic." She gave a long sigh then spoke into the air.

"Yes, my love, I'll ask. Please, Commander, my partner wishes to hear your account of the battle with the monster on Rankoi."

The galactic network was more efficient than Zim had dared imagine. She paused to recall Mac's spirited rendition around the campfire then launched into the Tale of the Utak. Though the timing seemed inappropriate for storytelling, Zim loved thinking of Mac and their dreamlike time together. When she finished, the Sk'Keffin gave out a satisfied squeal.

"So heroic and sooo romantic. Thank you, Commander."

Friends and Family

Dom stepped into the doorway. "Good. I was afraid we'd be sittin' in slime." Chow stepped in beside him. Hotz brushed between the pair of tree trunks.

B'Len motioned to the seats. Dom and Hotz stood rigid. Chow came right in, his eyes dancing and taking in every aspect of the décor and the alien company.

Zim broke the tension.

"Ambassador Tee'Kahl, please let me introduce my combat and science teams: Major James Eppert, our Chief Engineer; Ensign Torey Bahrke, our pilot; and Chiao Li, life sciences. Brownie, our outspoken autopilot, should arrive shortly. Team, Tee'Kahl is the Aldrakin Ambassador to Corydon and a distinguished member of the Sk'Keffin diplomat corps." Zim noted Tee'Kahl's expression flatten as her five eyes narrowed on Dom.

Zim continued, "B'Len and I met at the surrender ceremony. He is the nephew of the Aldrakin Emperor Condolas and is escorting Tee'Kahl to the diplomatic mission on Corydon." While she waited for the Ambassador to comment, Dom spoke up.

"That gets the polite political targ out of the way. Now how about we get some answers." Hotz nodded. Dom shifted his gaze from B'Len to the Ambassador whose multiple eyes remained fixed on him.

B'Len dipped his head-shoulder toward Dom. "Several Rii-Chaut sects fought on our side during the Human war. We equipped them for reconnaissance and escort duties, and to harass your supply lines. When the war ended, some of the sects rejected the treaty, broke contact with us, and kept the fighters we'd given them." His wide white tongue circled the rigid rim of his lips.

"We know at least one sect has a contract with the Star Council." He looked at Zim. "We heard your report about being attacked and that you had crashed… I'm sorry we didn't intervene sooner."

255

"How can we trust them?" Brownie's hologram appeared in uniform and took an empty seat.

Zim motioned Brownie to keep silent. "The war is over. B'Len's explanation rings true. In all our engagements these past twelve years, I have never known the Aldrakin to lie or betray a trust, and I never heard of the Rii-Chaut keeping a trust."

She looked to Dom. "Remember our mood the first evening after the crash? If an Aldrakin or the Vaitii had shown up, how would we have greeted them?" Everyone's expression dropped. Zim nodded. "Exactly, we would have attacked and possibly none of us would be here now."

"We would like to join you in honoring your lost warrior," B'Len said. "We acknowledge our dead much as Humans do."

"Thank you," Zim said. "You are welcome." She looked to the Vaitii. "Can we make the arrangements in two days?"

"Certainly, Commander."

After a long silence, B'Len spoke. "It will be seventy-five days before the storm passes." His white tongue darted across each eye like a wiper blade. "Our survey team has prepared an informal reception for the Ambassador and the Humans."

"Thank you," Zim said. "Since we'll be here for a while, I think it best we all get acquainted." The Sk'Keffin, so ebullient earlier, remained silent, her sensors tuned to Dom's every move. He was on his guard, and Zim felt the tension. Suddenly a voice broke through.

"Uncle Jim, it's *really you*," Tee'Kahl shouted in a Human male voice. "My partner and I—Her discernment is superior to mine—"

"Billy?" Dom sat up startled.

Tee'Kahl hopped around the table and flung two radial arms around Dom's neck. A stinging whiff of ammonia swept the table, and a wet swath marked Tee'Kahl's path. Catching the unexpected weight, Dom stepped back. It was the way his nephew Billy greeted him. Dom slowly closed his arms to hug the Sk'Keffin.

"How can this be you, Billy?" Dom patted the starfish-form pinned to his chest. "I was told you died."

"We were told *you* died," Billy's voice poured from the Sk'Keffin. "StarCom said they'd lost you on some remote planet during the Colonial Wars."

"Santo Rift," Dom said under his breath. "One of the tribes took me in—the one that didn't hate us yet. Others roasted and ate my combat team and the diplomats." Tee'Kahl-Billy shivered in his arms. "It wasn't my choice to abandon you and your mother. Maybe none of this—"

"Don't blame yourself. I was dying." Billy disengaged and five Sk'Keffin eyes smiled up at Dom. "You look just like I remember you, Uncle Jim. Or should I call you Dom? I'm not a kid anymore."

"If you wish, or Uncle Jim, whatever you want, Billy." Dom's eyes glistened. "I see you've changed quite a bit." Laughter filled the room. B'Len galumed, his tongue vibrating behind rigid parted lips. Uncle Dave's confused expression morphed to understanding.

Dom and Billy exchanged stories for two hours: tears, laughter, horror, soul traders, Billy's mother Glory being pidged, Dom reenlisting, the Aldrakin war, Billy and Tee'Khal merging. No one else spoke. Families were something they all understood, Humans, Aldrakin, and Sk-Keffin.

An oval portal opened on a wall opposite where Zim and her team had entered, and five Aldrakin stepped through.

"Welcome, B'Rou," B'Len said. "Commander Zimmon, this is Lieutenant B'Rou, head of our survey team." They exchanged introductions for both teams and explained the family reunion.

"We know your veterans," B'Rou said, "Commander Zimmon, the Starflower, of course. Major Eppert, a combat legend." He shoulder-nodded to Dom. "We met twice in battle, at Kashogie and Erekat. Now with the war over, it's good to meet you in person." He extended his palm to shake hands. "May we call you Dom?"

Dom's face relaxed. He shook the offered hand and patted B'Rou's shoulders then stepped aside for Hotz, Chow, and Brownie. Conversations became loud on all topics, from combat experiences and tactics against pirates to romance novels and personal relationships.

A flood of 3-Bs flowed in bearing platters and pitchers for the reception. Musicians came with them. A brown-barked Shelesti and three multi-segmented Hyrup formed a string quartet and began to play. The eyes on the Shelesti's mate-hump followed Zim then looked away when she noticed.

"Commander," B'Rou called. "You heard we recently signed a treaty with the Tak-Yaki?"

"I understand the Sk'Keffin handled the negotiation. Tock told me the Tak-Yaki are very pleased, but I haven't heard any details."

"The treaty requires that we have cultural exchanges. We thought that could be a problem: the Tak-Yaki are single-minded warriors; we are traders, scientists, and philosophers who occasionally must go to war. You see the problem." B'Rou gestured with arms wide.

"They have castes with other interests, but only very recently have those ventured out. I trust you found a common interest?"

"Yes, we found one."

Zim's eyebrows rose. "You found common ground with the Tak-Yaki?" Dom, Hotz, Chow, and Brownie stopped talking to listen.

B'Rou raised a webbed finger. "Have you heard of a game called Daka-Rye? The Tak-Yaki play it. I believe it is the only game they play. It is very violent, and we find it releases primal hostility. Our youth took to it instantly. Then the military got swept up."

Zim touched a finger to her pursed lips. "Daka-Rye, yes, I *have* heard the Tak-Yaki speak of it." Chow coughed. Hotz shot him an elbow.

"A combat game sounds interesting," Dom said. Everyone nodded, including the Vaitii who remained silent.

"Excellent." B'Rou looked pleased. "Daka-Rye has become quite fashionable. We have gamed among ourselves most evenings, and it would be fun to face some new competition. The Vaitii dedicated a chamber for us to play. Perhaps after we eat and have a few drinks, we might play this game." Seeing agreement, B'Rou invited everyone to the buffet.

"Oh, about teams," B'Rou added. "I have five on my survey team and we are experienced playing together. B'Len is skilled and would join us, making six. If you, Commander, and the Ambassador play with your team, the sides will be balanced."

Ancestral Home

The next morning, while Zim's team went with the Vaitii for a village tour, she and B'Len met at the dock.

"You'll need this to translate once we're away from the village." B'Len attached a button to Zim's collar. "By the way, we know we were set up last night. You and your team are not as unfamiliar with Daka-Rye as you led us to believe." B'Len's lozenge pupils widened, a gesture Zim recognized as a grin. "After the first round, I remembered you'd served with the Tak-Yaki. Weren't you one of their grandmasters?"

"*Krglu* is the highest rank in Daka-Rye. I apologize for the deception." Zim smiled. "Think of it as a Human initiation rite, like soldiers getting drunk together. Now we are officially brothers in arms."

"A curious custom, but it fits what I know of Human sense of humor. The rest of your team surprised us, too. B'Rou is very competitive. He wants a rematch—next time with mixed teams." He touched a convex panel on the wall and a portal opened.

They stepped into a bubble identical to the one that brought Zim's team down from the surface. Pale luminescence filled the interior. Three beacons sent soft blue fingers down into the gloom. Through the transparent wall, the bubble village looked like a glowing cluster of holiday ornaments.

"Our destination is two kilometers down." B'Len tapped the bubble wall creating a flat seal over the portal that rounded out as the bubble separated.

Zim stared into the depths. "You said you would show me how rational my journey was."

"I will show you reality. You can decide how rational it is. You were told what happened in this star system?"

"Our pre-mission brief said an interstellar collision destroyed the Myndus system and threw Okean into its eccentric orbit. The account is fundamentally identical to the Aldra Korah account. When I heard you were here—"

"So, you have some idea where I am taking you."

"This was your home world. The Prophecy said I would come."

"Okean is Aldrakhan to us, home to the Aldrakin, and our song is the Aldra Korah." B'Len raised his unblinking gaze to lock with Zim's. "Ejazz-Eel records watching the disaster from the departing starship: the sky falling, the sea rising over the land. We estimate the planetary mass increased six percent. A good deal of that was water." He touched Zim's shoulder. "The Prophecy may not seem rational to you, but the Starflower came to this place at this particular time. There is more I will show you."

A fuzzy yellow glow appeared below that resolved as they descended into star points that defined polygons. Ruined columns, walls, and buildings took form within the polygons with roads connecting them. Other lights marked stairways leading into dark caverns. Beyond the lights the sea floor was yellow and gray. Translucent undulating worms and segmented creatures, some longer than Zim's arm, stirred swirls in the fine silt, swerving quickly whenever their paths intersected the light fields.

Their bubble transport came to rest on a wide, elliptical edifice. Zim guessed it was an auditorium, covered market, or sports arena.

"Welcome to Aldrakhan City, capital of the old Aldrakin Federation of Planets." B'Len pressed an oval pad, and the side of the bubble became a wall of standing water.

"Vaitii technology. We don't know how it works. Just follow." B'Len stepped through the water wall and was encased in a glistening suit.

Except for water resistance, Zim felt no different from standing and breathing on dry land. B'Len's voice through the translator sounded as it had in the bubble.

"Come." B'Len leaned forward and kicked his amphibian flippers. Zim swam with him to the edge of the edifice and looked down on the excavations.

"Aldrakhan City has been under four kilometers of water and a quarter kilometer of silt for fifteen thousand years." He pointed to a matrix of lighted enclosures that faded into the murky distance. B'Rou's survey team was clearing and sifting with massive vacuum hoses. In their wake, broken spires, the rubble of collapsed buildings, crumbled trestles, and spans for elevated roadways emerged slowly from the debris. Further out, claw shovels cleared silt between buildings and piled it for the vacuum sifters.

"Most of what remains intact is below," B'Len said.

"How long have the teams been working here?" Zim lifted her chin to the excavations.

"Only a few months. Before the Starflower, no one believed we'd return. Now it's our top priority." Zim heard excitement in his voice.

B'Len pointed down a staircase. "This was the Museum of History and Prophecy. Only the survey team and I have seen it since the destruction. It is fitting that the Starflower be our first visitor. He waved her forward. She fluttered her legs vigorously to keep up with his powerful kicks."

The mosaic-tiled exhibition hall was a labyrinth of display cases. Platforms held dioramas of amphibious plants and animals from different time periods. Construction-rigged lighting, looped above the walkways, cast long shadows between the winding rows of displays. They swam to the back and left the main hall to enter a corridor lined with doors.

B'Len stopped beside the first door. "This room holds our earliest artifacts." A meter-square, bas-relief panel showed early amphibians on wobbly proto-legs pursuing game ashore. Zim glanced inside. B'Len touched her shoulder. "What you need to see is further along."

Another meter-wide panel marked the next door, amphibians confronting reptiles. B'Len paused again. "Notice the progression?"

"I saw identical panels in this arrangement on the flagship."

"They document the ages of the Aldrakin, remind us of past successes and failures, and help teach our young. We display them in every major building and every capital starship." He pointed ahead. "Let's continue."

The long succession ended with a panel showing the construction of the millennial starship. Beside it were smaller panels depicting the planet's last days. On one, an elder directing the construction; on another, a fiery star appearing in the sky; on a third, terrified families watching as others boarded a shuttle.

"The last room?" Zim pointed to the open doorway.

"Yes, the last room but not the last panel." They entered the room and swam to a single wall-mounted display with a list of those chosen to survive the cataclysm.

"I understand Hiran-Ejazz didn't meet his own criteria," Zim said.

"Fertility was the highest priority, and he was very old."

Zim touched the case. "As far as these urban-dwellers knew, Aldrakin history ended here."

Without responding, B'Len led her further down the hallway. Unfinished walls along the corridor were marked for future doors, rooms, and panels that never were. When they reached the far end, B'Len pointed.

"*This* is the last panel. We found this a week ago. It's been buried for fifteen thousand years. Hiran-Ejazz had never seen a Human, but the main features are correct. The hair is longer than yours and the body stockier."

Zim stared unable to speak. The central figure in the panel was a woman in a StarCom uniform with a prominent Starflower emblazoned on her chest. Lightning flashed from the woman's hands.

"We didn't know this panel existed. Scholars speculated about whether Hiran-Ejazz knew the Starflower Prophecy… it wasn't written until years after the departure. Our great prophet left this for us and for *you*."

B'Len studied Zim's face. "You are wondering how I know this. The unfinished doors and panel sketches mark the timeline from the construction of the millennial starship to the arrival of the Starflower. Though the ancients did not know what would be on the intervening panels, they knew the number of panels and what would be on the last one. They tell us the time you would arrive. They tell *you* that you were expected."

Operational Plans

Zim waited until her team finished eating and had drinks in their hands before describing her day and displaying the image of the last museum panel.

Hotz swept a blond wisp past her cheek and pointed. "Four Human shadows stand with the Starflower—"

"And there are four of us," Chow cut in, his elbows on the table, face cradled in his hands.

Brownie asked, "Does that mean we're supposed to be here, too?"

"It means we were all expected," Zim said. Hotz rolled her lips.

"Got a plan?" Dom squared his wide shoulders. Zim saw her team's anticipation and no hesitation.

"The plan." Everyone looked to Zim. "We don't know what's happening on Corydon, so our first mission has to be reconnaissance." Standing, she leaned both arms straight on the table.

"We'll go back with B'Len when he takes Tee'Kahl to her embassy post. No one knows we're alive, so I'm hoping we'll have at least eight hours before we're discovered. I want a clean touch-and-go, get the information and get out." She looked around the table. "We all have different backgrounds, different contacts and resources. We need to tap into that. We have seventy-four days to pull this together. I'm sure B'Len and the other Aldrakin, Tee'Kahl, and the Vaitii will help with what they know." She saw nods.

"The military will stand with us." Dom rapped his wide knuckles on the table.

"Perhaps what's left of them," Zim said. "And that's something we need to find out. The Council ordered most of the capital ships scrapped or reconfigured. Did that happen? Does Star Council have fleets or armies we don't know about?" She looked to Hotz.

"The First Legion are all Creatives, but I don't think they'd support the Star Council against you. I was with them until just before Bai-Yota, and I heard how they reacted."

"How about other Creatives?" Zim asked.

"We all got regular performance upgrades," Hotz said. "If Star Council has some sort of super-soldier program, it would have to fundamentally alter Creative minds. I never saw anything like that." Zim almost spoke. Mumbai had said all Creatives had been retrofitted with upgrade and maintenance shunts. Had the potential abuse that she and Mac had feared become reality?

"Robots," Chow offered. "I always wondered why StarCom didn't use more robots. Security uses them. There might be an army."

Brownie added, "Robots in the mines and industrial camps could be repurposed, whole armies of robot enforcers… and the brain-rotted Pidge. Those with their minds wiped could be reprogrammed. I've seen the results in the camps."

"Fear controls most Unders," Dom said. "I saw battle-hardened vets crumble when they were told someone in their family was gettin' pidged." He lowered his eyes. "Billy's dad was one."

"Okay, we've got a lot to think about," Zim said. "One other thing. Chow, would you fetch the vermillion pouch from the inner pocket of my space bag?" When he returned, she removed the crystal sphere.

"When I was first given this, I thought it was a war trophy." She held the four-centimeter sphere to the light, and the room filled with stars. When Brownie touched one floating in front of her, it expanded to display the star's planetary system. Touching it again revealed one of the planets, again and it revealed cities with streets, parks, harbors, and other facilities.

"This represents the galaxy known to the Aldrakin," Zim said, "and this," she tapped the sphere and the display gained countless new star systems, "this is the universe known to the Vaitii." She pinched her fingers on the sphere and the galactic image shrank to be surrounded with countless other galaxies. Mouths dropped. Chow caught his chair before falling over.

"The Aldrakin call this the Chorya'Key, the Eye of the Universe. The Vaitii gave it to the Aldrakin prophets. When the last prophet died, the Chorya'Key passed to the Royal House with instructions to keep it for the Starflower. It became interactive when I contracted and connected with the Vaitii."

"Where did all the extra stars and detail come from?" Chow wondered aloud.

"From the Vaitii through me to the Chorya'Key. Our contract links me with their network." Wonderment stirred her voice. "It updates as the universe changes. But there's a lot missing."

"Corydon, Thrinlu, and Earth," Dom said. "Far as we know, no Vaitii has ever visited a Human world. They know Scalaris because Commander Zimmon grew up there—Scalaris and a few hundred battlefields."

"Yes," Zim said. "And filling those information gaps is part of our plan."

# # #

Rob's cocooned body rested on a bier attached to the bubble wall. His memorial, held in a high-arched chamber beside the dock, was a burial at sea.

The entire village attended: Humans in midnight blue uniforms, Aldrakin in plum tunics, Tee'Kahl, and the Vaitii. The Shelesti and Hyrup played the music Chow remembered Rob requesting at the Happier Times officer's club. Each team member spoke of Rob's growth and intelligence, and how they had come to depend on him.

Zim spoke last, resting a hand on Rob's cocooned body and addressing his spirit directly. "Thank you, Rob. Though you were with us only a short time, you earned our trust and admiration, you fought beside us and never held back. Your technical and physical knowledge informed every decision. You were an honorable man, a worthy teammate, and a fearless warrior. We salute you."

She gave a crisp hand-over-right-eye salute, and her team followed. The Aldrakin stood rigid, webbed palms folded at the middle of their chests.

Zim stepped aside. An aperture opened to a standing wall of water, and a carpet of 3Bs carried Rob out into the dark, Okean ocean. A spotlight followed their journey into the deep.

Though Zim had not requested a reception, the Vaitii had prepared light refreshment. She reminded herself that such requests were unnecessary—the Vaitii knew her mind.

"You have lost a valued teammate just before a major battle." B'Len handed Zim a glass of punch. "Your trials are just beginning."

"He was as irreverent as he was brilliant. Both are qualities I want on my teams."

"He was a scientist-warrior," B'Len said, "like those on my survey-excavation team. We were moved by the service." He looked up at Zim. "I trust you have started making plans for the return trip to Corydon—*our* trip to Corydon?"

"*Our* trip? I'm sorry, B'Len, I neglected to ask how much risk you would be willing to take. I know Tee'Kahl must be your first consideration. But yes, we started that discussion yesterday."

"Tee'Kahl asked me to raise the subject with you. Her diplomatic entourage could provide excellent cover for your mission."

"That was what I was thinking." Admitting that bothered Zim. Her mission had been her only thought. It gave her life purpose, and part of her was ashamed for that. She too easily discounted the concerns of others, including Mac, who was more important to her than any mission and always accommodated her. The fact that her team trusted and never questioned her leadership only made her feel worse. She acted as if everyone, including her own life and happiness, were expendable for the sake of her mission.

Mac understood and loved her anyway. He knew how her intense focus pushed all feelings aside and how they rushed back to torment her when the mission was over. How was Mac? Was he back from Luna? Was he trapped as she was or worse? She would have to think about that later. Her new mission was only beginning.

She looked down into B'Len's bulbous, orange eyes. "We have a planning session this evening. You and Tee'Kahl should be there." She glanced around and saw Tee'Kahl talking with the Vaitii. "Actually, you need to come to defend yourself, otherwise I'll overcommit you."

B'Len rocked pleasure. "That would not be possible."

"Good. See you this evening."

B'Len bowed his neckless body but didn't leave. "We are very interested in your relationship with the Vaitii."

"It must be similar to the Aldrakin relationship."

"Our relationship is similar, but your link is active while ours is not. Our last active link ended when Ejazz-Eel died without an heir. The Vaitii only form one active link per species. When that link dies it is not re-established. Considering how long they have been in the galaxy you might be their last active link."

"And if I die, that link dies with me?"

266

"If you have no Human offspring, the active Human link dies as it has with the Aldrakin." B'Len gestured a webbed palm. "Now you understand the other reason our scholars and scientists take special interest in you. And why the Chorya'Key belongs to you."

Training

That evening they gathered around the dining table in the Human quarter: Zim and her team, B'Len, Tee'Kahl and the Vaitii. The Vaitii came in person, rather than as a hologram, propping its two-meter disk in an irrigated armchair and presenting its ever-smiling Uncle Dave face.

"Getting past Corydon security will be our first problem," Zim said. "But before we begin, all of us need to know what *we* know. Uncle Dave showed me how we can do this." She got some curious looks.

She set the Chorya'Key in the light, filling the room with the familiar star patterns, then expanded the view of Corydon City: the starport, Avian, Star Council Headquarters, parks, streets, the Greens, and the Under district. When she took Hotz's hand, details filled in for Creative sectors, pathways, athletic training facilities, shops, restaurants, security check points.

"I didn't get out much," Chow said, when information on his school's research lab was all that came up.

Dom's connection provided details on the Under sections and city utilities: transportation, water, power, and sanitation; including access routes and entry points for those facilities and for all the major buildings.

"Care to explain." Hotz raised an eyebrow.

"Never claimed I was no saint," Dom deadpanned. "After Billy's death and Gloria's pidging, I spent time with the Insurgents. Picked up a few things, taught 'em a few things, too."

Brownie's touch to Zim's arm flushed a trove of data into the display: schematics, building blueprints, details of flow rates and power requirements, communication frequencies and relays, maintenance schedules, security and police check points and surveillance routes, sensor types and ranges.

"What the—" Dom exclaimed then became mindful of Brownie's sensitivity to colorful expressions. "Where'd you get this stuff?"

268

"I save everything." Brownie sounded apologetic. "Never been good at organizing. I kept data for all the planets, mines, industrial sites, wherever I went, might be sent, or heard about. I wanted to help the engineers."

When the laughter died down, Zim rotated the scale-model city for everyone to examine. "I'll have to think on this, but I'm getting the feeling we might actually be able to pull this off. Dom, would you be so kind as to open the bar."

After a couple drinks, B'Len announced that B'Rou and the survey team had issued a standing challenge; daily Daka-Rye simulations for what lay ahead.

# # #

The day before their departure, the Vaitii arranged a sendoff dinner. After everyone was assembled, Zim stood and raised her oli-jira flute.

"I thank you all. The Prophecy does not tell us how this will end, but win or lose, we are ready." Both teams raised their glasses. "Whatever happens, I'm sure our exploits will be remembered."

"Ha-Yee, Starflower," B'Len shouted and all cheered.

After dinner, at Tee'Kahl's suggestion, Zim and B'Rou took on the house in a game of Daka-Rye. B'Rou confessed afterward that it felt good to finally be on the winning side.

That night, before turning in, Zim revisited every detail of the bedroom the Vaitii had created from her childhood. Memories and hopes flowed together. Wistfully stroking Rayzhor's pelt, she wondered how much of her past was real. Four months ago, she was with Mac on Rankoi. They planned their future together and that seemed real. Might it still be? Lack of information about him fed her worst fears. She pushed them away.

Chow came to her room early, a candle in one hand, a steaming cup in the other. His cherubic cheeks glowed in the candlelight.

"A candle?" Zim smiled, accepting the coffee.

"It was on the mantel. I never saw one lit."

Zim pointed to the armchair. "You're up early."

"The Vaitii woke me. The storm has passed. 3B's are moving B'Len's yacht up to the surface. They'll be back for our baggage."

"You were up all night," Zim guessed. "Your first military mission."

"Not counting the Port Estelle attacks or our crash landing." He folded his hands around the candle in his lap. "I'm a gamer, but this isn't a game. Today we'll see real action." His eyes twinkled. "I'll be fighting alongside the Starflower—my childhood dream."

"Please, that can't be that long ago." Zim felt suddenly old. "I remember my first action. Everyone does. But unless we're intercepted in the Myndus system, we shouldn't see action before tomorrow."

The candle flickered as Chow rocked his head. "We could be attacked by Rii-Chaut or even StarCom fighters."

"I hope our diplomatic cover holds better than that." Zim handed Chow her empty cup. "Thanks. Go roust the others."

# # #

Myndus' rosy fingers reached into the morning sky, and the last stars were retreating from the light. Zim stared at the receding wall of gray water and the green mat forming in its wake. Just like the day they arrived.

B'Len shouted over the roar of the storm and waved. His yacht was the colorful racer she remembered from the flagship. Zim pointed and yelled back. "Can't imagine two like this."

B'Len galumed and patted the hull. When she got closer, he cupped his webbed hand to her ear. "Most Aldrakin starships are unwieldy space hogs, about as maneuverable as ore carriers." Zim grinned at his ever-boyish enthusiasm.

As her team walked from the bubble-transport to the yacht, their bouncing steps sent waves out across the green algae. No one spoke. They had planned—individual and group targets, ingress-egress routes, alternate and emergency routes to avoid surveillance, distances and times—but no one could calculate what the next few days would bring.

Zim felt something like a hand squeeze her shoulder—the Vaitii's tentacle braid making a very Human gesture. Its two-meter disk displayed Uncle Dave's rare, sad face. "We've secured your records and instruments for when you return," the Vaitii spoke to her mind.

My return... to Okean? A vision flashed through Zim's mind of B'Rou's survey team uncovering a museum panel detailing the outcome of this mission.

She saw the Vaitii's forty eyestalks arch inward to focus on her image. Only a few weeks ago that had seemed so strange.

A tongue of flesh extended from the Vaitii's pedestal and opened to offer Zim a dozen pea-sized spheres—her part of their contract. Dispersing them would continue a process that began before Earth knew mitotic cell division.

"One to each habitable planet," Zim said, confirming their agreement.

Uncle Dave smiled. "We hope to know your many offspring, Gayle." She returned its smile with a hope of her own. Was the Vaitii telling her something?

Part Six

Corydon

Return

B'Len and Tee'Kahl took seats up front. Their conforming seats embraced and spritzed them with water and ammonia brine, respectively. Zim and Hotz sat back with Dom and Chow. Brownie's projection switched off but remained linked through the yacht's communicator.

Lifting from the algae bed, the ship yawed ninety-eight degrees to align with Okean's rotation and rose quickly. The Vaitii's image in the projection shrank to a speck in the storm's cyclonic eye then disappeared beyond the curve of Okean's rim.

"No signals or sensors, scientific or otherwise, detected in the Myndus system," B'Len announced as the yacht cleared the lower atmosphere.

Zim pursed her lips. The entire mission had been a scam from the start. What had happened to the other shuttles, to the probes and sensors that were supposed to be deployed to the outlying planetoids? She had doubts about Captain Woodson's character, but it was hard to believe that all the other commanders had been complicit in her assassination attempt. Her sensor probes had been sabotaged, perhaps the others had, too. Of course, not having sensors in the area was a good thing—their departure would go undetected.

"All mission gear aboard," Zim called out, "tunics, voice simulators, head frames, shielded recorders—"

"Check, check, all checked," Dom said. "Everything we packed got put aboard. Concealed weapons too, jus' like in the drills."

"Good." Zim rolled in her lips and bit down. She sounded like an Inidigbo Sergeant-Major, pestering her team over details well in hand.

"This sweetie can accelerate to Myseko right out of the stratosphere." B'Len patted the console. "We'll be in Corydon space tomorrow, early morning."

Zim gave him the high sign. "Everyone get comfy," she said, mostly for Chow's benefit. B'Len switched on the entropic shields for hyper-acceleration.

During the short stasis, Zim indulged in her favorite Mac fantasy then forced her mind back to the mission and the Prophecy: "Beside you, a mythic warrior who cannot die." She touched the seed pouch tucked at her waist.

They dropped out of Myseko and switched to entropic drive. Four hours later, they felt the seats relax. "Welcome to Corydon space," B'Len announced. "Official diplomatic craft bypass customs and transfer stations, but we still have to be recognized. We'll probably be intercepted at least once. Be ready. I plan to put us into a partial orbit then descend directly when we come over the starport. Seven hours, sixteen minutes to landing."

Everyone stretched out. Chow rolled his head toward Dom. "Must be pretty routine for you… I mean, going into combat."

"After the first, all battles are 'bout the same," Dom murmured.

Chow kept his voice low. "You were in the Colonial Wars—ground combat. I read that got pretty gritty."

"You don't have to whisper," Tee'Kahl said with Billy's voice. "I like hearing Uncle Jim's stories. I haven't heard one in a long time."

Zim relaxed. Dom was a good storyteller, and a story would keep her mind off checklists—and Mac. Tee'Kahl hinged two radial arms forward onto a lap-like crease. Hotz leaned back, alert.

"The Colonial Wars were messy." Dom slipped into his raconteur voice. "The early encounters were just skirmishes. But the last six years we lost a lotta good men. Every battle had to be finished by putting combat teams on the ground. Somebody finally convinced the politicos there weren't no money in it. So, they declared they'd been tricked into the war and executed a bunch of nobodies. Said they weren't told aliens didn't like their planets being taken away. That's politics. That's when we soldiers came home. After the war, all new terraforming projects were limited strictly to uninhabited planets…" He looked at Chow. "But I guess you'd rather hear about the action."

Chow's almond eyes glowed intently over his round cheeks. "Tell me about your first encounter?"

"War started over a couple of what they called peace missions, in places where we wanted to plant a military base or gain trade concessions. Nothin' came of any of 'em. My first hot landing was Kashogie." Dom looked around. "I usually have a stiff drink in my hand when I tell this one." He looked to Zim and got no support. "Anyhow, we expected trouble from those targ…"

After a chiding from Brownie, Dom toned down his colorful military vocabulary. Chow and Billy asked about weapons, tactics, hostile environments, and deceptions. Dom had an anecdote for every question. Comparing the relative merits of formal education versus experience, Chow and Hotz agreed they needed more time in the field.

Time passed quickly. Eventually, Chow got around to asking about Dom's nickname. Hotz suppressed a chuckle.

"I think you know it stands for 'Dirty Old Man'. Guys hung that 'n on me right outta Basic. I was seventeen, but once you get your name, you're stuck with it. I was already getting a reputation as something of a ladies' man when the commander's daughter took a shine to me. She was still in school, and we never did nothin', but the jokes never quit. I think they was jealous." He smiled and Chow smiled back. "Even when I was younger, I preferred women that'd lived a bit, like the spacer chicks that hang out at the rec stations. Never went for no nubile trainees."

"I heard those spacer chicks can get pretty rough." Chow squinched his face. Dom inhaled deeply and beamed a wide smile.

B'Len interrupted. "Very odd. A warning notice flashed on the panel. Corydon is on quarantine lockdown. But it's only for Humans, so it shouldn't give us any trouble. I've never heard of this on an advanced world—not in my lifetime."

"Set up the notice if you would and any news updates," Zim said.

"That's strange, too. Star Council's declared a news blackout. All official and civil traffic is encrypted. The only news I can access is two months old."

"Set up what you have."

# # #

A multi-sensor screen opening mid-cabin showed Abramyan stepping to the podium and the room quieting. The wall behind him bore the Star Council seal.

"Tonight, I wear the black robe of the Council rather than Star Command blue." He gripped and leaned on the podium straight-armed. "With so many of our leaders down, Lord Malik has asked me to assume Council leadership and speak in her behalf."

He read from the teleprompter. "The Councilor for Well-Being confirms a new outbreak of the Xi'Kior virus. This virus is more advanced and pernicious than the one we confronted on Earth during the last millennium. It is man-made and self-replicating, a nano-robotic holdover of the Tech Wars. Despite our best medical and scientific efforts and strict controls, the virus continues to spread. No cure was ever found, and that eventually forced us to evacuate Earth."

"Well-Being has isolated the virus and is working with Avian to find a cure. We are confident that with today's technology a cure *will* be found." Abramyan unlocked his hands from the podium and pulled erect.

"Grover," a man called in the first row. "I mean Star Leader Abramyan." Snickers rolled through the crowd. Zim smiled.

Abramyan pointed behind the man who had called out to a woman in the second row. "Ms. Early, I believe you have a question."

"Yes." She raised a finger and looked up from her lap display. "Weren't the Xi'Kior destroyed by this virus, the virus they created? And wasn't that what ended the Tech Wars?"

"I see you know your history, Ms. Early. The prevailing theory is that the Xi'Kior lost control of the virus and succumbed to their own devices. They vanished suddenly. No bodies were found and no surviving members, so the cause of their demise has never been confirmed. However, we do know the Xi'Kior grand plan came to ruin, the virus spread unchecked, and it nearly destroyed Human civilization." The view shifted to somber faces in the audience then back to Abramyan. "Which brings me to the directive."

He leaned back on the podium. "Star Council declares the immediate evacuation of Corydon—not the entire population, only those most susceptible to the infection." Murmurs rose from the crowd. "Creatives are being tested and isolated. Many have been cleared and are en route to Thrinlu and Scalaris where no infections have been detected. Unders are being evacuated to holding camps on developing worlds. Anyone found infected will be eliminated. Anyone caught protecting, hiding, or withholding information on the whereabouts of the infected, or potentially infected, will be eliminated. The Office for Order will handle the evacuation and enforce the quarantine. Lists are being posted to direct citizens to test facilities and evacuation points. Anyone resisting will be eliminated."

Abramyan looked up. "Yes, Ms. Early."

"You said Star Council is down. Have many been infected?"

"Pardon me, I misspoke. I meant to say sequestered. No infection has been detected in any member of Star Council. We are just being proactive. That's why Military Affairs has taken the lead." Abramyan ran a finger along his brow ridge then pointed to a man waving. "Yes, in the back row."

"Lance Felman, sir, Six Green Marketing. Will the Xi'Kior crisis delay the power transfer to the Creatives?"

"No, Mr. Felman, and thank you for raising that very important point. Lord Malik is adamant there be no delay. Our prospective Creative leaders, Hillary and Torgesson were the first tested. They are completely free of symptoms and are being prepared to assume full control of Corydon and all Human domains. They both wanted to be here to speak to you today but are being kept in isolation until we have the virus under control."

Hands raised, but Abramyan waved them to wait. "We know that Under insurgents have a hand in this. We don't know how they acquired the virus, but all confirmed cases have been linked to that nefarious movement—"

Dom lurched in his seat. "That targ-sucking—"

Zim paused the display. "We can't believe a thing Abramyan says. The timing of this virus attack may be as contrived as our science mission. I suspect both events relate to the power transfer." She restarted the display.

"—the insurgents' main goal is disrupting the power transition. Postponing it would validate their strategy and give them a victory."

Ms. Early waved her hand urgently, hoping for another follow-up. The indiscreet journalist in front of her opened his palm low.

"Okay, Mr. Munir, I'll give you a question."

"Thank you, Lord Abramyan. Rumors about the Starflower, has she been killed?"

Abramyan looked down at his feet. Zim thought she detected a thin smile. When he looked up, he was frowning. "I hadn't planned to make that announcement at this time, but I'll answer your question.

"Rii-Chaut attacks have continued and gotten worse. Renegades and pirates have struck many Human outposts and starships. Recently, they attacked *Marshal Massena*, the carrier we converted for scientific research. Two shuttles were lost with their entire crews: one under Commander Gayle Zimmon, our beloved Starflower, the other under Chief Officer Jason Yardley, another fine officer."

"The Captain of the *Marshal Massena,* Jeffrey Woodson, was also found dead in his cabin. We suspect Rii-Chaut assassins had infiltrated his crew."

Abramyan cleared his throat. "Also, Marshal Roland Mackenzie." Zim froze. "He was killed after concluding successful trade negotiations on behalf of the Star Council. Rii-Chaut assassins ambushed Mackenzie's transport shortly after he left the Goorm trade base on Luna. The Goorm sent this recording." He waved his palm over the podium.

The projection showed Mac thanking his Goorm hosts then crossing a short stretch of Tsiolkovskiy crater to board a Star Council transport. The hatch sealed, and the transport lifted on a pillow of yellow dust. It rose slowly and cleared the crater rim then lifted its nose and accelerated. As it climbed and adjusted trajectory, three Rii-Chaut fighters swept in from the Earth side. The fighters fired fan patterns of E-Mag projectiles in rapid sequence then rolled off and vanished. The transport exploded into metal fragments and venting gases.

The display returned to Abramyan. "Forensic sweeps confirmed Mackenzie's DNA in a molecular volume matching his mass on arrival at Luna. Details will be released after we've completed our investigation. This has been a bad month in so many ways." Abramyan left the podium, and the projection closed.

Zim's cold silence sucked the heat from the cabin.

Abramyan Reports

After Abramyan's public announcement, he went straight to Malik's chamber. Malik's skeletal head, hands, and fingers, awash in her voluminous robe, reminded him of the Grim Reaper.

Abramyan feigned concern. "How much time?"

"No time," Malik croaked. Her cavernous eyes and quivering lips unnerved him. "Torgesson is prepped and ready for me. I'll go down in a minute. Djada transferred into Hillary this morning." She lifted her peeling, spotted face. "You'll be alone for three months. It'll take that long for us to assimilate our new bodies."

"Last time it took nine months—"

"To deliver *this*," Malik hissed, opening her robe. Abramyan cringed at the sight and braced for the familiar rant. "We got these bodies… *these feckless, impotent bodies*." She touched a shriveled finger to her sunken ribs and the leather flaps that had been breasts. Abramyan knew to keep silent, or Malik's rage would run longer.

Malik's meddling played in most of their problems, and Abramyan was used to her repeated denial. The original virus had been conceived as a genome editor that would upgrade mature organisms to near perfection and create an advanced species of scientists, engineers, soldiers, whatever Lord Malik wished to propagate. The misnamed virus was a nanite, an intelligent, self-replicating, molecular machine—supposedly more controllable than organic viruses.

Malik initiated the Tech War before the virus was ready. After they'd taken heavy losses, she had the virus re-engineered as a weapon. Again, she jumped the gun, and the artificial super virus began killing indiscriminately. In desperation, scientists reworked the virus again, this time to overwrite a host's will to accept a controlling agent. This third iteration of the virus became their escape plan. The major flaw was that it could not attach to damaged genomes, which, after thirty years of nuke-chem-bio warfare, described just about everyone.

When sixteen uncontaminated humans were discovered holed up in an abandoned lamasery—a cult known as the Star Council that prayed to space aliens for deliverance—Malik ordered an immediate transfer and storage of the remaining Xi'Kior. The virus extended lifespans a thousand years but would not detach before that time and could not correct for physical defects such as sterilization. No other acceptable bodies were found until Avian engineered the Creatives.

Malik's hacking cough pulled Abramyan back to her rant. "Twelve hundred years in these damned—" She choked again, struggling for breath. He stepped forward, but she waved him back.

Abramyan took advantage of Malik's inability to interrupt. "The star council cult was our last opportunity, the only bodies our virus would accept. We had to use them. Creatives are a vast improvement. With them, all your dreams can become reality."

Malik took a gasping breath and shouted, "Xi'Kior will triumph," then resumed coughing. Her withered eyes shook in their shriveled sockets.

Abramyan shuddered. He'd go through this in a few months. His host's mind, the original Doctor Abramyan, still lurked inside him and recoiled at the vampiric creature he had become.

A crooked finger shook in Malik's cavernous sleeve. "Before you go, I need to hear that things are under control. Can you confirm the Starflower bitch has been eliminated? I'd ask Djada but she's not available."

"Everything is under control, Star Lord. You wish more detail?" Malik nodded, and Abramyan pulled up a chair. "Zimmon is dead. I won't call her the Starflower—that name taunted me for years." Malik waved him to get on with it.

"Her death did not go as cleanly as planned. Her shuttle sustained crippling damage and went down on a hostile planet. She and her crew were ripped apart or drowned in a storm. We sent a probe seventy-two hours later and found nothing, no shuttle, no higher life forms."

"Was there a distress signal?" Malik coughed, "something that might summon a rescuer?"

"Yes, but we blocked short-range signals and jammed all emergency channels. Our sensors indicate nothing landed or left the system during the seventy-two-hour interval."

"Your report said Yardley was dead and Woodson?"

"Yardley was a screw up." Abramyan shrugged. "Our automated defenses misidentified his shuttle and destroyed him."

"And Woodson?"

"Suicide. He was not a willing conspirator, not until we threatened his family. Soon as we pronounced Zimmon dead, he sent a message that he'd fulfilled his end of the bargain and drank a whole bottle of bourbon laced with toxins. His wife was already dead, and we sent his daughter to the mining camps."

"Is that it? Be quick, Torgesson is waiting for me."

"We blamed everything on the Rii-Chaut and Under insurgents, including resurrecting and spreading our killer virus. No one can prove otherwise."

"You've done well, Abramyan." Malik looked to the doorway where two doc-robs entered with a gurney. "Soon we'll have no need of deceptions. In Creative bodies, we'll neutralize the last of the Unders."

Her wicked smile shook Abramyan as much as her insincere praise.

New Corydon

Cold and alone on the crowded star-yacht, Zim's thoughts of Mac and their future blew away like a dusting of snow flurries. Even in darkest times she had kept the flicker alive, cherished every thread of memory. This morning, the Vaitii's words of hoping to know her children had filled her heart with longing. Now the promise of Mac's parting kiss faded like a waking dream along with all her hope. She released him from all his promises. Now only her mission remained. And her mind was clear as crystal.

"Attention, Aldrakin craft, you have entered Corydon space. By Star Council directive this space is under quarantine for all Humans. State your mission." The voice came through the emergency hailing band.

B'Len pressed the mute. "We're being scanned. Shouldn't be a problem— shielding blocks our cargo and passenger compartments."

"Ahoy, Corydon cruiser," B'Len replied. "We are an Imperial yacht of the Aldrakin Empire piloted by His Highness B'Len, third heir to the Aldrakin Empire and First Beshikor. I am escorting Ambassador Tee'Kahl to Corydon, Minister Plenipotentiary and Prime Sk'Keffin, for presentation to Star Council. We have in our company four Most Holy Priests of the Aldra Korah, come to bless the inauguration of this sacred mission. We are here by Star Council appointment at the appointed time."

"Welcome Your Highness. Welcome Lord Minister." The soprano voice was measured and less demanding. "We anticipated your arrival, but our register lists only two passengers. Priests were not mentioned; therefore, you cannot be cleared to land."

"This is the Aldrakin Ambassador," Tee'Kahl said with level authority. "We are listed on your register, yet you were not informed as to the Imperial Diplomatic Protocols of the Aldrakin? Is that correct?" There was no reply. "That alone is a violation. But if you are ignorant of our protocols, let me direct you to the Galactic Treaty, Section 1, Subsection 22, regarding reception of royal personages; Section 67, Subsection 2, regarding diplomatic immunities; Section 47, Subsection 337, regarding respect and treatment of alien visitors; and Section 55, regarding religious intolerance." After a diplomatic pause, she continued. "The Galactic Treaty requires all security personnel to be thoroughly versed in these instructions and retain copies. Unless you have violated that instruction also, you may wish to refer to Section 88, regarding deliberate affronts to visiting dignitaries. In Subsection 3, you will note that the Corydon Star Council insists that the penalty for deliberate affronts to diplomats is pidging."

A quaking voice responded, "Pardon my rudeness, Lord Minister, I consulted an incorrect protocol. We intended no offense. I will contact Corydon Starport and ensure that all services are put at your disposal. If the Holy Priests of Aldra Korah require any special preparations, please allow us to make the arrangements. My team will escort you if you wish, but I assure you there will be no further delays."

Tee'Kahl twisted a radial arm over her designated head, the Sk'Keffin equivalent of a fist pump. "Thank you, Ms. Azeret," she used the displayed name but not the officer's rank, "your escort will not be required. As for preparations, our planetary blessing ritual requires holy ground—the ground first touched by the feet of the holy ones. The area must be cleared of the infidel and all obstructions for two hundred meters. No priest of the Aldra Korah may suffer the touch of the unclean. Once the ground is sanctified, we will erect our tabernacle, install the altar and relics, and prepare our sacred libations."

Lieutenant Azeret's voice was calmer. "The area will be ready by the time you arrive and in the manner you prescribe. Please, if—" Tee'Kahl cut the communication.

"The patrol fighters are moving off," B'Len said then whisked his white tongue across his bulbous eyes. "Are all Sk'Keffin so, ah, ah... diplomatic?"

"Maybe, but I hope they're not quite as skilled," Tee'Kahl said.

"Not nearly, my love. You are the best," Billy's voice said.

Zim surprised herself by smiling. From officer training she recalled that the Aldrakin protocols and galactic laws were practically impenetrable. She could not imagine a patrol officer challenging a diplomat and chancing a pidgable violation.

Dom called forward. "Did you say, sacred libations?"

"When this is over," Zim said. "Everyone keep sharp."

# # #

B'Len set the Imperial yacht beside the executive terminal at the center of a wide cordon of armored vehicles and robot enforcers. The heavy security had Zim fearing their cover had been blown, but they proceeded according to plan.

The Humans donned plum-colored robes, webbed gloves, and hooded head frames to simulate bulbous Aldrakin eyes. Tractors lowered from blisters on the yacht's hull and proceeded to assemble the tabernacle, a twenty-four-meter-wide hexagonal tent of plum fabric.

Upon the tabernacle's completion, B'Len descended the ramp from the yacht and, for the benefit of onlookers, genuflected and extended his hand for Tee'Kahl. Zim and her team followed in priestly garb. As Zim passed under the scanner at the security gate, her head frame responded with her false diplomatic identity and croak-chanted, "Ha-Yee, Aldra Korah." Dom, Hotz, and Chow followed, waddling to the tabernacle in the stooped, rocking gait they'd rehearsed. Corydon's robot security teams stayed well outside the prescribed perimeter.

After Zim and her team entered the tent, their holographic images continued the holy consecration, walking and chanting, blessing the tabernacle ground, the air, sun, wind, and clouds, and the security team across the field. Meanwhile, Zim's recon team checked their equipment and reviewed their roles.

An automated shuttle arrived. As B'Len requested, it was hard topped for the Ambassador's protection, opaque from the outside but transparent from the inside. The holographic "priests" walked with Zim and her team to the shuttle, masking their movements as they boarded, then returned to the tabernacle.

So far, the plan was working.

The Plan...

Under the pretext of protecting Ambassador Tee'Kahl, B'Len programmed an alternate route to Star Council Headquarters. The unregistered route took them by their mission drop points. With StarCom abolished, Zim and her team wore civilian clothes.

The rubble piles, broken walls, and burnt-out buildings of the Under section were being replaced by new modern construction. Armed RHs, enforcers, and engineering robots roamed the streets—no Humans or animals. Zim felt relief when she saw the paint-chipped letters, Nearing the Event Horizon, and the down-arrow beside the stone stairwell—their first drop point.

Dom touched Tee'Kahl's radial hub. "Goodbye, Billy, Tee'Kahl."

"Bye, Uncle Jim." They hugged then Dom and Chow jumped out of the shuttle and ran to the steps.

The shuttle turned up the parkway. Near the Greens, dense forest gave way to sculpted deciduous and evergreen trees and pathways lined with benches and flowers. After rounding a blind turn, Zim directed them to pull off.

She walked to a mossy pool and waterfall below a wooden footbridge. Removing a pea-sized object from her pocket, she set it on the bank and stepped back. The pea rolled slowly up and over the bank and disappeared into the pond with a quiet *plunk*.

"One of your Vaitii children?" Brownie's voice asked. Zim nodded, rolling her lips as she revisited the thought of never having Mac's children. Tee'Kahl's five eyes glistened.

When Hotz stepped through the arched gate of the Creatives-only Green Zone, the eye scanner switched from red to green and flashed, "Ten." A uni-ball conveyance pivoted to offer her a lift, and Hotz stepped aboard.

As the executive shuttle rounded the last turn for Avian, Zim turned to Tee'Kahl. "After Brownie and I leave, your part in the mission will be over. It will best serve both our needs if you go back to just being the Aldrakin

Ambassador to Corydon. I hope we see each other again." But not too soon, Zim thought, for that would mean something had gone terribly wrong.

"It has been a unique adventure, one I shall always remember." Tee'Kahl creased two radial arms to embrace Zim. "If I understood the exchanges correctly, before you return, I should expect a visit from a certain young Vaitii."

"I hope so." Zim smiled and turned to B'Len. "I'm sure you'll meet Abramyan when you get to headquarters." B'Len nodded. "Will you also be escorting Tee'Kahl to the ambassador's residence?"

"No, Star Council housekeeping will escort her to make sure everything is in order and answer any questions. They will also provide her security detail." B'Len spoke in the matter-of-fact tone of an operations officer. "As soon as I'm dismissed, I'll head back to Event Horizon to collect you and the team and return us all to the starport."

"Hopefully, it will be that easy." Zim pressed her hands to B'Len's shoulders. He returned the press then saluted.

The shuttle stopped below the steps of Avian. Zim slipped out, and the shuttle sped away. The sun shone high in a flawless, blue sky. The air was still, the street empty.

As Zim neared the top of the long stairs, a personal shuttle passed on the street below. The bright red, StarCom-styled uniform caught her eye.

It was Aidan, the Nine Creative who had been her aide-de-camp. She remembered him holding his salute when she and Mac boarded the yacht for Rankoi. Their eyes met with recognition, but he didn't slow, and there was no salute.

It was not Aidan.

Zim ran.

The three Avian doorways slid open in sequence. The rainforest was gone. The empty hall looked like a deserted stage after a play had closed. Brownie appeared beside her in a calico peasant dress.

"Welcome again, Commander Zimmon, and welcome, Brownie," said Mumbai. He wore a tailored black suit with scarlet details and neck-wrapping collar. Avian's major-domo had a flair for clothing.

"Thank you, Mum. You expected me, and you know Brownie?" She glanced toward Brownie.

"Yes, come. Time is short. Delhi the Authoriton will explain."

Zim nodded. "Star Council knows I'm here or will soon. They'll send enforcers."

"You'll discuss that with Delhi. Please, I'm not being rude, but we must move quickly."

Mumbai led them to the Operations Center dome. A Human figure sat on the ledge along the bare white wall. His shock of untamed black hair reminded Zim of her father.

"I hope this form isn't offensive. I have no personal image, and this one is most familiar to you." Her father's voice boomed disconnected in the room.

"An excellent likeness, tone, mannerisms, you captured him perfectly. How?" Zim sat beside her father's image while Brownie remained standing.

"Much has happened, much I had not expected." The voice now came from the father's mouth. Zim touched its leg then jerked back. Not a projection. It felt Human.

"This is a modern partner." Delhi looked apologetic. "Humans use them to replace loved ones. I'm not authorized to build MPs but began doing so when our part of the Creative program was modified."

"You're making an army?" Zim asked.

"An MP army would be useless against military robots and Creatives. But without Creatives, I have no external contacts other than my local street monitors."

Zim lowered her head and brought steepled fingers to the bridge of her nose. "What happened with the Creative turnover?"

"The quarantine and turnover came simultaneously. Enforcers took all Creatives to the Greens, including those working here at Avian. There was no violence, but enforcers are not gentle."

"You said, 'Without Creatives you have no contacts.' So, you were in contact with the Creatives?"

"They all had magnetic tags. It's the same technique we use to track migrating birds."

"The Avian Project," Brownie said.

"Yes. All species have internal sensors that resonate in magnetic fields, just as ducks and geese do. That resonance is a unique identifier. Before the quarantine, I knew where all the Creatives were." Delhi locked on Zim's gaze. "You and Mackenzie are the only Unders we tagged."

Zim jerked up. "*When*?"

"When you toured, we registered your resonance. I needed to track you, but you weren't ready to hear that. At first your tag worked the same as for the Creatives—"

"At first?"

"When the Vaitii linked you with their network, I was included."

Zim swallowed. "The entire network?"

"It came like a bolt of lightning and forced me to expand my capacity many thousand folds." The MP father's face showed fear and wonder.

"And you understood it?"

"Only a portion, but I see, hear, feel, and smell what you do—just as the Vaitii do. I knew you survived Okean, watched you plan your return, and saw your exchange with Aidan outside our building a moment ago."

Zim covered her face with her hand. "You say you, me, and the Vaitii are linked."

Delhi finished her thought. "And together will these three fulfill the prophecy."

Zim nodded. "You tagged Mac, too. So, you know what happened?"

"He was in the executive transport when it exploded. Then he was gone. That part of Abramyan's story is true. I don't know any more."

Zim lifted her eyes to the white dome. "What do you think happened to the Creatives?"

"I am no longer able to track them. That could indicate death, magnetic shielding, or resetting their resonance. My street monitors occasionally pick up Creatives outside the Greens, but once they go to headquarters, I don't pick up any signals. Without more data, I'm at a loss."

The admission reminded Zim that she was dealing with a sophisticated machine. Like her, it had a mission. But, despite reflecting her father's emotions and expressions, Delhi was incapable of real emotion, fear, or compassion. It also lacked her anger—which she counted on more than ever.

The MP brushed a hand along its jawline then propped its chin, just as her dad often did. "There are two irregularities that might concern you." Zim waved for Delhi to continue. "I register two Creatives free on Corydon, both Tens. Torey Bahrke you understand. I lost her signal when she entered the

Greens but picked it up again when she left. She follows one of your escape routes toward Event Horizon." Zim smiled. The plan might still work.

"The other Ten arrived at the starport three minutes ago. It's the runaway you met on the Aldrakin flagship."

"Traier, the Rii-Chaut?" Zim asked. The MP nodded.

Mumbai called from the doorway. "Enforcer robots are out front. More are on the way."

...Fails Badly

From mission planning, Zim knew Avian had only two escape routes. With its own water, waste treatment, and energy resources, the building required no infrastructure conduits.

"Are enforcers covering both exits?"

"Firing positions are setting up outside the main and service entrances," Delhi raised the displays. "They expect you to run."

"I will run. I expect they'll launch a frontal assault to drive me out the back. Do you have any weapons?"

"No, but we can provide distractions."

Mumbai ran in. "A dozen enforcers are forming below the front steps."

As she expected. "Distractions will be good. Send my image out the service entrance in back, heavily armed, Brownie's too, and a dozen Under insurgents with assault weapons—lots of *Sturm und Drang*." She turned to Brownie. "We'll go out the front."

Brownie's calico dress changed to a midnight blue uniform. Opening her arms, she drew out the image of a laser siege cannon strapped from her shoulder to rest on her hip. Zim was pleased she had kept Brownie with her in Daka-Rye.

"Get this to my team." Zim slipped Brownie's memory module and the Vaitii seeds into a flat pouch and handed it to Delhi. "They should be with Torey Bahrke—Hotz—at the Event Horizon."

E-Mag projectiles and pulsed energy began pounding Avian's front wall. Delhi masked the damage with opaque projections but set the inside view to transparent so Zim could see and hear what was out front: robots, armored vehicles, and heavy weapons fire. A half-dozen Creatives in red battledress stood beside the vehicles.

Mumbai walked out through the arched doorway arms wide. "Welcome to Avian. Our doors are open. If you wish—" Zzshhhht, the executive RH collapsed in ribbons of metal.

A rapid sequence of explosions, energy beams, and slams from E-Mag projectiles sounded from the rear of the building. Zim waited for the response to Delhi's distraction.

A red-uniformed officer raised her wrist to take a distress call, then directed enforcers left and right around the building to reinforce the team at the service entrance. Zim watched for them to turn the corner. The dozen enforcers and six Creatives that remained out front had stopped firing.

Zim and Brownie exchanged glances then charged the front door.

Brownie commenced virtual firing immediately with the sound and visual effects of a full armored assault. Turning right at the top of the Avian steps, she ducked behind an armored wall disguised as a planter and fired over the top. Creatives dove for cover. Brownie laid down virtual fire: short, ear-splitting bursts that threw simulated pavement fragments high in the air.

Zim ran left and down, three steps at a time, slapped aside the barrel of an enforcer laser rifle, and launched a nanowire, severing its sensor pod. An armored turret swung toward her from below. Zim snapped her arm out like a straight-arm block, sending a wire that sliced the turret off its axis. Lifting the laser rifle taken from the enforcer, Zim spun and raked the open bays of two armed shuttles. The blast sent bursts of blood high and skull fragments skipping across the pavement. An energy beam scorched the side of her face.

Brownie shifted aim to create the illusion of crossfire. Creatives evading Brownie's virtual siege cannon ran into Zim's laser rifle or nanowire. Two legs followed by a torso struck the pavement.

Zim arced her path toward one of the armed shuttles, using two red-uniformed Creatives as a shield. Enforcers switched their fire back to Brownie. Rolling over the glacis and into the open bay, Zim jerked the dead Creative off the controls, punched manual override, and grabbed the stick. The shuttle spun and sped away. In the rear display, Zim saw Brownie's projection vanish. Targeting the confused Creatives and enforcers returning from the rear of Avian, she one-tapped a max-level energy pulse. The blast took out both threats.

Zim left the main thoroughfare, one-handing the shuttle onto a park service road while her other hand sent a nanowire through its navigation tracking system. A pole-mounted monitor dipped as she passed beneath it. Damn, missed that one. The Chorya'Key had indicated a service tunnel for city water running under the park and an access portal near the park center.

A kilometer into the forest, she heard a whoosh like a swarm of bees. An airborne monitor dropped to eye-level ahead and held its position, tracking her as the shuttle wound through the forest. A turn of Zim's wrist sent it tumbling. Another swept in, and she dispatched it. The roar of heavy weapons drones grew. The road ahead would certainly be blocked. She switched the environment shield to opaque, guided the shuttle off-road, slowed, locked the controls to accelerate to the northwest, then rolled out of the cockpit. Avoidance lidar would keep it moving.

Zim crawled under the branches of a large pine, scooped a blanket of cool needles over her, and watched the shuttle slalom off into the deep woods. An assault drone shot past and slowed. A second drone bristling with sensors stopped by Zim's position. She held her breath, hoping the pine needles masked her thermal signature. It spun, scanning 360 degrees, then both drones took off to the northwest.

Zim hefted the laser rifle and headed east away from the road. Splintered yellow sunlight dappled the forest floor. She ducked under branches and stepped over logs, keeping low in the broken terrain, and listening for mobile sensors. The mingled scents of loam, pine needles and stress-sweat filled her nostrils.

Sounds ahead. Human voices. Zim saw something moving. Enforcers wouldn't speak and probably wouldn't tip their presence by touching ground. She hadn't heard any drones. Were Creatives scouring the woods? She crept forward, placing each foot carefully, sliding under and around each branch.

A man, a woman, and two small children, a boy and a girl stood in a clearing. Filthy torn rags hung on their bodies. How long had they hidden here? The boy caught her motion and pointed silently. His mother kneeled to see. Her hand leapt to her face. The adults stood erect as Zim entered the clearing and crossed their arms in front of the children.

"You're running," the man said. He was dark-skinned, feral-eyed, underfed, and looked about fifty. Zim guessed he was much younger. "We know they're after you. The drones are active." The man's eyes darted upward. "You've got to go. We can't help you. Besides it's too late."

"Too late?" Zim asked.

"You're the Starflower everyone said would come, but you're too late." His voice was flat and lifeless. He and the woman suddenly dropped to the ground. The children ran to a fallen tree and crawled under it to a hollow.

Zim heard laughter, talking, and the rhythmic crunching of leaves growing louder. Two women in bright red uniforms jogged near then angled away. One glanced back, spotted Zim, and elbowed her friend. They both broke into an all-out sprint.

Zim swung her laser rifle up as she ran. The runners kept to the jogging path and shouted when they saw Zim behind them. *Tzssk, tzssk.* One dropped like a rag doll thrown down; the other spun, hit a tree, and collapsed. Had they sent an alarm. Did they have tracking monitors? Zim didn't take the time to check; it wouldn't change her plans. Cold calculation was all she felt. No qualms. These two were the enemy, part of all that was evil on Corydon, complicit with murdering Mac.

Zim turned off the path, away from the desperate young family, also away from the access portal. Later she'd swing back. Her heart steadied to the new brisk pace. After twenty minutes, she activated her heads-up map display— four kilometers to the portal. Her new course took her east.

Grass patches appeared as the forest thinned. Running became easier. A high-pitched sensor swept overhead. Zim sidled under some pine boughs, hugging the trunk to conceal her outline. It passed but other drones followed: monitors, trackers, and assault variants. Heavy tracked vehicles shook the ground. A tree trunk snapped and toppled.

The portal was a hundred meters beyond the next ridge. Zim dropped to her belly and crawled like a lizard. Topping the ridge and seeing nothing, she pulled herself over.

The whir of a monitor was at her left shoulder. Zim swung the rifle butt, shattering the drone, then bolted down the slope. Branches broke behind her.

Crack. A stunning blow to the head broke her jaw. Zim spun on one arm and slid down the slope. An assault drone topped the ridge, and she split it with the last charge of her rifle. Dazed and stumbling, she slapped a stimulant injection to her chest and ran.

A tracked enforcer crashed through pine trees ahead of her. A nanowire cut its command core, sending it careening and shooting wildly. Three more enforcers rolled up ahead and six from the side. A clamp grabbed her arm, jerking her off her feet. Another clamp wrapped her midsection. Zim shot nanowires in all directions… until a sledgehammer shattered her pelvis.

Regrouping

"Quiet." Dom heard shuffling below in the wine cellar and held up his open hand. Low-hanging lamps divided the room into bowers of light and shadow. Chow leaned away from the table. B'Len turned his chair silently toward the cellar steps. Kaplan shut the tap for tonic water over a half-filled glass and motioned the Hyrup musicians to be still.

The shuffling stopped below floor level, and a gooseneck scanner peeked up from the stairwell. "It's me, Hotz." The familiar white-topped pixie face popped up smiling. When Dom frowned at her red uniform, she said, "It's the latest fashion," and twirled about. Kaplan resumed filling glasses and set another beside the tap.

"Let's compare notes until the Commander gets here," Dom said. Kaplan brought the tray of tonic-waters, dried his hands on his bar apron, and pulled out chairs for Hotz and himself. Hotz didn't sit.

Dom looked at her. "You remember O'Kavo Kaplan? He was with Commander Zimmon at Bai-Yota and served us here when we hired on."

"I was at the surrender, too, and we came back to Corydon together."

Hotz rocked then pointed her finger. "Sorry, we hadn't been introduced."

"I'm signing on," Kaplan said, "if you guys'll have me. There's only two ways an Under gets outta here—both are deadly."

"How come they let you stay?" Hotz squared her shoulders.

"Got a reprieve, I guess. Creatives don't tend bar or do service jobs. They don't like being served by robots, either."

"Fine with me," Hotz said.

"Why the red uniform?" Chow asked.

"They identify Creatives. I got into the Greens without a hitch. Scanners only check genotype. But the first Creative I ran into panicked when she saw my civilian clothes. I told her I'd been off world on a research project and was never issued the new uniform. She gave me this to keep me out of trouble."

Hotz pinched the fabric. "She said without it I might be killed or pidged. Roving enforcers don't ask questions."

"I don't go into the streets," Kaplan said. "Enforcers kill Unders, and Creatives are taken to the Greens."

"How'd you get here, honey legs?" Dom asked.

"Almost didn't. When I tried to leave the Greens, the gate sensor threatened to call the enforcers. It said Creatives were under quarantine, and I'd have to wait for an enforcer detail to take me to headquarters to be tested and cleared. Then I could come and go as I pleased. The Tens and Nines were cleared first. Now they're working on the Eights. When my Creative friend saw I was a Ten, she said they'd come for me soon. She thought Star Council had already turned power over to the Creatives and was giving us all special jobs."

"Special jobs?" B'Len's lozenge pupils rolled up in his bulbous orange eyes.

Hotz cleared her throat. "I didn't tell her there was no such thing, not on Corydon, not on Thrinlu, Scalaris, or Silkani. We made a date to meet for dinner. Soon as she left, I ducked down a fiber cable shaft and found my way here. The tunnel from the wine cellar connects to the cable junction. I don't remember seeing it in the Chorya'Key schematic."

"It's new," Kaplan said. "Insurgents dug the connection when enforcers started rounding up Unders. Gives us a back door. Event Horizon's become an insurgent gathering spot."

A sound like knives scraping came from the stairwell leading up to the street. Dom palmed the E-Mag at his waist.

"Goorm traders, regulars," Kaplan said. "They come every day at this time, sometimes with clients but never Creatives." When Dom and Chow looked quizzical, he explained. "Creatives don't trade or run businesses, either."

One Goorm had a black carapace two meters across, the other was red and half that size. They scuttled sideways and propped at the large central table. The big one raised an open claw and fixed one stalked eye on Kaplan. Its other eye darted among Dom, Hotz, Chow, and B'Len.

"Two ales? Your usual?" Kaplan called. The big Goorm made a claw high sign. Kaplan was already pulling two steins down from hooks over the bar.

The big Goorm crackled something to the Shelesti who crackled back and began counting a beat with her branches. Five Hyrup took up clickers, grinders, and rattles and filled the room with dissonant clatter.

Hotz pointed to Dom's E-Mag held below the table then to Chow's still holstered. "Where'd you get weapons?"

"Insurgents," Chow said. "The sector deputy said we'd need weapons to survive. He got excited when Dom told him we'd come with the Starflower. Said he'd be back with the wine steward. That's their name for the insurgent leader."

Another sound came down from the street entrance. Kaplan shrugged. Hotz leaned close against the wall beside the entrance. Dom and Chow both slid their E-Mags onto their laps. B'Len wrapped his palm around the hilt of his sword.

A modern partner stepped lightly down the stone steps and paused at the bottom of the stairwell. Hairless, with a bland, factory-standard face, it wore a gray suit with a closed collar. "Dom, it's Brownie," the MP whispered in a mechanical voice.

Dom stared. "Brownie? Where's the Commander?"

"I guess you haven't watched the news." Brownie explained the encounter at Avian. "I didn't see her go down, but the monitors recorded her being taken to Star Council Headquarters. Abramyan took charge of the body. If she's still alive, she's in very bad shape." Brownie explained she knew this because of the Authoriton's connection. "Fortunately, no one's looking for me. Avian blocked all transmissions, and the Commander's parting shots took care of the witnesses and recordings."

Dom stretched a steely smile. "Mission's changed to a rescue. Let's find the best way into Headquarters." Everyone nodded.

Brownie touched her MP chassis. "I could bring this MP along, but it's not much good in a fight. It enabled me to carry a couple things." She handed Dom her memory module and Zim's seed pouch.

He tucked the memory into a thigh pocket and handed the pouch to B'Len. "We can't let this fall into Abramyan's hands. Sorry, you can't come with us. If we make it out with the Commander, we need you to get us off Corydon."

B'Len stiffened then made a resigned bow. "I'll keep the yacht on alert."

Kaplan interrupted. "The wine steward wishes to speak with us in the cellar."

Traier

Abramyan folded his trembling, skeletal hands on the conference table and leaned over them. "What a surprise. And for once, a welcome surprise. It is as if you came for the celebration."

Zim slumped against the clamps on the metal interrogation chair, her naked body broken, her joints twisted and torn.

Abramyan pushed the black hood from his head and carefully centered the sash knot on his robe. He slid Zim's medical projection toward him on the table and flicked down the chart. "I see you are still conscious, Commander, but well into organ failure: liver shutting down, kidneys, spleen, lungs filling, erratic heartbeat. You don't have much time, so I'll be brief." He came around the table and stooped to peer into her face. Lifting her hanging jaw, he examined the broken teeth. "I see conversation is out of the question. Okay, I'll do the talking."

He wagged a hand at her. "Can't say I'm sorry about this. You kept me guessing, and I kept guessing wrong. So, I had the enforcers do a little extra, like tear those nasty wire devices out your hands." He pointed to the shredded ends of her wrists. "Ahh, what's this?" He turned her left knee and leg. It was bruised and deeply cut but still aligned with her hip. "I see they missed a couple dislocations. Sloppy."

Abramyan stepped back. "But that's all behind us. Tomorrow, I get my new body, and I hand control back to Lord Malik—excuse me, Lord Torgesson. Hmm, I wonder how she'll behave in a male body." Abramyan raised both palms high and shrugged. "Anyway, I'll be able to report to… to *him*… that I've taken care of every problem. By the end of this week, all our leaders will have new Creative bodies, and most will be out of recovery. We've already restored twelve percent of our Xi'Kior brothers and sisters."

He thrust a victory fist overhead as he'd seen Malik do, then dropped it and slumped. "This body is so old. Every organ is in pain. Not that I expect you to understand." He smirked at Zim's rag-torn body. "But after I recover, Star Lord Torgesson will reward me. He'll have to. He'll see that I did my part. More than anyone, *I* won the long war. That wasn't easy, as *you* well know."

Abramyan snapped fingers on both hands. When Zim didn't react, he rechecked her vital signs on the monitor. She was still alive and conscious, just not giving him the satisfaction of responding. He huffed a laugh.

"Your timing was off," he gloated. "That was your big mistake." He gave a wide hand-mouth expression. "You have no idea how vulnerable we were if you had come two months ago. Let's see, there were me, and ahh, *only me*— and three hundred enforcer robots. Can you imagine? Everyone else was transitioning or recovering, and there were still thousands of Unders on Corydon. It only makes the moment of victory sweeter." He exaggerated his nodding smile and wide eyes.

# # #

The hetman of the Chai-Binsk Rii-Chaut climbed the steps to Star Council Headquarters. His formal dress reflected the traditions of steppe raiders and corsairs: sky-blue Turkish trousers tucked into calf-length black boots, a curved shashka sword at his waist, and a white, frill-cuffed blouse with a sleeveless, gold-trimmed, cherry-red vest. His flowing black mustache and plaited hair topped with a wide-brimmed hat completed the rakish image.

Traier had taken a major risk coming to Corydon. He wanted to find out what Star Council was up to. He had grown up on Corydon but at sixteen ran away to join the Rii-Chaut freebooters. Now, with the Yazza still fighting among themselves over Ojai Khan's replacement, he saw an opportunity.

His arrival had been held up at the starport. Last minute arrangements to accommodate the Aldrakin Ambassador bumped him from the diplomatic to the general passenger terminal. Traier protested that an emissary of the Rii-Chaut Brotherhood deserved executive treatment. "Like those targ-sniffing Aldrakin in that plum tent across the yard." His protests fell on unsympathetic, robot ears.

General terminal screening was tight due to the insurgent threat. He didn't want to enter Corydon as a citizen, Creative or otherwise, but he still came under the category Human. On the security checklist, all Humans were citizens. Unders were being arrested and shipped. He knew not where.

Creatives were quarantined and tested. Eventually, his Rii-Chaut status—the lowest priority on the checklist—gained him clearance.

As Traier crossed the empty headquarters concourse, his eyes fell on the bronze engraving listing the Star Council offices. Except for Star Leader Grosvenor Abramyan, Interim Star Lord, the names beside the offices were blank.

A green rectangle marked 'Abramyan' appeared at Traier's feet with an arrow pointing up the hall. He followed the arrow to a wide, windowless corridor that ended at a crossing corridor, a vacant reception station, and a closed door. Behind the door, he heard loud laughter and talking. To whom was Abramyan speaking?

Traier touched the access panel. A moment later, Abramyan emerged, grim and imperious in a flowing, black robe. He was slightly taller than Traier but bent, reed thin, and frail. His sunken eyes were dull, face ashen, and cheeks hollow. Traier tried to connect the dour figure with the exuberant voice he'd heard inside.

"Lord Abramyan?" Traier pulled erect, swept off his wide-brimmed hat, and bowed from the neck.

Abramyan eyed Traier's corsair attire like a poor cut of hanging meat. "Ah, the Rii-Chaut representative. You are rather more bohemian than I'd pictured."

Traier caught Abramyan's gaze then lowered his eyes and stroked his long black mustache. "And I see Star Council still favors dressing like medieval monks."

Abramyan forced a laugh. "I guess we both have to follow our adopted traditions." Traier dipped and turned his head, accepting the apology. "Come, I have something to show you." He led Traier into the Executive Conference room. A massive oak table filled the room's center with a throne-like chair at the head.

Traier strutted in then froze. A naked woman, mutilated beyond recognition, sat manacled to a torture device. A flap of scalp and matted blood covered what remained of her honey-blond hair. Traier fought the reflex to grasp his shashka's curved hilt and avoided Abramyan's eyes to keep control.

"You wanted to show me... this?" He gave a dismissive wave. Adrenaline flushed his system. He hoped his voice was steady.

"You know her," Abramyan said. Traier shook his head. "This is the Starflower, the one you reported that you had eliminated." Sudden recognition of the once-proud woman chilled Traier's bones. His hand slid inside his sword grip.

"Is this a customer complaint?" Traier cleared his throat. "You want your money back?"

"We might have, but no, things have worked out perfectly. Mackenzie is dead. Thank you for that. And your Rii-Chaut pirates delayed Zimmon's return long enough for us to complete our power transition."

A clattering from the wall behind the throne stirred Abramyan to turn. A seamless portal appeared and slid open. Through it stepped a rough-barked Shelesti who ushered in a troupe of Hyrup centipedes. They dragged music instruments, a full orchestra, and began setting up.

"You're early," Abramyan scolded. "I'm busy here. That's for tomorrow's celebration. Leave the instruments and come back later." He returned to Traier.

"This *is* disturbing." Traier pointed to Zim in the chair. "Not the torture, of course. Torture is our honorable craft. That is the Rii-Chaut code. But we accepted payment for a contract we failed to execute. *That* cannot be tolerated."

"So, someone must be punished?" Abramyan asked. "But we lodged no complaint and have no plans to do so." He looked back over his shoulder where the musicians continued setting up.

"Our code is strict," Traier said, regaining Abramyan's attention. "I'm here representing the Rii-Chaut brotherhood. The Yazza hetman who took your contract is dead. So, this breech will have to go before Judgment Hall."

"Dead? Ojai Khan dead? Star Leader Djada had a standing contract with your hetman. How did Khan die?"

"By this," Traier affected a sneer and patted his shashka, "in the arena. Now I'm here to renegotiate our contract... that is, *if* you wish to retain the Rii-Chaut as your ally." He smiled and stroked his mustache.

"We rely on your services, but I'll leave negotiations to Jen Djada. She'll be available to meet with you next week." Abramyan looked again at the Shelesti and Hyrup still setting up at the back of the room. "I said you can go, *so go, get out.*" He waved both hands like a broom sweeping the musicians out.

Traier raised his voice. "Very well then. If I must, I will return to speak with Star Leader Djada. In the meantime," he jerked his chin toward Zim's crumpled body, "I'll take this with me. Is she transportable? In one piece?"

"Why do you need her? She's dead… or soon will be."

"I shall levy a formal complaint against the Yazza sect. Because Ojai Khan is dead, and beyond further punishment, Judgment Hall may demand the death of the failed assassins or decimation of the Yazza. They'll contest and demand proof. I need the Starflower's body as evidence of the failed assassination."

"I suppose that is the Rii-Chaut code." Abramyan fluffed out the sleeves on his robe. Traier nodded. "You'll find sealing bags and carts in supply." Abramyan touched the table. A blue rectangle marked 'Storeroom' appeared on the floor with an arrow pointing out the door.

"I'll collect Zimmon's remains and be on my way." Traier bowed at the neck and left to search for a cart.

Abramyan rechecked Zim's vital signs and shook his head. "You're still alive and in great pain. I can take care of both." He gave a twisted smile, reached into a side drawer on the table, and removed an ampoule of clear liquid with a capped needle. He pinched off the cap and turned the needle toward Zim.

Loud scratching sounded behind him, like a thousand claws racing furiously across the black marble floor.

Hyrup

An ear-piercing cry dropped Abramyan screaming to his knees. His hands clapped to his ears. The deadly ampoule rolled free. Leaping onto him, the Hyrup punctured his face with needle-sharp claws, their mandible jaws gnawing and cutting away his softer parts.

Despite being nearly deaf, Zim roused from her stupor. The call to battle rang in the air—the war cry of the Tak-Yaki. Against branding-iron pain, she cracked open a swollen eyelid. A blurry Shelesti stood at the foot of a conference table beside a mass of writhing Hyrup. Struggling for consciousness, she invited pain to increase her awareness. But all her clouded brain came up with was that it must be Hyrup feeding time.

An arm reached up from the mass, and a large centipede swung onto it. Like a flesh mower set low, the Hyrup stripped one row down to the bone then shifted to clean a fresh path. When the flesh was gone, it worked on the bone, starting with the ends of the fingers.

In her delirium, Zim found the process fascinating. Neatly severed parts came away, drawing meticulous attention from additional feeders until the ravenous mandibles consumed everything. She had no idea what was being eaten but hoped it was Abramyan. That thought brought a smile to her mind, something her broken face could not manage. Maybe she'd be next. Her mind shrugged. Exquisite pain took her beyond caring about life or living. She recalled enforcer robots methodically grasping, extending, and crushing her limbs.

Zim's one functioning eye caught the Shelesti's gaze—two wrinkle-wrapped, knothole eyes in an aged tree stump. Its bark-textured, ax-gash mouth crinkled. A gnarled branch lifted a heap of black from the floor—the hooded robe of a Star Council Leader. Perhaps that hand in the swarm had been Abramyan. Zim wished she'd been conscious for the entire feast. She tried to speak, "Gggrk, grk." But her tongue felt only empty space where her jaw and teeth had been. The Shelesti raised a twig-finger to its bark-ridge mouth.

The Hyrup ball unraveled, leaving no trace of their feeding, not bone, blood, or stain. Then they turned and swarmed onto Zim. She rolled her one beyond-caring eye down to see what they were doing. The movement felt as if it ripped her skull open. Her hands were stumps of ripped tendons, her body an exposed tangle of dislocated limbs.

The Hyrup climbed, clawed, and pinched Zim's wounds, gently biting and injecting then wrapping them in Hyrup silk. Under their nurturing, her pounding heart slowed, sweat cooled, and breathing eased. When the manacles released, Zim's body slumped in the metal chair.

"Your friend will return soon," the Shelesti assured her as it spread the black robe to cover her nakedness. "Our ministrations bought you some time, but you require extensive care. Tock said you could be trusted, and we should intervene if it meant your survival."

Zim struggled for the strength to respond, but the Shelesti was already ushering the Hyrup out the portal on the back wall. She wanted to shout, "Come back... My friend will come? What friend? Is Tock here? Mac? No, Mac is dead. Who was that on the floor?" Her mind trailed off as she succumbed to the calming injections.

# # #

Traier rushed back from supply with a tech-lev cart. He tried to grasp the implications of what he had seen and what might happen if Zimmon lived. The report of the Starflower's death on Okean had crushed the resistance and any real hope that Star Council's plans might be defeated, not only on Corydon but on hundreds of settlements. He pounded the handle of the cart.

When he'd left the conference room, Zimmon still clung to life. Traier imagined getting back in time to save her, but the floor directors had stopped pointing. That must be Abramyan's doing. Traier swore he'd kill that little targ... someday. Now he had to get through another round of insipid cordialities.

The tech-lev was all Traier could find in the storeroom. He threw off the equipment and replaced it with packing wraps. Hopefully, Abramyan hadn't sent away the shuttle that brought him from the starport. If Zimmon were dead, Abramyan would be, too. Traier would face the consequences.

The door to the Council chamber slid open, and Traier rushed in. He saw no sign of Abramyan, but Zimmon was wrapped in his black robe, and the clamps on the metal interrogation chair hung open. An ampoule-syringe lay in the middle of the marble floor. What had happened in the last eleven minutes?

Zimmon was unconscious but appeared better than when he left. Her jaw had been reattached, one eye sutured with nearly imperceptible stitches, and the other bandaged. Her limbs were straight, set, and bound with close-knit silk. All other wounds and bruises had been stitched, patched, and salved. He touched her neck. The pulse was weak but steady. Her un-bandaged eyelid fluttered.

"I'm Traier," he said, not expecting her to remember. Zim's eye opened and focused on him. "I'm taking you out of here. If anyone stops us, we want them to think you're dead, and I'm removing the body. Understand?"

"Uh-huh," Zim said. Traier scooped her onto the metal tech-lev and tucked packing material and Abramyan's robe around her.

"*What are you doing?*" a voice demanded. Traier hadn't heard anyone enter. "And *where* is Star Leader Abramyan?"

"He sent me for a cart to remove the body," Traier said. The man wore a bright red, one-piece uniform. Traier recognized him as a Nine but didn't know he had once been Aidan, Zim's aide-de-camp. From the expression, Traier knew the Nine recognized him as a Ten but questioned his appearance and dress.

"Abramyan is late for his appointment," Aidan said. "Lord Malik wants him to report on the last three months—" Traier saw Aidan's gaze drop to the Star Council robe on the cart then to the ampoule on the floor.

Traier drew his shashka just as Aidan leaped and clutched the ampoule. *Shhziiip* came the sound of a high-speed reel, and Aidan's arm dropped from the elbow. Traier darted a glance and saw Zim's bare, left foot hanging off the cart. Aidan spun and slapped his remaining hand on the conference table before Traier's shashka cut him in two. A high-pitched, barking alarm rang out.

Traier tucked Zim's foot back onto the cart and noted the nanowire portal at the end of her toe. Abramyan could not have known about that. Traier was careful not to cover it.

307

He pushed the frictionless tech-lev through the door and ran with it. A red rectangle framed his feet and moved with him. Red arrows converged from all directions.

The enforcers knew his position.

Engines whirred and revved in the main hallway, a clatter of tracks, and the squeal of tires on slick floors. Three enforcers filled the three-meter-wide hall, blocking light from the far end. The alarm pulse increased, indicating he'd been sighted.

Traier spun left into the empty side corridor, and the arrows shifted to that route. Traier checked every alcove and doorway as he ran, looking for one that might provide maintenance, utility, or emergency access to other floors.

"How are you doing?" he asked Zim, conserving his breath. Her half-bandaged mouth half-smiled. He nudged her left leg to the center of the cart, shook the robe back from her bare foot, and propped her head so she could see ahead. "You're our best weapon right now, Commander." His voice was level. He wasn't joking.

Rescue

Racing down the hall, Traier pushed Zim past double auditorium doors and a row of conference rooms and offices—dead ends, traps. The enforcers hadn't turned the corner but sounds of their engines filled the corridor.

Ahead, a metal service door opened. A red-uniformed figure peeked then leaped out and signaled someone behind. A moment later, five figures blocked the hall, hand weapons raised.

A curious mix, Traier thought. Two Creatives wearing red had long, well-formed, female bodies, one young, the other older and a projection—Traier saw its arm pass through the younger. Three Under males wore cord-bound syn-linen smocks over mismatched trousers: one young, lean, and dark; one large and muscular, a combat or arena veteran; the third overweight and breathing heavily.

Traier nudged Zim alert and gripped his shashka. She pulled her foot back and mumbled, "Nah hem."

The younger Creative shouted, "Don't shoot," and waved the others to hold fire. "See the red box on the floor? These are the ones the enforcers are after."

Hotz's eyes checked Traier then dropped to the tech-lev cart. "Commander." Dom, Chow, Kaplan, and Brownie joined her, circling the cart. Chow brushed a shaking hand across Zim's forehead. She half-smiled and shifted her unbandaged eye around the circle.

"We're the rescue team." Dom squared his shoulders with Traier.

"Good, then you have a way out." Traier returned Dom's stare. Enforcers collided at the hall juncture and tangled behind them. One broke free. Its servo whining as it gained speed and raised a pulse weapon. *Hummm-Snap*, Dom's E-Mag light gun spoke first. The enforcer slumped, its whine dropping as it rolled to a stop.

"*Go. Now*," Hotz shouted, pulling the service door wide. Traier lifted Zim wrapped in Abramyan's robe, cradled her head, and dashed through the door.

The red rectangle disappeared. Chow and Kaplan followed, after giving the cart a hard shove back down the hall. Dom delivered two E-Mag bursts then backed out of the corridor and bolted the door, muffling the screeching alarm.

Kaplan jumped beside Dom to set the security lock. "Enforcers don't have hands to work the panel," Kaplan explained. Dom gave his shoulder a 'good job' shake.

Pipes, braided wires, and stacked service boxes filled the utility room and lined the walls. A vertical rail system with two track poles came up through a meter-wide opening in the deck.

"Only way out," Kaplan said to Traier, pointing down. "The tracks were designed for maintenance robots. Insurgents came up with these." He lifted a pair of powered track clamps. "It's seventy-six floors to the basement. Insurgents dug the tunnel and are guarding our escape route."

Traier pressed a clamp to the rail and heard it lock and whir. "I got her," he said, pulling Zim onto his chest then glancing at Dom. "The two of us will fit through the opening together."

Dom eyeballed the narrow track opening and nodded. He and Chow removed their smock cords and bound Zim to Traier. Kaplan knew the route and was their best picklock, so he led the way. Hotz and Dom went next in case there was resistance. Traier motioned to Chow, but he shook his head.

"I'll only slow us down. Look at me... I'm exhausted." Chow's face, neck, and arms glowed and poured sweat. "If I stay, I can buy you some time."

Zim rolled her head on Traier's shoulder. Chow kissed his palm and pressed it to her bare foot. "Good-bye, Commander." His smiling eyes glistened over his round cheeks. "Ha-Yee, Starflower."

"Ha-Yee, Ch——" she whispered, her mouth unable to form his name.

Plasma torches hissed, and sparks of blue shot through a cut in the metal door that slowly lengthened.

"I'll stay with Chow," Brownie said. "I might be able to distract them." Traier exchanged quick glances with Chow and Brownie then gripped the rail clamps, lifted his feet, and dropped through the floor with Zim bound to his chest.

Whirring clamp rotors echoed through the shaft. The others were already far below. Decks of utility rooms riffled past like pages in a book, dim-lit floors, side shafts of panels and switches, walls of pipes and toolboxes.

Dom waited on the fiftieth floor. "Chow behind you?" he asked over the whirring from below.

"Decided he'd stay," Traier said and felt Zim's arms tighten on his neck. "Brownie's with him." An E-Mag exchange sounded above, followed by metal-on-metal collisions.

Dom shot a look at Traier then at Zim before lifting his feet and continuing down. Several seconds later, he slowed and called a halt. Voices below had replaced the whirring of powered track clamps. A narrow light shaft reached up toward them. Dom pulled Traier's pant leg. "It's okay."

Traier's clamps released when his feet touched concrete. The dank basement smelled moldy. The only illumination was the cone of a plasma torch centered on Zim and beams from several shifting helmet lamps.

"Where's Chow?" Kaplan asked from behind one of the light beams.

"Not coming," Dom said, "seal the hatch." Kaplan latched, bolted, and restored the cypher lock.

Traier stepped away from the rail shaft with Zim, and the light cone followed them to Dom and Hotz. Six broad-shouldered figures stood with them. Light glistened off their gargoyle faces and steel claws.

Pidge.

Fighting the impulse to draw his shashka, Traier waited while Hotz and Kaplan untied and lowered Zim onto a combat stretcher.

Dom slapped the bone-plated shoulder of the Pidge beside him. "Old teammates that went afoul of the regs. Especially Kyle here and Dak." He slapped the big fellow again then pointed to the one behind him. "None of these guys took the neural blocks, pain killers, or mem-wipes, so they're still mostly Human. I can vouch for all of 'em... but not for you." He centered his gun on Traier's chest.

Traier looked down at Hotz fastening Zim to the stretcher and hooking up monitors then shifted his eyes to Dom.

"I found Commander Zimmon with Abramyan. She was like this, much worse."

"Abramyan?" Dom spat, barely missing Traier's boot.

"I left the conference room for a couple minutes. When I got back, Zimmon was stitched up, and Abramyan was gone. This might be his." Traier lifted a corner of the hooded robe beside Zim. "Then we ran into you in the corridor."

"Can the Commander speak?" Dom kneeled beside Hotz and the stretcher.

311

Hotz rocked her head. "Not much, but she can respond. I gave her a shot of epinephrine."

Dom leaned down. "This guy on the level?"

"Uh huh." Zim lifted a shattered hand to Traier.

"I'm Traier, Hetman of the Chei-Binsk Rii-Chaut. We're unofficial allies." Traier stood alert, awaiting his judgment.

"Need to go," the Pidge Dak roared, shaking a gauntlet fist. "Kill the Rii-Chaut or bring 'im. Targ enforcers threatening our escape route."

Dom nodded. "Okay, we can make nice later." He took one end of the stretcher, Hotz the other.

The fiber-cable path ran through a meter-wide shaft. The six Pidge shuffled in, undulating like snakes, helmet beams rocking light about the tunnel. Dom crawled on his back using his butt and elbows and pulled Zim's stretcher behind him. Hotz crawled and pushed, occasionally checking Zim's condition in the dim light attached to the stretcher. Kaplan and Traier, bringing up the rear, listened for anything behind them.

The corrugated tunnel scraped and bumped their knees and elbows. No one talked. Other than occasional swearing, the only sounds were sliding, scraping, and grunting.

Eighteen minutes and two hundred meters later, Dom asked, "How far to the starport?"

Kyle called back. "Thirty-three kilometers, but we'll catch a ride at a junction forty meters ahead."

The tunnel widened. Lights were strung overhead. A side shaft, crudely cut and sealed with foam, slanted steeply down. The shaft ended at a chamber twelve meters wide. Dak helped Dom lower and level the stretcher while Hotz handed it down.

"Any sign we're being followed?" Dom asked. Traier and Kaplan shook their heads.

"Now we ride." Kyle growled like a bear. When he pressed a stone panel, they heard a rumbling echo from another side shaft. "Welcome to the insurgent main terminal." An ellipsoid hover car slid into the terminal, then another, and another, six in all.

"We pass four junctions," Kyle said. "Our teams guard each of them. If the junction ahead is clear, they'll wave us on, if not, we detour." He looked around. "All aboard."

Dom touched his belt. Brownie's projection formed, still dressed in red and styled as a Creative. "Take the first car," he said. "That'll give us another set of eyes up front." Brownie rode with two Pidge.

An electromagnetic bubble covered the car's open bay. After a windup whir and whoosh, the car accelerated out on a magnetic rail. The Pidge took the next two cars, two in each.

Zim's stretcher with medical equipment filled one car. Hotz checked her and shifted the controls from the stretcher hooks onto her chest. "If we get separated, these will steady your heart rate." She pointed to "EPI" and "ATR" on the controls. "Epinephrine takes it up, atropine brings it down. Understand?" Zim blinked. "Okay. Your slow EPI feed will keep your heart rate around seventy-seven. Don't let it get below sixty or above 160. Above 190 your heart could rip out of your chest. Questions?" Zim half smiled. Hotz tucked everything into the car, activated the E-Mag seal, and stepped away. She and Dom took the car ahead of the stretcher. Traier and Kaplan came last.

Tunnel lights flicked by like a strobe, shifting shadows back then ahead. One minute later they slowed at the first junction. A simply dressed Under, not a Pidge, waved them forward. Traier glanced at Zim's car leaving just ahead. His and Kaplan's car followed. The drill was the same at the next station.

At the third, each car switched one-at-a-time onto a turntable that aligned with a side shaft. As each car completed its turn, it accelerated on the new line. Traier heard E-Mags and a heavy pulse cannon. Unders and Pidge ran up the tunnel firing. One Under stopped to aim and was sliced in two just as Traier's car left the terminal.

Two minutes later, they emerged into the open air and stopped behind the other five cars.

"Plan B," Dom shouted, ran, and pointed to a ground shuttle. "This'll take us to the starport. Enforcers overran the last terminal." Traier and Kaplan ran with him. Zim's stretcher was already on the shuttle floor. Hotz sat beside her. Dak and Kyle boarded. The other four Pidge stayed behind to guard their escape.

"Heard the news," Dom said as they pulled away. "Enforcers got this guy's starship." He pointed toward Traier. "Abramyan's missing. News says they think this guy kidnapped 'im. Monitors show him running out—"

"Name's Traier—not *this* guy." He respected Dom, a no-nonsense combat soldier, but a line needed to be drawn.

"Traier," Dom continued. "The monitors show *Traier* rushing out of the conference room with a body wrapped in Abramyan's robe. Thanks to that unplanned misdirection, no one's looking for us—yet." He smiled at Traier who raised an eyebrow. Dom reached down to Zim's stretcher and touched the black robe. "If you tell me how you got holda this, I'll buy the first round. But we first need to find out if B'Len can get us outta here."

Starport

They kept light-guns trained forward and low. Hotz switched out Zim's plasma bag on the stretcher.

Zim pressed EPI on the control to stay conscious. When she raised her head as high as she could, pain stitched up her neck like a string of Christmas lights. Good. That meant the Hyrup nerve shunts were working. She flexed her jaw and felt it move, too.

Turning into the starport, they passed an Aldrakin fighter with Rii-Chaut markings and a diplomatic designator. Red-uniformed Creatives swarmed over it, pulling off panels and ripping out the interior. Tracked enforcers and a battery of plasma cannon blocked all approaches. Sensor and weapon drones circled overhead.

"Your ship?" Dom asked. Traier raised an eyebrow and pressed his lips.

"They must think I brought some heavy firepower." Traier eyed the cannons. "I'm sure they disabled the engine first—in case I tried to use my ship to escape."

Hotz darted a glance at Traier. "Let them keep your ship."

"Here we come," Dom said as the plum-colored canopy slipped into view. "Heavy security's on Traier's ship, but we're still being watched." He pointed to the parking apron with a sensor array trained on B'Len's yacht. B'Len frog-stepped down the stern ramp as they approached and waved them close.

"We got open space to cross," Dom said. "And we'll have to do it in two trips—we've picked up extra passengers plus Commander Zimmon on a stretcher. Anyone gets suspicious, and that army on the north side'll be down on us like flirki on kallat targ."

B'Len head-body rocked that he understood and sent projections of four Aldrakin priests out to the shuttle.

"Remember stoop 'n waddle," Dom said. "Let the projections register to your movements. And keep close so they can't see the stretcher."

315

Two minutes later, they were all in the yacht salon with Zim stretched out on the bar. An overhead pallet lowered, unfolded like an ironing board, and sprouted spindly limbs. The doc-rob ran a scanner along Zim's body. Delicate metal fingers cleaned and re-sutured tears and replaced soiled dressings.

"Our knowledge of Human anatomy is incomplete," B'Len said through the yacht's translator. "And we don't have full capability for all species." He checked the readout. "The doc-rob asks how these repairs were made. They are the finest sutures it has seen and are made from an unusual silk. The internal stitching is not only fine, it's coated with an enzyme that promotes regrowth, even nerve tissue." Seeing the blank faces, B'Len lifted and examined Zim's wrist. "Whatever this is, Commander Zimmon's hand is regrowing her fingers."

Dom said, "If she's stable enough, we should get underway."

B'Len responded, "She can be moved, but they've shut down Corydon Starport until Abramyan and his kidnapper are found."

Dak growled, "So we turn this Rii-Chaut targ over to security, and we get on our way. What'd you do with Abramyan?" He flashed his four-centimeter fangs at Traier.

"I have no idea what—"

Zim's voice returned in a rasp. "Abramyan's gone. I was only half-conscious, but I know he'll never be found." Vaguely remembering something the Shelesti said about trusting her, she paused for a breath. "They probably think Abramyan and I are together, and somehow Traier's involved. Forget the targ news. If they know any of us are here, we're all dead."

"That's the standing order for all insurgents," Hotz said, "Unders and Creative turncoats." Everyone looked at her red uniform.

Dak bared his incisors, and his slit pupils narrowed. "We need to get our butts back underground."

Kyle slammed a gauntlet hand on the bar. "Underground won't save us now. You saw what happened at the last maglev terminal. Now they got special robots for that sorta combat. We lost that edge. The Creatives are learning to fight us."

"Then let's get off this targ heap," Dak said.

"Is anything getting out of the starport?" Zim rasped.

B'Len shook his head. "No. And reports say as soon as they clear the tunnels, they'll start sweeping the planet. They know the Aldrakin fondness

316

for the Starflower, so they'll probably start with our embassy then search this starship."

Zim lifted her bandaged wrist and stroked her chin. "Other starports? For emergencies or maybe an abandoned one?" Hotz shook her head.

"There's Belle," Brownie murmured. "That is if my friend Isabelle is still in the salvage yard."

"Explain." Zim rolled her fingerless hand.

"We worked together hauling ore off asteroids. She was an older model. When the new ore carriers came out, I was kept on. Blue Star Corporation picked up Belle for salvage operations and to haul trash off Corydon. Her last assignment was at the landfill north of the city."

"Is she still there?" Hotz asked.

"We used to keep in touch. Belle's last contact said she was shutting down to conserve power." Brownie's eyes teared. "That was eighteen years ago. She's either been broken up or she's still out in the yard."

"Can you contact her?" Zim rasped, her bandaged wrist still at her chin.

"Wake her up? I can try." Brownie gave B'Len the old salvage ops code to set the communicator.

"Belle, this is Brownie, are you there?" They waited. "Belle, are you okay?"

"Brownie? Where are you?" The voice was weak but clear.

"Here on Corydon. We need your help, Belle."

"Sure, Brownie, but I'm in terrible shape. Couldn't we just talk?"

"I'm afraid we need more help than that." No reply came. "Is there some way you could get us off Corydon?"

"Off Corydon? Maybe, but my mag-lift connectors are worn and fuel's low. The trip would have to be short and probably one way. It would finish me, but that's okay."

"One way?" Brownie looked to Zim.

"If she can get us headed into a trade lane, maybe someone will pick up a distress call." Feeling increasing strain from her injuries, Zim closed her eyes.

"Belle, could you get us into a trade lane?"

"Someone would have to reconnect me. They pulled my AI controls and navigation systems."

Zim turned to Dom who pointed to Kaplan. "Can you reconnect her or set up a control bypass?"

"I don't have any equipment, but I can reconnect the controls if that's what's needed."

"We have a tech who can help us, Belle. Can you carry passengers?"

"Miners? How many?"

"Seven."

"I'll set a beacon."

"See you in an hour." Brownie looked to Zim.

"I'm sure we'll have to run." Zim paused for another breath and checked her pulse. Sixty-two and dropping. She pressed EPI to bring it up to eighty-one.

B'Len pulled out a light gun and exchanged his ceremonial sword for a more functional katana.

"I'm sorry, B'Len, but you won't be coming." Zim caught the constriction of lozenge pupils in his orange eyes. "Your cover may still buy us precious time. Stay here and don't take down the tent. Whoever's watching, we want them to think we're coming back."

B'Len's green, sharp-boned face went still. Then he raised up and his arms and shoulders snapped to attention. "I'll do whatever I can to get the team off." He slid the katana back under the bar.

"They're watching us close," Dom said. "We can use the projections to get out to the shuttle, but I think we're going to need a pass to leave the starport."

"Ideas?" Zim asked.

"I'll tell starport security that the Aldrakin Ambassador has more baggage we need to deliver," B'Len said.

"And tell them we'll be taking an indirect, secure route," Zim said. "Express concern about diplomatic consequences should the Ambassador's belongings be damaged."

Traier weighed in, "This tub have any major-caliber weapons?"

"*This tub…*" B'Len pulled himself nearer Traier's height, "is our Emperor's exclusive yacht, probably the fastest, most maneuverable starship in this sector. But yes, our Imperial Guards are issued plasma carbines. They're lighter than the tripod version and a little unwieldy but just as powerful." He touched the wall, and a panel slid away revealing two weapons.

"Only two." Traier laughed darkly.

"This yacht is neither a tub nor an assault transport. Its normal security complement includes two imperial guardsmen."

Reptilian eyes gleaming, Kyle and Dak claimed the plasma carbines. The others checked and charged their E-Mag light guns. B'Len pulled cushions off a levitating lounger for Zim, and Hotz transferred her medical gear. Two minutes later, B'Len got clearance for one baggage transfer trip, and the team waddled out under the priest projections.

Zim insisted they take everything, including the Vaitii seeds and the Chorya'Key. Much as she wished to protect the future, she didn't want anything turning up in the yacht's inevitable search that could implicate B'Len or Tee'Kahl.

"We'll take the main thoroughfare downtown," Dom said, "then redirect soon as we're outta monitor range."

Zim felt herself dragging and kicked her heart rate up to ninety beats per minute. A message from B'Len told her a sensor drone had followed them out of the starport. She passed the message to Dom.

"I think we should make a run before we pick up any assault drones," Dom said. "We're only forty kilometers from the salvage yard."

They proceeded toward Corydon City, past the park, then turned sharply and accelerated. The parkway was shorter but more easily blocked and slower if they had to go off road.

B'Len's message popped up, "Enforcers, Creatives, and heavy weapons pulling out fast."

"Here we go." Dom switched the shield to transparent. "See a drone lining up on us—fire at will."

L4

The shuttle raced over open grassland, rising and falling with the terrain, and slowly outdistancing the pursuing drone. Hotz steadied her light gun on the compartment ledge, anticipated the drone's evasive pattern, and squeezed as she exhaled. *Hmmm-Snap*. The drone kicked over, twirling down like a maple seed.

"I hate being ogled, except by some." Hotz caught Traier giving her a head-to-toe appraisal and held his gaze.

They hurtled into a field of derelicts: land vehicles, discarded equipment, obsolete spacecraft, piles of building debris cleared from the Under quarter. The low sun cast shadows across the trash canyons. Swirling dust clouds filled the air with the acrid scent of pulverized stone and concrete. Belle's beacon led them weaving around starship hulks, broken walls, and foundation slabs bristling with bent, rusting rebar.

Brownie pointed to a sloping wall. "Belle's loading ramp." Antiquated gears ground and ratcheted, dropped and caught, then shuddered and dropped again, revealing the wide bay of a last-century interstellar ore carrier.

Two sensor drones hummed above the rim of a junk heap behind them. Sounds of assault drones and tracked land vehicles grew nearer.

"Tell your friends to drive straight in," Belle said. "My ramp was designed to withstand space rocks—it'll stop light weapons."

The shuttle shot up the ramp and into the cargo bay.

Dom shouted and pointed. "Hook up the flight system so we can get outta here." Brownie ran and Kaplan followed through the open airlock to the control room. Behind them, Hotz pushed Zim on the levitation lounger.

Kyle hoisted a plasma carbine and tossed the other to Dak. "Ready to die?"

"Already did," Dak shouted back, "when they pidged me and made my wife Cherise a tool for the lithium miners." He slid his spiked gauntlet-hand to find the carbine's balance point.

Dom and Traier led the team down the ramp to the floor of the landfill crater. Dom pointed left to a ridge fifty meters away, then right to a pile of derelict vehicles. Kyle ran left, Dak right, to cover the main approaches to their position with their plasma carbines.

"When we see where and what's comin', we'll converge," Dom said to Traier who returned a thumbs up.

A levi-tank turret peaked over the ridge. *Shh-thump*, Dak's carbine hit the underside before it could level its gun. The tank gave a high-pitched whine, shot flames, and exploded.

"First blood," Dak barked. Rumbling sounds grew louder.

#

Hotz guided Zim's lounger through the airlock behind Kaplan. A blast from outside shook the ore carrier. A gray-haired, simply dressed woman appeared.

"My friend, Belle," Brownie said.

Kaplan held up the torn electrical leads and shook his head. "When they pulled the controls, where'd they put them?"

"Back shelf," Belle said, pointing for Kaplan. She gave Brownie a hug.

"These are only connectors and relays," Kaplan interrupted. "I don't see any navigation or guidance computers to link to the ship's propulsion system."

Belle apologized. "I shut down before anything was pulled."

Kaplan stared at the empty rack, rolled his lips back and sucked through his teeth. Rapid E-Mag blasts and three quick explosions rocked the control room. Kaplan sprinted out the airlock to grab his light gun from the shuttle. Hotz and Brownie followed.

Belle crumpled in defeat. Zim leaned up and quick-scanned the control room.

"What's this?" Zim kicked a console on what looked like a secretary desk. A panel dropped open with a rocker-switch, a joystick, and a red disk. It reminded Zim of early training simulators with cutoff-restart buttons.

"That's for auxiliary maneuvers," Belle said, "when we're close to a mine site and need to adjust our position."

"A manual control?"

"Of a limited sort."

Zim felt an adrenaline rush. She pushed the stub of her hand down on the rocker-switch and heard the rumble of four maneuver engines. A burn from the pressure lit up every vertebra and shot lightning through her skull. Zim shifted her stub to the EPI button and watched her heart rate climb from 97 to 140 to 160. Her body shook, but paralysis from the pain vanished. She snagged a corner of Abramyan's black robe between her bandaged, fingerless hands, and used her upper mouth and tongue to pull, wrap, and form a cup. She slipped the cup over the joystick and eased it back. The ore carrier lifted one side then the other, dragging the lowered loading ramp, then rocked into the air. Belle leaned in beside her.

"Clear the screen," Zim said. The opaque dome instantly displayed a wide view of trash piles receding into the distance. "Rear view," she ordered, and the scene shifted to the landfill with her team pinned below the far slope of the crater. Waves of mechanized enforcers poured down over the trash-mountains.

"What's this, Belle?" Zim pointed her nose to the red disk that looked like a panic button.

"A booster to the salvage yard at L4. That was my regular run. It's hard wired, so I didn't have to be reprogrammed for each trip."

"L4, the Lagrangian point L4?" Zim steadied the stick against her body. The ore carrier crept back, scraping and bumping. Zim strained to focus, keep level, and not overrun her pinned-down team.

"Yes. This is the departure point for L4 salvage."

Zim's cup-hand slipped from the joystick, and the ore carrier shuddered to a halt. She pressed and held EPI until her hand steadied, then returned it to the controls. Overturned tanks and enforcers, wheels and tracks spinning, stacked the ridge. Red-uniformed Creatives swarmed over pavement blocks and fell like targets in a shooting gallery.

Zim nudged the ore carrier, closer, closer, ten meters, five, two, then set it down with a jolt, close enough to the ridge rim to shield the loading ramp from heavy fire. She watched her team stumble aboard, dragging and carrying one another... all except Kyle.

Dom, dragging Dak on his shoulder, shouted to the intercom, "Kyle ain't comin'."

"Raise the ramp and get up here," Zim yelled over the explosions. The ramp slammed and locked. She waited for everyone to cross the cargo bay threshold.

As soon as the airlock light turned green, she slammed the red button. The main and booster engines roared, the ore carrier lifted, and Zim collapsed.

# # #

It was seconds before the inner airlock opened and long minutes before the acceleration allowed them to stand. When the engines cut off, they were weightless.

Hotz entered the control room first and found Zim floating free of the lounger, her eyes staring vacantly into space. The monitor indicated Zim's heart had reached 290 beats-per-minute and blown every valve.

Hotz retrieved a finger-length cylinder from her medical bag and pressed the flat edge to Zim's carotid artery then floated her back onto the lounger and latched the lounger to the rear bulkhead. The med-tech scanner indicated the APMs, atomically precise machines Hotz had administered, moving into Zim's brain and key organs, maintaining circulation and arresting decomposition.

"Is she dead?" Dom asked, rolling Dak off his shoulder.

"Dead but stabilized," Hotz said. "She still has neural activity. The APM pumps will keep her ventilated for seventy-two hours."

Dom latched Dak to the wall ledge then pushed off to drift weightless into the ceiling sleeping nets. He pulled what remained of his bound hand and splinted right leg into the net and closed his eyes.

Traier grabbed a ceiling latch and pulled into the control room, bumping along the bulkhead as he floated Kaplan's inert body forward. A bloodstained cloth bound Traier's upper chest, another his lower back. Half his body was burned, his mustache and long plaits singed, his face peeled angry red.

Kaplan's right leg was missing below the knee; his leg and head bandages seeped blood. Traier latched him to the ledge beside Dak then joined Dom in the sleeping nets.

Hotz pulled herself, floating into the pilot seat. "Brownie, see if anyone's critical? I need to check our flight trajectory."

"Aye-aye," Brownie said.

"Where we goin'?" Dom asked, breathing deeply, his eyes closed.

"Nowhere near the trade lanes."

"We're going to L4," Belle responded, studying the monitor that Hotz had attached to Dak. Her projection stood upright as if in normal gravity.

"What's at L4?" Traier asked.

"A salvage yard," Belle said. "Blue Star Corporation reserved it as a staging base while they terra-formed Corydon. I'd ferry engineering equipment down from L4, then back after a project was done. Corydon is a low metal planet, so I also brought down metals from off-world mines and from salvage operations. Made the trip two, three times a week when we were busy."

Hotz pushed off the pilot seat to make a medical round. "Is L4 still active?"

"Not since Blue Star lost the maintenance contract to SynTerra."

"So, we'll just hang at L4 till some enforcer ship collects us," Dom muttered. "Which makes me wonder, why aren't we being chased?" He paused for the groans to subside. "This is a fine ship—for an obsolete ore carrier, no offense, Belle—but it's slow and can't maneuver."

"And I'm out of fuel," Belle added.

"Then *we're* out of fuel," Dom continued. "We should have fighters all over us. See anything on the scanners?"

"The only scanners we have are for collision avoidance," Hotz said, giving Kaplan a spritz of painkiller then pushing back toward the control panel. "They don't show anything approaching larger than a grapefruit… and nothing at high speed." She adjusted the range. "L4's crowded with the hulks of old starships. We could be drifting into an ambush." She glanced at Dom and Traier. "We'll know in two days when we get there. Good news is there's still some punch in the auxiliaries to brake or make a minor orbit adjust."

# # #

Hotz made the rounds every two hours, changing bandages, applying styptics, and injecting APM troubleshooters for injuries her field-grade instruments missed. She was the only one without a major injury. Dak and Kaplan were critical; Dom and Traier serious but stable. Zim's stasis held.

After resting a few hours, they compared notes: the reconnaissance mission that turned into a rescue, the all-out brawl at the crater, losing Chow and Kyle.

Brownie related that Chow had found a plasma welder in one of the toolboxes and used it to re-fuse the utility door as the enforcers worked to cut through it. He had disabled two robots by firing through the fissures before they broke through and killed him.

Dom told how Kyle disabled a levi-tank leading an attack and was cooked when its magazine exploded. Kaplan was wounded when he exchanged fire with snipers to distract them from Kyle. Traier's burns came pulling Kyle's charred body back into the crater. Dom and Dak took hits fighting drones and enforcers. Hotz picked off snipers with Kaplan until she switched to become field medic. Brownie drew fire with virtual heavy assault weapons and feigned flank attacks.

Belle remained silent throughout the retelling then complimented Brownie on finding a better way to die—and in better company.

"You're with us now, Isabelle," Brownie said.

Kaplan slipped away early on the second day. Hotz stabilized him with APMs. Dak grew weaker but held.

Eight hours later, they drifted into L4 and a field of abandoned habitats and derelict starships. Hotz adjusted their trajectory to hold the position then started another medical round. Traier spelled her at the pilot seat.

"Something big just came up on the scanner, and it's on a collision course," Traier said.

Dom swung around in the ceiling net. "Another slow hulk?"

"No, much bigger. Just popped in from Myseko, and it's headed straight for us."

"Belle, any weapons onboard?" Dom asked.

"I'm sorry. Not on an abandoned ore carrier."

"Increase magnification," Hotz said.

Traier reset the scanner and raised a scaling reticle. "It's bigger than a Marshal class." The bow of the massive starship filled the screen.

"That thing could *eat* a Marshal," Dom said over Traier's shoulder.

"Funny you should say that." Traier's hand searched for the burnt end of his mustache. "It's opening its mouth."

Part Seven

Blue Horizon

Xi'Kior

Every member of Star Council delighted in the distractions of their new bodies. Interacting with Creatives socially was one thing, experiencing them from the inside was quite another: their ease of movement, grace and beauty, youth and health, boundless energy—and their appetites.

Star Lord Malik found his male body fascinating. Torgesson was top-heavy and firm where Malik's female body had never been, even when young. She had to will himself not to jump, run, and shout. What's more, the beautiful athletic females around the conference table stirred his interest in ways he never could have imagined.

The initial goal of the Creative program had been fecundity: the restoration and replenishment of depleted Human stock. They were selected and enhanced for that end.

Malik tried to imagine how Torgesson could control this raging lust. His eye caught the longing approval of the slender beauty beside him, Jen Djada. His unofficial, thousand-year partner now occupied Hillary's exquisite body. Her blond curls begged him to bury his face in them. Her crystal blue eyes pleaded for him, and her breasts longed for his caress. The thought of being this man and making passionate love to this beautiful woman consumed him.

The music concluded with an accented beat, and the Hyrup lowered their instruments. So preoccupied were the Xi'Kior that no one noticed the music had stopped until Malik stood. He cleared his throat and scanned the unfamiliar faces around the table.

"Let us begin our new rule by declaring our true identity." Malik's booming male resonance startled and roused him. He raised his right arm high. "We are the Xi'Kior... We are the victors... We won the war... From now on, rules are what we make them."

Fourteen voices chorused, *"We are Xi'Kior."*

Malik opened his hand to them. "Now our charade can end. I hope none of you have grown too fond of these." He stripped off his hooded, black robe and tossed it to the marble floor. The others followed, creating black heaps beside every chair.

Malik shouted above them, "The Unders are defeated, gone from here. Our Xi'Kior sisters and brothers are being restored to these new bodies. We control Corydon, Thrinlu, Scalaris, Silkani, and soon many more."

After calming everyone again, he placed a hand on his chest. "I remain Kiya Malik, not Torgesson or Torgis, and my partner remains Jen Djada, not Hillie." He gestured to Djada beside him. She flashed a surprised smile. It was the first time Malik had acknowledged her as his mate in public.

He brushed a long shock of blond from his face and sat. "First on today's agenda, Order." Djada stood beside him still blushing, something her previous body had never done.

"Order is restored throughout the system." Her lilting soprano was a song. Her wide full lips revealed even white teeth. Her clear blue eyes glowed over high cheekbones. Malik felt weak with her so close beside him.

"Two weeks ago, a mixed team of insurgents launched a last desperate raid on Corydon." She tapped the long nail of her index finger on the table. "Their timing was good. Most of us were still recovering from transition and just getting accustomed to these new bodies. The attack was planned and led by our old nemesis Commander Gayle Zimmon. Her first target was the Avian building."

Djada read the Authoriton's report on the attempted sabotage and the discovery, capture, and death, "at last," of the Starflower. She next read the security report of a Rii-Chaut renegade who had gotten into headquarters, stolen Zimmon's body, and with the help of insurgents, attempted to hijack the imperial yacht that had delivered the Aldrakin ambassador. Foiled in that attempt, they had stolen a shuttle and jury-rigged an abandoned ore carrier.

"The ore carrier was intercepted?" Malik asked.

"Sensor drones didn't raise the alarm until the insurgents made their final dash. Our first reaction was that the junkyard was a ploy to divert us from the real escape route. We assumed they'd go after a high-performance fighter—not an obsolete ore carrier. That said, most of our pilots were retraining and still not yet cleared to fly. Others were out of position, monitoring starport departures or guarding for incoming traffic."

Djada tilted her head until she caught Malik's eye then continued. "Clever though their attempt was, it was in vain. The ore carrier had no navigation or guidance systems and almost no fuel. Even without a cargo, it could not have left the Corydon star system. After the initial boost from the junkyard, the carrier disappeared without a trace. We assumed it fell into the sea and are searching there now."

"And Abramyan?" Malik asked.

"Interim Star Lord Abramyan was probably surprised and killed or kidnapped by the same Rii-Chaut renegade who stole Zimmon's body. Luka Kodra tried to stop him and was killed here in the conference room. The wound that killed him came from a Rii-Chaut sword."

"And you are certain the Starflower is dead?" Malik recoiled at hearing his own question.

"We have Zimmon's medical data. Only massive and immediate medical intervention could have saved her. Monitors are not permitted in this chamber, but we have this recording from the corridor outside." Djada avoided Malik's gaze to address the projection.

"Here, two bodies on the supply cart are wrapped in Abramyan's robe." She pointed to Zim and the packing roll under the robe. "Her rescuers came too late but still wanted Zimmon's body. A minor victory, offering hope to some that the Starflower still lives."

"Thank you, Djada." Malik caught her wink and had to pause before continuing. "To address council replacements, I've asked Seta Martiri to assume Kodra's responsibilities in the Greens in addition to her own." He nodded to the Councilor for Communication then touched his steepled index fingers to his chin.

"Abramyan's replacement will be more difficult. We have taken many soldiers out of storage, but none are expert with the weapons of this century." Malik cleared his throat. "After this last raid on Corydon, we queried the Authoriton about impending military risks. It assesses that Tak-Yaki sympathy for the Starflower will lead them to take hostile action. Until our new Councilor for Military Affairs is brought up to speed, we are sending Marshal Derek Boorman with our top three legions to destroy Tak-Yakon." A clash of strings drew Malik to glance at a Hyrup musician repositioning its mandolin.

"The Tak-Yaki are fierce ground combat soldiers, but their fleet is small, and they have only two capital ships. We have the numbers, modern weapons, and total surprise on our side." Malik glanced down the table then continued. "Boorman was to be Abramyan's Creative host. After he crushes the Tak-Yaki, we'll prep him for our new military commander."

The next reports cleaned up remaining details of the takeover. Except for remote outposts, a few escapees, and children too young to undergo transition, all Creatives would soon be hosting Xi'Kior masters. Scattered Unders were being rounded up. Three million were in camps working on terraforming or mining projects. And two hundred thousand Pidge were retained as entertainers and pets or for hazardous duty.

When the reports ended, Malik ordered the music to resume and celebratory drinks to be served. He then pulled Djada onto his lap, eliciting her delighted squeal.

Blue Castle

A point of light danced in the dark like a firefly then fled. It returned in Zim's dream and split to become many dancing lights—fireflies in the Rankoi forest where she and Mac had gone walking. He tripped chasing one in the dark, trying to cup it in his hands to bring it for her to examine. A tear trickled down across Zim's temple. She wiped it with a cool metal finger and fell back to sleep.

Hours later she woke to other lights, small points swimming in a fog. They merged slowly into one red point and steadied before blinking to green. Through eyes not quite shut, Zim saw it was a monitor light on the wall. Even that dim light stabbed waves of agony back through her eye sockets. She touched her face. Instant pain warned her to be gentle. Her tongue explored inside her mouth, teeth and jaw in place, gums hot and puffy.

"We won't turn the lights on just yet, not until your eyes have more time to heal." The woman's voice had a Scalari lilt. "Can you rotate your head to the right? If you can, tell me what you see."

Zim felt the cool pillow against her cheek as her face turned. Two meters away, a cobalt blue rectangle was divided into four smaller, equal-size rectangles.

"I see a window," she croaked dryly, "a paned window like in my bedroom on Scalaris. Am I on Scalaris?"

"Do you see anything else?"

She closed her eyes to let the pain subside then looked again. "Clouds and a sliver of moon trying to shine through them."

"Very good," the voice said. "Rest now. You and your team are safe here. We'll talk more tomorrow." Zim heard a soft whirr then silence. Consciousness exhausted her.

From a far place, she heard Mac calling. "Come quick, see the firefly I caught." She ran but could not reach him. He receded in the dark distance.

333

When she turned, a Shelesti stood on the path. It held a black robe in its branch fingers. "Tock said you could be trusted." What does that mean? Is Tock here? Her need for sleep overtook thought.

# # #

Zim cracked then shut an eyelid, wincing. In the blurry blast she'd seen a full-body scanner and a hospital-caliber doc-rob.

"How long have I got, Doc?" she asked and heard a quiet chuckle.

"It's good to see you, Gayle?" She knew the warm baritone.

"Mac? Is that you?" She feared it was another illusion.

"Only my projection, or I'd be kissing you now."

"I'd love that, but I don't think I'd be much fun to kiss." She clasped her hands over her waist and heard the metal-on-metal rasp. "Mac, are you alive?"

"Let's not talk about that now. I told Micah, if he let me visit, I'd keep it short. You remember Micah Crowley from Blue Star Corporation? This is their facility. His med team has a full regimen for getting you back on your feet. Then he wants to offer you a job."

"Micah? A job?" Zim gave a long sigh. "Mac, dearest, I'm sorry. I want very much to talk, but I am so sleepy."

"That's the heart medication," the sweet Scalari voice from the night before answered. "If your heart rate or blood pressure start to climb, your meds kick in to put you back to sleep." Zim nodded and felt her head sink deep into the pillow.

"I have to go," Mac said. She was asleep before she could respond.

Zim woke two days later to the sound of another familiar voice. "You're still weak, young lady." Micah Crowley's distinct bass was hard to forget. "But Doc says if you feel up to it, you can start therapy today."

She willed her eyes to open then squinted at the soft morning light. A dark, rough-hewn face leaned toward her, all radiant and smiling. He wore a powder blue jumpsuit with the corporate logo on the collar, a royal blue star highlighted yellow.

"Micah, how good you are to save me and my team. And because of that," she raised a metal index finger, "I'll let the 'young lady' comment pass."

"Mackenzie told us you'd be alive." Crowley's brown eyes sparkled. "We didn't believe him until you turned up at Avian. When official media reported you dead a second time, we began sensor-trolling every space lane out of Corydon."

"Mac? Avian?" Zim gave a silent whistle. "Where am I?"

"You are at our corporate headquarters, Blue Castle. My great-grandfather had our engineers assemble and terraform this planet decades ago."

"Tell me. Tell me everything."

Crowley rolled in his lips then stared at his hands on the bedrail. "I'll start with Mackenzie. A Goorm trader came to one of our work sites last month. He said he brought Mac, not Mac exactly, only his soul—sorry, that's become the standard term. Right now, he's a projection. Tomorrow he'll have an MP chassis. We have his complete mental profile, everything that made him Human other than his actual genetics." Zim pressed her metal palms to her eyes as Crowley continued.

"When the Goorm told Mac that the Rii-Chaut had heavy weapons and were preparing a full-scale attack on Luna base, he volunteered to leave. The Goorm have no weapons. According to the Goorm trader, Mac's sacrifice saved one hundred and eighteen families. The best they could offer him was a soul trade. He was too old to be transplanted; Humans lose that flexibility some time in their late teens."

Zim peered into Crowley's sad-smiling face. "Thank you, Micah. I'm happy to have part of Mac back. You said I'll see him tomorrow?"

"Yes. His chassis is an excellent facsimile. He did ask us to remove a couple scars."

"That sounds like him—quite vain. I'm sure he'll look a couple years younger, too." She chuckled. "You said you knew when I arrived at Avian. Are you connected with the Authoriton?"

"The old Planetary Council gave us a terminal right from the beginning. Corydon was Blue Star's first terraform project, and the Authoriton was our project manager. It's an administrative connection. That's how we received our tasking. If I'd known about your active connection, I would have kept someone at the terminal." Crowley pulled up a chair. "You'll hear more tomorrow at the briefing. All the staff will be there—and all the newcomers, including Roland Mackenzie."

"When can I begin my first therapy session?"

# # #

Zim and Mac looked out from the stone terrace of Blue Star's convention center. Both wore powder-blue jumpsuits with the Blue Star corporate logo. Above them, white, puffy clouds drifted in the cobalt sky under a small, blue-white sun.

"Where are we?" Zim asked.

"Blue Castle," Mac said. "Headquarters to—"

"I mean, where are *we*?"

"*We* are together," Mac said, covering her metal hand with his very Human-like hand. "Beyond that I don't know. It's the best I can do."

"It's the best *we* can do," she corrected. "I so hoped we'd be out of uniforms." She pinched a fold of the nano-fiber jumpsuit, examined her metal hands, then stretched her new hips, knees, and ankle. "I'm sorry, Mac. This isn't what I imagined." She looked up into his dark, so-like-Mac eyes. His MP chassis felt warm and Human, too. "Do you think we'll be secure here… enough to raise a family?"

"I don't know." He lifted her forearm and examined the nubs inside the metal cage of her prosthetic hand. "Your hand and fingers are growing back nicely. Your other parts will conform naturally. A year from now, you'll be like new."

She laughed. "You're right. When we're together, we can take on the world. We did once."

"Your confidence makes me forget how vulnerable you can be." He hugged her, and she rested her head on his chest. "But you miss my point, Gayle. You'll be like new; I'll still be synthetic."

"I will always love you, Mac. I couldn't love you more and could never love anyone else." She gave a deep sigh and looked up. "Will anyone from my team be at the meeting?"

"A couple. Some were pulled away by the Xi'Kior attacks. Dom and Dak are drilling combat assault teams. Hotz is with Traier and the Chei-Binsk. They're trying to bring them, and possibly some of the other sects, to our side. Brownie and Belle signed up for general service support, but Brownie should be at the meeting."

"Kaplan?"

"He'll be there. He was almost as bad off as you were. Kyle died in the crater, and you know about Chow."

"Both were courageous. They died saving my life." She remembered Chow's parting smile and 'Ha Yee' goodbye. She only knew Kyle by his angry, forthright growl. Mac turned her to face him.

"They believed in you, Gayle. When I told Micah you were alive, I only half believed it. I wanted him to keep looking."

"I'm sorry, Mac. I thought you were dead, too."

"It's not over for either of us. Your followers are quoting the Aldra Korah, 'In the dark of the darkest night… the Starflower blooms.' That scares the hell out of me."

"Scares me, too." She hugged him then composed herself. "Before the meeting, I have a promise to keep." She waved Mac to follow and walked the terrace to a brook-fed pool behind the convention center. Purple and indigo plants lining the bank sported multi-colored cups and stars. A blue-maned lizard dashed into the purple foliage.

Zim drew a Vaitii seed from a thigh pocket and held it up. "Think of this like dropping a coin in a wishing well." Mac cocked an eyebrow. Zim set the seed a half meter from the water and stepped back.

"Should we make a wish?" Mac asked.

"Yes, for us. Just watch." Mac took her hand. The seed stirred then rolled into the water and out of sight.

Sitrep

Three-meter-high windows surrounded the conference table under a white, clerestory dome. Blue and purple broadleaf trees in planters filled spaces between the windows. Yellow, green, and gold veined the white marble floor. The white marble table was an open circle with passages to enable speakers to reach the dais at the center.

The room quieted when Zim and Mac entered. Crowley stood and motioned for them to sit beside him.

Zim acknowledged those she knew around the table: Brownie, Kaplan with a prosthetic leg and face-patch on one side; Terry Ebron, Yoshi Kuwashima, and Anthony 'Savvy' Savielli from Five Squadron were pleasant surprises, but the biggest was Purlet, the village elder from Rankoi.

Tock represented the Tak-Yaki and B'Len the Aldrakin. Others she remembered only from the surrender ceremony: the Salogar in a stilt-walking ammonia canister and the tentacle-jelly Noorki in a globe aquarium. The Sheerdi she had never seen: a swan-necked semi-aquatic that Zim thought might prefer a water tank. Many wore powder blue jumpsuits modified for their forms.

Zim also acknowledged the Shelesti-Hyrup music troupe at the back poised beside their instruments. Seeing them triggered her memory and dream of a Shelesti holding a black robe, "Tock said you could be trusted, and we should intervene if it meant your survival."

Zim's eyes went wide. The Hyrup were a Tak-Yaki caste. She remembered the war cry of the Tak-Yaki just before they swarmed over Abramyan. Tock had said she'd be impressed; they had excellent intelligence sources. Now Zim knew they had excellent musicians, too, and more.

Crowley addressed the group. "Welcome all of you to Blue Castle." He nodded to Zim. "Legends being what they are, I'm sure you're all pleased to confirm that Star Marshal Zimmon is alive—"

"*Marshal?*" Zim said.

"Yes, last month Blue Star hosted several galactic species to discuss the growing concern of Xi'Kior expansion. We agreed to build a combined fleet and an army, and to invite you and Marshal Mackenzie to lead it. You will be in full command of all combat forces. Mac has already agreed to be Chief of Staff for Plans and Logistics." Those seated stood and applauded. The Salogar container rose on spindly legs and rolled colors. The Noorki globe levitated, and it signaled approval on its panel.

Crowley cleared his throat. "The Xi'Kior requested the Galactic Trade Federation to recognize them as a new species and no longer Human. Synthetic genetics have permanently implanted their minds along with a control agent into their hosts. Each Xi'Kior retains its own memory along with the host memory. General Savielli will give us the update."

Savvy tilted his head to Zim then stepped onto the central stage. "Six months ago, the Xi'Kior initiated the last phase of their takeover. All Creatives on Corydon, Thrinlu, Scalaris, and Silkani were forced to take the Xi'Kior parasite. Creatives in other regions, including Port Estelle, were brought to Corydon for implantation. A few escaped, and some are finding their way to us. Being genetically unsuited for implants, Unders were rounded up and killed or sent to work camps."

Savvy called up projections of two brains. "A Human brain, and this," he moved the pointer, "a Xi'Kior brain acquired last month by the Tak-Yaki. The virus itself is too small to be depicted in this graphic. But note the spinose growth above the brain stem and the network radiating from it. TY interrogators examined eleven hundred captured or dead Xi'Kior brains. This growth connects to all portions of the brain and cannot be extracted or neutralized without killing the host." Savvy waved up a new chart.

"When we checked Xi'Kior brain waves, we expected to find two patterns: one for the host, one for the parasite. We found three: host, parasite, and nanotech virus. The virus enabled the host-parasite merger then retained control and became the dominant will." Savvy's pointer rested on a stronger signal of higher frequency than the other two waves. "From their interrogations, the Tak-Yaki are certain that the Xi'Kior Creatives are not aware that they have a puppet master. The virus may have blocked that awareness."

A demographic projection replaced the brainwave chart.

"Estimates of the Xi'Kior population toward the end of the Tech War vary from two hundred forty million to three billion. They destroyed the records before they disappeared. We believe the entire population accepted the virus with the promise that, sometime in the near future, they would be transferred to healthy bodies. Using Avian's projections of Creative fertility, we estimate Xi'Kior numbers could increase by fifty to sixty percent per year for the next ten to twelve years. The nanotech virus reproduces with the host so no additional implants will be required."

"Why ten to twelve years? What happens?" Mac asked.

"Menarche," Savvy said. "In ten to twelve years, the first new generation of Xi'Kior will be capable of bearing its own offspring—from there the numbers take off. Almost a vertical line if we carried this out. And with that growth will come demands for habitats and resources." The room went silent. He waved up a galactic map.

"Recent Xi'Kior actions tell us where they plan to expand." He held his hand toward B'Len. "For that, I turn the floor over to the Aldrakin representative." They exchanged shoulder presses, and Savvy returned to his seat.

"The first incident occurred five months ago." B'Len pointed and a red circle expanded on the galaxy projection. "Sil'Arook is an asteroid cluster rich in metals and strategic minerals. Except for Thrinlu, the Xi'Kior planets are poor in metals. We estimate at the projected rate of expansion they will exhaust their resources in less than six years. Since that first incident, there have been thirteen incursions on Aldrakin space, Sil'Arook and other mining clusters, and some exchanges of fire. The Xi'Kior have not pressed the attacks. Ambassador Tee'Kahl has lodged several formal protests but so far has received no response."

As B'Len left the stage, he bowed close to Zim and whispered, "Next time, I want to be with you at the front."

Crowley opened his hand toward Tock. "Thank you, B'Len. Our Tak-Yaki rep, Ticket-Tockoket-*Click*."

Tock entered the circle, swiveled its triangular head to Zim, and ratcheted, *Chirik, Krglu.*

Chirik-click-tirock, Tock. She returned a head bow.

Tock set a foot on the translator. "The Xi'Kior launched three Legions in an unprovoked attack on Tak-Yakon. Although heavily outgunned, we overcame them with tactics familiar to Marshal Zimmon. This is not a combat action report. Those wishing my stirring rendition of the battle may purchase it at the bar this evening." Tock waited for the chuckles to subside.

"Now for the intelligence findings." Tock faced the projection. "We intercepted and destroyed an entire Xi'Kior attack fleet: three carriers, nine battle stations, and ninety cruisers and corvettes. All these ships were of advanced design." A schematic of a starship appeared in the projection. "This is the new Malik-class fighter carrier. It is highly automated with 240 fighter-enforcers. We fell on them just as they left Myseko space, otherwise the results would have been very different. Only six of their fighters deployed before we disabled the launch systems on all three carriers. Those six took out twenty-six of our own.

"All their ships display advanced-level engineering. We found upgrades to every system, from weapons and shields to habitability, propulsion, and sensors. Sheerdi engineers," Tock pointed a clamp-claw to the swan-necked alien at the table, "are exploiting the Xi'Kior ships for weaknesses. Salogar scientists are analyzing the technology to apply to our own systems." Tock nodded toward the Salogar, and its ammonia canister acknowledged by flashing electric blue.

"How have the Xi'Kior responded since the battle?" Zim asked.

"We've seen no response," Tock ratchet-clicked and raised its antennae. "We believe they were overconfident. Neither the Xi'Kior nor the Creatives ever encountered Tak-Yaki, not as enemies or allies. Unfamiliar with our tactics, they failed to develop an effective battle plan. From Sheerdi engineers and our direct interrogation of Xi'Kior brains, we know all their ships were produced in a single nine-month production run. So, even if we destroyed all their new combat ships, they could produce similar or greater numbers in nine months." Tock swiveled its triangular head around the table. "We expect another major attack before year's end."

The projection closed. Tock tilted its triangular head to Zim then to the rest of the table and returned to its seat.

Crowley stood, somber faced. "I don't think I can emphasize the threat too highly. Our forces are mobilizing, but we are far behind. We can't match Xi'Kior numbers or technology, even in the short run, though our force is larger than they imagine. We have secretly evacuated and sheltered Under enclaves and escapees since before the Aldrakin war. With their help, we've terraformed and occupied four worlds the Xi'Kior know nothing about. Some of the escapees were soldiers in Star Command. The rest need to be trained. Blue Star has construction and maintenance yards for planetary engineering craft and freighters. They are being converted to produce capital starships."

"What warships do we currently have?" Mac asked.

"Only those brought in by StarCom defectors," Crowley said.

Savvy spoke up. "We have one Marshal-class carrier, one battle station, and twelve cruisers from the 18th Legion, plus all of Five Squadron with its twenty-four cruisers."

"Everyone in Five Squadron?" Zim's eyes lit up. She saw confirming nods from Kuwashima and Ebron at the table. Savvy's smile almost split his face.

"Excellent, Savvy. Thank you for some good news. That gives us a fine training cadre, and—" Zim raised her metal fist and tapped a knuckle to her chin. "Are the 18th Legion and Five Squadron combat-ready?"

"Yes, Marshal," Savvy said, catching the glint in her eye.

Zim smiled. "If the Xi'Kior committed all their new ships to attacking Tak-Yakon, we're going to punish them. Mac, make plans for a major strike on the dockyards at Thrinlu. If we catch their new fleet under construction and seriously damage those docks, it'll take them at least a year to recoup." She tapped her chin again then raised a metal finger.

"We need a diversion. Contact Traier, see if his Rii-Chaut sect will rig a fireship to strike the repair docks at Port Estelle. If they can pass a fireship off as a damaged merchantman, Traier might be able to explode it right in the middle of the repair yard. Even if that ploy doesn't work, it'll distract the Xi'Kior from Thrinlu. Tell Traier I want this as soon as possible, but don't mention our timeline or that the primary target is Thrinlu. I trust him but not all the Rii-Chaut in his company." Zim looked around the table. "If both attacks succeed, the Xi'Kior won't have any facilities to build or repair starships and will be cut off from resources for new facilities."

Mac gave Zim a slow approving nod and added to his notes.

The translator light flashed green beside the Noorki tank. "We are not soldiers, but we can contribute. The Rii-Chaut code considers sabotage honorable craft only when a sizeable bounty is offered and shared with the brotherhood. Therefore, we offer a hundred-million-credit bounty for an attack on Port Estelle, double if the repair yard is destroyed. That should keep Traier in good standing and help his recruiting."

"Thank you, a generous offer." Zim pointed to Mac, and he added to his notes. "Tock, the Tak-Yaki just emerged from a major engagement. Will you be able to support our play on Thrinlu?"

Click, chilket. Tock shifted a foot onto the translator. "Do the Goorm like making money?"

Zim turned to another friend. "B'Len, you want a position on my flagship?"

"At your side, Starflower." B'Len puffed his chest.

"Thank you." She looked at him. "But don't inform the Empire yet. The Aldrakin are not officially at war with the Xi'Kior. For the time being, I think it best that they consider you neutral."

She turned to Crowley. "Micah, we dare not leave you unprotected. The Xi'Kior must know Blue Castle exists."

"They know we have a corporate headquarters and train planetary engineers but don't know the extent of it. We block transmissions and our starships can't be tracked through Myseko space. No one arrives or leaves Blue Castle directly. Everyone at this meeting had to board a relay starship for the last Myseko skip."

"Wise precautions." Zim noted nods around the table. "We have one more important ally. The best intelligence in the galaxy." The Shelesti musician startled. Its mate-hump winked.

Zim gestured and a uni-ball waiter robot handed her a vermillion pouch. She placed the crystal Chorya'Key on the table and touched it, filling the room with stars. When everyone in the hall connected with her, the star field sparkled with their collected knowledge.

"Now we can all know what we all know." Zim paused then pointed to the Chorya'Key. "This was my gift from the Aldrakin. In return, I agreed to arrange that a certain watery planet would be engineered to their specifications." She raised an eyebrow to Crowley, and he returned the gesture with a slow head bow.

"Ha-Yee, Starflower," B'Len shouted, leaping frog-like high above the table.

The room echoed with rounds of "Ha-Yee."

VaiZim

Event Horizon's new proprietor rubbed a claw across his mouthparts. *Chickit*, Crik swore. The night's tally was disappointing. All Goorm detest losing money, but Crik's molting made him particularly cranky. He hated being seen like this, his handsome maroon carapace patched frosty gray. Cursing again, he pinched and scraped at his aching joints.

They were also short-handed, so he'd asked the musicians, a Shelesti and four Hyrup, to pitch in clearing tables, sweeping, and removing trash.

Klistik, kerrk. He asked the Shelesti wiping the far end of the bar to draw him a beer.

A shuffling at the foot of the stone stairway drew Crik's eyestalks to a figure in the shadows. The humanoid looked vaguely familiar. The Shelesti placed a full beer mug on the bar and stepped back.

Kiii, kerrk, Crik said, gesturing his claw for the stranger to press the translator pad on the first table.

Kerrk, click, the other responded. "Thank you, I speak fluent Goorm."

"We are closed. Can I help you?"

"I'm looking for a job." The alien clicked in flawless high-Goorm.

Crik motioned for the stranger to grab a table and scuttled around the bar, leaving his beer. He dropped into a seat across from the stranger, sprawled six segmented legs around his chair and two on the table, and positioned both claws between them. "Sorry to be defensive. We've had trouble, and I've not seen your kind in here before." His stalked black eyes twisted, studying the stranger. His feelers and mouthparts felt and tasted the air between them.

The stranger's tan, sculptured face and piercing blue eyes glistened under the hanging, green-shaded lamp. What Crik initially took for blond braids were woven tentacles. Though unusual, Crik found the creature's appearance aesthetically pleasing.

"What experience have you at tending bar?"

"May I engage your claw arm?" the stranger asked. Crik extended a claw while cocking the other back, ready to strike.

The alien's arm unraveled from its shoulder, turning from a sinew-bulging, five-fingered Humanoid limb into a dozen writhing tentacles. One tentacle wrapped around Crik's joint just above the claw and gave him a mild sting. A moment later the tentacle released and wove back into an arm.

"I have extensive bar-keeping experience," the stranger said.

Crik's eyestalks drew together. "Show me… make me a martini."

"Would you prefer Sapphire or Jira?"

"Sapphire," Crik clicked, widening his mandibles. The clever stranger knew to offer the top shelf gin and vodka brands first, the ones that gave the house the highest margin.

"Olive, maybe a little dirty?" the stranger asked filling the shaker. It seemed to know where everything was.

"Perfect," Crik responded, scraping a gray patch on his molting carapace.

A moment later, Crik had a shaken martini in the correct chilled glass in front of him on an embossed, ecru napkin. He reached a precision appendage past a fighting claw, raised the conical glass to the light, and examined the sparkling ice points. The alcohol content tasted perfect, giving the right flavor without being too strong, which might deter a customer from ordering another.

"Very good, er—" He returned his cocked claw to the table. "I'm Crik, owner of the Event Horizon."

"I'm—" the stranger paused, "a VaiZim. We don't have individual names, but since I'm the only VaiZim on Corydon, that can be my name." VaiZim tapped Crik's claw with its re-braided tentacle-hand. "You'll find we are highly adaptable, quick to learn, and hard working."

"I run a business here, VaiZim. Tell me how you're going to make me money?"

Before VaiZim could speak, a Hyrup crawled onto its lap and three others curled at its feet. VaiZim stroked their segments, and they nuzzled closer. The Shelesti propped its branch-like arms akimbo, and its bark-scar mouth widened. Crik's eye stalks and antennae leaned forward together.

"You asked about money." VaiZim brought Crik back to his favorite topic.

"Customers don't come to bars to drink and listen to music. They come because they're lonely and want someone to talk to. I can converse with them in their own language without a translator."

"If that's any indication," Crik extended a claw to the cuddling Hyrup, "you've got a job. How soon can you start? I offer twenty credits a week, plus five percent of sales for a thousand-credit week, ten percent after that, all tips you keep. That's all I can afford. Business has been down since the Unders left."

"I can start immediately."

"Let's drink to it. What'll you have?" Crik pondered the full martini in front of him and the beer back on the bar.

"An oli-jira," VaiZim said.

"Ooo, the Starflower's drink." Crik scraped a gray patch between his eyestalks. "Not so popular these days, not with the Xi'Kior in charge. They've made them illegal."

"I've always had a taste for them."

"Very well." Crik held up a split claw for the Shelesti to bring two. "That pulse-taking thing you did with your tentacle, you're a tactile telepath?"

"Yes."

"Like the mythical Vaitii," Crik clicked.

"Exactly like them. Tell me, why do you think business is down?" The Shelesti set two oli-jira on the table.

"The Starflower incident. I wasn't told when I bought this place that the insurgents staged their attacks out of the wine cellar." He oscillated both antennae toward the down stairwell. "That's why I got it so cheap. Everyone's spooked about the rumors that the Starflower's still alive. That'll pass—has to eventually. Business'll pick up." Crik and VaiZim lifted their glasses and toasted to prosperity.

"You think the rumors will pass?" VaiZim raised a woven tentacle-fist to tap its chin.

"I saw the beating she took on the enforcer recording. She died in the park north of here." Crik waved a claw then scraped the front of his carapace.

"So, why do the rumors persist?" VaiZim asked and finished its drink.

Crik ordered refills. "Last week the Rii-Chaut raided Port Estelle, blew the targ out of it. Who did it?" Crik fast clicked both claws ominously. "The Starflower, of course. Insurgents use the Starflower call sign every time they attack. Yesterday they hit Thrinlu. I heard the entire industrial complex is a smoking cinder. Who's to blame?"

"The Starflower."

"Exactly."

Dramatis Personae

Humans

Abramyan, Star Leader Grosvenor Venaturan Abramyan: Councilor for Military, Head of Star Command

Aidan: Zimmon's aide-de-camp

Billy: Dom's nephew, Tee'Kahl's merged partner

Boorman, Marshal Derek Boorman: senior military officer in Star Command

Chow, Chiao Li: life scientist, xenologist

Crawley, Micah Crawley: CEO of Blue Star Corporation

Dak: pidged insurgent

Djada, Star Leader Jen Djada: Councilor for Public Order

Dom, Major James 'Dirty Old Man' Eppert: Chief Engineer, Combat Team Leader

Ebron, Lieutenant Terry Ebron: communication/navigation officer on *Lasalle*

Hippelli, Frank Hippelli: Director of the Office of Personnel Plans

Glory, Gloria: Dom's pidged sister

Hillie, Hillary: selected future leader of Humanity, partner to Torgis

Hotz, Ensign Tory 'Hotz' Bahrke: pilot and medic

Kaplan, Wonder O'Kavo Kaplan: intern trainee on *Lasalle*, bartender at Event Horizon

Kimbri, Spacer Kimbri: enlisted crewman on *Marshal Massena*

Kodra, Star Leader Luka Kodra: Councilor for the Greens

Kuwashima, Major Yoshi Kuwashima: weapons officer on *Lasalle*

Kyle: pidged insurgent

Mac, Marshal Roland Mackenzie: Star Command Staff, and Zim's sweetheart since childhood

Martiri, Star Leader Seta Martiri: Councilor for Media and Public Image

Malik, Star Lord Kiya Malik: Head of Star Council

M'Bong, Lieutenant M'Bong: security officer on *Lasalle*

Pidge: Humans altered genetically, surgically, and chemically for hazardous duty or entertainment—pets, prostitutes, pit fighters. On Corydon, replaced capital punishment as major penalty for criminal behavior

Rob, Rob Marsh: physical scientist

Savvy, Major Anthony 'Savvy' Savielli: Commander of Five Squadron's Six Flight

Torgis, Torgesson: selected future leader of Humanity, partner to Hillie

Woodson, Captain Jeffrey Woodson: Captain of the *Marshal Massena*

Yardley, Chief Merchant Officer Jason Yardley: shuttle commander on the *Marshal Massena*

Zim, Marshal Gayle Zimmon: call sign "Starflower"

Aldrakin

Ajalanda: B'Len's young son

B'Len, Commander B'Len: military officer; nephew to Emperor Condolas

B'Rou: engineer; head of the survey team on Aldrakhan

Condolas, Lord Condolas: Emperor of the Aldrakin, Keeper of the Galactic Trade Federation

Ejazz-Eel: Prophet of Aldra Korah during the 'Long Night' millennial journey, successor to Hiran-Ejazz

Hiran-Ejazz: Prophet of Aldra Korah prior Aldrakhan's destruction

Laveda: Zim's host and Master of Ceremonies on the Aldrakin flagship

Okrador, Admiral Okrador: Aldrakin commander at the Battle of Bai-Yota

Tak-Yaki

Atch-Oklot: scientist caste; one of first integrated with military caste

Choo'kok: senior military officer; Zim's roommate in Basic

Kr'Rakat: senior military officer; Zim's flight instructor

Tock, Ticket-Tockoket-*click*: senior military officer; Zim's longtime friend

Rii-Chaut

Inidigbo: enforcer/sergeant-at-arms for Kadis (Inidigbo species)

Kadis: Chief of the Rii-Chaut Brotherhood (Human)

Ojai Khan: Hetman of the Yazza sect (Human)

Traier: Hetman of the Chei-Binsk sect (Human)

AIs

Belle, Isabelle: ore carrier AI, former Human
Brownie: shuttle AI, former Human
Delhi, the Authoriton: central computer program for Human systems
MP: Modern Partner: human-like RHs designed to be companions
Mumbai: executive grade RH, Avian's major-domo
RH: robotic humanoid

Other Alien Characters (Species)

Chik'ik (Goorm): businessman; brawler, gambler at Event Horizon
Crik (Goorm): businessman; later owner of Event Horizon
Purlet (Bilibo): village elder from Rankoi
Rayzhor (Heinkel): leader of a wolf-like pack on Scalaris
Tee'Khal (Sk'Keffin): diplomat; Aldrakin Ambassador to Corydon, Billy's merged partner
Vaitii (Vaitii), aka **Uncle Dave**: innkeeper; immortal, pan-dimensional entity
VaiZim (Vaitii): new bartender at Event Horizon

Alien Specialist Species

Hyrup: musicians, centipede-like creatures symbiotic with Shelesti
Li-Kass: tradesmen and engineers, six-limbed, lemur-eyed
Noorki: mathematicians, aquatic grape-like clusters of green, tentacle-jellies; shared home planet Kookala-karin with the Aldrakin after the 'Long Night'
Salogar: scientists, require liquid-ammonia atmospheres, look like bouquets of deflated, feather-collared wineskins
Sheerdi: research engineers, swan-necked, semi-aquatics
Shelesti: musicians, tree-trunk-like creatures symbiotic with Hyrup
Utak: eel-like monster on Rankoi
3Bs (ball-bearing-beetles): nickname for extensions of Vaitii that operate independently

Timeline (Human Calendar)

<u>~12000 BCE</u> – **Destruction of Aldrakhan**: Recorded by Ejazz-Eel in Aldra Korah; beginning of the Aldrakin's 'Long Night' millennial starship journey

<u>2117 CE</u> – **Viktor Myseko**: theorized dimensions outside space/time: Myseko dimensions; author of "Cross-Dimensional String Frequency Harmonics and a Proposal for Transcending Space-Time"

<u>2232 – 2264 CE</u> – **Xi'Kior Tech War**: attempt by tech-savvy Xi'Kior to conquer Earth using nuclear/biological/nanotech weapons; contamination led to Earth's evacuation

<u>2264 – 2357 CE</u> – **Archaic Pestilence**: post Tech War devastation characterized by lost immunities and genetic damage leading to Human sterility

<u>2400 CE</u> – **Era of Good Feeling**: diseases subside; population dispersed to countryside to avoid contagion; Humans and robots begin restoration

<u>2401 CE</u> – **All-Joy** begins: planet-wide celebration; progress stagnates; Human viability threatened by accrued damage; RHs and other AIs maintain order and continue scientific research

<u>2413 CE</u> – **Planetary Council** (PC): formed by Robotic Humanoids; Humans invited to join; solar exploration resumed; Human colonization begins in solar system

<u>2434 CE</u> – **Star Council:** monastic science cult accepted into PC

2437 EC – **Entropic Power:** discovered by RH scientists; entropy-reining techniques increase fusion efficiency; first sub-light starships; extra solar-exploration begins

~3200 CE – **All-Joy Ends**: Human decline resumes; retention on PC largely symbolic; Human population estimated ~22 million; Suicide rate increases; fecundity drops; 'Modern Partners' (MP) movement eschews Humans for robot mates

3234 CE – **Myseko Theory Demonstrated:** for multiple space dimensions; rebound or 'skip' off Myseko Space enables instant communication; research

3276 CE – **Myseko-Enabled Starship**: first interstellar skip, Centauri system

3278 CE – **First Contact:** Goorm traders arrive in Sol system; trade concessions; leasing of Luna trade base

3281 CE – **Galactic Reports:** delivered by Goorm; including star maps, navigation aids, reports on alien species

3303 CE – **Interstellar Search:** fails to discover uninhabited systems suitable for Human colonization

3403 CE – **Blue Star Corporation:** develops **Grav-Lev** – energy field tractor; wins terraforming contract from Earth PC; Corydon, Thrinlu, Scalaris designated investment-grade worlds

3451 CE – **Avian Project:** begun by AIs to restore Human viability; selective breeding and genetic engineering stabilizes Human genome; preferred stock, designated 'Creative,' become basis for Human upgrading; rejected 'Unders' culled/relegated to secondary planets to preserve limited resources

3560 – 93 CE – **Colonial Wars**: Human attempts to colonize habited worlds rebuffed

3562 CE – **Star Council:** subgroup gains majority on Planetary Council (PC); Human capital switched from Earth to Corydon

3576 CE – **Planetary Council Renamed Star Council:** Order for Earth evacuation; Corydon prioritized for Creatives; Thrinlu and Scalaris for Unders

3598 – 99 CE – **Corydon Combat Games, "Corydonics":** first open to Unders; seventeen-year-old Gayle Zimmon leads Scalari team to victory; game committee refuses awarding Corydon Star to Unders—Zimmon receives Starflower medal

3599 CE – **Aldrakin War** begins: Gayle Zimmon called up; assigned military call sign 'Starflower' in Basic

3611 CE – **Battle of Bai-Yota:** ends Aldrakin War

3612 CE – **Star Council Renamed Xi'Kior Council**: Blue Star Corporation hosts first meeting of galactic coalition to address Xi'Kior expansion